CANISTER OF EVIL

CANISTER OF EVIL

Joseph "Champagne Joe" Militello

authorHOUSE®

AuthorHouse™
1663 Liberty Drive
Bloomington, IN 47403
www.authorhouse.com
Phone: 1-800-839-8640

First published by AuthorHouse   09/15/2011

ISBN: 978-1-4634-3126-6 (sc)
ISBN: 978-1-4634-3125-9 (hc)
ISBN: 978-1-4634-3124-2 (ebk)

Library of Congress Control Number: 2011911673

Printed in the United States of America

Any people depicted in stock imagery provided by Thinkstock are models, and such images are being used for illustrative purposes only.
Certain stock imagery © Thinkstock.

This book is printed on acid-free paper.

Table of Contents

FOR
LORRAINE

Glossary Of Terms

Milkshakes   P. 62 An outlawed procedure forcing bicarbonate thru a thoroughbreds' nostrils to aid its' breathing capacity.

Hagganah   P. 156 Israeli freedom fighter group.

Chador   P. 207 Mid-eastern dress similar to a burka.

Kofta Kari   P. 208 Popular mid-eastern meatball dish.

Chapter One

A Day at the Races

"They're at the post!". The crisp British accented verbiage sliced thru the low level murmu kings English and Australian outback slang would be accepted by the racing fans at this track. Henson, of the crowd with precision and clarity. This sharp edged voice was new to Duke Charga, and had actually startled him somewhat, causing him to jump back a foot or so. Charga had been leaning his 6 foot, 200 pound frame heavily on the trackside railing, concentrating on the scheduled group of entries on the card for this upcoming 8th race. This was the first time he had heard this recently hired race caller who had been signed on as a replacement for Harry Henson, following Hensons' earthly departure. Charga questioned whether this white south African with the high pitched vocalizations and accent that seemed a cross between Britains kings English and Australian outback slang would be accepted by the racing fans at this track. Henson with his more base toned voice was, for years, a most highly regarded and respected icon of the thoroughbred racing world, and had been a familiar staple at the Arcadia race track, and had earned a place in the racing hall of fame. He had actually become a household name in the world of thoroughbred race calling, a very uncommon accomplishment for someone whose face was, for the most part, unfamiliar to the majority of his followers. He had completed over two decades as track announcer and race caller before he had succumbed to the not uncommon variety of senior age ailments, arthritis, heart problems, and ultimately cancer, Still,

Charga recalled reading an article about this former Johanasburg resident who was attempting to fill the shoes of old man Henson, He remembered it to be highly positive. In that article was a report that this new track announcer possessed the unique ability to almost instantaneously memorize the names of all the horses in a race, and to report their running positions in any given race with 100% accuracy. His reputation had preceded him and was reported to be almost legendary in his native country. Somewhere it had also stated that he was very possibly the very best ever in his job. As far as Charga was concerned, the jury was still out on that.

"This Denman character seems okay" Charga mused to himself, "But, he'll never be able to replace Henson." He was unaware of the public at larges' reaction toward the new race caller, which was 100% positive, since this was the first time he had visited this great race track since he had been involved as an investigator in a case where one of the track employees had been found dead just outside the barn area some months earlier. That was back when he was working as a Lt. detective in the homicide division of the Arcadia police department. The court ruling in that case was that no homicide had been committed. However, as far as Charga was concerned, there had been some evidence of foul play, but as it turned out, the court ruled that the decedent had simply slipped by stepping on a spot of dirt that had been urinated upon by a passing thoroughbred, and that he had fallen backwards hitting the back of his head on the corner of the stall, causing a fatal aneurism in the brain. But, as in any case of a non disease related death, the circumstances of the event were subject to review and investigation. He remembered clearly how the spouse of the decedent back then was so understandably distraught, and how every one of the working grooms and all of the jockey colony had come together on her behalf, donating all kinds of money, goods, and services in a worthy and gallant effort to help her thru that trying time. It was during that investigation when Charga had become acquainted with several of the shedrow workers, stable hands, grooms and jockeys, and many of the involved thoroughbred horse trainers, that he had gained a better knowledge of the sport and a healthy respect for those who worked behind the scenes. What had begun as a relatively routine inquiry had resulted in his becoming much more interested in the sport of kings, which he had subsequently grown to really enjoy, albeit at a distance, via news stories and TV simulcasts. Another pleasant result was that a few of those newly acquired track acquaintances had morphed into a kind of steady, yet also long distanced, friendship between himself and those he had interviewed for that case. Unfortunately, since leaving the force to become an independent P.I. he had found it difficult to free up the extra time or the extra cash that would have allowed him to spend all the days he would have liked at the races, and in so doing to have more fully cultivated those acquaintances and friendships. Still, he considered a few of the grooms and jockeys his friends, and was certain they regarded him as such as well. One really good outcome stemming from that investigation was that while at the track he bumped into Adriana Messina, and they seemed to click. They dated several times and their relationship seemed to be growing, at least until she traveled back to Sicily to continue her studies. Even then, they had kept in touch via mail and an occasional phone call. "Well" he thought, "Today may be a perfect day to try to revitalize my friendships with the people here at the track." He had just collected a cash payment from his latest client, a suspicious wife who had asked to have her husband put under surveillance in order to prove her suspected case of infidelity in a possible divorce action. It had been an easy gig, a simple week long 7-24 surveillance, for an easy "nickel" pay check. The cheating husband in this case had been very accommodating. He had made no secret of the fact that he was indeed having an affair with his doctors' nurse. It was one of the more productive, money wise, investigations Charga had contracted in the past few weeks, and since this client had preferred to pay in cash, and had asked that he come to her office in Duarte to collect, figured it to be a great opportunity to skip on over to the nearby racetrack and take a shot at growing that $500 bankroll with a few well placed wagers. The videotape, photos, and chronological OAR (observed activities report) he submitted would definitely provide her lawyer incontrovertible evidence in the cause of her pending litigation, if she continued the action, thus almost guaranteeing a favorable decision in the divorce action. It had been impossible for Duke to not have noticed how this client had been so very, very pleased with his submitted report, and by virtue of her purring words of gratitude, and her inviting body language, he had sensed she had been offering more than simply the cash as payment for services rendered. Rather she was offering more for services she hoped were yet to be rendered on this sunny spring afternoon. Charga had been gently fondling the stack of fresh twenty dollar greenbacks she had just handed him. It was the most cash he had earned and handled in quite a while. He was counting and re counting the twenty five crisp new bills, meanwhile, unbeknownst to him, she had already discreetly removed her shoes and kicked them off under her eight foot wide oversized, over polished desk, lifted herself from the big leather chair, and had surreptitiously, very quietly and deliberately tip toed around and had positioned herself directly in front of him. She had rested her perfectly shaped derriere on the forward edge of the desk, and even before Charga had taken notice, stretched her long legs and began to seductively straddle his right leg. He looked up. She smiled. "Is there anything else you may need?" she asked, "Can you stay a while?" Charga, himself 36 years of age, figured her to be just a bit older, late thirties, maybe early forties, still she was a very handsome woman, blonde, about five foot ten in heels, not super model thin but slender and well proportioned, an intelligent and successful real estate broker with what appeared to be a bright and cheery outlook, considering the circumstances, and a rather charming, most alluring personality. Fully aware that the private investigators' primary function is to observe and report, and not to pronounce judgment on either client or subject of inquiry, he had found in this case, he was truly unable to understand what would possess a man to jeopardize any relationship with this most sexual woman. "I'd love to hang out with you, Mrs. Micelli" he had blurted out, "But you're actually still married, and I wouldn't want to screw up your case,"

"Lousy choice of words" he thought, then went on, "maybe another time. Today I planned to see a man about a horse." He had been contemplating spending a day at the races, and with the cash he now had on hand had determined this might be just the right day to take a shot. He removed her hand which had found its way up from his knee to resting ever so gently on his upper thigh. "But I certainly won't forget you" he had whispered. He rose and started to leave, but stopped with his hand on the door knob. He turned and added, "Like I said, maybe another time, okay?".

"No sense slamming this door shut!" he thought to himself. Still, to refuse and resist her generous and sensual hospitality had been, for him, a monumental exercise in self restraint, but he really did have other plans for the day, and if Duke Charga was anything, he was stubborn in his persistence. Maybe sometimes a bit too stubborn, he thought. This may have been one of those times. He had picked up the money just after three PM and the tarck policy of allowing free admission after the 7th race was another inducing factor to go on over and try his luck, after all, he was in the vicinity, and why not? So, he had made the short drive, and had walked on up to the entrance gate. As he expected, he was stopped, had to show his weapon carry permit, and luckily the entrance security guard had remembered him and did not pressure him to check the Glock. Now at the track, he was concentrating on the entries in the upcoming race. He had earlier doped out this 8th race as being a two filly race between the fillies Kostroma and Flawlessly. "Too close to separate" he thought, and so he decided on placing a boxed exacta using them both. Now, looking down at his program again, then back up to the odds tote board, he was sure he had made the right play. Flawlessly had been listed as the probable favorite with morning line odds of 7 to 5. She had been bet down to post time odds of 4 to 5. That's considered odds on. Kostromas morning line odds were listed as 2 to 1, and she had been bet down to 6 to 5 while the publics wagering pattern had pushed the rest of the field to odds of 8 to 1 or more. Kostroma was number 4 on the program, Flawlessly was number 7. He checked his wager ticket again. A $50 exacta wager of the 4 with the 7, and a $50 exacta wager of the 7 with the 4. He had risked 20% of his bankroll on this one boxed play wager. He slid the program and the wager ticket into the inside breast pocket of his suit jacket, removed his jacket handkerchief and briskly wiped his forehead. He ran his fingers over his closely cropped dark hair, and was surprised to find the top of his head slightly dampened with perspiration. Was it the unusual southern California April heat of the day, or the fact that he had been traveling around all day abuttoned up suit and tie? He had purposely kept his jacket buttoned up in order to keep concealed the shoulder holstered 16 round .45 caliber Glock automatic which he kept strapped on at all times when he was dressed. That was a habit he picked up during his active police days. Or was he becoming overheated due to having ventured beyond what some racing aficionados had come to call a personal wagering excitement-pain threshold? That certain point at which a gambler of any kind, places a wager where the excitement the wager presents is not on a par with the pain one may encounter when and if that wager turns out to be a loser. He recalled the trainers and jockeys trading stories concerning the horse player excitement-pain threshold, and how many of those players who ventured beyond their individual threshold had soured totally on the sport. Could it happen to him, he wondered momentarily, but then shrugged off the notion. "Never happen." he thought aloud, "Not for $100 anyway."

The British accented voice crackled across the track once again. "They're all in and set." There was a momentary pause, then the starting bell rang out, the gates flew open and the race was on. "And away they go!"

Charga strained to see the early positioning of the horses as they raced along on the backstretch. The new race caller was reporting the thoroughbreds changing positions within seconds of their movements. Charga was impressed by the running race call. "Say" he exclaimed, "This guy is really good."

Every filly in the race had been called in their respective position, but all he wanted to hear was how Kostroma and Flawlessly were running. Flawlessly had run off to the lead, she was in front by two lengths as the field reached the far turn. Kostroma was lost in the pack, running five lengths behind the leader. Now the horses were past the halfway mark and Flawlessly had maintained her front running position. At this point Kostroma was called as running fourth, four lengths behind, but just as Flawlessly led them into the turn heading into the stretch, he heard "Here comes Kostroma in the middle of the track!". Kostroma was demonstrating her fabled closing kick. Charga was into it now. He began shouting. "Come on Kostroma!". It was a great closing run, but Kostroma had come up just a head short of beating the favored Flawlessly. Still, Charga had the exacta, though he would have preferred it if Kostroma would have finished first. A Kostroma to Flawlessly exacta would have paid out $14 for every $2 wagered. This exacta of Flawlessly to Kostroma was returning a paltry $9.40 for $2. Charga had it 25 times for a total return of $240.

"Just short of a yard and a half he thought. "Not bad." He smiled as he quietly congratulated himself. "Not bad at all."

This had been the feature race of the day, so he waited around a bit before going to cash his winning ticket, to watch as the horse, jockey, trainer and owner converged in the winners circle for photographs and post race interviews, while the losing jockeys dismounted and began walking back to the jockey dressing rooms. At the same time, the losing horses were being led by their grooms and handlers to their respective stable areas, and they all passed just beyond the rail upon which he had been leaning. One of the grooms, Juan Zella, a true veteran hard boots stable hand, who during his more than ten years of track employment had worked at not only every southern California race track, but at both major northern California tracks, and down at the old Aqua Caliente race track in Tijuana, Mexico as well, spied Charga out of the corner of his eye. He stopped and called out. "Hey! Lieutenant Charga! How you doing?". Zella had been one of the persons most affected by that stable workers death Charga had investigated. Charga remembered Juan Zella most vividly. It was his testimony during the initial interrogation, and at the formal inquest which proved instrumental in the final court ruling of accidental death in the case of Juan's sibling, little Pepino Zella. It had been just two weeks prior to that fatal incident when Juan Zella had wired the passage money for young Pepino and his bride in order for them to emigrate to the United States from their native Argentina. Juan had then used his respected position and influence, earned thru his many years of trustworthy employment for numerous big name thoroughbred trainers and owners in the various race track shedrows, to get his younger brother immediately hired on as an assistant horse groom. On the day of the incident, Juan had been hot walking one of the thoroughbreds, along with that thoroughbreds' trainer, when they both heard a short holler, "Oww!", followed by a thumping sound emanating from just behind the John Steen barn. Juan was aware his brother had been working in that area. He had immediately handed over the lead reins to the trainer with him, and scurried off to find the source of the sounds, and to be of any assistance, if in fact any assistance had been needed. It was then that he found his younger brother Pepinos' body lying prostrate just in front of the number 3 barn. There was a fast growing pool of blood spreading on the straw covered dirt beneath his head. Juan had excitedly called to his trainer to immediately notify the track medical department, and to call 911. A track ambulance was on the scene within five minutes. The track team of paramedics had made every effort to restart the young boys heart, to no avail. The 911 emergency ambulance arrived ten minutes later. Both medical teams were too late, and both teams concurred, the 21 year old Pepino Zella was declared dead on the scene. It appeared he had fallen backward, hitting his head on the corner of the barn. Initial determination was simply that he had slipped after stepping in a small puddle of equine urine. The skull trauma had caused a brain hemorrhage and almost immediate death from internal sanguination. The track medical team had found Juan sobbing like a child. Little Pepino had died cradled in Juan Zellas' lap. A CSI team, the county coroner, and the Arcadia P.D. had been called in, and detectives Charga and Dunne had been dispatched to investigate the incident. They had arrived within twenty minutes of the call. The scene was fresh, but on that day Juan Zella was totally unable to respond to any questions. He had been so thoroughly shaken from the incident, he was not only unable to finish that day at work, but remained grief stricken and guilt ridden and was off work for two weeks following. Had he not sent for his brother to come and work with him at the track, this unfortunate incident would never had happened. His sister in law would stay in America just a few weeks, then with the help of friends and co workers would return to Argentina, sadly minus one young husband. Although he had witnessed many a shedrow accident, he never dreamed he would personally be on the scene at his own brothers' demise. Charga and Dunne had interviewed several others, including the trainer who had accompanied Juan, along with other stable workers, horse grooms, farriers, and some jockeys who had been nearby at the time, before getting to Juan Zella two days later. Charga was never totally satisfied with the initial and final determination in this case. He had suspected there was something more to the story and so had returned to the track barn area three additional times in order to clarify some relative facts. There had been no signs of any attempt on Pepino Zellas' part to halt his fall. No hand or arm indent in the moist soil next to or under the body, signifying a possibility that when Pepino had fallen backwards his body was already limp. Charga had suspected some sort of foul play. Had he been in a fight, was he hit in the head from behind? His instincts were seldom erroneous but he had finally acquiesced to the ruling of the court hearing judge on this case, death due to accidental circumstance. His partner, Mike Dunne had said "Let it go. we've got other cases to cover." and so he did. But now Charga was a bit surprised that Juan Zella had recognized him. "Hello Juan" he answered, "You remember me?"

"Sure. I remember you plenty good."

"But how did you pick me out of this crowd?" Charga asked, "I'm not that unforgettable am I?"

"It no that you be unforgettable" Zella answered with a smile. "It's more that you sure stand out from everybody else. You're hard not to notice."

That was so very true. Duke Charga really didn't fit in with most of the track attendees around him. Fully dressed in his dark blue gabardine suit, he stood out amongst the ordinary racing fan in that area who were mostly dressed in sport shirts and dungarees or khaki pants. Charga was clean shaven, lean and fit, and sporting dark green sunglasses that completely hid his ice blue eyes. He liked those glasses and felt they added something to his dark Gregory Peck type look.

"But I'm no longer with the police" he said, waving his hand as if to emphasize the statement, "I'm a private investigator now."

"I saw something about that" Juan Zella said in return, "On TV a few months ago."

Charga had also seen the local TV report concerning his voluntary resignation from the Arcadia P.D. He was happy that the newsman assigned to cover that story had been a bit on the lazy side, and hadn't bothered to delve any deeper beyond the public relations statements jointly released by himself and the department. Had he done so, he may have uncovered the true facts that precipitated Chargas' resignation. About how Charga had been under fire internally, and under investigation by the IAB (Internal Affairs Bureau) for allegedly abusing a suspected drug dealer in his custody. The alleged abuse however, had elicited information which in turn had led to the arrest and swift conviction of the czar of a major international drug cartel, but that fact obviously, had been irrelevant to the investigating IAB officers. Charga had been reprimanded and was about to be put on a 30 day suspension for his action. That had struck him the wrong way! It had been the proverbial straw that broke the camels back. After 8 years on the force, initially as a foot patrolman, then up to sergeant, and on up to detective and lieutenant detective, Charga had discovered that being a peace officer could be simultaneously rewarding and frustrating. He had been taught in academy that the mere presence of a uniformed patrolman acted as a deterrent against most criminal activity. As a beat cop he felt he was indeed performing an essential service for his fellowman in general, and society at large, by preventing the commission of many acts by would be criminal perpetrators, and by arresting those individuals involved in the actual commission of any crime. Even then however, he was somewhat frustrated as well in that, in many instances, the apprehended suspect of a given criminal act would be released hours before an arresting officer could complete the crime and arrest paperwork required by city, county, or state statute. He became even more frustrated when, as a detective, he was assigned to the homicide division where investigating crimes involving suspected homicides, after the fact, required a special attitude, a monumental degree of self restraint, an extensive knowledge of the law, and of the limits of the law, and required every detective to operate within certain pre approved boundaries. "We have rules" he often said, "But they don't!". Also, an abundance of intestinal fortitude was a strength to be called upon in almost every case, simply in order to cope with the sights and scents of gore and death, the inherent aftermath of any homicide. In any case, and especially those cases involving a homicide, the investigation of the crime, the gathering of evidence, questioning of persons of interest, and eventual apprehension of suspected perpetrators was tightly regulated by law, and all officers involved were required to operate within the limits of mandatory and court imposed rules of conduct. These restrictions, Charga had always felt, gave the edge to the criminal element. He had made it a personal strategy to push these rules to the edge of legality, and to skirt the limits of his police authority. This personal policy had garnered results. His arrest and conviction record was among the highest on the force. It was his off beat and sometimes labeled "rogue" tactics that had led to his reprimand and order of suspension. Rather than accept that determination, Charga had opted for resignation. He opined he could better serve society at large and satisfy his own sense of true justice, by embarking upon a career as a private investigator. As a P.I. he was less encumbered by most of the court imposed restrictions placed on the police, and so just maybe, he thought, he could turn the odds in his favor, and in favor of the general public and against the street criminals and thugs. With him it was simple, white is white, black is black, good is good, and bad is bad. There were no grays or in betweens.

"Yeah" he continued the conversation with Juan Zella, "I left on my own. Just got tired of all the bullshit and politics."

He was still holding Zellas hand in a firm gripped handshake.

"I saw that" Zella replied, "So como sta now? How you doing today? Any winners?"

"Just hit this exacta" Charga answered proudly, a self praising smile crept across his face.

Zella leaned in toward Charga and whispered conspiratorially,

"I gotta good one next race."

"Really? Charga was interested, "Who?'

"Numero quartro, number four." Zella whispered again, "He's been working real good, very sharp, he looks ready. No bulla crappa."

"You know for sure?"

"Si! I ma sure. I know!"

"Great! Thanks Juan." Charga released Zellas hand, reached into his inside vest pocket, pulled out his wallet and removed several business cards. He turned one over and wrote a number.

"Here's my cellular phone number" he said, handing the cards to Zella. "Call me if you get any others in the next few days, okay?"

Zella took the cards. "Sure lieutenant" he said, "No problema." Then, noticing the cards read M. D. Charga private investigations, asked "What's the MD for? You're not a doctor too, are you?"

"No" Charga replied with a snorting laugh, "My father was a big John Wayne fan!"

Juan Zella, not being a big movie fan, and not understanding the inference, but not wanting to display ignorance, simply shrugged and nodded his head.

By now, the winning horse, trainer, jockey and owner had left the winners circle and were making their way back to the barn area.

"I got to get going" Zella said, motioning toward the oncoming entourage. "Whittingham and Stevens are coming."

"Good seeing you again, Juan" Charga called out as Zella started walking away with his horse in hand, then added "Call me okay?" Zella looked back over his shoulder, and smiled. "Okay" he said, then continued toward the paddock and barn area.

The winning horse, trainer and jockey strolled by, very near where Charga was standing. "Nice ride Gary!" Charga called out as he caught the jockeys eye. Then added "Good job Charlie!". The big bald headed trainer nodded his thanks, and both he and jockey Stevens smiled triumphantly as they walked on past.

Charga looked up at the tote board. Number four was at 6 to 1. He immediately went to cash in his winning exacta ticket and place a wager on the number four in the next race. He never even looked in the program to see the horses' name. It would be the final race of the day. With nothing planned for the next day, he decided to head on home to his apartment in Century City. He figured he'd return on the morrow if the number four was a winner. He trotted briskly out to parking area number C-3. Located his new dodge Dynasty, and proceeded to pull out onto Huntingdon boulevard heading toward the freeway. Charga loved this jet black vehicle. It had come equipped with all power accessories, brakes, windows, locks and steering, and he had found, for him, it was super comfortable. He settled into the soft cloth covered drivers' seat and gazed proudly over the vehicle. If nothing else, his hitch in the P.D. had at least earned him this car. It had a body style so similar to that of the bigger Chrysler New Yorker, one had to get up close to notice any differences. The contours of both these vehicles also closely resembled the body type of that years Cadillac Sedab De Ville. Smart buyers chose the Dynasty since its' purchase price was about half that of either the New Yorker or the Caddy. He had bought this vehicle all cash, using the bulk of his savings along with his earned severance pay from the P.D.

"It was a good buy." he thought as he pressed down on the accelerator, "What pickup!"

It was the right decision to get on the road early. Even on a Saturday one could get jammed up in freeway traffic congestion, especially when the local ball game and the horse races ended at about the same time. He decided to go a bit out of his way, down to Anaheim, and stop in for an early evening Italian dinner at Mommas Place. It was a popular spot, and at about this time Momma would be just beginning her busy Saturday night dinner action. Charga figured he could slip in just before the rush. He was right. Had he waited just another half hour he would have needed a reservation to get a plate of her famous spaghetti. Mommas Place was a small family owned and operated restaurant situated in the middle of a tiny, twelve store shopping mall. The restaurant itself consisted of just two rows of six tables each, one row against the south wall, one row down the center, all twelve covered with what has become the traditional red and white checkerboard table cloth, a standard to be found in most Italian restaurants of any self vaunting authenticity. A set of four booth tables hugged the north wall. Each table top was home to a rather large container filled with Parmesan cheese, as well as a smaller jar of oregano, along with the usual shakers of salt and pepper. The sweet aroma of Italian home cooking lent a certain ambiance that could hardly be found in other Italo-American restaurants in the area. Charga hesitated at the door just in order to inhale and enjoy the first appetizing scents of that home cooked Sicilian sauce and the various aromatic cheeses that effectively roused his gastric juices. That aroma brought back memories. With every visit here he found himself momentarily reminiscing over the many times he and Adriana had dined here.

"Man" he thought, "I really did enjoy her company. Maybe I like her more than I realize."

He pictured her face. Her dark eyes and silken black hair perfectly suited her smooth olive complexion. The vision of her inviting, lush and full lips oft times floated thru his dreams, especially so when he was at Momma Garlattis' place. Charga had been introduced to Momma s some time earlier when Adriana, who was an Italian exchange student at the time steered him to it, claiming the taste of food served there was the closest to authentic Sicilian in all California. Because of his own unique family heritage, Chargas' father was of Spanish/Mexican origin, while his mom was of Italian descent, he discovered that he really did thoroughly enjoy the special, topical semi-spicy taste of Sicilian dinner fare, and found himself returning again and again, back here to Mommas. At Mommas he was now considered a regular.

"Hello lieutenant, come on in." Angelo, the youngest of the Garlatti family, greeted him warmly. "I'll set you up in the booth right here."

13

Angelo was the baby in the Garlatti family. His two brothers handled the buying and preparation of the food, he simply waited tables and bussed, however like his siblings, he weighed in a bit on the heavy side. Momma Garlatti now simply took care of the books, but it was her own home cooking recipes that were followed in the kitchen. Angelo stood iust five foot eight. was barrel chested and rather wide in the middle, and he carried over 250 pounds, undoubtedly the result of daily sampling of Mommas |pasta and pizza. Slightly balding, his short necked rounded head gave the impression of being an NBA basketball with eyeballs and a perennial smile. Charga heldthe notion that had Angelo gone into professional sports he could easily have become a big league catcher, he had the perfect body for it, kind of short and kind of wide. Angelo led Charga to the first booth nearest the storefront window. "Vino?" he asked.

Charga nodded. Angelo knew the wine. He knew Charga preferred Barbarone out of the Sonoma valley vineyards.

"I'll be back with your wine and a menu." he said as he turned and walked toward the back room scullery area.

"Thanks Ange" Charga said, fiddling with the cheese container, "You know what I like."

Charga sat quietly, physically still, but mentally alert to excess. This was the booth he and Adriana had shared when, at Adrianas insistence, they first dined together here at Mommas. Seated here, he was finding it very difficult to brush the many pictures of Adriana from the memory screen of his mind. His thoughts were traveling back and forth now, between those good moments with her, and some of the bad moments with the Arcadia P.D., along with a pressing present concern regarding his $200 win ticket, the result of which, to him, at this time remained unknown. He calmed himself by remembering that Juan Zella had already recommended two other plays, both of which turned out to be winners. That was during and shortly after Chargas' investigation into the circumstances of Pepino Zellas death. Owing to that he felt somewhat assured in the veracity of Juan Zellas' inside dope. Still, a $200 win wager was a lot more than the $20 each he had plopped down on the previous two tips. "How had Zella known?" he wondered to himself. Were those races on the up and up? "No!" he said half aloud, "I won't go there. So what anyhow."

He reached into his inside shirt pocket to retrieve the ticket and began pondering his action once again just as Angelo returned with the wine and a menu. Charga looked up. He anticipated the inevitable next question. Angelo had asked it every time Charga had come in solo, and as usual he was not disappointed. "So, how is Adriana?"

"Fine" Charga answered, "She's still back in Sicily, but we keep in touch."

Then, really half in an attempt to change the subject, and half to satisfy his own curiosity added, "Angelo, did you hear who won the last race today?"

Charga knew the brothers Garlatti were avid horse race fans.

"My brother Mike is cooking tonight, he always listens to KNX. He should know."

"Could you find out for me? I'd appreciate it."

"Sure. No problema. I'll be right back." Angelo turned and started toward the back of the restaurant.

"Hold on Ange!" Charga called out, halting Angelo in his tracks.

"I'll have the ziti with mommas meat sauce, okay?"

"Right." Angelo took back the menu and disappeared through the doors marked 'Kitchen Personnel Only'.

Charga stared down at his $200 win ticket. He convinced himself.

"Win or lose, it was worth a shot."

Angelo returned shortly, ziti in hand, and smiling as usual.

"Here you go lieutenant." he said as he deftly positioned the plate of hot ziti on the table directly in front of Charga. "And by the way, be careful the plate is hot." Then smiling even more broadly, "Mange, enjoy." He remained standing near the booth, then bowed slightly toward Charga and said in almost a whisper, "Mikey says it was a 4, 6, 3 in the nitecap at the track. Is that good?"

Charga smiled. He flashed the $200 win ticket on number 4 so that Angelo could understand the reason for his own wide grin.

"Bono!" Angelo exclaimed, "Tutta bono!"

Charga dug into his ziti. It was doubly enjoyable this night.

Chapter Two

Visits, Violence & Vice

7 A.M.

The rising, warm southern California sun had already begun
its' gradual and tenacious burning away of the usual Los
Angeles area layer of low hanging clouds and coastal eddy fog, leaving
behind a film of morning dew on grass, leaves, and all surfaces
horizontal as lone evidence of their existence. Even Chargas' beloved
Dynasty, despite being parked under a covered carport, had not been
spared. The golden rays were now penetrating the window panes of
Chargas' one bedroom Century City apartment, falling across his bed,
providing both light for the room, and a rather soothing warmth for
his shoulders. Charga rolled over to face the ceiling. The sun warmed
his face. Normally he slept on his side or on his back, but this night
he had fallen asleep on his stomach, his face resting snugly on the
hewer of his two down filled pillows, a sure sign that the four glasses
of Barbarone wine he had drunk while scarfing down Mommas' ziti
with homemade meat sauce, followed by the customary signature
Sicilian after dinner cordial of a small glass of Anisette liquor had
been just a bit of an overly copious quantity of alcoholic beverage. He
rubbed some of the sleep from his eyes, then kicked the single cotton
sheet off his unclothed body, at the same time knocking the second
pillow from his double wide bed to the floor. Southern California
spring nights were seldom cool enough to warrant being covered
with more than one sheet, or one lightweight blanket at best, for a

person to sleep comfortably. He focused on the bedroom window to his right. The early light was beginning to pour in now. It would be another unusually warm day, even for L.A. A good day to be at the races, he thought. He hoped he would be as hot at the track today as he had been the day before, two bets, two wins. He sat up and quickly became cognizant of the fact that he was unconsciously sporting a healthy morning erection, undoubtedly equally the result of some sexual dreaming, combined with a full kidney and bladder brought on by his excess intake of fluids the night before. He picked up the pillow which had fallen atop his shoes and socks next to the bed, tossed it back onto the bed, and started toward the bathroom to immediately relieve himself.

"I'll pass on these today" he thought, stepping over the set of barbells and hand weights he used in what had become for him, until just lately, a virtual morning ritual. Was he becoming lazy or was he simply bored of these weights? He had been advised by his investigative partner detective lieutenant Bill Dunne, back when they were first assigned together in the robbery division at Arcadia, that a well prepared officer should not only be mentally sharp, but physically fit as well, and that it would be wise at all times to keep himself in tip top condition. It was in this way, Dunne had opined, that an officer of the law could stay one step ahead of the criminal perpetrators. It was advice well meant and well taken. Charga had learned to pride himself on his lean and fit physicality. He had, until very recently, made it a must do routine to work out with his weights for at least fifteen minutes every day. In addition, he had also signed on with Tai Kato, a Korean Tae Bo instructor, for an intensive six month semester of training in that Asian fighting technique. Upon completion of that course he had become quite proficient in the oriental arts of both defense and attack. He quickly shaved, showered and toweled off, then still naked, hesitated momentarily, as he purposely took a longer than usual glimpse of his reflection in the bathroom mirror. In addition to the over the bathroom sink mirror, another full length mirror had been installed on the inside of the bathroom door. It came with the apartment, along with the stove, fridge, microwave, and built in air conditioning. These were all normal accessories for the apartments in the area. He flexed his sinewy muscles and grinned triumphantly. Despite his recent tendency toward skipping some morning workouts, his body was holding together in excellent physical shape, and he mused that he, like the mirror firmly hanging on the door, could also be described as being "well hung". He stepped lightly out of the bathroom and headed down the short hall that led to his apartments' combination dining/living room and kitchen. He checked the kitchen for his favorite kitchen appliance, the Mr. Coffee coffee maker machine. It sat on the countertop in its' usual spot, next to the kitchen sink, ready for its' customary morning action. He set it up for two cups, dropped in two tablespoons of coffee, added the water and got it going. Then he simply gazed around the room as the coffee began rapidly dripping into the carafe below. He was anxiously awaiting that first, always delicious cup of morning coffee. The aroma was always just so inviting. It was a rather small kitchen area, based on most Century City apartment standards, just ten foot by ten foot of floor space, but with lots of countertop space and overhead wall cabinets. Charga hadn't found too much use for all the cabinetry, he kept but a minimum of plates and pots, one complete set of dishes, service for six and two pots and one frying pan for when he woke with enough ambition to prepare himself some eggs, sunnyside up, as he liked them. The all electric stove was situated just to the left of the fridge, and left of the stove, in the corner, was a countertop microwave oven, then a nice double stainless steel sink just below the centrally located kitchen window. The kitchen area opened to a small dining area. Here Charga had placed the 3 foot by 5 foot wooden dining table which he had picked up at a garage sale some months earlier, along with 4 triple slatted back chairs with woven cane seats, none of which fit into the basic overall more modern character of most of the other furniture in his apartment. The dining area worked into the living area where Charga had set up a large black leather couch facing his large screen TV, and stereo equipment. A small tiled floor area sat just to the right of the TV set at the foot of the apartment entry door. The short hallway leading to the bedroom and adjoining bath made up the remainder of the apartments 750 square foot living space. It was enough for him, at least at this point in his life. He opened the fridge, more instinctively rather than for any particular purpose, hoping maybe to find some morsel of food that might go with his coffee. Nothing much. Just two cans of Miller light, one of which had already been opened, "And probably flat by now" he thought, remembering that it had been two days back when he had popped it open for a cool slug just before heading on out for a final round of surveillance on the gallivanting Mr. Micelli. There was a half head of lettuce, some over ripened tomatoes, and a cut green bell pepper lying limply on the bottom shelf. The remnants of a well intentioned, but quickly abandoned health food diet that he had tried out for a grand total of three days. He had found a strictly vegetable diet just did not provide him the inner feeling of strength to which he had become accustomed. Maybe that was why he had lately been skipping his morning workout regimen. The coffee made, he poured himself a cup, added a teaspoon of sugar, took a quick sip, then returned to his bedroom, coffee in hand. He took a longer sip, placed the hot cup atop the track program from the previous day, which he had tossed on his dresser along with his $200 win ticket, and began to dress. As he pulled up his boxer shorts and tucked in his open armed undershirt he heard the gentle ding dong of his apartment doorbell.

"Who could be ringing at this time?" he asked himself as he hastened back down the hallway still holding a single sock in each hand. The bell rang again. This time it seemed to ring with a tone of urgency. "Keep you pants on!" Charga called out, "I'm coming." He stopped at the door and peered through the security peephole. It was his former police partner, Mike Dunne.

"Mike!" he exclaimed, more in surprise than anything else, "Hold on."

Charga hurriedly slid back the door safety chain, released the deadbolt lock and opened the door. "Mike, what brings you here?" he asked, "Especially at this time."

Charga figured it had to be something relatively important to motivate Mike Dunne to be out and about before nine A.M. His recollections of Dunne was that of a chronic slow starter. With him it was always two or three cups of coffee, a donut, and a long drawn out discussion of the work schedule of the day, before beginning any plan of action at all. Dunne was a typical career cop. Fifteen years in uniform, now over ten years as detective. He was big. Big all around. Over six foot, wide shouldered with a short strong neck, a powerful 44 inch chest and 20 inch biceps. Slicked down salt and pepper hair, dark eyebrows over dark brown eyes, but with a prematurely gray, almost white moustache over a set of heavy lips. His face was pock marked, the unwelcome aftermath of his time of teenage hormonal turmoil. He could easily be taken for a professional wrestler. Dunne was also not especially noted for personal tact, and true to his reputation was as brusque as he was burly. He brushed past Charga, stopped suddenly as he was about to seat himself on the couch, then questioned, "Is that coffee I smell?", and headed on into the kitchen. Charga closed the door and followed. "Nice to see you too, Mike" he said, his tone more sardonic than cheerful.

Dunne had already opened and closed two overhead cabinets in an eager search for a cup. His third try was successful. He poured himself the last cup of fresh brew, and replaced the empty brew carafe, then opened the fridge and growled. "What? No milk?"

"Not today" Charga answered, "Sorry.".

"Ah, that's okay" Dunne mumbled almost inaudibly, "I'll just take it black." He looked back at Charga. "Get dressed." he ordered, "I'll wait."

"That's what I was doing." Charga replied. Then as he walked on back to his bedroom added "By the way, unplug my Mr. Coffee." Mike Dunne yanked the cord from the outlet in his usual manner, using more force than necessary, then strolled after Charga, still taking in the hot coffee in quick short sips.

Chaga picked out a fresh shirt from the group of two dozen hanging in his closet, donned his favorite blue pants, checked his Glock, slipped it in his shoulder holster and strapped it on. "Still favoring that oversize cannon, hey?" Dunne half asked referring to Chargas weapon. He really didn't expect an answer, and received none as Charga just smirked, and shot him a look implying it was still none of Mike Dunnes' business. Dunne had always chided him about carrying such a weapon. Charga had always liked his big Glock. It had become a running discussion back when they worked together. Dunne looked around. This bedroom hadn't changed much since he last was here. That was almost a year ago. Same ordinary dark wood bed, dresser and night tables, same lamps, nothing elaborate. The dresser mirror still needed a good cleaning. It was as streaked as ever. He scanned the dresser top and quickly eyeballed the track program under Chargas' coffee cup, and the $200 win ticket protruding out from under the program.

"Been to the track, hey?" he queried, now in a more serious tone. This time he was expecting an answer. Charga nonchalantly slipped on his socks and shoes, picked up his coffee and drank most of it down. "You noticed, so?' he replied, answering the question with one of his own. "Is that why you stopped in, to get a tip?"

"Maybe something like that." Dunne shot back, fingering both the track program and the wagering ticket. Charga noticed he was frowning. He was about to again ask of the real nature of this unexpected early morning visit when the ring of the front doorbell momentarily interrupted his chain of thought.

"Who could that be now?" he wondered to himself, then said aloud, "Seems like it's gonna be a busy morning." and started toward the door.

"Don't bother peeking thru the hole" Dunne said, keeping just two steps behind, "That's my partner Brad. I had him park the car in back."

Charga opened the door. He found Dunnes' present partner still anxiously leaning on the bell button.

"That's my partner." Dunne announced almost sheepishly, "Detective sergeant Brad Street". He motioned toward Charga.

"Meet my ex partner Marion Duke Charga."

Street was an extremely tall man, over six foot six, and appeared to be very lean and mean. He was well dressed, in a light blue gabardine suit over a silk gray shirt and silk charcoal black tie. His face was drawn. Thin lipped, with closely set cold blue eyes, a high forehead with short cut blondish hair that drastically receded at the temples. He addressed Charga in a cool standoffish tone, and made it a point to not offer his hand to shake.

"I've heard about you." His voice was deep. Charga imagined that had he heard this voice while blindfolded, he could easily believe he was hearing the voice of the base baritone of the Platters. He ignored the intonation. He was well aware of the fact that he had earned a less than favorable reputation with most of his counterparts at Arcadia, and had come to accept a certain amount of animosity from them. He stepped out of the way and waved his hand in a mock royal invitation.

"Mi casa es su casa." he said as he backed toward the couch, felt it behind his calves, and eased himself into the end seat.

21

"Captain Dunbar still setting up the assignments?" he asked, turning to Dunne with a raised eyebrow.

"Yeah." Dunne answered, "So what?"

Charga chuckled. "It's just that it's good to see he hasn't lost his sense of humor."

Dunne appeared slightly puzzled.

"Dunne and Brad Street!" Charga blurted out with a mocking grin, "Very nice team up."

"Wise guy!" Street interjected, "I didn't think it was so funny."

Even Duke Charga, who wasn't one to scare off easily, found Streets' commandingly deep voice a bit intimidating.

"Old Dunbar!" Charga explained, almost apologetically, "He was always doing things like that. He called us, Mike and me, the candy cops." He looked up at Street. "Get it? Mike and Marion. M and M." Street remained rigid just within the open doorway. He didn't smile.

"So what kind of name is that anyway? Marion?'

"My Dad was a big John Wayne fan." Charga replied. The explanatory retort was obviously beyond Streets' perception, and went totally unrecognized. "Forget it." Charga said as he waved his hand as if to wipe away the words. "So what brings you two down here? You still haven't said."

Big Mike Dunne shifted uncomfortably, finished his coffee, then set the empty cup in the kitchen sink. He was reluctant to broach the subject but knew it was part of his job, no matter how uncomfortable it might be. He had to ask some serious questions. The idea that an ex cop, his own former partner, could be involved on the wrong end of some criminal activities, and that he had been assigned the task of leading this investigation, put him in a position he did not at all relish. He walked deliberately back to the living room, folded his arms and asked, in a slow and serious tone, "Do you know John Harborstone?"

Charga leaned back. The name seemed familiar, but it was not a name that conjured up a face nor an incident. "I know that name from somewhere" he said, "but can't say from where. Why?"

"Just look in your racing program." Dunne barked as he trudged into the bedroom. He promptly returned, track program and wager ticket in hand. He dropped both in Chargas' lap.

"Last race." he said, "Horse number four. And who is the trainer?" Charga flipped thru the program pages. Dunne was right. Harborstone was the trainer of the horse he had bet. He looked up. "So?" he asked, "What's that got to do with me? And with you and . . ." motioning to the tall detective Street, "with stretch over there?"

"It's why we're here wise guy." Street shot back, his base voice now more tinged with defiance than before.

Mike Dunne shrugged, nodded, and turned back toward his partner. "Okay. Just take it easy Brad." he ordered, "We'll get what we came for, just relax and let me do the talking."

Charga took a final sip of coffee, set the cup down on the table next to the couch, and leaned back again. He looked up at Dunne and Street. They made a formidable duo. Dunne, with his all around bigness and professional police attitude, Street with his extraordinary height and seemingly hair trigger temperament. Another excellent team up job by captain Dunbar. He stared up at Big Mike Dunne, wondering where his line of questioning was leading. Now it was Chargas' curiosity that was piqued.

"Where are you going, Mike?' he asked, "What is it you really want to know?"

Dunne turned slowly, silently, and trudged into the dining area. He was deliberately moving in a manner designed to be intimidating. In one motion he pulled a chair away from the table, straddled the seat and leaned his upper torso over the chair back, resting his powerful arms on the top slat. The chair groaned under his weight. "Where do you come off laying two hundred smackers to win on a horse?" he asked. Then added, "On a Harborstone horse yet."

Before Charga could even begin to offer a response, Street, who had remained standing in the open doorway, slammed the door shut and grunted, "C'mon! C'mon! Speak up wise guy!"

"Hey Mike!" Charga blurted out to his former partner, "Rein him in, Okay?."

Mike Dunne raised an open hand, palm out, toward the taller detective. "Shush!" he whispered, and the lanky detective Street tightened his lips and took a slight step back.

Dunne faced Charga. "Harborstone was found beaten half to death early this morning." He spoke in a matter of fact tone.

Charga perked up. "What? Where? How? And anyway what's that got to do with me?"

"Your card was found in his pocket with your cellular phone number written on it." Dunne replied, then asked, "We need to know, what's your business with him?"

"No business" Charga answered, "I just happened to bet on one of his horses."

"And I guess you're going to tell me you didn't know that the CHRB is looking into his horse business?"

Charga answered that question with two of his own. "How would I know that? What's really going on here, Mike?"

Detective Street folded his long arms across his chest and interjected, "Here's a better question, wise guy. How can you afford that cell phone and that new Chrysler New Yorker you've got parked out back?"

Charga was becoming a bit agitated now. "I need that phone for my business, and by the way, it's a Dynasty, bud." His intonations had now become defiant. His friendship with Mike Dunne notwithstanding, it could not offset the obvious animosity which had so quickly risen up between himself and Dunnes' overgrown new partner.

Street snarled back. "Yeah? Well we know you've got no paper on it. Bought it cash, hey?"

Charga couldn't help but notice the hostility in tone and demeanor of the big man standing at his door. Detective Streets' jaw had tightened, the muscles in his face were taut, and his right hand had balled into a fist. Charga fully recognized that, when on the force, he had alienated several of his fellow officers, both in uniform, and from his own detectives squad because of his lone ranger style, and he was well aware that he had not been universally loved by any of his superior officers up the chain of command. This situation had come about primarily due to his unorthodox criminal investigative technique which relied almost exclusively on his own singular lone wolf approach toward solving crime. Because he had rarely enlisted assistance of any kind from other detectives in his unit, many felt he was a kind of self serving glory seeker. Well, he admitted, in some ways he did relish the notoriety. At the time he was a working Arcadia detective, Duke Charga had considered himself the most efficient investigator in the squad, and his top rated arrest and conviction numbers had certainly served to reinforce his self confidence. A bit of the ill feelings toward him could be ascribed to plain old jealousy, mostly from the older, more veteran members of his detective unit. He had been the hot shot, the zealous rookie detective with fresh ideas and an inexhaustible reservoir of energy. They were mostly burned out from the unending grind of viewing the sights and the sites of criminal homicides. Still, he wondered just what over exaggerated fairy tales had been passed around the squad room to affect Street so intensely, though he knew some thought of him as a rogue cop, and some others said he was just plain bad, just because of his one major slip. Charga decided it was best to change the subject, and terminate this exchange with the tall detective, an exchange of words which had so quickly turned so adversarial. Purposely ignoring Streets' question, Charga turned back to his former partner. "Honestly, Mike" he said, "I had no business with Harborstone. He definitely got my card from someone else, I sure didn't give it to him.".

Dunne shifted slightly, rubbed his forehead as if to imply he was wondering aloud. "We'll find out, Duke" he said, "I can't figure where you fit into this yet . . ." he hesitated for a few seconds, then added, "But it sure looks funny from here."

"How do you mean?"

"One. He's got one of your PI cards" Dunne held up a finger with each new point. "Two. You've got a nice two hundred win bet on one of his nags. Three. He's being investigated for some kind of racing infraction or finagling, and four, he turns up almost dead from a beating.".

"So, where do you figure I do fit in?"

"I worked with you for a year plus some." Dunne answered, "I know how you can get yourself involved with things.".

"Come on Mike, I . . ."

Dunne held up his big open palm in the universal motion for stop. "I'm not saying you had anything to do with Harborstones injuries. Just that you might know something without knowing you know it. Know what I mean?".

"Now, what could that something be?" Charga queried. He had already run the info Dunne had related thru his thought process center and was certain his link to Harborstone, although peripheral, was connected to Juan Zella.

"This is just a preliminary investigation." Dunne began explaining, now almost apologetically, "You know the routine. We have to check all the angles."

"Sure, Mike" Charga acknowledged, "I know.".

"Well, what about it?" Dunne asked suddenly, pointing to the track program and the $200 win ticket. "What's the story? And don't bullshit me."

"Nothing much to tell." Charga answered, smiling and holding the wager ticket. "I just took a shot on this nag." He knew the wily veteran detective wasn't about to buy so simple a response, but it was all he was inclined to deliver at this point anyway.

"But why would Harborstone have one of your cards on him?" Dunne asked again, his voice dropping an octave or two.

Charga shrugged and shook his head in response. Actually he was almost certain of the answer to this question, but was really unwilling to offer it up before first checking out Juan Zella on his own. Were Zella and Harborstone jointly involved in some sort of racing improprieties, and had he been given a winner because Juan had known of an impending pre arranged outcome? Before Charga would give up Juan Zellas' name, he would have to check into this on his own. His lone ranger instincts were kicking in again.

Dunne smiled, the smile of one who could not be easily fooled. "You know I don't believe a word of this, right?' he asked, his tone dripping with sarcasm. Charga smiled back and shrugged again. "Okay then," Dunne continued, "Where'd you get the dough to make such a nice size wager?"

Charga stood up. "That's easy" he said, as he slipped the ticket into his shirt pocket. "I just finished a surveillance gig, and got paid a small bundle. Then I won some more. So I had money to burn."

He went to the kitchen, opened a drawer and removed a spiral notebook. It was the book wherein Charga kept all his clients names, job descriptions, and income notes. "Want the name of my last client?" he asked. "Now you know I don't have to give this to you right? But here, you can check it out for yourself." He tossed the notebook to his former partner. "Last entry, last page written on."

"We will" Dunne assured, as he rose. He walked toward the entry door, and handed the notebook to Street. "Copy the last entries" he ordered, "We'll check this part of the story.". Street fumbled through his jacket pockets for his own pad and pen. Locating them, he hurriedly wrote out the last page entry, then dropped the notebook on top the TV.

"Before we go" Dunne began again, "So now, how did you say Harborstone got hold of your card?" Thinking maybe he could irritate Charga into blurting out a truthful answer. The strategy didn't work. Charga simply smiled and shrugged again.

"Would you believe, coincidence?" he asked mockingly.

"Let's go Brad." Dunne murmured, then to Charga "We'll be in touch."

"So what do you figure it for, Mike?" Charga asked, raising himself up off the couch, "A straight out mugging robbery?".

The three men stood together now just between the doorway and the TV. Charga picked up his client notebook and riffled its pages with his thumb. Mike Dunne ran a forefinger across his whitened moustache wiping off the last few lingering drops of coffee.

"He had over a hundred bucks on him" he answered, "To me that rules out a mugging for money.".

"So what then?" Charga pressed. He really wanted to get a feel for Mikes' take on this assault. He had always admired Dunnes' expertise in perception regarding motive and intentions of possible perpetrators. "What's your take?"

"Seems personal." Dunne went on, "Seems like somebody just wanted to beat him up." He paused momentarily, "Question is, who and why?"

"So you've got no idea of motive, why or who?"

"Can you give us one?" Street interjected, "You're the KIA in here, aintcha?"

Street was alluding to Chargas' reputation as a wise guy cop. KIA was short talk used by officers and detectives down at the P.D. to describe an officer who carried himself like he had all the answers. It stood for a Know It All.

"Took place in the early A.M." Dunne continued, ignoring his partners comments. "Someone probably knew his routine, knew when he normally arrived down at the stable, knew he would most likely be alone, sat in wait and caught him unawares." He shook his head slowly, "Then just beat the hell out of him."

"You mentioned the California Horseracing board. Maybe something to do with that?" Charga asked.

"I don't even know what they were looking into." Dunne replied as he buttoned up his suit jacket. It appeared he had put on some extra pounds since first purchasing this suit as the jacket pulled tautly against the buttons. His .38 caliber snub nose now clearly outlined beneath the jacket just under the left armpit. "I just met them at the hospital when Brad and me went down there to see if we could get a statement."

"Did Harborstone say anything you could use?"

"Nah. He couldn't talk. He was out of it. Doctor said maybe later today would be okay." Dunne now unbuttoned his jacket. "Damn jacket shrunk!" he grumbled, "Dry cleaner must have used too much fluid.".

Charga smiled. "Right!" he said, knowing full well it was Mike Dunnes' morning donut ritual that was to blame here. "Too much fluid, sure."

Dunne continued, "It was the CHRB who mentioned their inquiry. Said his stable was winning an outrageous percentage of races lately. Guess they figured it was information we might be able to use."

"Probably some kind of race fixing." Street cut in.

"Don't mind him, Duke" Dunne half whispered, "He's against all kinds of gambling. Thinks it's all crooked."

"Figures." Charga chuckled, then nodding toward the tall man, added "Much too uptight."

Street began to say something in response but was restrained once again by Dunnes' big open palm, held just in front of his face. "Enough!" Dunne exclaimed. "We'll be going in a minute." He looked squarely at Charga, "I still like to know how he came to have your card with your hand written cell phone number on it and . . ."

"Can't really say" Charga interrupted, "I already told you that." "I know what you told me, Duke, but I sure get the feeling that you know more than you've said here."

"Honestly Mike" Charga turned both hands palm up in a pleading gesture, "I probably know less than you." Then added, "But if you like, I'll check around down at the track."

"We can do that ourselves" Street cut in, now seemingly annoyed at his partners' ongoing conversation and hesitance in leaving, "We're on our way there now."

"You know Mike" Charga continued, "most of the stable hands down shed row are illegals." He was speaking to his former partner but intentionally staring at the tall detective. "You know how they avoid the law any way they can, and they certainly won't want to be questioned by you two super white guys."

Dunne nodded. He was well aware of the illegal status of many shed row workers, and he could not disagree. He knew his former partner was right-on regarding the shed row track employees. He had already thought back to when he and Charga, working together out of the Arcadia P.D. were assigned to investigate the death of a shed row employee some months previous. He remembered how the illegal alien stable hands had suddenly disappeared like the cats in a Siegfried and Roy illusion show, how it had been so difficult to have any of them voluntarily come forth, much less be willing to tolerate any kind of investigative inquiries, once they knew that he and Charga wore badges and represented the law. At that time, because of Chargas' ancestry and heritage it had been prudent for Dunne to allow his younger partner to take the lead in the investigation. Charga had wanted it so, and Dunne concluded it wise to acquiesce. Voluntarily relinquishing his position of lead detective was not an action Dunne relished, what with his many years of seniority and ranking in the Arcadia P.D., still he had thought it a smart and correct move in that particular case. The deciding factor was that Charga was fluent enough to understand and converse in the workers' native Spanish.

"They probably would respond better to someone who speaks their language and doesn't carry a badge." Charga said, his eyes locked onto Streets, all the while thinking, "So I'm a KIA? Well maybe in this case I really am." He directed his next remarks straight at detective Street. "That's right. I can talk to them in their language, so I'll surely get more out of them than you guys could." he said, now smiling a smile of confidence. "And as soon as I get something relevant I'll let you know about it."

Street grimaced. Though still somewhat of a novice in detective work, he instinctively knew what Charga had said likely was true. A badge could scare illegals from surfacing, much less allowing themselves to be available for questioning. In addition they would likely play dumb if they could even be rounded up.

"So where is Harborstone now?' Charga asked, maintaining his stone cold stare. He was already formulating a plan of action. His quick mind had long since processed the tidbits of information Dunne had volunteered. Question number one. What was Harborstone doing with his card? Answer. It seemed obvious that Harborstone was in need of some sort of personal or confidential assistance requiring the services of a private investigator. He undoubtedly must have mentioned something to Juan Zella in regards to a personal matter where he had need of a P.I., or more possibly, since he had been found rather beaten, a bodyguard. He was sure Zella would not have handed over the card without Harborstone first broaching some such subject. Question number two. Why was the California Horse racing Board investigating Harborstone? Answer. Since Zella had already tipped Charga onto several winners, long before they stepped on the track, it was likely Zella was privy to some inside information, or he was simply a genius at handicapping. Possible, but not likely, Charga thought. More likely the scenario included something a bit more devious, and also likely Harborstone was involved. And it was also very possible Harborstone remained in some sort of trouble, and maybe in some sort of danger as well, and was still in need of some kind of personal and confidential service, the type of service that could only be provided by a private investigator. The attack on Harborstone could very well be connected to something related to racing. He would talk with Harborstone first, then back to the track to question Juan Zella. Dunne finally answered the question. "He's in General Hospital in Duarte.", then asked one of his own, "Why do you want to know?".

"Just curious." Charga replied coyly. "I'm hoping he'll be okay. He's a pretty good trainer."

"I'd really prefer you don't put your nose in this, Duke." Dunne said, knowing full well that if his former partner had already decided to poke around, his advice would go unheeded. "But I can't really stop you." He paused for a moment, adjusted his shoulder holster, purposely exposing his police shield hooked onto his belt. It was his not so subtle way of reminding Charga that he was the one with the badge. "Unless, of course, you hinder or obstruct our official investigation."

"Sure Mike" Charga nodded his acknowledgement, "message received loud and clear."

"Okay Duke. We'll be going, but we'll be in touch, right?"

"Right Mike." Charga offered his hand in an assuring gesture of goodwill. "Where do you figure to start in this?"

"We'll be going on down to the BCH stable, then probably back to Duarte later today to see if Harborstone is able to give us something to go on by then."

"Good luck." The two smiled and shook hands. Detective Street grimaced once again. He was by now very visibly annoyed with this show of genuine affection and friendship between his partner Mike Dunne and this former detective of notorious repute. Despite their differences in approach to investigations, the bond which had built up during their time working together remained evident.

Although Street admired and worked well with Mike Dunne, their team-up had not yet evolved to the still close partnership so obviously enjoyed by Dunne and Charga.

"I'll get the car" Street growled, "We got nothing here."

Dunne and Charga, hands still clasped, watched as Street angrily opened the door and briskly trotted away toward the apartment complexes' rear parking area.

"Not everybody down at P.D. is like him." Dunne remarked, nodding toward the door. "Some of us still believe you were an okay cop."

"Yeah. Well I thought it best to get out when I did" Charga answered, "I may have acted a bit prematurely but I was really pissed back then." It was his way of rationalizing his precipitous resignation. Although he had been relatively successful as a P.I., his heart remained in straight forward police work. Sometimes he regretted his action.

"I know" Dunne assured, applying just a bit more pressure to his hand shake to emphasize his words, "but I should have tried harder to change your mind."

"Not your fault Mike."

"Part of it is" Dunne went on, "I was your partner. I should have said more to the IAB. I should have come out stronger in your defense."

Charga released his grip and placed both hands on Dunnes' shoulders. "You did what you could" he said, "It was my own fault. I was way out of line, I just . . ."

"Maybe" Dunne interrupted, "but it was just one incident, and you were kinda personally involved."

Dunne was referring to the drug dealer Charga had pistol whipped. It was that same dealer who, six weeks earlier, had headed a gang of four thugs who had themselves beaten Charga when the group they worked for believed him to be a bit too close to building a solid case against their cartel. Their instructions from the cartel leaders in Bogota were to beat him so badly as to scare him off the investigation. It had been a major miscalculation. They hadn't figured on Chargas' drive. The effect of that beating was negative. Rather than have him back off, it served to bolster Chargas' resolve. Charga became more focused, seemingly obsessed with a more ferocious determination then, to not only destroy the entire operation of that particular Columbian drug smuggling group, but to gain for himself his own full measure of personal revenge, and immediately following his recuperation, he set upon an unrelenting crusade to bring down the ruling family and hierarchy of that particular cartel. He was totally committed to this one and only case file, and his subsequent seven days a week, sixteen or more hours a day, month and a half investigation eventually brought him face to face with his main attacker. That's when he lost it!

Mike Dunne had stepped in, in an attempt to restrain his partner, but by the time he did, Charga had already brutally battered their suspect dealer. He had already jammed the muzzle of his Glock .45 into the dealers mouth. These unsanctioned and totally unauthorized actions, although powerful and intimidating enough to elicit all the vital information needed to steer the federal agents onto the international drug operation resulting in a good number of arrests and convictions, were obviously totally illegal, and were witnessed by not only Mike Dunne, but other R.D. officers as well. When questioned by IAB investigators, these officers, rather than perjure themselves, were left with no choice but to report truthfully as to what they had witnessed. Charga was subsequently brought in on charges of misconduct, battery, and attempt to commit murder. Unbeknownst to either Charga or Mike Dunne, had it not been for Dunnes' own forceful testimony on Chargas' behalf, plus some behind the scene maneuvering by an assistant D.A., Charga was in line for not merely a suspension, but a full discharge, and he faced the possibility of having criminal charges brought against him in a formal court of law where incarceration upon conviction was most probable. It was not the first time Mike Dunne had actually saved Chargas' ass. He had done the same at least twice while the two worked together on the streets investigating crime for the Arcadia P.D. Once by tackling a thug who held a .22 caliber Smith and Wesson pointed at the back of Chargas' head. Once again by stifling Chargas' sharp wise guy tongue while the two of them were confronted by a pool hall full of armed coke heads. A wrong word there could have ended with their both being badly hurt or worse. In that instance Dunne had advocated self restraint and caution, which included a tactical retreat. "Sometimes silence and retreat is the better part of valor" he had said later, after both he and Charga were sitting comfortably in their police vehicle. "You have to know when to hold 'em, and when to fold 'em." Mike Dunne enjoyed the game of poker, and when engaged in a tense situation would often offer a quote that referenced the game.

"Well Duke" Dunne continued as he placed a hand on the front doorknob and prepared to leave, "I'm still of the opinion that you made a mistake in quitting back then." He opened the door and peeked out to see if his present partner had retrieved their vehicle. He had. The car was now standing, motor running, on the driveway just in front of Chargas' apartment. Street sat anxiously behind the wheel, noticed Dunne in the doorway and shot an angry stare toward him.

"Brad is waiting" Dunne went on, "So I got to get going." "Caio, Mike" Charga said, "thanks for clueing me in on the Harborstone deal."

"Had to" Dunne offered in response almost apologetically, "had no choice but to follow up your business card."

He stepped gingerly over the Sunday Examiner newspaper now laying just outside the door. "By the way" he added, "Your paper's here."

Charga nodded and smiled. "Take care of stretch" he said as he stooped over, picked up the newspaper and waved goodbye to Street. Street did not react, and showed no acknowledgement in return.

Charga shrugged. "Oh well" he mumbled to himself, "You can't please everybody." He closed the door and picked up the telephone.

"Time to get cracking" he said aloud, as he proceeded to dial.

Dunne hopped into the car. "We're off to the track!" he announced in an authoritarian tone.

Street put the vehicle in gear, and pulled out onto the main street. He did not reply.

"I know you've heard stories about Duke Charga" Dunne began, "But you don't know all of it, or even half of it." Street nodded. "I've heard." he said, rather coldly. He was feigning disinterest but this encounter with Dunne's ex partner, and Dunne's obvious bond with him, had churned Streets' natural curiosity. If Charga was the rogue cop he had been told he was, and Mike Dunne was the oft decorated career cop he knew he was, how could these two be so close, tied together with what was clearly a warm and genuine friendship? Shouldn't a bad cop be anathema to a good cop? Shouldn't a cop who represented all the best things in police work, be the harshest critic of a cop who could precipitate a city wide departmental scandal by acting in the most opprobrious manner by abusing the very fundamental precept represented by those wearing a badge? The question had gnawed at Streets' guts since his team up assignment with Dunne. Street had never heard Dunne in any way denigrate Charga, or Chargas' police record. On the contrary, Mike Dunne's statements, if and when he did on rare occasion speak about his ex partner, were consistently commendatory. That fact had stuck in Streets' craw. From what he could ascertain, he was at least as good or even better as a police detective and as a partner than Charga ever was or could ever be.

"He was more than a hot pencil when he was in uniform." Dunne continued, "Did you know that?" His reference was to the fact that Duke Charga had earned a reputation for writing a disproportionate number of minor civilian and traffic violation citations while patrolling the streets, both as an Arcadia beat cop, and later as a roving vehicle patrol officer. Dunne resumed his monologue. "He was a natural born policeman."

Street continued staring straight ahead, sitting stoically, but listening intently. He turned onto the I-5 freeway, sped up quickly and smoothly merged with the oncoming traffic.

"I've heard." he said again, momentarily glancing back at Dunne. "You've said that before."

"But I never told you the real reason he came so unglued back then."

"No" Street answered, "So, are you going to tell me now?"

"Yeah. I guess it's about time you know what I know about Marion Duke Charga."

Duarte general was a solidly constructed four story squared building situated on Montrosia Avenue just off the second avenue exit of the 210 freeway. The front of the building featured the main lobby entrance with a double set of automatic glass doors directly midway between groups of six ten foot high double paned windows. Centered in the ground level rear was the emergency entrance, a large garage sized doorway with a rollup door. There were parking spaces located in front and back with driveways running along each side. Charga took note of the more than ample number of available parking designated for handicapped motorists in front, and for emergency vehicles and staff in the rear. That left little room for visitor parking spaces. He drove around thru the front and rear lots once, unable to locate an empty space. Rather than drive in circles he opted to drive out and park curbside on Montrosia. It was Sunday so the parking restrictions along this main street were not in effect. He wondered how family visitors of those hospitalized put up with the parking situation there.

"Have to arrive early" he thought, "Or they'd have to park blocks away.".

He slid over to his right and exited his Dynasty from the passenger side. Instinctively hitting the all door lock button as he did. He semi jogged the more than 300 feet from the curb to the hospital main entrance. The doors slid open. He stepped in gingerly, paused and surveyed the scene. It was the first time he had been in this facility. The well maintained lobby floor of orange tone tile shone like a freshly polished citrine. Charga was impressed. There wasn't a scuff mark on it. He strolled to the big desk at the far end of the hotel style lobby. A rather heavy set, but pretty in face, fortyish woman in a spotless white hospital uniform looked up and smiled sweetly. "May I help you?"

Charga smiled in return. "I'm investigator Charga" he said, affecting a tone of assuredness and authority.

Her smile broadened, revealing a set of perfectly matched and manicured bright white teeth.

"Most likely falsies" Charga thought.

"Oh yes, you called earlier." she acknowledged.

Charga could readily understand the psychology of assigning her to front desk duty. Seated behind the marble topped counter she presented a friendly, apparently intelligent, somewhat authoritative introductory face to the total hospital operation.

"A good looking woman." he thought.

She wore her sandy brown hair pulled back tightly, and tied in a bun. Heavily penciled in dark brown eyebrows and carefully painted mascara lashes outlined a pair of bright, light green eyes with which she now was sensually scanning Chargas' face and frame. She flashed a suggestive wink, and slightly puckered her blush colored lips. "One moment" she purred as she began flipping through a stack of files. Chargas' eyes were naturally drawn to her full bosom pressing out from beneath her uniform top. The material was being pulled tautly against the front buttons. She noticed his attention and arched her back slightly, further straining her uniform top so that it now gave an impression that she was wearing a size smaller than her figure required.

"No falsies here" he thought.

Charga realized his stare was uncontrollably honed in on her full bosom. He knew it, and she sensed it without looking up. He took note of the name tag, bright blue in color with white lettering, pinned prominently on her white uniform top just above her well rounded left breast. It read 'Marilyn Miller' over the numbers 2364, and Duarte General. He glanced away.

"Nice lobby" he said in an attempt to show he was looking elsewhere beside at her breasts. She smiled again as she tore off a page from a little memo pad, wrote 406 on one side and another seven digit number on the other.

"Here you go handsome" she paused, "I'm off at three and I'll be home by four. My number's on back, in case you're interested."

"Good looking lady" Charga thought, "But just a bit above my dating age limit." He looked at the note, folded it over once, and quickly handed it back, holding it delicately between two fingers.

He had decided to be gentle. "Thanks Marilyn" he said with a flirtatious wink, "But I'm what you could call committed."

She shrugged. "The good ones usually are" she sighed, then pointing across the lobby, "Elevator is over there."

"Right" Charga replied, "and I understand detectives Dunne and Street were here earlier." This to help reinforce the impression that he was also a fully authorized officer. During his earlier phone call he had introduced himself simply as an investigator. These were the oft used ploys of successful P.I.s. He had learned well the art of implication and misdirection.

"That's right." she smiled again, this time rather weakly, "There were two detectives and two race track people here, and I understand they were all informed that mister Harborstone probably would not be fully conscious and available for questioning until later this afternoon. At least that's what I was told."

"I know. That's the story I got as well, but I'll just go on up and make a fast check. Thanks."

She shrugged again, as if to indicate his efforts were being wasted.

"Up to you" she added, "Suit yourself."

Harborstone was in a semi private room. There were two beds, both with older gentlemen patients. Medical charts hanging over the steel bed frames at the foot of each bed listed the names and condition of each patient, but Charga had no need to check either of them. It was obvious which patient was Harborstone. The bed to his left held a patient with multiple bruises on one side of his face.

He appeared to be sleeping rather comfortably. In the bed to his right lay a gray haired gent who was actively engaged in watching a religious service on the room television. He glanced toward his room mate. "Hasn't woke up yet." he blurted out, "but at least he's stopped moaning." The old characters' voice was scratchy and hoarse, like the strained vocal chords of an over excited football fan after a day on the fifty yard line. Charga was familiar with the sound. His own father, in his more senior years, suffered the same vocal condition, a consequence of smoking two packs of cigarettes a day for twenty plus years.

"Well, I guess that's an improvement." Charga nodded, slowly.

"Yeah! I wouldn't like him making noises while my TV church is on!"

"Right." Charga nodded again.

"You another cop?"

Charga smiled. At this particular time he was in no mood to carry on an extended conversation about his past police career, or his present status as a P.I. In any event, he knew he mustn't say outright that he was a cop, as that would br a felonious act. His plans were to get in, get some info from Harborstone, and get out in as least time as possible. "Just watch your TV" he said, in as pleasant a tone as he could muster.

"Awww! You cops are all the same." the old man grumbled in return as he upped the volume on the TV. "Just keep it down over there."

Charga pulled the bed curtain around Harborstone, reached into his suit jacket side pocket and removed a packet of ammonium carbonate. He removed the oxygen nasal cannula hooked into Harborstones' nostrils, broke open the packet and waved it back and forth under Harborstones' nose. Harborstones' head jerked to the side, his eyes opened.

"Wha?" he mumbled once, then again, "Wha, what?" as he felt his brain clearing and his eyes beginning to focus. "What's going on?"

"You're in Duarte General." Charga explained, "And I'm Marion Duke Charga."

"Oh yeah" Harborstone stuttered, "I wanted to talk with you."

"Okay. From this moment on I'll consider you my client. We can work out the details later on. Now I need to know why you need me."

"I got some phone calls" Harborstone began, "From someone, I don't know who, t-t threatening calls."

"About what? Why?"

"Whoever it was told me to watch my step, to stay away from his woman."

"What woman was that?" Charga asked, hoping to elicit as much information as he could before the effects of the ammonium C wore off.

"Th-that's what I asked too, what woman? Harborstone moaned in response.

"So?"

"I don't have any women." Harborstone blurted out loudly, "You see, I-I'm gay!"

"So?" Charga asked, "Do you think those calls have anything to do with this mugging?"

"Ha-have t-to" Harborstones voice was now beginning to trail off. Charga waved the ammonium carbonate packet under Harborstones' nostrils once again, effecting him with yet another jolt of temporary conscious lucidity. The horse trainer reacted.

"Wha, wha?"

"Try to stay awake, Harborstone!" Charga demanded, "Did you recognize the person who attacked you? Can you describe him?"

Harborstones' eyes rolled back in his head. Charga took him by the shoulders and gave him a shake. "Wake up! Did you recognize him?". The suddenness of that shake, combined with the malodorous fumes of the ammonium C had brought him back. His eyes focused once again, his mind became activated, triggering his recall. "Kinda big, crew cut, a bruiser type. Had a kinda reddish blotch on his face."

"Did he say anything?"

"Hit me twice in the face first off, said something like this is for Louise, then I just can't re-remember."

He was falling back into unconsciousness. Charga shook him again. "C'mon! Stay awake!"

"Hey! Quiet down over there!" The rasping voice came from across the room. "What the hell are you doing?"

The bed curtain suddenly was pulled open. A solidly built African American hospital orderly, arms folded defiantly, now stood between the two beds. "And just what do you think you're doing?" he questioned antagonistically.

Charga raised his hands in the gesture of surrender, and stepped back away from Harborstones' bedside. "I was just leaving."

The big black man unfolded his arms and looked down questionably at Harborstone, then back to Charga. "Who let you in here?" he asked.

Charga was running thru his options. This black orderly was physically built like Mike Dunne, only a bit taller, and a whole lot younger. An almost perfectly round, clean shaven head stood atop his over muscled neck, and his well proportioned biceps and triceps indicated he was most likely a dedicated weight lifter/body builder. His deep set dark eyes reflected no fear, while his body language clearly indicated he would more than relish a physical confrontation. Charga drew on Mike Dunnes' lessons. Sometimes a tactical retreat is the better part of valor, and the wisest move at hand. Hoping to continue his facade, Charga took one more step back and answered in solemn tones. "I'm investigator Charga. Here to check on this mans condition."

The black man seemed to relax some. He looked back at Harborstone, noticed the oxygen nasal tube loosely laying on his neck. "How did this come loose?" he asked, as he checked the oxygen flow and repositioned the tube in Harborstones' nostrils.

"Well, he was talking and it just kind of fell off."

"He was talking?", the orderlies tone was incredulous. He obviously was aware of Harborstones' condition and medical prognosis. "How in hell did he wake up?" he asked while straightening the blanket covering the horse trainers chest. Charga played dumb. "I don't know. You're the doctor." He answered as he stepped even farther away from the bed.

"Didn't say much though" he continued, "But there'll be two detectives coming in later today from Arcadia. They'll question him further then."

"And what's that ammonia smell in here?'

Charga shrugged, feigning ignorance, then waved at the old man in the next bed. "So long Pop."

"Yeah, yeah!" the old man graveled back.

Charga exited the room, walked quickly to the nearest stairway and rumbled down the three flights, two steps at a time. He had found the elevator coming up to be a slow mover, and he wasn't about to press the down button and wait for it to come back up. It was a good move on his part. Just as he hit the street level lobby and headed for the front doors, the orderly in Harborstones' hospital room discovered the opened packet of smelling salts.

Detective Street turned off the freeway and onto Huntington boulevard heading toward the Arcadia race track. Huntington was an extra wide two way boulevard with tall full birchwood and oak trees on either side which partially hid the palatial fronts of widely spaced, very upscale twenty room adobe brick homes. These mini mansions were set back approximately 100 feet from curbside to front door on plots of a quarter acre and more. He thought back to the time he had first driven along this thoroughfare. It had been Streets' first Arcadia P.D. investigation out of robbery division following his transfer up from the uniformed street patrol unit. He remembered how the sweet scent of freshly mowed grass had wafted up from the meticulously manicured lawns and tailored hedges, and how he had been so impressed with the cleanliness and fresh look of this area. He had mentioned that to his then partner, Paul Carson, on that first day, and Carson had stared back silent response. Carson was not an overly friendly sort, and was obviously and often outwardly prejudiced toward certain segments of the population at large. He often roiled against the poorly dressed Latino men who could be found scrounging the Arcadia area in search of a days employ. It appeared Carson actually disliked Latinos more than he did blacks or Asians, for whom he also held no great love. Why that was so, Street had never questioned. He was the new man in the detective section back then, and thought it wise at the time to simply try to fit in without making waves or raising controversy over personalities. "That was then" he thought. Right now he was teamed with Big Mike Dunne, a solid, much more fair minded man with whom he worked more easily, and for whom he had much respect. He hit the window down button and inhaled deeply. Funny, how now the noxious fumes of gasoline and diesel exhaust seemed to overpower that fresh cut grass scent. Or was it that he had become so familiarized with these surroundings that he no longer appreciated the quiet beauty of this neighborhood, but now more readily noticed and dwelled upon the negative rather than the positive? That seemed the bane of all detectives. Because they constantly dealt with the seamier side of human endeavor, they learnd to view the world through dark colored lenses, and more readily accepted the iniquitous over the honorable. He stopped mid block to allow a well dressed Caucasian woman to cross, followed by a Latino female carrying an armload of packages. "If Carson was here" he thought, "He'd be raving about this!".

Mike Dunne had finally completed his ywenty minute soliloquy on the virtues and exemplary traits of former detective Marion Duke Charga. He had been talking non stop since the start of the ride. "Well, that's about it" Dunne concluded. "Like I said, aside from his quick temper, he was a born cop."

Street shifted himself slightly in his seat behind the wheel. It had been a bit uncomfortable listening to his partners' panegyric praise of a previous partner, but he understood that Dunne and Charga had indeed worked well together, and that the distinct and special bond which builds between partners, that unique feeling of trust and camaraderie between officers working together over a course of time, had not, as yet, fully blossomed between himself and Dunne. There were however, many budding signs, one of which was Dunnes' opening up in regards to his experiences while on patrol with his previous partner. Street rightly surmised that this demonstrated a growing sense of trust between Dunne and himself, and he immediately recognized that particular reality when Dunne had first initiated this twenty minute non stop veralization on his own. Street had to admit if the stories Mike Dunne had related were only half true, then Duke Charga had really been an above average member of the detective robbery/homicide squad. Street had already become aware of the healthy competition that existed within the various squads at Arcadia P.D., however if one were to believe Dunnes' version of past events and circumstances, and of Chargas' past action and interaction among and between other detectives and squads, then the stories and rumors that swirled around in the department could have been borne, as Dunne suggested, more from envy and personal animosity, along with an underlying level of southern style prejudice, rather than from anything stemming directly from Chargas' lone wolf attitude. He mulled over Dunnes' dissertation and began to mentally dissect it. Maybe it was true, he thought to himself, that Duke Charga did possess a good deal of courage under fire, and had been always so very loyal to his partner, still his capricious temperament, that same almost fearless temperament, as Dunne had described it, which had led them bith into and out of so many tight and dangerous situations, and which had led to an extraordinary number of solid arrests and convictions, had also led to a number of very strong reprimands and a suspension without pay, and Chargas' inability to maintain his volatile emotions under control directly precipitated his abrupt, yet voluntary resignation. Street again shifted slightly in his seat as he spied the road sign that read 'Racetrack Two Miles Ahead'.

"Well" he said, in a rather serious tone while glancing toward his partner, "From what you've told me today, Charga may have had great investigative instincts, but it seems his Latino-Italian personality probably put you both into situations you could've avoided." He paused momentarily, then again glanced toward Dunne and added, "That doesn't sound like what a born cop would do. Anyhow, in the end he screwed himself, didn't he?" Dunne wore a dejected expression. Before he could answer Street continued "I know you liked him," Street went on, "probably still do, but you got to admit he was a bit of a cowboy. Maybe still is." "I guess so, on that point." Dunne grudgingly had to admit it. Street nodded, then added, "But you know this is the first time I've ever heard anything positive about him."

"How would you?" Dunne snapped back, "You've been working with Carson. You must've already figured out that Carson is nothing but a prejudiced S.O.B."

"Well, he told me how Charga banged that perp around, and how he got in all that trouble." Street said quietly as he steered their vehicle past the sign reading 'Arcadia Barn Area. Employees only." He flashed his badge at the gate guard and continued on down the dirt road leading to the racetrack shed row.

"Yeah. He did go off bad that time." Dunne replied, "But I told you why he did, and by the way, Carson did plenty slapping around too."

"But Carson was never caught at it." Street half chuckled, "Okay. You told me why Charga went off, but how in hell did he get away with it? That's what gets me. In front of half the squad! They all figured he'd be doing jail time right now. So what's the story there?"

"I'll tell you" Dunne went on, "I did what I could, but you know that A.D.A Cortez? You must have seen her. Cute little thing. Dark hair, nice figure?"

"I think I know who you mean."

43

"Well, she had a thing for Duke." Dunne smiled impishly, "Covered his ass by making a deal with the perp. Perp didn't press charges and she gave him full immunity in exchange for that and some testimony."

"You mean she let the perp walk?"

"Yep. And Duke was handed a suspension with a stipulation that if anything, any even little thing, ever cropped up again involving excess force, well, he would lose everything. She said she probably wouldn't be able to save his ass twice without someone higher up looking into her own actions."

"So how come he resigned?" Street asked, "He got a pass."

"Didn't trust himself I guess." Dunne answered with a shrug, "Maybe it was the right move for him. He thinks so, and like you said he did have quite a fast temper. I have to agree with that, and . . ." Dunne went on, "he was in love with a certain style of car and wanted to pay cash for it, so he grabbed all his severance pay and what he had vested in his retirement and went right out and just bought it. That's the car he has now, that new Dynasty. Also, I think he had become a bit soured with the job. After all, we do deal with all the scum and lowlifes of the world, don't we?"

Street pursed his lips and nodded acknowledgement. "Well" he said, "We're almost there." He drove past the first row of buildings marked 'Stables 1 thru 10', and '11 thru 20', turned right at the marker designating Seabiscuit Avenue and pulled up in front of the big green building with the letters BCH prominently displayed at each end. The BCH stables had earned a reputation as the best maintained barn building at the track. It was a well deserved accolade. Although the building itself was a bit older than many of the others along this shed row, it was in much better condition. The BCH organization stabled some of the very best top rated thoroughbreds in North America and so, in order to keep their equine stars in the best possible of facilities, had made it a point to keep their assigned buildings in good repair, cleaned twice daily, and routinely painted at two year intervals. This was an ongoing effort made in order to maintain their superior ranking, as well as acting as an inducement for owners of other top rated horses to stable their thoroughbreds at BCH. BCH was also well known as one of the largest purchasers of highest quality hay, grain, fodder, and equine vitamin supplements. It seemed no wonder they produced and ran so many thoroughbred winners.

Juan Zella was overseeing the bathing of one of the BCH thorough-breds when he noticed the two jacket clad detectives approaching. As the BCH stable manager he prided himself on his powers of observation and ability to recollect incidents and faces.

This aptitude was a key prerequisite for any shed row worker if they were employed by BCH and desired elevation to the position of stable manager. Zella could spot an emotionally upset horse as readily as he could an injured one, and he also had acquired the ability to touch, rub and feel hot spot potential future injuries prior to their becoming evident to most trainers and many equine veterinarians. He immediately recognized the barrel chest detective as one who had assisted in the investigation of his brothers death some time back. Before Zella could utter a word, both detectives made their badges visible. Dunne by unbuttoning his tight fitting jacket, his badge was hooked on his belt, and Street by holding his badge in hand, stretching his arm in front of his body and aiming his badge directly at Zellas face and waving it menacingly, a motion specifically and deliberately meant to intimidate.

Zella rattled off some orders to his subordinates and strode toward the detectives. He was not in the least intimidated and his posture reflected that fact. He had dealt with police and immigration officials many times before since becoming the BCH stable manager some years back. Street quickly replaced his badge and I.D. wallet into his suit breast pocket.

"You're here about mister H, right?" Zella questioned.

"And just who are you?" Street retorted in an obvious attempt to regain the power initiative.

"Chill!" Dunne ordered as he extended his open hand toward Zella, "Hello again." he said, "You're Juan Zella are you not? Remember me?"

"Si! Hola detective."

They shook hands, but not in an overly friendly manner, it was more of a businesslike handshake, still Street wore a surprised look.

"You know each other?"

Dunne looked back at his partner. "Yeah." he answered, "We met a while back. This guys' brother had a kind of suspicious accident around here, and me and Charga were assigned to check it out."

He turned back to Zella. "So what can you tell us about your boss' mugging, anything?"

"Not me" Zella replied, "I wasn't here. Mister H comes in before anybody. Garcia here . . ." he motioned to one of the grooms who was hosing down the thoroughbred just a few feet behind where the trio was standing, "he found mister H when he came in this morning."

Zella whistled sharply, then called out. "Yo! Jose! Ven aqui (vena key) he ordered. Jose Garcia looked up. His dark brown skin and sharply cut nasal and jaw line features clearly betrayed his Aztec Indian ancestry. A red baseball cap with the letters BCH prominently stitched in yellow thread partially hid his thinning jet black hair which hung out long in back and over his ears. Deeply set dark brown eyes hiding behind blue tinted sunglasses began darting from the detectives to Juan Zella and back again. He stroked the growth of hair under his nose and hesitated momentarily. He appeared ready to run. He crimped the hose, then handed it off to the other BCH groom.

"No emigre!" Zella assured.

Garcia strolled haltingly toward the threesome.

"Es bueno" Zella added, "Es okay. Ven aqua." He was aware of Garcias' illegal status and so, was quick to alleviate any fear of capture and possible deportation. Zella knew that only immigration officers were interested in undocumented aliens, and these were regular Arcadia police who likely couldn't care less.

"Si. Es okay" he again assured, then turned back to again face Dunne and Street. "He doesn't speak much English" he said, "But he understands okay."

Dunne nodded acknowledgement, smiled weakly, then addressed Garcia. "Well, did you see or hear anything unusual or out of the ordinary this morning? Anybody here who shouldn't have been?"

"No. Nada" Garcia replied, "I no see nada. I find le bossa solomenty".

"Solomenty?" What's that mean?" Street asked. He knew very little Spanish.

"He says he only found mister H, but didn't see anything unusual." Zella explained.

The interrogation of Jose Garcia continued for just a few minutes, with Zella acting as interpreter. When it was clear nothing of any value could be gained thru further conversation with him, Dunne again turned baack to Juan Zella. "What about him?" he asked, motioning toward Garcias' co-worker now finishing hosing off the chestnut thoroughbred a few steps away.

"Well, he did come in a few minutes after Jose here."

"Maybe he noticed something" Dunne said, "I'd like to question him as well.".

Zella shrugged. "Okay. But he speaks less English than Garcia, and understands less than that."

"So you can translate." Street interjected in his authoritarian manner, "Like you've been doing."

"No can do senor." Zella offered apologetically.

A cocky smirk spread across Streets' thin lips. He felt he had at last taken control of the conversation. "Why not? He demanded, "Are you now refusing to co-operate?"

"It's not that" Zella replied, turning his palms upward as an expression of disdain rolled across his face. He looked at Street, then back to big Mike Dunne and whispered rather apologetically, "He's not Hispanic."

Streets' head bobbled back a bit, "Wha? He sure looks Mexican to me."

It was an honest statement. True. To any eye untrained in distinguishing cultural or ethnic differences between brown toned peoples, this man, Salaam Achmed Mahdi, when intermingled amongst a group of Hispanics, could indeed be easily taken as just another member of that group.

"So what is he?" Dunne asked. He was a bit perplexed. "He looks Hispanic to me too."

"No sir" Zella replied, "He's some kind of Arab, from Lebanon I think."

"So how do you communicate?" Dunne queried.

"We have another one like him here, Achmed Zada Basara, he speaks Spanish and relays my instructions. We call him Zada for short."

"So go get him!" Street demanded, "We'll wait."

"He'll be in later" Zella answered, "He starts late."

"Well then" Dunne interjected, "How is this guy gonna work, if you can't communicate with him?"

"He's been here a while. By now he knows most what to do."

The detectives exchanged looks of frustration. Dunne focused on Zella. "So now we're back to you. I ask you again, think about it, are you sure you didn't see or hear anything different around here?"

"No, not really" Zella answered, wondering how he could be of any assistance whatsoever since he hadn't arrived that morning until a half hour after Harborstones' first discovery.

"When I came in, Jose had alre ady called 911, and the hospital ambulance was already loading mister H, and Mahdi there was just standing around doing nothing, and Jose was nervous about the whole thing."

"I thought it was you who called 911" Street broke in, "At least that's what the dispatcher said." He looked down at his little notebook. "Caller was recorded as Juan Zella."

"Jose used my name" Zella said in response, "Then he kinda just disappeared, he tries to keep in the background." Dunne nodded.

He knew why that would be, then continued. "Maybe something unusual in the past few days? Harborstone acting strangely? Did he seem troubled? Was there maybe somebody hanging around back here, or maybe asking questions about him? Anything like that?"

Zella shook his head slowly, "No." he answered falteringly, then as his stare slowly focused skyward, his head tilted slightly starboard, added, "But there was this one guy who came up to me after the last race yesterday, asked about how did mister H get so many winners out on the track," he paused for a second or two, then went on, "But with his hot streak of winners that's not so unusual. We've been getting those kind of questions lately, but there was something about this guy. I dunno. He just seemed strange, and angry."

"And then you said what?" Dunne asked.

Well, I did tell him that mister H starts every day at four in the morning, and doesn't leave until after the very last race every racing day. He even comes in when there's no racing scheduled. Mister H and this whole stable work hard for those wins."

"And so" Street joined the questioning, "What did he look like? Anything unusual about him beside his attitude?"

"Big guy" Zella answered, "Wore a cap, sunglasses, had a red mark on his cheek. Kinda like a bum maybe."

"Do you remember where and when this guy talked to you?"

Zella rubbed his cheek as he answered, "Well, it was alongside the paddock walk just after the last race. I remember because we won that race, and that was the winner I tipped to your partner."

Dunne looked at Street. "You?"

"No! Not him." Zella cut in, "Your other partner. That other detective, Dunne nodded as he spoke while looking over at his partner. "Sorry, Brad. I should've known."

"Figures!" Street added sarcastically, "I didn't think he was smart enough to pick winners on his own. And just how did you know for sure that horse was going to win, may I ask?"

Zella puffed up like a rooster strutting in front of a bam full of hens. "I watch." he said with a perspicacious smile, "I watch workouts, I watch feed, I watch everything, and I can tell." He patted his chest with an open palm. "Someday I will be top trainer for BCH!".

Street and Dunne exchanged surprised looks. Dunne rolled his eyes skyward. "People!" he thought "The boss is busted up, and right away this guy is looking to move up and take his place!"

"Well okay" he said aloud, "Now let me ask you this," Dunne turned back to again face Zella, then spoke slowly and precisely, "Did mister Charga give you his card?" He was almost positive he already knew the answer to this question.

"Yeah" Zella answered, "About six cards, but how did you know that?"

Dunne ignored the question, answering with another, "And you gave one of those cards to John Harborstone, right?"

Again Zella showed surprise. "That's right! He noticed them on my equipment table when I was changing my shirt after the last race. We were getting ready to go home and he just picked one up and asked if I knew mister Charga well?".

"Why would he want or need a private investigator? Any idea?"

"I don't know and I didn't ask. He's my boss and I don't butt in his business."

"So what did you say about my ex partner?"

"I told mister H that mister Charga seemed to be an honest man, and that he treated me good when he was looking into my brothers' accident." Zella looked apologetically at detective Dunne, then added, "You too, you were good with me and my brothers' wife too."

"Well, something must have been going on with Harborstone if he was interested in a P.I.!"

"Maybe" Zella said quickly, "I hope I helped you. I've got to get back to work now. Do you think what I told you could be anything important?"

"Well, it's something" Dunne acknowledged, "And it could be something important." He extended his hand again, and Juan Zella clasped it. This handshake was well meant by both. Zella appreciated Dunnes' disregard of Jose Garcias' illegal status, and Dunne appreciated Zellas' sincere attitude and co-operation.

"Did I help some un poquito?" Zella asked, then whispered, "I like mister H, you know? Even though he's a gay man."

"He's a homo?" Street blurted out loudly.

"Shh" Zella admonished, "That's supposed to be a secret." He pointed over his shoulder. "These guys wouldn't respect him as much if they knew that." Then added, "You know Hispanic values and all, comprende?"

"Got no relevance as far as we know" Dunne said. He elbow nudged his partner. "Let's go. We got all we could from this end."

"Where to now?" Street asked as he and Dunne returned to their vehicle.

"To the track security office." Dunne replied with a half smile. "Could be our red faced character made a few bets. We'll check the security tapes. Maybe we can find something there that could help us identify this guy and track him down."

"That could take all day or more." Street complained.

"We've got all day!" Dunne answered gruffly, "And we got nothing else planned, so let's go."

Street u-turned the vehicle and drove on back toward the barn gate heading for the race track front entrance area. As they passed the exit gate Street waved to the guard who paid no heed, but instead turned to greet the driver of a shiny new Mercedes Benz on his way in. Street then turned onto the roadway leading to the front parking area and main track entrance. Neither he nor detective Dunne took notice of the other vehicle, a black Dodge Dynasty, which was passing thru the main entrance on its way to the barn area security gate.

The tires of the black Mercedes raised a small cloud of brown dust as they skidded several feet before the shiny vehicle came to a full stop just in front of the BCH stable building. The driver pushed the automatic trunk release button, and the trunk popped open, exposing a well oiled, hand tooled brown leather saddle. Juan Zella ran out and opened the driver-side door, half bowing as he did. "Good morning Senor Colton.".

Brian Colton was the 'C of BCH stables. Now just turned fifty two years old, and just about ten pounds on the paunchy side, he struggled just a bit to exit the vehicle gracefully. He ran one hand thru his still rather full bodied head of slightly graying hair, peered studiously at Zella thru his gray green deep set eyes, and frowned a thoughtful frown. It wasn't often that Colton visited the race track barn of BCH, and it was obvious his mind was working on recalling Zellas' name. He chomped down on the half smoked Bering cigar clenched between his perfectly designed and fitted set of dentures, threw his head back, and rubbed his chin. "That's Juan, right?" he smiled as he spoke.

"Yes, sir."

"Thanks" Colton said rather abruptly. He waved toward the rear of the vehicle. "Take that saddle into the upstairs office. That's a good man."

Colton stepped in front of the Mercedes and scanned the BCH building. He placed his hands on his hips, leaned back just a bit, and took a deep breath. Then he let out a long sigh. The Colton family had long been in the horse business, and this building, known as the BCH stable, had at one time represented just one more example of the Coltons' old dynasty. He nostalgically recalled, somewhat regretfully, how this old building used to carry a large sign that read 'Colton Stables'. The words had covered the entire west side of the building in six foot high letters of deep green paint. Every visit here seemed to resurrect his memories of the Colton legacy. Brian's great, great grandfather had begun the family's century old horse business history, working roundups and breeding horses way back during and just after the Civil War. That was Luke Colton. He had been a roaming cattle hand before he learned of the Union Army's offer to purchase as many healthy horses that could be supplied to them. So, from 1863 to 1870, he and two other cowboys of the time went about scouring the open ranges of the Arizona and Colorado territories, capturing whole herds of wild horses, breaking them at the Army outposts of the west, and selling them to the U.S. cavalry in ride readiness. The trio made a bundle of solid U.S. gold dollars. Following the peace agreements signed at Appomattox the territory of west Texas turned into a wild, wide open area. Gambling and prostitution were rampant. Unfortunately for them, Luke Coltons' two partners tended to drink and party with the proceeds of their horse sales while he had opted to diligently save his portion of the profits with an eye toward using these monies more wisely. In 1871 he bought over one thousand acres of prime Texas land where he set out to build his horse empire. The family prospered there for eighty years. Then, in the summer of 1950, Brian Colton's father, recognizing the new potential of California land ownership, sold the family ranch in Texas, and moved the entire operation to the Simi valley, just north of the burgeoning city of Los Angeles. It was there, at the Colton ranch in the valley, where he became interested in the business of breeding and racing thoroughbred horses, and it was there where Brian Colton senior had proceeded to build a kind of horseracing dynasty of expanded wealth and reputation. That was all prior to Brian Jr. taking charge of the business operation. This was the ranch where Brian Colton Jr. had lived from the age often on, and it was the only real home he actually could remember. He could not recall a single day at that ranch without seeing, touching, or riding horses. He really enjoyed trail riding back then, and had several favorite pintos and Arabians which where his alone to saddle and ride whenever he desired. He also could not remember any day when he did not get whatever he desired. He father had pampered and spoiled him, after all, he was an only child. He mom had died at his birth, and his father had never remarried, preferring to remain alone rather than take on a new wife. Brian Colton Sr. was of the old school, strongly moralistic, possessing a nineteenth century mindset, who believed to re-marry would be, in essence, a denial of his life with Brian's mother, a denial of their love, and a desecration of her memory. So Brian Jr. had been reared by a string of nannies, most of whom he had noticed, were more interested in the possibility of luring his father into a second marriage, rather than in his own proper upbringing. His father was consumed by the horse business, his nannies were focused on their own social elevation, thus, without sensible guidance, Brian was let free to do as he pleased. He began dating at sixteen, was married himself at just nineteen, and divorced at twenty two. That first wife had departed the scene with a hefty cash settlement of almost three million. His second wife who he had gone ahead and married at twenty eight, lasted a bit longer, and due to a tightly worded pre-nuptial agreement, walked off with less than one and one half mil.

For the past twenty years he had come close to a third marriage on several occasions, but always managed to somehow evade saying 'I do" again. He had since gained a reputation as a ladies man, and a playboy. It had been soon after his second divorce that Brian's father suffered a sudden, and fatal heart attack. At the same time the horseracing business went into a downward trend, and the Colton money began to dry up. He took another deep breath. He was well aware that the decline in the Colton family fortune could be laid at his own doorstep. His two ill advised and disastrous marriages, with their multi million dollar divorce settlements, had taken quite a bite of the Colton Inc. family bank accounts. Those settlements, followed by the subsequent years of his own dolce vita living, and his neglect and faulty mismanagement of family finances, coupled with the nationwide decline in horseracing revenues had further exacerbated the downward curve of assets and holdings of the once near great Colton fortune.

All these factors combined had driven him to seek out moneyed investors willing to join him in a partnership alliance. An influx of new money, he rightfully surmised, would allow him to continue his now habitually extravagant life style.

Thus he had found John Harborstone, a well respected and successful thoroughbred trainer with a desire to set up a stable of his own, but without the capital necessary to do so. Harborstone did however possess enough investment capital to buy into an already well established stable with a history of much success. That was the Colton stable. It had taken a bit of negotiating and compromise on Brian Colton's part, but in the end Harborstone had agreed to sign on as a one third partner with complete control of the breeding and training of the stable's equine stock. When the word came out that Colton was in some kind of cash flow difficulty and was seeking financial backers in order to keep the racing operation afloat, investors far and wide proffered offers of varied value in attempts to buy in, and catch a share in this fabled stable. Brian had chosen the offer of most largesse, put forth by an Arabian multi-millionaire horseman, the Sheik Abdul Bib Baddaffi. Baddaffi had offered not only cash, but a stock of twenty Arabian thoroughbred race horses as well. The Sheik promised non interference in either training, breeding, or racing of the stable. He claimed his interest was also not even in his portion of purse winnings, but merely in, what he called, the prestige of ownership of American racing thoroughbreds.

"That was a great deal." Brian thought to himself as he strode into the BCH building and up the eight steps to the second level office area, because the Colton stock had dwindled due to his selling off of the major stakes runners he had had in his own stable. Now the BCH stable was again well stocked with many graded stakes runners, along with some proven stallions and good breeding mares. All being well cared for out on his Simi valley ranch. Juan Zella had already shouldered the saddle from the Mercedes' trunk, up the steps and to Colton's office on the second level. He placed it gently across the back of one of the leather guest chairs, and waited for his employer to arrive to receive any further instructions he may be given. Zella knew that mister Colton, once on the scene, was wont to take full charge of all comings and goings and any stable related operations in the BCH building. Juan had always been fascinated by the wide glass window Colton had had installed in this office, allowing a full view of the interior of the stable. This second level, originally built as a hay loft and feed storage area, ran halfway down the north side of the BCH stable building. It had been converted to four separate stable hand sleeping and break rooms, with Colton's double sized office on the far end in the middle of the building. The large window offered Colton, when he was present, a means to oversee anything and everything taking place in the stables on the ground level. A four foot wide walkway ran the entire length of this second level, bordered by a four foot high railing. There were no doors to any of the employee break rooms, neither to Colton's outer office area, however there was one for the private desk area in Colton's office, and this door was always locked when Colton was away. The ground level below was now used as a saddle and tack storage area, and for hay and feed stockpiles. During the barn area renovation a few years back, a toilet restroom had been installed just under the steps, making it more convenient for the BCH stable workers to answer any urgent callings of nature while on the job in the area. This saved the few moments it had previously taken these stable hands walking the twenty yards back and forth between the old stable buildings. It was a time saving, thus a money saving renovation of the Colton stable operations. Twelve open top horse enclosures lined the interior south wall on the ground level. Six additional enclosures ran along the north wall beginning just adjacent to the saddle and tack storage area. Situated just below Colton's office was a small room designated as the head trainer operations center, consisting of a desk, two file cabinets housing horse conditions and related information, and three phones from which all training information, instructions and work assignments were delegated and reported in. One phone was hooked up to the wall phones installed at the opposite ends of the BCH building, a second phone afforded direct access to the track secretary's office to report any late changes in equipment, conditions, or late scratches. The third phone, with an outside line, was the general use telephone. This was John Harborstone's headquarters. Colton had wanted it this way. It was psychologically symbolic that Harborstone be situated directly beneath him. That was just the way he was.

It was less than two minutes before Brian Colton strode in, smiled weakly at Zella, then proceeded directly to his private office door. He unlocked it, opened the door, then turned to Zella. "Come on in, Juan" he gestured with an open hand, "Come in and take a seat." For a moment Juan Zella was taken aback. He had never been invited into Brian Colton's private office area. Normally he would be called by John Harborstone, and they would meet for discussion in Harborstone's office below where they would exchange ideas on the delegation of training duties for the other stable workers. Harborstone had been involving Juan more and more of late in the training and conditioning of the BCH thoroughbreds. When he had met with Harborstone and Colton up here on the second level, it would be in the outer office only.

"Yes sir." Zella half whispered as he hesitantly shuffled in and dropped his body in one of the fancy chairs in front of Colton's well polished six foot mahogany desk. "What is it, sir?" he asked. "Is he going to fire me?" was the real question floating in his mind. Colton smiled.

It was more of a smirk than a smile. "You're not in any trouble, Juan" he began, "So just relax!" Colton then opened a side desk drawer and removed a pre-printed form. "You know about mister Harborstone, right?"

Juan nodded. "Si."

"Well," Colton went on, "He probably won't be back at work for a while." He began writing on the form as he spoke, then looked up and smiled that smirky smile again. "So, I'm notifying the racing board and the track that you should be listed as assistant trainer under him on all the programs from now on."

Zella sat up alertly. "Gracias!" he blurted out. "Thank you so much."

Colton waved an open palm. "That's not all." he continued on, now rather more slowly and deliberately, "I want you to take over full training duties while he's out of action and . . ." he paused, looked straight into Juan Zella's eyes and went on, even more deliberately than ever, "and if you do well enough, I will recommend that you be given an opportunity to apply for a full trainers license.". He sat back in his chair. "What do you say about that?".

"Thank you senor Colton." Zella smiled. "I will do my best." He said.

"I'm sure you will." Colton replied as he handed the form to his now new assistant trainer. "Take this to the track office. It authorizes you to train BCH thoroughbreds and lists you as an assistant trainer."

"Si! Si!"

"We'll discuss who you may want to take your position as stable manager sometime later this week, okay?"

"Si!"

"Okay now. Go ahead. Get this paper filed in their office right away. I will call and let them know you're on the way up."

Colton stood and extended his hand. Juan Zella almost jumped up and grasped it firmly. "Gracias!" Zella exclaimed once more, "Gracias!".

"I think you deserve it." Colton answered, "Okay now, get going.".

The two men exchanged smiles once again, and Zella bent forward like a Chinese coolie bowing in subservience. He looked down at the assistant trainer recognition form, half bowed again and blurted out, "Gracias! Muchos gracias, senor Colton." then turned like a top, and quickly made his exit. He needed only three steps to float down the stairway. He paused for just one second in front of Harborstone's office. He grinned. Maybe his patient waiting for a break had finally paid off. He was now one step closer to becoming a full fledged recognized thoroughbred trainer.

Chapter Two . . .

Part Two

Charga wasn't at all surprised at how easily he had passed thru the security gate leading to the track stable area. He had mastered the art of feigning authority by acting and speaking in a confident, matter of fact manner and was seldom questioned. It worked again. He merely slowed his Dynasty as he approached the gate guard, authoritatively hollered out the open window, "Harborstone investigation!", and flashed his investigator I.D. credentials. The security guard, who had had his head down reading the comics section of the local daily, took a glancing glimpse of the I.D., waved him past, and quickly returned to his newspaper. Charga then steered his vehicle onto the dirt driveway leading to the track stable area. He easily found his way to the big green BCH stable, and drove his Dynasty right up to just a foot behind the black Mercedes. He turned off the engine and set the brake. Exiting the vehicle, he simultaneously hit the all door lock button, and called out to a stable hand who was hot walking a roan thoroughbred into the BCH barn area. The stable hand appeared to be a Latino and Charga wasn't sure whether he was English literate. He decided to speak in Spanish. "Hola! Amigo. Donde es la officia de le grande bossa aqua?"

The man turned his head just slightly, looked back but never missed a step. He pointed to the stairs just outside the stable door. "Aya, arriba." he replied, then gave the big horse a strong tug on the bridle and kept on walking, kicking up the two inch deep straw layer covering the flooring down the middle of the stable. Charga ascended the wooden stepped stairway. It was sturdy, made of mostly two by four side planks and railings, and two by eight oaken steps, but the wood had dried out some since its' construction due to its exposure to the elements, and it creaked eerily under Charga's heavy stride. At the top of the stairs was a semi rusted out screen door that opened to the upper walkway. The door was unlocked and it screeched horribly as he pulled it ajar and stepped inside. Moving at a steady pace along the walkway, his eyes searching for someone who could be regarded as a person of authority, Charga's observance training automatically kicked in. He quickly made a mental note of the first room thru the open doorway. No one was in this room, but his peripheral vision caught glimpse of a red, green, and white flag with a leaf cluster center circle pinned on a side wall, and some brightly colored red and green striped blankets covering several cots set randomly around the room. "Typically Mexican." he thought. Most stable workers and grooms hailed from south of the border. Some were legal alien residents. Most were not. He strode on along the walkway. Hanging beads at the second doorway partially shrouded what appeared to be a simply set up coffee maker on a long table situated in the center of the room surrounded by eight or ten opened folding chairs. No one here either.

"A nice little break room." he mused, "But when do these stable hands get a chance to sit and enjoy a cup of Java and a smoke?" Charga was well aware of the busy work schedules of these hot walkers, grooms, and stall workers, since he himself had wasted half a teenage summer vacation employed as a student worker at a training complex out in San Bernadino. It was there where his minor interest in horses and horse racing had its' genesis for him. Charga peered into the third open room. The Empire state building, Twin towers, and Brooklyn bridge were easily recognizable landmarks among the many pictures and photos of the New York city skyline that covered the lower half of one wall with what appeared to be a flag of some kind hanging just above them. He didn't recognize the design of this flag, green with a yellow half moon and a star. "Most likely some south American nation" he thought as he continued scanning the room. One rather dirty looking person, dressed in denim shirt and pants, muddied at the cuffs and sleeves, was half reclining on a cot at the rear of this room. He was dark skinned, had longish black hair, which obviously hadn't been shampooed in weeks, and was sporting a scruffy beard. He turned his head slowly, and thru dark, deep set eyes, began staring menacingly at Charga. "What you want here?" he asked contentiously. Charga noticed some kind of foreign accent. One he couldn't place.

"Sorry." Charga replied as he continued scanning the room. There were more pictures of New York city on the opposite wall, along with photos of groups of people. At this distance he was unable to clearly define the locations or settings of these photos except that he did notice most of the people in them were bearded. There was a second cot along the wall, and a card table in the center of the room with four chairs around it. He moved on.

A state flag of California hung in the fourth room, along with a few scenes of the California coastline and mountains, obviously torn from the calendar which was tacked up next to them. The calendar had past days marked off with big red X's. A worn, well used sofa lined one wall on the far side of this room, in front of which sat an old model television set with an old fashioned rabbit ear antenna atop a small table. Several McDonald burger wrappers were next to the TV.

"A lunch room." Charga surmised.

Brian Colton, having heard the approaching footsteps of Charga, thinking maybe it was Juan Zella returning to the office area, possibly with second thought questions regarding his newly appointed assistant trainer position, began strolling toward the outer office doorway. Charga and Colton reached the open doorway simultaneously, and both stopped short.

Colton spoke first. "And who are you may I ask, and what are you doing up here?"

"I'm here to ask some questions about John Harborstone."

"Really?" Colton snapped back sarcastically. He refused to back up from the doorway and immediately assumed a defensive stance.

"And what if I don't want to answer any?" he shot back. Colton was laboring under the mistaken impression that Charga was another of the California Horse Racing Board investigators who had recently been nosing about his stable, an inquiry spurred on by the uncanny winning streak notched by BCH runners of late. It certainly had been a very unusual run of racing luck and good fortune. Even

Brian Colton had wondered about it. During the last two months his thoroughbreds, trained by John Harborstone, had been winning at an almost fifty per cent clip. It was an open secret that the CHRB suspected some sort of possible illegal activity had been instrumental in the posting of these very unusual numbers. If even a hint of skullduggery could be uncovered, it was their investigators' job to do so, and to do so ASAP. To that end the CHRB investigators had daily been seen roaming around the BCH stables, asking questions of everyone on the premises. Colton had already been grilled twice as to what he may have seen, overheard, or personally instructed his stable hands to do. A primary function of the CHRB was to investigate and ferret out any activity that could be construed as having a negative impact on the sport, and because of their policing efforts, the business of thoroughbred horseracing in California had been practically blemish free since years back when the suspicious, sudden demise of Phar Lap served to blacken its' name. Now, before Charga could utter another word, Colton began again, "Look," he said, a tone of defiance, mixed with a touch of undisguised contempt dripped from his every word, "I've said all I'm going to say. We've just been extra lucky lately and John is just plain and simple a very good trainer, so if you CHRB boys want anything more than you've already got, well then, you've come to the wrong man again, get it?" Charga had been taken aback by this short tirade, but quickly realized what was going on. He raised both hands in an 'I surrender' motion. "Whoa! I'm not from the CHRB. Take it easy. I'm just here trying to get some info about who may have attacked John Harborstone this morning."

"Oh." Colton stepped aside hesitantly, "But that still doesn't answer my question. Who the hell are you?".

Charga removed one of his business cards from his wallet, and handed it to Colton. "I'm Duke Charga. Private investigator."

"Sorry" Colton said, "Those CHRB boys have been all over us of late. They've been questioning our latest winning streak, as though they think we've been doing something wrong, and they seem determined to pin something on John. I think they believe he's been doping our horses, or maybe doing milkshakes on 'em." He waved his hand just below his chin. "I've had it up to here with them."

Colton's demeanor had softened. He studied Charga's card. "So how are you involved?" he asked.

"Harborstone hired me." Charga replied, extending his hand, "You must be Brian Colton."

"That's correct." Colton stepped aside, motioning to the cushioned chairs. "Come in. Sit down. How can I help?" he asked. His mood had changed in an instant. Although he thought of his trainer as an underling, still Colton genuinely liked John Harborstone and was more than willing to help find the person or persons who had so brutally beaten him. He knew Harborstone as a mild mannered person, not overwhelmingly effeminate, but one who could aptly be described as a sweet man. His predilection in sexual preference most likely the underlying factor in his character. Colton thought, "Harborstone sure would make an easy target."

"That's okay" Charga said, "I'll stand." He removed a small pencil and notebook from his jacket pocket. "Just a few questions." Colton strolled to the big glass window overlooking the barn interior, stared down at a hot walker stable hand leading a chestnut toward the rear double doors, then began half whispering, and very deliberately. "I'll help however I can" he said, "I'm just sick of those board investigators. They just don't know John Harborstone. If they did, they'd know he would never engage in any such activity. He's actually a very moral man, even if he is a bit quirky.", "By that you mean . . ." Charga paused, searching for an unobjectionable adjective, then continued in a tone suggesting a question yet inferring a knowledge of the fact, "you mean could we say . . . gay?" Colton's head swiveled, his body remained facing the window, but his eyes were focused intently on Charga's face.

"You know?" he shot back, "How?"

"I visited him this morning in the hospital. Just came from there. "He told me himself."

Colton furrowed his brow, he placed his ever present cigar between his teeth, removed a gold plated cigar lighter from his pants pocket, and began re-lighting the half burned stogie, puffing heartily as he contemplated his next combination of words. "He told you?" he began dubiously, "and why did he tell you, and why were you visiting him in the first place?" He paused momentarily, then before he could be answered continued with another series of questions. "What are you, an ambulance chaser? Are you one of those sleaze balls who try to cash in on other peoples miseries? And what is it exactly that you want from me?"

"Hold on. You've got me wrong!" Charga said as he unconsciously began to fondle the soft leather of the horse saddle straddling the couch style chair just to his right. "Let's put it this way" he said, "I'm not someone who's crazy about being awakened by the Arcadia P.D. asking questions about a man, John Harborstone in this instance, whom I've never met personally, and only know through his reputation," he paused, and I was curious myself as to why one of my business cards was discovered on this guys' beat up body."

"Yes, go on." Colton nodded. "Is that what prompted you to see him in the hospital?"

"Right. And Harborstone hired me on the spot to look into things for him. He was half awake but conscious enough to realize that if I, as an independent investigator, could track down his assailant, that I could maybe keep the fact of his sexual preference out of the news around here."

"Well, that makes sense." Colton interjected, "He wouldn't want that to become public knowledge. You know, horse racing is strictly a mans business."

"That being the fact, then how come he told me that the man who attacked him told him to stay away from his woman?" Charga wiggled his fingers, "Was he acey duecy?" "Acey duecy?"

"Yeah. Meaning he goes both ways."

Colton snickered. "Funny you should use that terminology." he said.

"How so?"

"It's an old horseracing term actually meaning that one stirrup is shorter than the other on a saddle, but . . ." Colton went on, "to answer your question, no. Far as I know he was just a gay fool in some ways, and had I known that before I allowed him to become my partner, well then, he never would have become my partner." Colton bit down on his stogie, took a deep puff, then added, "like I said, horseracing is a mans' business. I don't even like the fact that there are now some female jockeys and trainers." He held up his hand in a 'stop' motion. "Hold on a minute!" he said, in a commanding tone, as he strode closer to the big glass window. Colton peered intently at the lower level of the stable, then took three determined steps toward a small table at the rear of the room upon which, Charga observed, was what he recognized as an overland trucker's civilian band radio outfit, very similar to the units installed in police patrol vehicles. Colton switched the set on, picked up the hand microphone, depressed the talk button and spoke. The sound of his voice filled the entire BCH stable. "Attention! This is Colton. You there! You hot walking that bay!" Charga looked down. There were two stable hands in the building. One was mucking out a stall. The other was leading a horse toward the rear doors. Both stopped momentarily upon hearing the sound of Colton's voice. The mucker, realizing Colton was not concerned with him, went back to what he was doing. The other stable hand had stopped moving and was now looking up at Colton's office.

"Stop yanking that bridle!" Colton ordered, "Just lead the horse at a steady pace! Comprende?".

Colton glanced back at Charga. "Have to watch these wetbacks all the time." he said as he replaced the mike on its' hook. "Especially now with Harborstone out."

Charga nodded. "Sure. Fine." he said, then added, "but back to the subject at hand. Why do you think someone would believe that Harborstone was fooling around with a lady, considering his sexual preferences.?"

"Beats me." Colton answered, "Maybe somebody mistook him for me." He smirked unabashedly, "I've got that kind of rep don'tcha know?" There was a definite hint of pride in his voice as he spoke. "The ladies are drawn to me and I to them I may add, and . . .".

"That may be so" Charga interrupted, "but you're not known to be in the barn area at four in the morning, are you?"

"Well now, that's true." Colton answered, "I usually only show up down here when I know Harborstone may be out, and on big race days, and never before nine A.M."

"Interesting." Charga's investigative analysis immediately clicked in gear. He began thinking aloud. "That means someone was here stalking and waiting specifically for Harborstone and that means . . ."

Colton completed the thought. "They knew he'd be here."

"Right!" Charga was impressed. "This guy may be a bit on the cocky side but he certainly is no fool." he thought. He continued thinking, but now was thinking aloud. "And that simply means either the perp knew on his own or someone told him that Harborstone would be here at that time of the morning.".

"Who and why would anyone want to do that?" Colton queried.

"Could have gotten that info from anyone, either purposely or by a simple slip of the tongue. When I figure that out I'll be close to figuring out why and who his attacker was.".

While mulling over this idea Charga found himself unconsciously gently stroking the saddle laying over the back of the big chair.

Colton noticed.

"I see you're impressed." He motioned toward the saddle.

"Can't help but to be." Charga answered, "It's a beauty.".

Colton smiled broadly, a smile that quickly morphed into his trademark sneer. "I call it my sex saddle." he said.

Charga frowned. "Now what's that all about?" he thought.

"Let me explain" Colton continued, "I had it made special. I let my lady friends ride it. Especially in the late afternoon when not too many people are around the track. "I'll take one of the outriders' horses and together we ride over the race track turf. They're really impressed with that, and it puts them in the mood for . . ." he paused, took another puff on his cigar, then smiled again, "Well, you know" he added, and that curious smirk appeared once again.

"Riding around the track?" Charga asked, "What . . . ?".

Colton pointed at the saddle. "Just take a closer look at it." He suggested, wryly grinning like a mischievous boy who had just successfully stolen a Playboy magazine. "Notice how it's just a bit higher in the back, and how the curvature from side to side is just a bit more angular?".

Chargas' curiosity was piqued. He examined the leather seat. There was definitely something just a little different about this saddle compared to the saddles to which he was familiar, but unless one was told about it, the subtle changes from a normal saddle would be difficult to spot.

Colton continued, now moving his hand softly along the seat area.

"See how it tilts toward the front?" he chuckled, "Now grab hold of the horn.".

Charga hesitated. This saddle horn, now that he looked at it more closely, also seemed different somehow.

"Go ahead!" Colton urged again, "Touch it!" He smiled his smirky smile once again. "Notice how it's not as stiff as normal saddle horns usually are? And check it out . . ." he pointed to the tip of the horn, "Notice how it's just a bit bulbous at the end?"

Colton was smiling widely now. "This keeps the chicks pushed forward and rubbing it. That gets them erotically excited and they don't even know why."

Charga looked up as Colton continued. "After a ride around the track I bring them up here, a glass of wine, a little this and a little that, and well you know what I mean."

Charga nodded. "Yeah. I know what you mean alright." he said rather disgustedly, all the while thinking, "This guy is slimier than a water snake in a mud puddle.", then he shook his head, feigning admiration. "You're something else." he said, not wanting to alienate this character whose help he night need later on.

Colton bit down on his now unlit cigar, and puffed up his chest. He believed he had impressed his visitor, and as far as he was now concerned, this young fellow had been made envious of his own lifestyle. "Anything else I can do for you?" he asked.

"Not right now, you've been a big help." Charga answered, at the same time thinking, "Sometimes I just don't understand some people's mindset." He again rubbed the finely tooled leather saddle, and maintaining the facade toward Colton, smiled admiringly. "This guy is definitely perverted." he thought.

To Brian Colton, however, there was nothing perverted about inducing women to desire a sexual encounter. "Glad to help." He said extending his hand, "Whatever I can do, okay?"

Charga disliked shaking hands with this slime ball, but grinned a fake grin and took Colton's hand. "I'll let you know. Thanks again. So long for now."

Charga took one step toward the doorway, then hesitated and turned. "Maybe just one more thing." he said.

"Go ahead."

"Who benefits from Harborstone's absence now that he'll be out for a time?"

"Well!" Colton answered, "I just elevated our number one stable hand to assistant trainer, and I've given him all the authority to maintain the training schedules John had already set up."

"And who is that?" Charga queried readying his pad and pencil.

"Juan Zella." Colton replied, "He's been with us for quite a while."

"Interesting." Charga whispered, then aloud, "Just one more thing."

"Go on"

"Any ideas as to why Harborstone would have needed the services of a private investigator? Maybe he owed out some heavy money, or maybe problems with one of his boy friends? Anything you may know of?"

"Nah!" Colton was emphatic, "Nothing like that, but he did mention once that he was having some trouble with one of our stable hands. I told him to just get rid of him."

"And did he?"

"Funny thing." Colton explained, "He never did. Said he could handle it and not to worry."

"And when was that?"

"Just about two weeks ago or thereabouts." Colton paused, "Unusual that he didn't do as I suggested. He usually took my advice."

"And who was it he was having problems with? Do you know?"

"Yeah. It was one of those new guys. One that didn't speak English or even Spanish. My other partner brought in a few of his people from his stables in Arabia. It was part of the deal when he bought in to my stable here. Maybe that's why John wouldn't fire that man. Didn't want to upset Shiek Baddaffi."

"Makes sense." Charga acknowledged, "What's this guy's name?"

"Don't know." Colton began crushing his half burnt down cigar in an already overflowing ashtray set on the table beside the CB radio. "I'm not up on all those funny names."

"That's okay." Charga replied as he continued making notes in his pad. "I'll just have to speak with both Zella and Harborstone again to fill in the spots."

He looked up and nodded slightly. "You've been a really big help. Thanks again." he paused just a moment, then added, "And try to go easy on those poor bastards," he pointed down to the barn first level, "you know, those people down there."

Colton snickered. "Yeah, sure." he said, "So long as they do what they're supposed to do!"

Charga half saluted Colton as he exited the outer office and strode onto the walkway leading back to the old wooden staircase, and down to the ground level. The visit with Colton had proved somewhat useful. Charga deduced that Harborstone more than likely had been set up for that beating. It was only the why, then the who, that was problematic now. He knew he had to talk with Juan Zella as soon as possible and figured he could catch him sometime during the morning before the actual races began, and question him then. At this time Juan could be considered a suspect since he did profit in some way by Harborstone's absence. Also, who was this stable hand that had given Harborstone a hard time? He'd have to ferret him out and get some answers form him as well. For that he might need an interpreter. Charga's train of thought was broken by the crackling voice ot the track announcer which suddenly blared from afar. "Welcome to arcadia race track!".

"That's right!" Charga thought aloud, "It's early post Sunday!". He felt inside his jacket pocket for his winning ticket from the previous day. The number four horse had won at 7 to 2, so his ticket was now worth just over nine hundred dollars.

"Guess I'll just go around front and cash this while I'm here.".

He hopped into his Dynasty and drove out of the barn area and onto the main parking lot in the front of the track. The lot was already half full.

"Surprising." he thought, "This being Palm Sunday.".

He walked up to the entrance windows that read 'Clubhouse Entry', pulled out a ten dollar bill and slapped it down. "One!".

The ticket seller asked, "You want a program?"

Charga really had no need for a program since he intended to simply cash his ticket and then go find Juan Zella, but figured, and rightly so, that had he said no, the ticket seller would think of him as being a real 'cheapo', so he answered in the affirmative. He knew how these track workers could make a big thing out of nothing.

"That's two bucks more, bud." was his growling response.

On this day no one even noticed the bulge under his jacket, and he passed right in without any trouble at all.

69

Brad Street steered his vehicle toward the 'Authorized Vehicles Only' parking area, flashed his badge at the security guard, and simultaneously placed the 'Police Business' placard on the front dashboard. The guard took note of both with much disinterest and waved the vehicle thru. Dunne motioned to a parking space nearest the press entrance doorway. "Park it there." he ordered.

Another uniformed track security officer strolled on toward their vehicle. He leaned in the window. "Can I help you?" he asked.

"Maybe." Dunne answered as he lifted his big frame out of the car and slapped the door shut behind him. "Where's the room where the video tapes of the track can be found?".

"You mean the race tapes or the general surveillance tapes?"

"Surveillance. Parking lots, ticket windows, like that.".

"That would be the A V room. All the tapes are kept in the A V room.".

"So why did you ask if we wanted the race tapes or the general surveillance tapes if they're all kept in the same room?" Street shot back. The track security guard just shrugged. "And so where the hell is this A V room?" Street demanded, the question dripping with sarcasm and annoyance.

The guard answered with civility, not wanting the exchange to become adversarial, after all these were the police. "Take the press elevator to the fourth level. Look for the audio visual room up there. It's to your left off the elevator."

"Thanks." Dunne said, almost apologetically, "Thanks a lot.".

Then he motioned to his partner to follow his lead. "Let me do the talking from now on, okay?" he said. "You have a knack of getting people pissed over nothing.". Before Street could answer that remark, Dunne went on, "It's your tone. Your tone, man! Sometimes you can get better results and more help by just lightening up a little.".

They found the elevator and hit the number four. It started up with a jolt. 2, 3, 4. The elevator doors slid open and the blue sign on the wall was plain and simple. An arrow pointed to the left with the words 'Audio-Visual' in clean white lettering. The arrows also showed Press and Lunchroom to the right. Thirty steps to the end of the hallway to the door with ten inch letters A V. They didn't bother to knock. A rather small man, gray haired, in his late fifties or early sixties looked up from behind a rack of VHS tapes.

"Yes?".

Big Mike Dunne towered over him. He looked down, "Likely a former jockey, retired, given a job here by the racetrack management" Dunne thought, "Most likely not a big winning jockey but a veteran rider whose life remained centered around racing." Aside from the stable workers most other racetrack employees were just that.

"We need to check some video from yesterday. Not the races, but the surveillance tapes. You got them?".

"We got tapes of all areas of the track but . . ." before the little man could finish, Street held up his badge, straight armed it into his face, almost striking the little man in the nose. "We're APD. Need to see tapes of the paddock area after the last race yesterday.".

Intimidated, the little man sputtered, "Uh, oh, s-sure. Come this way."

The detectives were led to another part of the room where one wall was lined with eight television monitors. Another mid sized gentleman was seated in front of the monitors.

"This is the AV manager." the little man motioned to the TV's.

"He'll help you.". Then he called out rather loudly, "Mister Demondo, police are here!".

Mister Demondo, a lower level executive of the track board of operating managers, was a former thoroughbred owner, who had been kicked in the side of the head by one of his horses while walking in the stable area of the track, and subsequently, because of that kick, had lost all hearing in one ear. That incident had precipitated his giving up on horse ownership and moving to a desk job with the track. He had said he never again felt at ease or safe in the stable areas or anywhere near horses, but still loved the sport of horseracing, so any job at or around the races suited him just fine.

Demondo had a curving scar on his left temple, a perfect half print of a horses' shoe. He was rather dark, weather beaten, a few too many wrinkles for his fifty five year age, with balding light brown hair, thick eyebrows, with a wide nose and somewhat thick lips between which he rolled a well worn toothpick. He turned slowly, and with an obvious Texas drawl, asked "So now what y'all poolice want up he ya?".

Dunne answered. "You know what happened to trainer Harborstone, right?".

"Ye-ah.".

"Well, in conjunction with that investigation we'd like to see who Harborstone's groom was talking with after the last race yesterday.".

"Yee-ah?"

"So do you have a tape of the paddock area?"

"Yee-ah."

Street impatiently spoke up. "So can we see it?"

Dunne glanced back at his partner with a quick admonishing stare. Demondo slowly picked up a pair of eyeglasses from the desk like space in front of him, flicked them onto his nose, then peered up at Street with a curious expression. "Ye-ah" he repeated, then spun around in his chair to once again face the TV monitors.

"Now! Now please!" Street demanded. Mike Dunne gave him a look of disappointment. "Chill!" he said, then to Demondo, "We really would appreciate it if we could see that tape.".

Demondo sat still, only his fingers were moving, directing the camera videos of various areas of the clubhouse, grandstands, and ticket selling booths. "I already jest told ya, thet you'all could see them tapes, jes slow down a mite thar, fellas." He cupped his mouth, then called out. "Chorlie!".

The smaller AV employee came out from behind some racks.

"Yes sir?".

"Git me tape fo six woon from yesterday, it's in rack numbah fo."

Demondo turned back, looked up at the two detectives. "He used to be quite a jockey in his day." he said.

"Figured." Dunne acknowledged.

"Fell at Sunland park, bad spill, tough break."

"Right!" Dunne had figured this guy to have been a jockey. "It's a tough business." he replied, "Maybe riskier in some ways than what we do."

"Yup! In some ways, but shore is more dangerous than most jobs.".

He turned back. "Chorlie," he said, "Set it up in video screen ny-an. Gents, pull up a chair and enjoy!".

Dunne and Street did just that, setting two of the four chairs on rollers directly in front of the TV monitor marked number nine which was located on the southernmost wall, off to the left of the main console. The screen first showed colored bars, followed by a scanning picture of the horse path leading from the track to the paddock area, then the wording 'Paddock Area', and the date and time appeared at the bottom of the picture digitally monitoring the hour, minutes, and seconds.

"How long do these tapes normally run?" Dunne asked.

Little Charlie answered. "It's a three hour tape, sir.".

"Okay. Forward it to the minutes following the last race.".

The former jockey nodded, hit some buttons at the bottom of the screen and said, "Here you go. This is just when the horses were returning. Is this what you want?".

"That's it." Dunne answered, "How do I pause it if I need to?".

"Just hit that second button.".

The two detectives stared intently at the tape replay of the horses coming off the track. The winner, the number four horse, was the last to be returning to the paddock and stable area.

"There!" Dunne pointed, "That's Zella leading that horse.", he paused, then added, "and that's the guy with the red mark on his face stopping him right there.".

Street nodded. He asked "Do you have any tapes where we can track this person's movements?".

Demondo, who had been monitoring his panel of eight TV screens, but had also been aware of the goings on to his left, turned.

"Chorlie!" he called out, "Git tape numbah seven fo fo.", then addressed Dunne and Street directly, "This'll show ya where da people walk and the parkin' lot area out front. We keep track of everything goin' on in the lot as a precaution against lawsuits.

Mebbe this'll halp ya too.".

"That's perfect!" Dunne blurted out. "Maybe we can track this guy to his car and get a shot of his plate.".

"Wouldn't it be too far away to make it out?" Street asked.

"Not if we can take the tape to our police lab, they can enlarge and clean up anything.".

"Oh right. Modern technology." Street agreed, "they have that new super enhancer down there now.".

Dunne nodded. "If we can follow red face to his car, it's possible we could be able to somehow get a shot of his plate. We'll take the tape to the lab for enlargement and enhancement, then we'll go back to Duarte General and try to get some answers from Harborstone.".

"Jes find what y'all want and ah'11 make y'all a copy. Thet's no problem, gentlemen, no problem at all.".

"Any coffee up here?" Dunne asked.

Detective Street leaned back in his chair in anticipation of an extended stay examining an assortment of video tapes.

"Ave got some watah hay" Demondo pointed to a cooler sitting at the side of video monitor panel, "Halp yerself." . . .

The two detectives settled in for what they both suspected could be a time consuming tape viewing session.

"Ah kin fast forward these tapes fo ya." Demondo added. He just was never happy to have strangers seated alongside him in his AV room. "And you'll be outta here in a jiff!".

"Well, that's good of you." Street answered. "Wouldn't be too much for you would it?"

Demondo didn't like his tone. He just grumbled a bit and hit the fast forward button.

Meanwhile, out front, Duke Charga headed straight to the nearest ticket seller/cashier window. He was anxious to cash his big win ticket, as anyone would be. The window was about 200 feet from the entrance gate, yet it seemed more like 200 yards to him. It's a known happening, time and distance do have an uncanny way of changing speed and perception when one is anxious for an event to occur. He quickly, gingerly yet gently, removed the ticket from his shirt breast pocket, took a second to covet it one last time, then picked up his pace once again. Just five feet from the window an elderly lady with bluish white hair stepped in front of him. If she wasn't eighty plus she was definitely just shy of being an octogenarian. Charga almost bumped into her backside. Oldsters, both male and female, seemed to be taking over the sport. He looked to his right, then to his left. They were everywhere, and they tended to move not just a bit slower than he'd like.

The old lady turned abruptly, glanced ominously, then spoke coldly, sharply. "Young man, please!". Charga stopped in his tracks. Another moment or two wouldn't make a difference, even as anxious as he was to grab onto that small wad coming to him. "Just short of one thou" he had figured. "After all" he thought, "I've held on to this winning ticket all night.".

With her blue white hair held stiffly sprayed in place against the southern California morning breeze, she shook her head side to side and murmured, "Teh! Teh! Always in a hurry to place a bet! No respect!".

She pursed her lips firmly, and the wrinkles encircling her mouth seemed to intensify. Then she waved a finger admonishingly. "You just wait a minute now, young man!".

Charga simply smiled a weak smile, shrugged his shoulders and replied, "Sorry M'aam.".

After several minutes during which the female octogenarian had kept up a running questionnaire and conversation with the young man in the seller/cashier booth, she turned and waved a wager ticket in Charga's face. "See?" she said, with a tinge of sarcasm, "I've got my two dollar wager, and there's plenty of time for you to get yours.".

Charga smiled meekly once again, then noticed her ticket was actually nothing more than a two dollar wager to show. His smile turned to a grimace. "All that talk for a two buck bet for third!". It was a rather annoyed stare he gave her as he stepped up to the booth window and watched her slowly shuffle past.

"Wanted to know who was the favorite in the first." the teller growled, nodding toward the slow walking woman, "I had to look up the program 'cause she didn't get one, that cheapo!".

Charga placed his winning ticket on the small counter area in front of the teller who never even glanced down. "Wanted to know who was riding, what was the trainer's name." he continued grumbling under his breath.

Charga interrupted. "I'm just cashing." he said.

The cashier went on with his quiet rant. "So I look it all up for her, then she tells me she wants a two buck bet on the fav for show!".

He shook his head in a display of total disbelief. "For show!" he exclaimed. "Imagine! The mentality of some of these oldsters!".

"I'm just cashing." Charga said again, pointing to his 200 dollar win ticket.

"The favorite for show!" The teller grumbled again.

"My ticket." Charga said, tapping the counter.

"Oh yeah, sure, any bets?".

Charga laughed. "No, I'm just cashing.".

Without looking at the wager amount, the teller slid the ticket into the slot marked mutual payoff.,

"Holy crap!" he exclaimed as he looked down at the amount, then back up to Charga "What a nice hit!".

The teller smiled. "Sure is nice to see not everybody bets two bucks to show on the favorite!".

He looked down once again. "That one went off at seven to two, so how do you want it?".

"Hundreds." Charga answered, trying vainly to control the obvious Elvis smirk from curling his lips as he spoke. The teller counted out nine hundred and forty dollars. Charga picked up the nine one hundred dollar bills, then said "The rest is for you.".

"Taxi!" came the loud call out as the two twenties were quickly scooped up. "And you have a great day too.".

As Charga folded the money into his wallet and began walking away he heard "If you win another nice one like that, be sure to come back to me to cash!".

Charga turned and gave the thumbs up sign. It was a nice feeling to have a decent sized bankroll in one's wallet, and Duke Charga was relishing that feeling. However, just now that feeling was secondary. He was actually here at the track on business, and now it was back to the business at hand. He planned to seek out Juan Zella, get some answers, then continue his private investigation as to who would want to beat the crap out of a gay trainer, and why.

He went directly to where he figured Zella could be found either the barn area, the paddock area, or somewhere thereabouts.

He didn't have to search long. Juan Zella was lingering just outside the paddock on the horse path leading from the stable area to the paddock.

"Yo! Juan!" Charga called, waving an arm, signaling Zella to come. Zella waved back, then quickly approached. "Hola!" he called back.

"Say Juan," Charga began, "I need some info, and I'm sure you're the one who can help me.".

"Sure, mister Duke. What you need?".

"You gave one of my cards to Harborstone, right?".

"Oh, yeah. Poor mister John. He was hurt bad, no?".

"Yes he was." Charga noticed that Juan Zella did not appear even a bit disturbed or concerned about Harborstone, as he spoke the words.

"Bad thing happened to him." Zella continued, "He's in the hospital now.".

"I know" Charga responded, "I've actually been up to see him there already.".

"You? Por que?".

"Cops came to me, wanted to know if I knew anything.".

Zella broke in. "Why did they come to you?".

"Because they found my card on him when they brought him to the hospital.".

Zella took a short step backward. "Oh! Qh si, si! That's right.".

"So what I want to know is why did you give him my card, and do you have any idea why he was beat up?".

"Well, the policia are working on this already, mister Duke.".

"I still want to know myself.".

"Por que?".

"Harborstone hired me to find out. The police will most likely write it off as a mugging or attempted robbery gone bad. They probably won't waste much time on this case. Could be they've closed it already."

"No mister Duke." Zella exclaimed a bit nervously. "They were here this morning.".

"They were?".

"Si! Asked me a whole bunch of questions.".

"And?".

"I didn't have too much to tell them.".

"Okay, but now just tell me.".

"They asked if anyone was asking about mister John.".

"And?".

"I told them si. There was someone asking about the BCH trainer.".

"Was it my old partner, Mike Dunne?".

"Si. And a tall mean looking man with him.".

"Okay, so what did he ask?".

"The policeman?".

"No. Whoever it was who asked about Harborstone.".

"He wanted to know about how we got these horses in such fine shape.".

"And you said what?".

"I said mister Harborstone worked hard. Came in every day at four A.M. and stayed late all the time.".

"Okay, what else?".

"The man said that four in the morning was awful early, and that's it's cold at that time.".

"And you said.".

"I told him that it didn't matter to mister H, since he always wore a heavy blue and white Columbia jacket. You know those jackets keep you nice and warm.".

Charga nodded. "Okay, now tell me exactly how and why Harborstone had my card.".

"Well, he told me yesterday that he had been getting some nasty phone calls . . .".

Charga interrupted. "What kind of phone calls, from who? About what?".

"He didn't say, but then you had given me a bunch of your cards and he noticed them on the table and just picked one up. He said he could probably use a private investigator.".

"Well, I figured it was something like that. That card is what brought the police to my door.".

"Senor Duke, I like mister H, and it looked to me that he must've wanted some kind of help, maybe to stop those calls.".

"I can't say I don't need the new business, but . . ." Charga paused. He removed the handkerchief from his suit breast pocket and gently wiped the gathering beads of perspiration from his brow.

The sun had fully broken thru the morning overcast, and was spreading it's golden warmth all across the un-shaded areas of the track. It was fast becoming a typical southern California spring day. Charga continued. "But," he said, "I'm wondering just exactly what that single card has gotten me into.".

Zella shrugged. "Sorry." he said meekly.

"That's okay Juan. Not your fault." Charga replied, then added, half aloud "Looks like it may be just a bit too hot today to be wearing this dark suit, and be standing out here in the sun.". He stepped back into a more shaded area along the edge of the horse path and motioned Zella to follow. "Just a few more questions, okay Juan?".

Zella obliged, and followed Charga into the shade, "Si! For you, sure." he said.

Again Charga noticed that Juan Zella appeared almost totally undisturbed by the fact that his immediate supervisor, a person he said he liked a lot, and considered his friend, had been savagely beaten and was lying in hospital at that very moment. Charga picked it up as being a mite un-natural.

"What's it mean to you, Juan, that Harborstone will be out of commission for a while? More to do? Less to do? What?".

Zella shrugged again. "Well, I'm sorry for him, sure, but . . ." he paused, then almost smiling, continued, "but now I am officially the assistant trainer.".

"You're what?".

"I no want it to happen this way, but mister Colton made me official assistant trainer today, and he's put me in charge of training all his horses." Zella puffed up his chest. He was definitely standing tall. "Maybe soon I become top trainer." Charga shook his head slowly.

"Do you know what you've just done?" he asked.

"No. What I did?".

"You've just made yourself into a number one suspect.".

"What you mean?".

"Well," Charga answered sympathetically, "Police will no doubt figure you as the one to gain most. They may figure you tipped someone to take Harborstone out, and with him out of the way, you moved up didn't you?".

Realizing what Charga was implying, Zella answered defensively.

"Si, I get promotion, but I no do that!".

"I don't think you would either." Charga agreed, as he again dabbed his forehead with his handkerchief. He stepped back further, pressed his shoulder against the smooth cool concrete wall, and glanced up thankfully at the building overhang providing the welcome shade. He spied movement at the corner of the paddock building. He blinked twice quickly, and focused his eyes. It was not a bird. "Say Juan, is that a camera up there?".

Zella turned and looked up. "Si, senor Duke. We have cameras on all the buildings.".

Charga smiled. "Well now, that's a break.".

"Como?".

"Are there cameras along the horse pathway by the paddock too?".

"Si. Cameras in front and back on both sides. They tape everything here, sun up to when it gets dark.".

"And what is done with the tapes? Do you know?.".

"I think all the tapes are kept upstairs in the surveillance room.".

"For how long?.".

"Now this I do not know.".

"Let's go and find out, okay? Lead the way."

"Okay senor Duke. I've got a few minutes before I have to get back to the stable."

Zella led the way to the rear of the grandstand past the concession stands, and around an interior corner to the employee and press elevators. He pressed the elevator call button.

"Security is up on numero quatro.".

They stood in front of the elevator doors for a moment, fixatedly staring up at the lighted floor numbers. 4,3,2,1. The doors opened.

Standing in the elevator was a well dressed blonde female, almost six feet tall in her six inch spiked heel shoes, nicely fitted in a tailored black pant suit. Her meticulously made up hazel eyes flashed a flecked muted green with every blink. Her semi tanned face was a perfectly contoured blemish free exemplification of the legendary southern California surfer girl, highlighted by what Charga considered the most kissable set of full lips since Brigette Bardot, or as in his own case, since Adriana Messina. It was funny, he thought, not hilarious funny but strange funny, how memories of Adriana had been crowding his thoughts lately.

"Nice looking." Charga whispered as he man-scanned her, up and down. He caught it that she was doing the same to him.

The statuesque blonde paused momentarily. She obviously liked what she saw, smiled admiringly and brushed by him rather closely. A bit too close for it to have been an accidental brushing. For just a fleeting second he felt the softness of her breast against his arm, then she was gone.

"Can't be more than twenty" Charga mused under his breath.

He and Zella stepped backward into the elevator as they watched her sashay down the corridor, swaying her chassis with just a little too much emphasis. She knew their eyes were following her, and they both knew that she knew.

"That was mister Colton's latest girlfriend." Zella whispered, "he gets all the good looking women, I dunno how, but he sure gets 'em!".

"I've got an idea about that." Charga thought to himself, "Lots of cash and a fancy saddle!".

Zella pressed 'four'. The elevator doors slowly slid closed.

"Have anything good going today, Juan?" Charga asked, in as pleasant a tone as he could manage.

Zella shrugged, then smiled. "We got only two going out today." He shook his head, "Neither one is any good really.".

"You're sure?".

"Si!" Zella answered, still smiling, "These two mister H hasn't shot up with stanozolo!".

"What the hell is that?" Charga asked. "Never heard of it. Is it legal?".

"Oh si! It's perfectly legal, but mister H shoots these horses up big time with it, more than he should, I think.".

"What's it called again?".

"We call it winstrol. It makes the chevallos very mean and builds up their stamina and muscles.".

"So it's a steroid?" Charga queried. He knew that certain drugs and equine performance enhancers were allowed while some others were not, but now his interest was piqued. Maybe this had something to do with Harborstone. Charga had already discovered that the California Horse Racing Board had been inquiring into the activities at the BCH stable. "Is that why you guys have been winning so much?".

"Er, well, si. Mister H sticks them in the feet just above the hoof.".

"In the feet? If it's legal why not just stick 'em in the ass?".

"He gives them too much. Over the limit." Zella answered excitedly, "Then he sticks the horses with lasix and that's a coverup so the vets won't find all the extra winstrol.".

"I thought lasix just helped them breathe easier.".

"Si!" Zella replied, speaking a bit more slowly with an air of superiority. He was relishing the fact that he knew so much more about thoroughbreds and racing than did this quasi gringo in his fancy fifth avenue custom fitted blue suit. "Si." he repeated, "But lasix is also a diuretic. After a race the horse pees out big time and flushes out all the excess fluids, comprende?".

"Okay, I got it." Charga nodded, "and I didn't know that." His voice trailed off as he noticed the number four flash on the elevator floor guide above the door. He lurched awkwardly as the elevator stopped abruptly. The doors slid open.

"This is it, down here." Zella said as he pointed to the door painted with the letters AV. Charga attempted to continue the conversation about the BCH horses and their extraordinary win streak.

"Is that why the CHRB is sniffing around you guys?" he asked as they strode quickly to the AV room.

Zella half answered. "Maybe." he said, almost inaudibly.

Charga pressed on. "Could that have something to do with Harborstone's injuries?".

"Maybe." Zella answered. He shook his head slowly, suddenly seeming a bit annoyed at Charga's questions. It was becoming obvious to Charga that Juan Zella had just realized he may have already said too much about the horses at BCH which would now, at least temporarily, be under his charge.

They reached the AV room. Zella didn't knock. He just pushed open the door and called out. "Charlie Cole! You here?".

There was no answer. Zella looked back at Charga. "Maybe he's out for lunch break." then took several steps farther into the room.

"Just follow me, mister Duke." he said.

Charga did just that, noting the handwritten dates on the rows of VHS boxes stacked on either side as he passed between several racks of stored video tapes. Each container was marked with an area designation, date and time. Charga took note of one in particular, 'Cashiers 1 thru 5, May 14 1992'. That was Mother's day of the previous year. He remembered it distinctly as that was the day he and Adriana had come to the track together on one of their early dates. Some boxes were even dated in the mid seventies.

"Didn't know they kept these that long" he thought. "Wonder when they started taping and storing?".

He knew there were film chronicles of past major races, and most races post World War two, but nevertheless found this extensive library of surveillance tapes impressive, to say the least.

"Nice collection." he mumbled, "You guys must tape everything around here.".

Zella half nodded, then again motioned for Charga to follow.

"Right thru here." he said, "Mister Demondo is always here. He never leaves for lunch. Charlie Cole gets it for him and brings it back from the press room.".

"Is that right?" Charga feigned interest, "And just who is mister Demondo?".

"He's the manager up here.".

The pair entered the monitor viewing area. Mister Demondo was seated in his usual position, operating the video scanners. His back was to them and he didn't turn. "Mo police?" he questioned, his slow rich southern Texas drawl stretching and emphasizing the 'oh' sounds. From his tone alone, Charga immediately sensed this man was annoyed at something. He surmised it had been Mike Dunne's new partner, since Brad Street had that strange ability to get people pissed off without even trying, and since Zella had mentioned that Dunne and Street had planned to visit the audio visual department to check out the paddock tapes. It was likely they had already been here and Street had worked his magic once again.

"No, mister Demondo." Zella spoke up hesitantly, just a bit apologetically, "This is . . .".

Charga interrupted. "I'm working on behalf of John Harborstone.".

Demondo almost turned. He glanced back over his shoulder. "Oh ye-ah?" the 'I don't want to be bothered' tone a bit softer now, "So yawl not police?".

"Nope." Charga replied. He sat himself down on a chair just to Demondo's right and offered his hand in greeting. Demondo peered over his bifocals. He smiled. It was a friendly smile. Charga continued. "My name is Duke Charga, I'm a private investigator.".

"And yore workin' for mister H? Good! I like him.". He grasped Charga's hand. His grip was strong, sincere. "John is an okay guy."

"Right. And Juan here is helping me quite a bit. We'd like to see . . ."

Demondo broke in. He had already guessed the reason for this visit to his work room. "The tapes from yesterday, ah know.".

He turned to his left, leaned slightly, reached under the counter and pulled open a metal drawer. He removed a VHS tape marked '461 Paddock'. "He'ya is what yo need to see.". He said, "Jes fast forward it a pinch past halfway.". It was more an order than a suggestion. He again reached down to the open metal drawer.

"Then you'all be wanting to check out this one he yah too.".

He removed another VHS tape. This one labeled '7-4-4 main lot'.

"I made short copies of these fo the police. They just left a few minutes ago.".

Charga had already depressed the fast forward button below the video tape player in front of him. "What's that tape?" he asked.

"He ya is the really important one." Demondo answered, sneering just a bit as he turned toward Charga. "This one he ya shows the plate numbah of that red faced man's car. You all will be wanting that too, right?".

Jualn Zella tapped Charga on the shoulder. "There!" he exclaimed, as the video screen displayed a view of the paddock area and showed himself being approached by a big, powerfully built man with a bright birth mark on his right cheek. "That's the hombre!".

"Check out those arms." Zella added, flexing his own medium biceps for emphasis. "He had some muscles.". He looked down at Duke Charga and added meekly, "To tell you the truth, I was a little scared of him.".

Charga returned his look. "I can see why." he said as he visually examined Zella's upper arms. "I can sure see why.".

Demondo broke in. "And he ya he is walkin' back to his vehicle."

He offered up the second tape, "Check it out.".

In one swift move Charga hit the eject button, removed the first tape with one hand, grasped the second tape with the other and slipped it into the player. "You're okay, Demondo." he said admiringly, "You're on the ball.".

As the second tape played, Charga sunk down some in his seat.

The surveillance video camera had been just a bit too distant from the parking area. The plate number could not be distinguished from that distance. It was just a blur of numbers and letters. "Well, it looks like a Chevy or Buick, but I can't make out the plates." He sighed, "That's why they took the copies!".

He hit the stop and eject buttons. "They'll use the enhancer down at HQ and get a clear picture of that plate. Damn! I was hoping we'd have something here.".

Demondo leaned back and laughed. It was a somewhat subdued laugh, yet enough of a laugh to cause his bifocals to slide a bit closer to the edge of his bulbous nose.

"What's so funny?" Charga asked. He was more than just a little confounded by Demondo's demeanor.

"I could've done it fo them." Demondo answered with another chuckle crowding in between his words, his heavy frame bouncing with his every exhale. "But ah jes didn't like their attitude.".

A momentary display of some exertion splashed across his face and he grimaced and grunted under his breath as he pushed his normally sedentary overweight size forty eight portly body up, and out of his chair. "Bring that tape he ya" he gasped, and he slowly and deliberately marched around to the side of the TV monitor panel board. He pointed to a video playback slot marked 'PF'.

"This is the photo finish close up tape enhancer." he explained, still breathing in short bursts, while almost lovingly tapping what appeared to be a much newer piece of recording and viewing playback equipment. It was obvious this piece of electronic gadgetry had been recently implanted into the side wall of the video monitor board. It was finished with a burnished stainless steel while all the other pieces of video devices wore plain blue metal skin outer panels.

"I kin set it to focus and enlarge the whiskers of a rabbit taped at a hundred yards out.".

Charga was impressed again. "Didn't know you had such equipment." The tone of his remark exposed a notably conspicuous combination of surprise and admiration. Demondo immediately picked up on it. His lips curled into a prideful smile and he nodded. "State of the art." he boasted, his chest noticeably expanding, now more with pride than deep breathing merely to catch his breath. "The race track has plenty cash and we git the best up to date equipment, that is . . ." he added with another burst of real pride, "whenever ah ask fer it! But ah didn't ask fo this, I demanded it!". He pointed to an eye level TV screen in the side panel, then pulled out a computer keyboard which was set on a sliding tray just beneath the counter. "Check it out, boy!", he continued as he began turning knobs and hitting the keyboard just below. He slid the tape in the input slot and forwarded the tape to a section where a view of the vehicle rear plates were unobstructed. Then he paused the tape. Charga watched with intent. Next, Demondo hit the caps lock, entered a code number password, then tapped the plus sign key several times. The plate number of the blue Chevy became larger and clearer with every tap on the keyboard.

In a moment it filled the screen, and slowly, surely became as clear as a closeup Nikon camera photo. "Thar ya go my boy!".

Charga removed his notepad and quickly jotted down the number. "I owe you Demondo!" he exclaimed.

"Naw! It's nothing' boy!". Demondo removed the tape and strolled back to his seat. "Back to my regular work." he said, "Gotta keep watch he ya.". Juan Zella, who had been standing back near the shelving, stepped forward. "So donde es Charlie?" he asked, turning slightly and gazing toward the door. "Should be back by now, no?".

"Probably out in the mens' room having a smoke." Demondo answered, "He needs to take a hit every once in a while. Just loves his seegars.".

"Cigars?" Zella queried, surprise un-mistakenly discernible, not only in his tone, but on his face as well. He had known Charlie Cole for all the years he had been working at the track, and had never seen him light up a cigar. "I didn't even know he smoked anything!" he said. Demondo turned to face Zella. "Well, jes don't spread it around. I shouldn't even have mentioned it. You know, they don't want us smoking' up here, and I really don't allow it in this room. A fire in here, with all these tapes would be a disaster and would be really tough to put out.".

"Oh, okay" Zella stammered, "I-I w-wouldn't say a thing. That's your own business up here, you're the boss.".

"C'mon, Juan" Charga gave Zella a head bob motion toward the door. "I got what I needed.", then extended his hand again to Demondo. "You've been a big help." he said earnestly. "A really big help.".

"Jes git whoever hurt John, okay?".

"I'll get 'em" Charga answered as the two shook hands once again, "Damn sure, I'll get 'em, mister Demondo, don't you worry about that. I'll find out who did it, one way or another, I'll find out.".

"I'm hoping you will" Demondo paused, "And you can call me Jack, okay?".

Charga smiled. "Okay, Jack, thanks again.".

"Thank you mister Demondo." Zella chimed in as he began leading the way back, thru the rows of tape racks, toward the door.

Just as they reached the door, Charlie Cole opened it. He was on his way in. He smelled of cigar smoke, and there was a lingering translucent trail of bluish white smoke rising gently in the passageway behind him. "Excuse me." he said, then looked up and added, "Oh, hello Juan.".

Juan Zella grinned, then returned the greeting. "Hola, Charlie.".

Cole nodded, but the quizzical look on his face prompted Zella to add, "We just needed to check a tape. Just leaving.".

"Well, you sure came to the right place." Cole said in return, motioning to the many racks full of videos. "We got plenty here alright. Well, I'll see ya around, okay?".

Zella and Charga exited the AV room and quickly walked to the elevator. They heard Charlie Cole call out. "I'm back, mister D!" as the AV door slammed shut behind them.

"Guess he got his tobacco fix!" Charga said sardonically, shaking his head as he spoke, "Lousy habit!" he added.

They found the elevator waiting for them. No one had used it while they had been with Demondo.

"I have to get back to the stables," Zella began, almost apologetically, "I have one filly going in the second. Have to get her ready. The vet gave her some lidocaine yesterday so I'll have to check her again before we put her out on the track.".

"Something wrong?" Charga queried. He had heard of lidocaine and knew it to be a pain killing substance. "Is she hurt?".

"Had a hot spot on her right front leg just above her sesmoid." Zella answered, "Race seems above her level anyway. If she's still hot I'll ask to have her scratched." He paused, then added, "Doesn't have too good a shot. Might be best to pull her out and look for a softer spot.".

"You can do that? On your say so?".

"Si, I am the trainer now, It's my call." Zella pointed to his chest with both hands, in a gesture of pride.

"Okay" Charga replied, then in a cautionary tone, "Don't get too carried away with yourself.".

"Zella looked at Charga and frowned. "Wha-what?".

"Forget it.".

The elevator reached the ground level and stopped with a jolt.

Charga began stepping out even before the doors fully opened. He had ridden on many elevators before, but this one felt just a bit shaky and it was a relief to be off it. "Think this thing needs an overhaul."

he said. Pointing back to the sliding doors which were closing with a squeak.

"Oh si." Zella acknowledged, "I know the track has called about getting all the elevators fixed up.".

"That reminds me." Charga said, "I've got to make a call.".

He removed his cellular phone from his jacket pocket and began to dial. He touched the numbers rapidly, almost without looking. It was a very familiar number, one he had often dialed before.

"I see you have one of those new portable phones." Zella blurted out. He had been wanting to buy himself one of those and was impressed with anyone who already had one.

"What'll they think of next?" he asked. It was really a rhetorical question, and required no answer. Charga simply nodded. He had already gone thru three other cellular phones, each one just a bit smaller in size and easier to carry. "Yeah." he said, "Great little invention.".

He heard the first ring, and on the second ring a familiar voice answered, "D A office. Petrone.".

"Hello Mike." Charga answered back, "Duke Charga here.".

He and Mike Petrone had worked together on several cases when Charga was part of the Arcadia PD. They had always maintained a close relationship, and he knew that Mike Petrone was one of his staunchest supporters when his excess force case was before the IAD review panel. Mike Petrone was now in his late twenties, of Italian American heritage, formerly a police records clerk who had helped Charga in searching police files for vital information relative to some cases Charga had worked. He had completed his study of criminal law and transferred up to a surrogate court clerk position. From there he had worked his way up and into the District Attorney's office, passed the bar exam and was hired on as a full assistant DA.

"Duke!" Petrone whispered back, "How have you been? I heard you're a PI now.".

"That's the story alright. But Mike, I'm calling 'cause I really do need a favor.".

"Well, that I figured already. You haven't called much since you left."

"I know. Sorry about that, Mike.".

"Okay. That's okay. What do you need?".

"I need you to track down a license plate.".

"Duke, I would if I could, but you must know I can't be doing things like that. People would get suspicious if I go around nosing thru the motor vehicle records department.".

"Why's that Mike?".

"I'm under their eye right now. Just got a promotion you know. It would be too unusual. I'm the newbie around here.".

Charga hesitated. "Damn!" he muttered.

"I heard that!" Petrone said, "Take it easy. Is it really very important? You know I'd like to help you out.".

"Yeah, really. It's got to do with a case I'm working.".

"Okay, here's what I can do. I'll transfer you over to Sylvia Cortez. She's top ADA now. No one questions anything she does around here. She's in line for the D A job. Rumor is the Republicans are going to run her as their candidate. Lots of power behind her right now.".

"Okay." Charga returned, "Thanks. I've worked with her before, and . . .".

Petrone interrupted. "I knew she had a thing for you, so she'll be happy to help you I'm sure.".

"So, you knew about that too, eh?".

Mike Petrone chuckled. "Everybody knew it!" he said laughingly.

"Alright Mike. Just put me thru.".

"Don't get upset ole buddy.".

"I'm not, really.".

"So how have you been anyway?" Petrone asked. He was sincere in his query, and Charga was just as sincere in his response. "I'm doing okay, but I do sometimes miss the old haunts, and some of the guys at the department.".

"Yeah, well some of us back here kinda miss you too. Try to keep in touch better, okay?".

"Will do. Promise.".

"Right. I'll put you through now. Take care buddy.".

"Thanks Mike.".

Charga heard the clicking sounds of the extension transfer. The phone rang once, twice, three times.

"C'mon." he mumbled, "Pick up. Pick up!".

Suddenly . . . "Sylvia Cortez.". The familiar throaty, yet totally feminine purr seemed to carry a more sophisticated intonation than one he remembered. "She's moving on up." he thought. Her voice brought back pleasant memories. Sylvia Cortez had unabashedly demonstrated an affection for Duke Charga when they had collaborated in gathering evidence during his very last criminal investigation for the Arcadia PD. He had indeed found her very attractive, not only in appearance but in character as well, and he had always felt a certain affinity toward her, but it was more as a friend and co-worker than anything else. Unfortunately he was unable to reciprocate her affections since at the time she attempted to come on to him, he was already involved with Adriana Messina who had had him totally mesmerized, yet he could readily picture her distinctly Latino good looks. The smooth, unblemished olive complexion, the shiny straight, jet black, shoulder length hair, neatly parted in the middle with short bangs draping her forehead, partially covering the deep set brown eyes, and meticulously mascara tipped eyelashes. He had also always been intrigued by her smallish, almost pug nose, but in Charga's opinion, aside from her shapely five foot five, one hundred fifteen pound frame, what really attracted every man's eyes were her perfectly shaped ruby lips. "Very kissable indeed." he thought as he stated his name in response, in what amounted to almost a whisper. "Duke Charga here. How are you Sylvia?".

"Duke!" she spurted out, surprise and glee apparent in her voice. "I missed you. How have you been?".

"Oh, I'm okay.". Charga was a bit taken back by her initial greeting. He knew she had had a crush on him, but figured by now she would've been over that. Apparently she was not. "It's so good to hear from you." she went on. "I was beginning to think you had forgotten me.".

"Now you know I could never do that." Charga exclaimed, figuring chivalry and a bit of honey would serve him well in this situation. "I think of you often.".

"Do you?" she queried, the much softer tone to which he was accustomed returning, "Why haven't you called before?".

"Sorry about that, but actually I've been very busy." Charga felt he wasn't lying, just being somewhat disingenuous. He had been busy, just not so busy that he couldn't make a phone call if he really wanted to.

"So how is Adriana?" It was a loaded and calculated question and Charga knew it.

"Oh well, we keep in touch. She's back in Sicily.".

"Long distance relationships rarely work out.".

"I've heard that too.".

"Okay then, but why exactly have you called?". Charga noticed her tone had again changed, reverting back to the business only coolness of her opening words after first answering the call.

"Actually I was talking with Mike Petrone, and he transferred me." Charga answered, then immediately thought, "Ooops! Wrong choice of words!".

"So, you mean to say you really don't want to talk with me?".

"No. No. I mean yes, but . . ." Charga recognized a verbal trap when he heard one, and saw himself falling into one right here. Maybe it would be best to come right out to the point. "Actually I needed a favor and Mike figured maybe you could help me.".

"Is that it?" The question was short, sharp and cold.

"Well, I also wanted to say hello to you and . . ."

"Get to it Dukey boy.".

"Well Sylvia, I need an address for a plate number. Mike figured you could run it without attracting too much undue interest.".

"Sure, I can do that for you . . ." Cortez paused, then added, "But only if you promise to treat me to dinner and a movie.". Her voice was soft again. She paused once more. Charga did not respond.

"Is that okay, Dukey?" she purred.

Women were hard to understand or interpret he thought. Now she was being seductive. A moment ago she seemed distant and passionless. Best to agree and avoid further complications.

"Love to." he said. He really didn't have to feign enthusiasm. Who wouldn't enjoy a night out with this attractive lady? And it likely would be fun reminiscing and renewing the old acquaintance.

"Just say when and where, and I'll be there." he added.

"What about Adriana?".

"Like I said, she's in Sicily. Not a problem.".

"Tonight. Seven. You pick the place.".

"Okay" Charga said, "Garlattis. Know where that is?".

"I do. Now give me the plate number and I'll bring all the info you need.".

Charga read off the number. "I really appreciate this Sylvia." He said.

"Actually, it's no big deal, but it will be great to see you again, Dukey." she replied, again softly and now with some passion in her voice, "I really have missed you" she added.

"And you know what?" Charga went on, "I really do miss you too.". He wasn't lying here. It was true, he actually did miss Sylvia. Maybe more than he had realized. Or was it just that purely male animal craving for female companionship? Tonight he would find out for certain. "Okay Sylvia, then I'll see you at seven.".

"It's a date Dukey.".

"Say Sylvia," he said, consciously, yet cautiously moving the conversation back to a more serious note, "maybe you could call me on my cell phone as soon as you get the name and address linked to that plate number.".

"What about dinner?" she asked rather suspiciously, "Would it still be on? Please?".

When it came to Duke Charga, Sylvia Cortez had no restraint, it had always been that way. She was an adamant believer in love at first sight, and she had been devastatingly smitten by Charga's good looks and personality right from the start.

Being a confident, self assured woman, she had no compunction in revealing her affection toward him, and even after several months during which they had had no person to person contact, it was obvious she continued to wear her heart on her sleeve for him, was still carrying a torch for him, and made no bones about it. "You know how I care for you, don't you?" she went on, then almost pleadingly, whispered "Please?".

Charga smiled. It was always an ego boosting situation for any man to have a woman like Sylvia Cortez, both beautiful and successful, all but fawn over him. "Yeah, sweetheart." he whispered back, using the most seductive, yet macho tone he knew, "I know.". He paused for a second, "Everybody knows" he thought, then added, "I'll be there. Count on it. Okay, baby?".

"Wonderful!" Cortez returned, "I'll call you on this number just as soon as I get through with my brief prep for tomorrows closing argument. If I don't call you within an hour, then you can call me. I could get tied up here. My case is first up on the Monday morning docket. That's why Petrone and myself are holding down the fort today. You know there's got to be someone in this office seven days a week.".

Charga was aware of that policy. The county District Attorney office had been manned from 8 AM to 6 PM seven days a week since the newly elected DA had come into office three years prior. He had claimed it was his way of maintaining a connection with the people. It was also a way to force the county to increase funding and hire additional assistant DA's. These additional ADA's were hired on thru direct interviews with the top District Attorney. Of the five newly hired ADA's, three were former law partners of his old law firm. The whole hiring deal smelled of cronyism, but then, as Charga had mused at the time, "That's politics.". "At least," he thought, "It had given Mike Patrone a shot to move up as well.".

"Well Sylvia," Charga remarked, recalling what Mike Petrone had said about Sylvia's possible candidacy, "Maybe the next DA will change that policy back to a simple five day, eight hours a day, work week. Think that could happen?".

"Damn straight, it will!" Cortez shot back, "At least if I have any say in the matter.".

"Wow!" Charga thought, "That's the strong woman I remember!". Now he liked Ms. Cortez even more! "Talk with you later, Sylvia." he said. "Okay. Bye for now Dukey.".

Charga snapped the cellular phone shut, slipped it in his jacket side pocket, and began walking back to the main track grandstand area. "The horses are on the track for the second race!" the sharp South African English tinged voice boomed out over the track speaker system. "Post time in fifteen minutes!".

"Might as well lay out a few wagers since I'm here anyway, and it's mostly track winnings cash I'm betting with." Charga mused, half aloud, then to himself, "I'll try a few plays before I leave.". He was contemplating returning to the hospital to check Harborstone's condition, or maybe if Sylvia didn't call in a half hour or so, to call her back to see if she had gotten the info he wanted, and if so, maybe following up on that straight away, and going directly to whatever address she may have come up with. "Well, in either case" he thought, this time silently, "I'll stay put here at least until noon.".

He strolled to the nearest ticket seller/cashier area, and made a quick check of the tote board, then made a just as quick wagering decision.

Not the best way to bet, but he was just following his first instincts. The number three horse had been posted as the morning line favorite with short odds of eight to five, but the number four horse was getting all the action. His odds were down to two to one from a morning line of eight to one. Due to that move, Charga assumed someone in the know was pouncing on that entry. "Smart money?" he queried himself. "Okay, I'll go with number four." He stepped up to the window. "Fifty win and place on number four." he said as he slapped a hundred dollar bill over the counter.

"Fifty win place number four." the ticket seller repeated. "You got it".

"Say, how come such an early start today?" Charga asked. He knew of the changes in starting times for the Sunday races, but didn't know why they started so early. The first race was normally sometime in the afternoon, now they were running the second and it wasn't yet noon.

"I dunno." The teller replied, "Something to do with simulcasting the races back east. You know there's a three hour difference. When it's eleven here, it's two in the afternoon there".

"I get it." Charga nodded.

The teller went on. He had said he didn't know but in reality he did. "And the TV sports network is covering the feature today. It's a Kentucky Oaks prep race".

"Right." Charga nodded again as he fished out the betting ticket from the auto 'totalizer' ticket printer.

"And . . ." the teller continued, it was obvious he liked to talk with his clientele, "this week they'll be covering the big Derby prep too, so I guess today they'll be getting all the kinks out and . . ."

"Right! I get it!" Charga said, sounding rather impatient, as he simultaneously turned and began walking back to the main track area. After six steps he could just make out the teller's angry vocalization. "Hey! Screw you! Just walk away like that! You asked, didn't you? I hope you lose! You jerk!".

Charga walked on down toward the rail separating the crowd from the actual race track. He nudged his way thru the railbirds and secured a spot right up against the rail, just ten yards from the finish line, and settled in to watch the race. He checked the tote board again. Ten minutes to post. The first race had gone to the favorite. "So the little old lady had actually won." He smiled.

"Good for her."

The horses had finished their warm ups and were heading toward the starting gate. Funny how the last few minutes before post time always seemed longer than normal. The track announcer's voice boomed once more. "They're at the post!", then after a short pause, "They're all in.", another short pause, the starting bell clamored and "And away they go!".

Charga's selection, the number four horse, raced to the front.

"Good start." he thought. Then around the first turn the favorite, number three, came up to challenge for the lead. Those two were two or three lengths ahead of the rest as the horses raced into the backstretch and came around the final turn heading into the stretch.

The murmur of the crowd became a roar. Charga included.

"Stay up there four!" he hollered excitedly, "Stay up there!".

Suddenly, seemingly out of nowhere, the number seven horse loomed up on the outside.

"Who's that?" Charga asked aloud, looking over to the guy at his right. This race fan, standing next to Charga all the while, had been very quiet and still throughout the race. He stared back at Charga and answered. "That's C J John from the BCH stable. They've been winning at a good clip here." He winked, then added, "I personally think they've been shooting up their horses.".

The track announcer called it, "And C J John takes the lead and wins going away! A photo for place, hold all tickets.".

Charga looked down at his win place ticket. "A loser." he said, "But maybe I'll get something back if he wins the photo.".

He glanced over to see the grinning face of his newly found friend.

"I got it!" was all that guy had to say, "Stick with BCH!". He turned and began walking toward the cashiers windows.

The photo results were posted. Order of finish 7, 3, 4!

Charga tore his ticket in half and tossed the pieces over his shoulder. He noticed Juan Zella smiling broadly in the winner's circle, standing with his jockey, the winning horse to the side, and with Brian Colton, cigar stub in tow, who had one arm completely wrapped around the waist of that gorgeous model type blonde.

"And Juan said he might scratch out!" Charga shook his head.
Maybe Zella didn't know, then again, maybe he just didn't want to say he knew. "Whatever!" Charga thought, Maybe I'll just hang on to the rest of my bankroll!". He headed for the exit. Now it was his mind that was racing. Maybe I should have checked the program more closely, then again, Zella had said the horse could be in over his head, so I likely wouldn't have played it even if I noticed it was out of the BCH barn, could have at least caught the place spot, did I bet too much? What if I played like that old lady? Fifty to show would have been okay. He began contemplating whether to return to Duarte General or push Sylvia Cortez for that address and go right over there first. "Maybe I can do both today.".
He was lollygagging along, not really looking where he was going. "Ouch!". Someone stepped on his toe. He looked down and saw a gnarly little white hand waving a wager ticket in his face. It was that same bluish white haired octogenarian he had encountered earlier. She had a two dollar show ticket on the number three. "So now it's you who's in a hurry, hey?", he cracked facetiously.
"Well, I want to cash in so just move it buster!", she replied, then pushed by him and briskly marched away with the energy of a twenty year old, and the form of a marathon speed walker nearing a finish line.
"Well, I know what keeps her going.", Charga said half aloud. "Funny what a winning ticket can do. Kinda keeps ones' spirits high!". He smiled as he passed the exit gate. Someone pointed toward him, then shouted out. "There's a winner!". It was the cashier who had pealed off Chargas' $940! Charga gave a thumbs up sign and kept on going. Maybe this would be a productive day after all, in spite of that last race result!

Big Mike Dunne gently stroked his whitened moustache as he marked Duarte General as the next stop in his police log. So far, this mugging investigation hadn't amounted to anything really important. As of now it appeared to be a simple commonplace irate boy friend or homosexual lover pouncing on an intruding 'wannabe' boy friend. Not much for a seasoned former homicide detective.
"Pull in here." he said, pointing to the driveway leading to the emergency entrance of the hospital.

Detective Sergeant Brad Street hesitated. "That's for doctors and emergency vehicles only, Mike.".

"Just put the PD placard on the dash.".

Being a stickler for following rules and regulations, Brad Street reluctantly steered onto the driveway, grunting slightly as he passed the large red sign that read 'Emergency vehicles Only'. He picked up the Arcadia PD placard from between the front seats and tossed it on the dash. "Okay?" he asked, a subtle tone of annoyance tinged his words, "Now what?".

"Just park anywhere," Dunne answered, "We'll only be a few minutes.".

He looked askance at his partner. "Calm down, don't worry! What's gonna happen?". He chuckled, "Nobody's gonna call the cops to give us a ticket. Remember, we are the cops!".

"That's not the point." Street mumbled. He shook his head slowly, "I just hope I'm not blocking a real emergency vehicle and . . .".

"Okay!" Dunne interrupted, "You stay here in the car in case you have to move it. Satisfied now?".

Funny how his partner had the innate ability to be annoying and get on some ones' nerves without even trying. It was just those little things, the tone of his voice, the sighs, the body moves, all combined, that could very easily get under ones' skin, ergo a rather even tempered person like Mike Dunne could be affected as well. And the insignificant cases Captain Dunbar had been lately assigning Dunne and his newest partner were certainly no confidence boosters. That was bothering Dunne as well.

"I have to work with him." Dunne thought, "Man, sometimes I sure do miss the Duke.".

He exited the vehicle, started up the walkway toward the emergency entrance double doors, then hesitated a moment to take one short glimpse back at his partner. Street had remained seated behind the wheel, straight backed as if in an 'at attention' posture, with the autos' engine running. He appeared to be pouting.

"What an asshole." Dunne mused, "Just a damn asshole!".

He entered the building. Two hospital workers in green uniforms stepped in front of him just as he passed beyond the doors.

"May we help you?". They seemed to speak in unison. Dunne flashed his PD badge and they quickly stepped aside. "Elevators?" he asked.

The pair pointed toward the right hall corridor, again their movement was in tandem. "Thanks." Dunne nodded slightly, then proceeded to the elevator, about thirty feet down the hall. He had been here earlier with Street on an initial visit, at the start of this investigation, so he knew to depress the number four in the elevator. John Harborstone was in 406 he remembered, that is, if he hadn't been moved since early that morning. The elevator stopped with a sudden jerk, and the doors slid open. Dunne followed the numbered wall signs heading toward room 406. As he approached the room he was confronted by a large black orderly. Mike Dunne was a rather big man himself, but in comparison to this big dude he appeared on the smaller side.

"Just where you going, mister?" the big man asked as he folded his muscular arms across his chest. Dunne noticed the bulging biceps.

"Police business." he answered, once again flashing his police badge. "To see Harborstone in 406.".

The big man was not intimidated in the least by either the badge or the facade of bravery. "I'll just stay with you, if you don't mind.".

"I don't mind, big guy." Dunne answered, "but I won't be needing you, thanks anyway.".

"This is my floor." came the quick retort, "and I determine if I'm needed or not!". The big man paused for a second, then added, "Got a problem with that?".

Now Dunne was really glad his partner had remained outside in the car. He didn't want a confrontation and Street would have certainly caused one here. "Of course not." he said and the pair entered room 406 together. John Harborstone appeared to be asleep.

"How's he been?" Dunne asked, motioning with a head bob.

"He's resting now," the big man replied, "so don't even try to wake him up again like you guys did this morning.".

"I didn't try to wake him." Dunne whispered, "When we were here the doc was here too, and we were told he couldn't be questioned at that time. That's why I'm back now.".

"Well, one of your guys came back and stuck smelling salts under his nose and woke him up!".

Dunne stepped back. "There's only two of us working this case, and neither of us came here alone.".

"Well man, somebody was here!". The big man made a fist and pumped it in front of his chest, "I almost got him." he said, "Just a minute too late.". He grimaced, then added, "I don't like stuff like that happening on my floor!".

"I heard him!" a raspy voice called out. Dunne glanced over to the next bed. A rather frail old gent, with thinning gray hair was sitting up, leafing thru the pages of a back issue of Playboy magazine, and munching on potato chips. "Young guy. I could tell by the voice.".

"Yeah!" the big black orderly added, "I kinda chased him outta here!".

"So you saw him?" Dunne asked.

"Sure did!".

"What did he look like?" Dunne continued. "Can you describe him?".

"Sure can! He was pretty good looking for a white guy. Kinda looked a little like that movie actor who was in that cowboy movie that was just on TV the other night." he thought a moment, then continued, "It was called 'Duel in the Sun' I think, yeah, that's it."

Duke Chargas' cell phone was vibrating furiously. He had been just about ready to steer his Dynasty down Huntington boulevard on his way back to Duarte General, instead he pulled off to the side of the road, kept the motor running, slid the transmission into park, and removed the pulsating instrument from his jacket side pocket. He flipped open the phone and extended the six inch phone aerial.

"Duke Charga here.".

"Hello Dukey.", the unmistakable voice of Sylvia Cortez purred in response, "I've got what you wanted.".

"Sylvia, you've got what any man wants." Charga flirted, "So give it to me.".

"Maybe tonight." Cortez flirted back. "Right now I'll just give you a name and an address.".

"Okay, I'll settle for that." Charga returned, "At least for now, anyway.".

"Here it is." Sylvia went on, "Got something to write with?".

Charga removed his notebook and a pencil from his inside jacket breast pocket. "Go!".

"Auto that goes with that plate belongs to Antony Taccio, AKA Tough Tony, AKA Tony the enforcer, a known loan payment collector for the old Fassa loan shark outfit. Supposedly he's gone straight since

we busted that outfit six months ago. Here's his last known address.".
Sylvia Cortez spoke more slowly now, enunciating each word
perfectly, articulating the number and the street name succinctly,
thus affording Charga ample time to accurately jot down each bit of
information. The procedure was not unknown to her. She had done
this before on many occasions, phoning in pertinent facts relating
to a given investigation or case in progress. Proper transferal of
accurate information was always paramount, as an error here could
send someone off to a wrong address, or in the case of an ongoing
court trial, could possibly jeopardize an otherwise solid prosecution.
She knew how to transmit information over the phone in a way that
the information given would be recorded correctly. "Got that?" she
then queried.

"Got it all down? Okay. Read it back.".

"I got it okay." Charga answered, then looking down at what he had
written, "This address looks like it's in the Little Lebanon section of
L.A. Am I right about that?".

"I think so Duke. Right on the edge.".

"I'm heading right on down there. Ciao, Sylvia, thanks.".

"Be careful, Dukey.".

"Don't worry. Meet you at Garlattis tonight.".

"I didn't forget. I'll be there, bye Dukey." Sylvia answered, then added
once again, "Be careful.".

Charga took the shortest route he knew down to the 'Little Lebanon'
section of the big city, steering his Dynasty south on Rosemead
boulevard, then on over to Rosecrans, thru 'Korea town' and the
Asian quarter, and into the neighborhood that had recently come
to be known as 'Little Arabia' or 'Little Lebanon'. The genesis of this
cognomen due to a sudden unusually large influx of middle eastern
types into this twenty by twenty street block area.

Here, old Spanish catholic churches and some Buddhist temples had
been overhauled, their pews and statues removed, and the flooring
covered with large colorful Persian wool rugs. These buildings now
housed Muslim Mosques. Store front signs and windows, formerly
painted up with Spanish wording, now featured Arabic writing, and
most men on the these streets sported unkempt facial hair, and wore
turbans and long robe type clothing. The women who shopped the

stores were wrapped head to toe in black or dark blue cloth outfits, with only their dark brown eyes exposed.

Charga shook his head in slight bewilderment. "Different strokes for different folks", he thought as he scanned the corner street name signs. "At least the street names remain in English.".

He instinctively knew these were, for him, mean streets, and he was glad now that he had opted for automatic door locks when he bought his Dynasty, since the ominous stares he was receiving from these dark skinned men was actually making the hair on the back of his neck stand on end. His body tensed, and unconsciously he became poised and ready for any possible hostile encounter. The strange cultural sounds of Arabic zithers and flutes permeated the surroundings. This continual euphony was broken only intermittently by the roaring sound of a commuter bus, an occasional auto horn blast, or a racing motorcycle. For Duke Charga, this was not only just a different neighborhood, in some ways it was a different world. Now he knew why Sylvia had been so emphatic in advising him to 'be careful'. His instincts were sensing trouble ahead. He loosened the fit of his Glock in its' holster. "Hey! You never know." he thought as he brought his vehicle to a slow drive, coasting to a semi stop at each corner. There were no stop signs on this main thoroughfare, just on the side streets, but he felt judicious scrutiny of all angles and corners in this environment was well advised. A lesson well learned from his former partner Mike Dunne.

"There it is." he said, half aloud, as he spied the Compton street sign. "Right down this street.".

He turned onto the street, noticed an empty parking space toward the middle of the block, just in front of a fruit and vegetable store, and neatly parallel parked in it upon his first attempt. "Pretty good!" he complimented himself after noticing the right side tires of his Dynasty were just six inches off the curbside. "Now to find six thirty two, apartment three R.". Of course it was possible, he thought, that Taccio may have moved within the last few months, and had left no forwarding address. Then again, he could still be residing here, and even if Taccio had moved, the local Post Office would likely know to where. That would be his task for tomorrow. "Only if necessary." he thought aloud, "One thing at a time.".

He meandered down the block, past several groups of dark skinned locals whose relentless stares appeared belligerent in their coldness, if not down right threatening. Charga ignored one group, smiled at the next, then nodded at the third foursome who were lingering just a few feet from the big red painted door with glued on numbers 6-3-2. "Hello" he said in as friendly a greeting tone as he could muster under the circumstances, "Nice day, eh?".

No answer. They merely stared back at him, then turned and began walking back in the direction from whence Charga had come. Charga hesitated momentarily. He turned slightly, visually following their movements to be sure they didn't mess with his 'baby'. They didn't, walking straight on by, past the fruit and vegetable store, and past his vehicle, right on down the block, disappearing around the corner. They never once turned to look back. Charga took a deep breath, then grabbed hold of the semi-rusted metal door handle and pulled open the door. The hallway vestibule was littered with old newspapers and flyers printed in Arabic, and some Wrigleys gum wrappers. The walls were painted brown with some newly spackled spots of white plaster doing their best to hold up the peeling paint and cover the age cracks. There were a half dozen postal mail boxes set in the left wall. Four of the six had doors, half of these were open and loosely hanging by one small hinge, the remaining two had no doors, and one was stuffed with candy wrappers. None of the postal boxes had working locks. Two of the them had names taped over their doors. Ida Basara 2R, and T. Taccio 3R. Charga looked around. There were no apartment bell buttons.

"Good. Still here." Charga thought. He pushed open the second door which separated the vestibule from the inside hallway and steps. "Three R" he mused to himself, "Top floor, on the right.". The stairs creaked ominously as he began to ascend the first set, stepping quietly, deliberately. The banister immediately groaned like an injured camel upon his firm grasp, and wobbled precariously under the slightest pressure.

"These are no help." he thought, and he released his grip and moved closer to the wall. At the second level landing, a door opened slightly, and a pair of dark eyes peered inquisitively thru the four inch opening. "Achmed?". The voice was feminine, rather soft, but Charga picked up a tinge of fear in it as well.

He turned. The door slammed shut abruptly.

"Right." he thought, "I'm not Achmed!".

He reached the third floor and checked the landing. On the left was an open door exposing a roomful of cardboard boxes, and some wooden slatted crates, all marked with Arabic calligraphy. To the right was a gray painted, unmarked, un-numbered door securely hanging on what appeared to be three relatively new black painted oversize hinges. There was a shiny brass key lock just above the gray painted doorknob. Charga stepped up to the door. In one smooth motion he lifted his Glock from his shoulder holster, then with his free hand, tapped the door with his car keys.

"Tony!" he called out, "You there?".

Some shuffling sounds rumbled from beyond the door, and the door slowly cracked open. A pock marked unshaven face appeared in the open door space. Charga recognized the red burn mark on the right cheek. He also noticed the brass metal chain lock which was holding the door opening to a minimum.

"And who the fuck are you?". The voice was deep, somewhat scratchy. It fit the face.

"Duke Charga.".

"And just who the fuck is that?", came the retort, "And what the fuck do you want?".

"I'm a friend of Nick Fasso, Tony. Just open the door!".

Charga was being just a bit disingenuous here. Sure, he knew Nick Fasso. Their paths had crossed several times during the days when he was working with the feds in the anti-racketeering division of the P.D. That was true, but he was definitely not a friend of Nick Fasso.

"C'mon, Tony!" he urged again, "Just open the door!".

"I don't know no fuckin' Nick Fasso! Get lost!" Taccio rasped back, and he began pushing the door shut, but Charga had already slipped his size eleven shoe in the bottom of the doorway.

"Listen, Tony," he half whispered, "The cops are wise to what you did today. I'm just here to tip you off.".

The ruse worked. The burly, former loan shark enforcer/collector shuffled back a few steps. "Hold on." he said. He fidgeted with the chain lock. "Move your foot.". Charga stepped back. The door closed momentarily, then opened wide. "Come on in.".

Charga stepped in gingerly, and immediately began mentally canvassing and assessing his situation. He kept his Glock by his side, holding it firmly against his thigh. "Nice place." he remarked sardonically as he visually scanned the apartment. The living area was small by anyone's standard. Just two small rooms. One, a kitchen area with a small gas stove, and an older model of Frigidaire, whose chipped porcelain finish had years ago turned brownish with age, lined one wall. In the center of the room was a small wooden table, flanked on three of its' sides with single wooden chairs. A pile of unwashed cups and dishes sat in the sink near the one rear window overlooking a yard replete with rusting auto parts, pit marked chrome car bumpers, and rotting old used up tires, giving credence to the idea that there may have been an auto repair shop at this location sometime in the past. A tiny bathroom with just a tub and commode separated the kitchen from the bedroom which was furnished with nothing more than a television set with a rabbit ear antenna sitting atop the fourth chair taken from the table set, and a single bed. The mattress was exposed, with no sheet or covering of any kind. Two pillows with stained pillowcase covers were tossed haphazardly across the bed. Charga took note of the butt end of a hand gun poking out from under one of the pillows. As he scanned the two rooms, Charga began to ponder. "Where is this investigation heading?".

The track surveillance tapes had implicated Taccio as a person of interest, the comments by Harborstone himself substantiated his description and identity, and now, the opening of the door allowing Charga entry to this run down dwelling was the topper. It seemed all too easy to this point. Charga once more ran over the particulars of this seemingly simple case; Harborstone was gay, but his sexual proclivity had been secretive, yet he had been receiving calls threatening bodily harm unless he ended an alleged male-female affair. Subsequently Harborstone is discovered beaten half to death on his way in to the stable at four A.M. Regarding the phone calls, how would Taccio have gained access to Harborstones' number? Then there was the lying in wait in the early morning. Could this be a case of mistaken identity? From this initial contact with the almost certain perpetrator of the assault on John Harborstone that possibility was viable, however seemingly unlikely. Charga concluded it extremely improbable that Tony Taccio, a low level criminal of limited intelligence, and known strong arm man for hire, had initiated such a scenario on his own. It would seem more likely that an actor like Taccio, had the purpose of the assault actually been to warn Harborstone off some woman, would have confronted Harborstone at a time when he was with that certain woman. "Has to be something more to it." he thought, "but what and why?".

Following years with the P.D., and now including his recent stint operating as a private investigator, Charga had totally mastered the art of deception, misdirection and misinformation in order to gather pertinent facts, and now he decided, was the time to put that skill into play. He was confident he could extract information from just about any individual without that individual being aware of his intentions, and Tony Taccio appeared an easy subject. Charga was now more curious than ever as to the whys and the whos in this case.

Taccio spoke up first. "How do you know about today?", he asked, "And how the fuck do the cops know?".

"Let me lay it on you," Charga answered, thinking on his feet, "I used to be a cop.".

"What the fuck does that mean?", Taccio interrupted, stepping back toward the bedroom. He appeared ready to go for the weapon atop the bed.

"Take it easy." Chaga replied, "I said used to be!". Taccio relaxed just a bit, "So what are you here for?".

"I told you. I'm here to warn you. To tell you to get going.".

"You used to be a copper?", Taccio asked, "and you said you fuckin' know Nick?". Charga nodded.

"That means you were on his payroll, right?". "I'm not saying." Charga went on, "but I heard you were going straight, and I don't want you to get hung up now, just for a punch hit.".

"How did the coppers find out? Did them fuckin' towel heads spill?".

"I don't know." Charga said, "but I know the cops are wise. Anyhow what towel heads are you talking about?".

"Fucking sand monkeys came up from downstairs two weeks ago. Said they knew I needed some dough. Said if I banged up this Harborstone guy they'd pay me a dime.".

"From downstairs?".

"Yeah." Taccio went on, "I've been out of work lately. Been slow down at the docks, you know I been working unloading down there at San Pedro. Making pretty good money too.".

"Yeah?" Charga asked, "But not like working for Fasso, eh?".

"No. Not anything like that." Taccio was at ease now as Charga was presenting a totally unthreatening posture and tone. "Shoulda got out of this fuckin' neighborhood a fuckin' long time ago.".

"Why didn't you?" Charga asked, seemingly uninterested in what Taccio had to say about the so called towel heads. "This is a creepy neighborhood.".

"Didn't used to be." Taccio answered, waving his arms emphatically, "Used to be Italian years ago. Then came the fuckin' Mexicans and the chinks. Now it's all sand monkeys!".

"So, why are you still here?".

"Rent's fuckin' cheap!" Taccio continued, "But you can't trust these fuckin' monkeys around here.".

"You think maybe one of them ratted you out?".

"Sure of it!". Taccio balled up a fist, "How else would the fuckin' coppers know I banged up that Harborstone character?", he paused, "Say, how the fuck do you know?".

"Still got some connections." Charga answered in a nonchalant tone, feigning a smirk, "But you know I'm not crazy about any of 'em!", then added, "Bunch of back stabbers!".

"Yeah!" Taccio agreed, "Just like these fuckin' towel heads!".

"So, what about them? What was their deal?".

"Ahhh. They came up and said I could make a fast thou by putting that Harborstone guy out of commission for a few days. Said he wouldn't hire one of them 'cause he was anti-Arab. Said he was giving their friends down there at the stable a hard time. Said all I had to do was beat his fuckin' ass and say it was 'cause of a woman. This way no one would be able to trace it back to them.".

"Really? That would be smart, but I wonder why they figured it was worth a cool thou?".

"I don't know and I don't fuckin' care either! They came across with five big, and they're supposed to be here today with the other five," he paused, then continued, very slowly, emphatically, "If they don't show, well then I'll know for fuckin' sure they dropped the dime on me!".

"But I'm telling you Tony," Charga went on, "the cops may be here before them.".

"In that case, I guess I'll just go on down and see Achmed right now.", Taccio said. He stepped over to the bed and picked up the old Army issue .45 caliber handgun, slid out the magazine, checked it, then snapped it back in place and pulled back the cylinder. It was ready to fire. "I'll get my dough now, and then I'm off to fuckin' Vegas!".

"Achmed isn't home." Charga said, holding up an open palm, "so just put that baby away.", then added, "And I'll put mine away too.".

"You fuckin' S.O.B.! You had that ready all the while, didn't you?".

"Hey!" Charga chuckled, "You never know.".

"And how the fuck do you know Achmed ain't home?".

"Spooky lady came out and asked for Achmed. Thought I was him. That was on my way up here.".

"Yeah." Taccio acknowledged, "He's probably at the fuckin' track working.".

"Was he the only one who hooked you up for that deal?".

"Nah." Taccio answered, "There was three of 'em. From down the block here, but he did most of the talking, him and that other rag head, called himself Ach Bin Haseed. Man, these sand monkeys have some funny soundin' names.".

"You said from down the block, where down the block?".

"Back at that fuckin' fruit store. Think I'll drop in on 'em down there right now!".

"Want some company?".

"Why would you want to come along? It's none of your fuckin' business.".

"Maybe I'm just curious, and maybe it's because we share an old friend.".

"Okay, mister. Two fuckin' guns are always better than one. It's your funeral, pal!".

Charga holstered his weapon just as Taccio stepped toward the bedroom door. Taccio partially closed the door, then plucked a wrinkled tan poplin jacket off a makeshift hook on the back of it.

Charga noticed the hook was simply a six inch nail which had been banged into the wood door and bent upwards. "Guess that works." he thought. Taccio wrestled with the jacket momentarily, then grunted as he stretched it over his size 44 frame. It appeared at least one size too small. He stuffed the .45 caliber into one of its' side pockets. Charga smiled and patted the big unshaven lug on the shoulder. "All set?" he asked.

"Yeah!" was the short reply.

"Funny." Charga mused, that despite big Tony Taccios' previous blemished, but well known history of strongarm tactics and exploits on behalf of the now convicted criminal loan shark and illegal bookie Fasjo, and in spite of his effluxion of expletive verbiage, Charga had somehow found himself not at all disliking this big brute of a man. Charga had discovered, some years back, thru his contacts with all sorts of characters and personalities, that there were some people he would find distasteful at the getgo, and others with whom he would attain an immediate rapport. In this case, with this character, he had surprised even himself.

"I'm with you, Tony!" he blurted out as Taccio bounded into the hallway. "Slow down.".

Taccio led the way down the rickety steps, stomping on each step like an angry bull elephant. The old stairway creaked and wobbled.

"Slow down!" Charga shouted once again, as he gingerly stepped along behind. Taccios' pounding hooves echoed thru the hall, and before he had reached the second level, a door was cracked open.

Once again the dark eyes could be seen peeking out from behind the traditional black cloth burkha. "Achmed?".

Taccio stopped, but just for a second. "Yeah!" he hollered, "I'm lookin' for that S.O.B. too!".

The door slammed shut.

"Freakin' female sand monkeys!" he snarled, "They're just plain fuckin' creepy!".

Charga didn't comment, just nodded. He figured any disagreement with this big brute, given Taccios' state of mind, would be nonproductive to say the very least, and as angry and seemingly unstable as Taccio appeared, could possibly lead to an unwanted confrontation with this strongarm specialist., and Charga certainly didn't want that!

In a moment they were at the street level, out the front doors and on the pavement, "the store is down here!" Taccio half whispered as he motioned to their left. Charga nodded again. He was well aware of the fruit and vegetable store on this block. He had parked right in front of it. He scanned the street and cement sidewalks, right and left. Unlike earlier, when the sidewalks were dotted with mid-eastern characters, and slow moving traffic gnarled the street, now both pedestrians and vehicles seemed sparse. The strange unremitting sounds of Arabian instrumental music continued, almost ominously now, to float over the entire neighborhood. Meanwhile, the immediate nearby area was eerily devoid of any activity at all. It was almost as if the neighborhood itself was anticipating some sort of trouble. Charga tensed instinctively, but Taccio seemed oblivious to their surroundings, and he continued to charge ahead in bull like fashion. He tunnel visioned his way along the sidewalk, almost tripping on a cracked section just six feet to the side of the store.

"This is it!" he muttered, as he grabbed hold of the front door handle, "Come on!".

Charga followed quickly. Once inside, Taccio headed straight toward the rear of the store. It was obvious he had been here before and he knew where he wanted to go. Charga at once surveyed the store interior, and made a quick assessment of their situation, location, and the layout of the store. Fruits, dates and figs to the right, corn, potatoes and some green vegetable items resembling asparagus to the left. The writing on the 'for sale' signs were all in Arabic. These fruit and vegetable bins sat atop a gray painted concrete floor, and low hanging fluorescent lights dangled some ten feet off the ceiling, down to just four feet above each bin. A man and a woman, both in traditional Arabic garb, hovered over what appeared to be a haphazardly stacked pile of white potatoes. Obvious shoppers, they were unhurriedly picking thru the pile, placing their selections into a plastic bag. Two wooden swinging doors with small rectangular see thru windows were hinged on the back wall. A lone bearded man, clothed in a black head scarf and ankle length black cloth robe stood just in front of these doors just a half yard away to the left. He was leering at them in a suspicious and menacing manner. That was no deterrence for Taccio. He stomped directly toward him. "Hey you!" he exploded, then almost in a holler, "Where's the big man? Ach Bin Haseed?".

The man didn't answer, he simply backed away from the doors while pointing to them. His demeanor had changed radically. Charga instantly noticed the unmistakable look of fear which was suddenly painted across his face. He shouted something, obviously in Arabic, to the couple sorting potatoes. They immediately put down their foodstuff, and all three scurried to the front of the store and ran out onto the street. With both arms outstretched Taccio pushed open the swinging doors, and burst into the stores' back room.

"Haseed!", he shouted, a definitive tinge of anger reverberated off the walls, "Where the hell are you? You little mother fucker!". Charga remained two yards behind, his hand firmly clutching the grip on his still holstered Glock, which he kept hidden under his jacket. The doors behind him continued swinging noisily, three, four more times, until finally slowing to a stopped position. Once inside this back room he quickly took notice of all around him. If there was just one thing his police training had taught him, it was when finding oneself in an unfamiliar setting, to always become aware of ones' surroundings. That lesson had stood him well during his days with the P.D., and also during his almost year and a half as a private investigator. Now the hairs on the back of his neck were bristling, an instinctive signal that he was definitely in some kind of hostile territory. He scanned the room. It was a twenty by twenty square room, dimly lit by a single incandescent bulb hanging precariously from the ceiling, held by one worn electrical wire, noticeably frayed in several places along its' length. A shaft of sunlight splashed in thru the rear door, propped open by a half full vegetable crate containing what appeared to be some kind of yellowish peppers. There was a pile of empty wooden vegetable crates haphazardly tossed against the south wall, and stacks of unpacked cartons and crates standing against the opposite wall. The gray painted concrete floor continued throughout the building, from the store area up front right on to the rear rooms and doorway. Deep scrape marks, undoubtedly from dragging cartons and crates, had cut a path from the rear door to the crates on his right. A round table, topped with colorful one inch tile work, sat in the center of the room. Three, obviously mid eastern men were seated at this table, taking turns at puffing on their shared arguily hookah which sat directly in the center of the multi colored tiled tabletop. Their arguily hookah was particularly ornate, a sign of wealth. It stood about a foot and a half tall, with a bright yellow base dotted with sparkling red and gold jewels. There were three leather hoses of matching red color, approximately three foot each in length, attached to the base with what appeared to be rubber mouthpieces on the ends. It looked somewhat similar to a magic smoking lamp Charga remembered seeing in a Rudyard Kipling Arabian Nights movie when he was a boy. The center glass tubing was awash with bubbles and smoke, and the space above the table was thick with that same bluish white smoke. Charga noticed the air in this room was totally permeated with the unmistakable pungent odor of Mideast hashish. All three of these men sported short beards which gave each the appearance of someone who hadn't shaved in a week. Their garb was traditional Mid eastern, wrapped neck to ankle in white cloth similar to European and American bedsheet material. Each wore a checkered scarf fully covering their heads down to their eyebrows. Two of the head scarves had red and white checkerboard designs, the third was in black and white. The man with the black and white head scarf stood, slowly turning toward Taccio and Charga. He took two steps forward, then defiantly stiffened his back, squared his shoulders, and positioned himself in what was obviously a 'ready to fight' stance. His deeply set dark eyes scoured both Taccio and Charga up and down. The scornful stare was so intense it caused big Tony Taccio to stop abruptly in his tracks. "What do you do here?" he said, his head cocked to one side. It was obvious this was the Haseed person Taccio had sought out. He spoke very slowly, very calmly, and very confidently, but hateful condescension and disdain dripped venomously with each syllable. "You should not be here.".

Big as he was, Taccio actually appeared to quiver a bit as this man spoke. Taccio reached into his jacket pocket and fondled his .45 caliber. That made him feel a bit reassured. Haseed took note of Taccios' movements, and judiciously slipped his own hand thru the side opening of his Arabic robe.

"I'm here for the rest of my money!".

Haseed smiled wryly. "Do not worry. You will get what is coming to you." he nodded toward Charga. "And who is this person? Your bodyguard?".

"Never mind who he is!" Taccio shot back, "I want my cash now, and I also want to know why you dropped a dime on me!".

Haseed squinted. "Dropped a dime? What means that?".

"You freakin' rag head! One of you creeps ratted me out! That's what it means!".

Haseed turned and muttered something to his cohorts who then stood up and away from the table, and positioned themselves six feet to either side of their leader, and two steps behind. Haseed then added a few more words. Charga could not make out or understand the language. It was guttural sounding and almost seemed as if Haseed was choking. The other two replied in kind, and snickered, nodding their heads in agreement with each other.

Charga sensed some sort of trouble yet to come. He stepped back toward the swinging doors and took a firmer grip on his Glock.

"We did not inform the authorities." Haseed shook his head slowly as he spoke, "Why should we do that?".

"I don't know! To save the freakin' five C's you still owe me, maybe that's why!".

"That would be foolish." Haseed answered deliberately, "Very foolish."

"Well, somebody squealed!" Taccio blurted out, "Otherwise how would this guy know about our deal? And howcum the bulls are on their way here?".

"It is unfortunate that you have now brought in this man, and now have led the authorities to us as well". He glanced menacingly toward Charga. "We did not want many to know of our activities here.".

"So what!" Taccio interrupted, "Just get my dough, and I'll be gone.", he motioned to Charga, then added, "And he'll be gone too.".

"Yes." Haseed smiled as he spoke, "That is true. You shall both be gone.". He turned slightly and called out something, and the other two men began to move forward. Then in one quick motion Haseed stepped forward, and removed his hand from beneath his robe. In it was a twelve inch curved blade knife which he plunged deep into Taccios' lower rib cage, while at the same time holding Taccios' right arm, preventing him from removing his .45 caliber handgun. Charga stepped back. Each of the other two had already whipped out similar blades and were coming at him. Charga un-holstered his Glock, but they were on him quickly. He felt a burning in his left bicep, and saw the reddened blade edge swing past his face. He hadn't completely drawn and raised his weapon, but he squeezed the trigger instinctively, then fell back into and thru the swinging doors. Just as his head made contact with the concrete floor he heard another shot ring out. Then everything went quiet and black.

Big Mike Dunne and Brad Street ran to the back of the store. Two bodies lay on the concrete floor in front of the swinging doors.

"Look! It's Duke!" Dunne cried out.

He knelt next to Charga to check his condition.

"Well, he's alive!" he exclaimed. "Call for a bus right away!".

"The one you hit is a goner, Mike, but what the hell happened here?", Street asked excitedly as he peered into the back room, "It's a freakin' blood bath back there!".

"Never mind that! Get on out to the car and call in. I'll check the back room and the alley out back.".

Dunne noticed Chargas' bloody sleeve and immediately wrapped it with his handkerchief. "Got to stop this bleeding first.".

That done, he stood up, pushed thru the still swinging doors, and entered the smoke filled back room. Two more bodies. One, a big burly Caucasian, with a cut throat, the other, obviously Arabic, was bleeding profusely from the groin. He scanned the room. Clear!

The rear door to this room was open. He checked out back. The alley was clear as well.

Street came running back thru the vegetable store.

"They're on their way!" he said, "Medics for Charga here, and for these other guys, the coroner!".

Chapter Two . . .

Part Three

Charga stirred. He couldn't determine if it was the bright white light that was seeping thru his eyelids, or the chiming bells he was hearing, that had awakened him. He could feel and hear his own heart beat, and with each beat came a sharp stabbing pain that shot from the back of his head to his temple. The throbbing continued, relentlessly keeping time with the beats. He slowly tried to open his eyes, blinking at first, then squinting, in an attempt to focus on his surroundings. The fluorescent bulbs set in the ceiling above, appeared at first, to be two white highway lanes, and the hanging curtain to his right like an orange tinged mountainside. He felt a burning sensation in his left arm. The semi fog was lifting from his mind, and the scenario of his last conscious moments was becoming clearer and coming into focus. The chiming bell rang twice again. A sweet mellow female voice purred, "Doctor Muller to three fourteen, doctor Muller to three fourteen.".

"Where the hell am I?" he muttered.

"You're in general." a deep voice boomed out in answer. Charga knew that voice. He peered toward whence the voice had come. The tall figure rose from the visitor chair, approached the left side of the bed, and positioned his face just a foot away from Chargas' half opened eyes. "We saved your ass.".

"Right!" Charga thought. It was the unmistakable sardonic toned voice of Brad Street, and now, with Streets' angular face just inches away, Charga could easily make out the crease lines around the mouth and eyes. He hadn't noticed these before. "Older than I figured," he thought, then spoke aloud, "Guess I have to say thanks!".

"That would be appropriate." Street answered, with much emphasis on the word 'would'. He was smiling wryly, "I think you owe us one now, don't you?". He was almost purring like a Chesire cat with a mouse in tow. Charga nodded. He still wasn't fully aware of what exactly had taken place, but he did know he definitely had been in deep trouble back there in that store.

"I cracked my head." he mumbled.

"That's right.".

"Then what?".

"Mike and I were on our way to track down Tony Taccio when we saw three locals running out of that store up the block from Taccios' last known address. It was like they had seen a ghost or something. We peeked in and heard a shot fired, then you came flying out those back room doors, landed flat on your back. Then a big Arab type came right after you with a freakin' snee . . ."

Charga interrupted. "With a what?".

"A snee. That's an Arabian mini sword. He was about to slit your throat when Mike popped him right in the head.".

"Good ole Mike! He was always a damn good shot.".

"We found Taccio in the back room.".

"So you got him?".

Street shook his head. "Nope. He was D.O.A. Sliced in the belly, and had his throat cut too.".

"That's too bad." Charga mumbled. He had kind of liked big Tony.

"Too bad. He was some character.". There was sadness in his tone.

"Really?" Street asked facetiously, "A friend of yours?".

"Actually, I just met him today.".

"And so you and he end up in a life and death situation together? So how'd that work out?".

"Really don't know." Charga answered. It was an honest answer. He still hadn't sorted out all that had gone on in that store back room. It had all happened too fast, and his head was still throbbing.

He was just bringing the picture into focus when Street broke in on his train of thought. "We'll unravel it all later, meanwhile you should know, those Arabs you tangled with, well, we got both of em . . ."

Charga broke in. "Both?". He definitely remembered there had been three. Street ignored the one word question and continued, "Yeah. Well actually CSU figured you really got one yourself.
Bullet from your big Glock ricocheted up from the concrete floor And ripped into one guys' scrotum, lodged in his kidney and . . ."
Charga interrupted again, "You mean I hit him in the balls?".
Street grinned. "Exactly." he said, then went on with his explanation, "That guy bled out before the bus could get him here.
Then, like I said, Dunne took out the other one.".
"What about the third one?".
"Third? There were only two.".
"No. There was another one, kinda like the ringleader.".
Street nodded. "We did find the back door open," he paused, "but we checked the back alley, and there was no one out there. Possible he ran off before Mike got out there.".
"okay, but never mind that right now," Charga went on, "How long have I been here?".
"About two hours.".
"Where's Mike?".
"He'll be here soon. Don't worry. He wants to ask you a few questions too.".
Charga was not that much out of it to forget his Dynasty. Leaving it parked curbside in that neighborhood for any long period was surely not a good idea. He could picture it being stripped, radio and wheels gone, up on blocks, and totaled. "What about my car?".
Street smiled again. "Mike knows how you love your cars, so he took your keys and said he would drive it to your apartment complex. A black and white followed, he'll get a ride back here from them.". He checked his watch, then added, "Should be here any minute.".
Charga looked down at his arm. "Son of a bitch got me!" he exclaimed, "came at me all of a sudden.".
Street uttered a sheepish sound. "Baa. No big deal. Just a little cut in the arm.". He shook his finger in mock admonishment, "Don't be a baby." he said, "You're just lucky we came on the scene or you could be joining your friend Taccio on a slab in the morgue!".
"Okay! Okay! I already said thanks.".
"You're welcome.".

"No. Really, I really mean it, Street." His tone was solemn, truthful. Street nodded slightly. "Really." Charga added once again, and he offered his hand.

"Okay. You're welcome." Street replied rather softly, as he accepted Chargas' hand and smiled, a genuine smile this time. They shook hands, both gripping firmly. It was not only a handshake of thanks, but a symbolic handshake as well, and both understood its' underlying meaning, that they were starting fresh. Shared near death experiences are known to do that. For those involved in such situations the most common manifestation is that they find themselves connecting at a higher plane, very often almost instantaneously, with a kind of subconscious instinctive bonding between one life saved and one life the savior, and now, despite their earlier confrontational encounter, the maxim had once again held true.

The door to Chargas' hospital room suddenly swung open. It squeaked just a bit. Both Charga and detective Street turned, their eyes falling upon a most lovely oriental female. She looked to be in her early twenties. Just about five foot tall, her slim size two nurses' uniform fit her neat and snugly, giving extra accent to the smooth curves of her slim bodice. Full strands of clean, shiny jet black hair fell loosely from beneath her white nurses' cap, perfectly framing her petite blemish free golden face, and accentuating her dark eyes. She had a cute slightly turned up nose, and sensuous lips which were curled in a Mona Lisa like smile. Her white sneakers squealed on the tile floor as she stepped to Chargas' bedside. "Hello." she purred. Without another word she took his right wrist in her hand, her index finger delicately pressing against the main artery, and checked her wrist watch for a few seconds. "Pulse is okay." she whispered, and smiled just a bit wider. "Hello." Charga whispered back in as flirty a manner as he could considering his condition. She rolled her eyes and momentarily stared at the overhead lighting. Her smile was replaced with pursed lips, "Teh, tch!". She answered, and shook her head slowly.

Charga stared admiringly at her nicely shaped bustline and took note of the name tag pinned above her left breast. "My Ling?" he questioned, "Is that how you pronounce it?".

She purposely ignored the question, removed a stethoscope from a side pocket in her nurses' outfit, then rolled out the free standing rack which had been parked next to Chargas' bed and upon which a blood pressure testing cuff was attached.

"My pressure should be high right now," Charga mused, "but only because you're near me."

The nurse did not answer. It was obvious she was deliberately ignoring him now. She wrapped the cuff on Chargas' right bicep, set her stethoscope in place in the crook of his arm, hit the button on the rack that automatically inflated the cuff, and again silently stared at her wrist watch.

"Do you flirt with every woman?" Street asked sarcastically.

Charga chuckled. "Nope. Just the good looking ones."

That comment drew a reaction. Her smile returned, somewhat wider this time. "You're fine." she murmured as she removed the pressure cuff and rolled the cuff rack back to its' place. Then she stepped to the foot of the bed, lifted the clip board which had been hung there and on which was Chargas' hospital chart, made some notations, and replaced the chart. She smiled again. "Just rest a bit." she said, "Doctor West will be here momentarily . . ."

"But I want out of here My Ling." Charga interrupted, "So how about we do lunch?".

Very slowly, she moved her head side to side in a deliberately negative motion. "No." she said, "But doctor West will likely check you out and discharge you today so just be patient." She spoke with a very slight Chinese accent. Charga found it most attractive.

"Will you be back?" Charga almost whispered the question.

Street shook his head. "Cut it out!" he droned.

My Ling, the nurse, refused to react. She simply spun around and quickly skittered across the room to the door, her sneakers continued squeaking like tiny mice under her feet, and out the door she went, waving a queens' wave as she exited. "Bye bye, sweetie." she called back.

"Yeah, okay, bye." Charga replied, but she was halfway down the hall before his words passed his lips.

"You know," Street said with a chuckle, "You're really something else!".

Charga smiled broadly as he spoke, "I make 'em feel good!" he said in return. They looked at each other for a moment, then both laughed together.

"I see you guys are okay!". Big Mike Dunnes' voice boomed out. He stood in the doorway, holding the door open with one hand, the other on his hip. "So what's the gag?".

"Nothing much, Mike." Street answered, still with a grin on his face, "We were just talking about some . . ."

"Thought you weren't getting along." Dunne cut in, "Guess I was wrong on that.". He strode with an authoritative gait to Chargas' bedside, placed both hands on his hips, and stood so straight up his barrel chest strained to burst the buttons on his shirt. "And how are you Duke? Okay now?".

"I'm fine, Mike." Charga nodded, "I'm ready to go."

"Yeah, yeah! You're always just fine." Dunne stroked his full gray moustache, then pointed directly at Chargas' nose. "But I want to know how you seem to always put your nose where it shouldn't be!", he paused, then motioned to Street, "You're just lucky Brad and I arrived when we did or you might be the headless horseman, you know that don't you?".

Charga didn't answer. He knew his over active curiosity gene had brought him into what had become a very dangerous situation. It really had been a close call, maybe too close this time, but yes, luckily it was big Mike Dunne who, as usual, had played the part of the rescuing cavalry. "I didn't figure . . ."

Dunne cut him off abruptly, "You never figure!" he exclaimed. "That's your problem, that's always been your problem.". He turned back to Street, "That was always his problem!" he repeated. "Goes where he shouldn't go, gets involved when he should just butt out!".

Street didn't answer, he simply nodded as if in agreement. Dunne turned back to Charga and continued, "So just what the hell were you doing down there? And how in hell did you get there? Why?". Charga began to respond, "Well . . ." but was again cut off by big Mike Dunnes' continuing harangue, "Shut up!". His voice was elevated, and that was unusual for the normally quiet and soft spoken big man. Charga determined it was best if, right now, he just did keep his mouth shut. Mike Dunne was upset and he had no reluctance at this time in showing it. "Always the lone wolf!" he went on, "Always sticking your nose in! Who asked for that?". He hitched up his belt so as to display his P.D. badge. "See this? You don't have one anymore!

Leave the police business to us. Just go on and keep on checking on the cheaters, and the insurance scams!". Then, with emphasis on the word 'your', continued,

"That's your business now, ain't it?".

"Well, I . . ."

"Just shut up! I'm doing the talking right now!".

Sensing that Dunne was about to commence one of his long winded monologues, Brad Street plopped his lanky body into one of the visitor chairs in the room. He sighed, and folded his arms across his chest. Considering how his partner had praised Charga earlier during their drive down to Little Lebanon, he figured that now Dunne was more upset with Charga for putting himself in danger, rather than for simply butting in on a police case. Charga rolled his eyes, then looked over to Street. He half smiled and Street smiled back and shrugged his shoulders. Street knew Dunne harbored genuine affection for his former partner, and after hearing the stories Dunne had recounted, his own feelings about Duke Charga had softened. It had dawned on him that his preconceived ideas regarding Duke Charga had been totally off base. The negative tales concerning Charga as told by Streets' former partner Paul Carson, were obviously mostly untrue and likely stemmed either from envy of Chargas' arrest and conviction record, or from Carsons' innate prejudice against those of Latino blood. It seemed the more time he spent with Duke Charga, the more he appreciated him, and the more he got to know him, the more he liked him.

"Here's your damn car keys!" Dunne slammed the set of keys onto the bedside night table. The table had a metal top, and the sharp sound of metal on metal caused Charga to wince. "Oww!" he moaned.

"CSU has your cannon." Dunne continued, "and I've got loads of paperwork to make out.". He took a deep breath. "Now," he paused, then went on in a more moderate tone, "you can tell me what the hell was going on, and don't BS me. How in hell did you end up in that store, in that neighborhood, and with Tony Taccio? C'mon, let's hear it!".

Charga began slowly, he was hesitant to divulge how he had gotten Tony Taccios' address, but how could he explain why he happened to be where he was without revealing that pertinent piece of information. He recounted his visit to the track audio visual room, adding, "I seemed to hit it off better than you guys with that southern cracker, so he was just a bit more helpful to me than he was with you.".

"Sounds like more than just a bit." Street interjected, "So you got the plate number, okay, but how'd you get to Taccio before us? How'd you know his whereabouts?".

"That's the number one question." Dunne added, "How?".

"I have sources," Charga answered guardedly, "and that's about all I will say about that.".

"Alright. We'll leave it like that for now, go on.".

Charga related his conversation with Tony Taccio, and what Taccio had said was the reason for the rough up of John Harborstone.

"Actually had something to do with not hiring somebody, that's what he said anyway.".

"Seems a bit far fetched." Dunne chimed in, "And one thou for a beat down seems out of whack." He stroked his moustache.

"That's permanent whack out money," Dunne continued, "not beat 'em up money!".

"Trouble is . . ." Charga said, "Taccio just doesn't know his own strength, and the fact that Harborstone is a queen didn't help him either.".

"So who really benefits from this deal?" Dunne asked. It was more a question to himself. "Got to be more to it.".

Charga propped himself up in the bed. "That's what I'm thinking too.". Then he went on to describe what had happened in the fruit and vegetable store.

"Did you or Taccio say something that got those two really pissed off?". Dunne asked. He massaged the side of his face, thinking.

"Call them some kind of name or something like that?".

"Not really.".

"Doesn't figure they would want to cut your throat out of the blue.". Dunne was digesting Chargas' story but not fully understanding the how and why of it. "Did they say anything that would give us a clue as to why they came at you?".

"Well," Charga answered, "They hollered something about a candy bar. I remember that.".

"A candy bar?".

"Yeah, Mike. I'm sure that's what they said. You know that sesame bar with the chocolate covering.".

"You mean the Joyva Halvah?".

"That's it!".

"What the hell . . ." Dunnes' voice trailed off, "What the . . .?".

"You sure you heard right?" Street asked as he pushed himself up out of his seat. He stepped over to Chargas' bed. "Maybe it just sounded like that. Could've been something else they were saying.".

"Like what else?".

Street rubbed his gaunt tapered chin. "Sounded like Halvah?" He murmured, "Halvah, Halvah . . ." He snapped his fingers. "Got it!" he exclaimed.

Both Charga and Dunne turned toward him and spoke in unison. "Got what?".

"You just think you heard Halvah," Street began, waving a pointing finger in the air as he spoke, "But these were Arabs, likely Muslims . . .".

"And so?" Dunne broke in, "Muslims, so?".

"It's more likely what they said was Alluhah Akbar.".

"And what the hell does that mean?" Charga asked.

Street continued his soliloquy seemingly ignoring the question. "A certain breed of Muslim, the wild ones, the ones who would cut your throat without a second thought, well that kind will holler those words before they come at you.".

"Really?" Charga was impressed. Street was speaking with authoritative conviction and seemed to know what he was talking about. "So again," he reiterated, "what does that mean?".

"It's almost like when the Japanese used to holler banzai! In Arabic it means God is great!".

"And just how do you know that?" Dunne queried, also a bit impressed by his partners' apparent knowledge of Muslim ritual.

"I used to date a girl whose parents were from Jordan. She told me a lot about the Arab culture.".

"I didn't know that.".

"There's a lot you don't know about me, Mike." Street smirked as he spoke, "We've only been partners a short while, remember?".

"The question remains why?" Dunne interjected, "Why cut up somebody seemingly for nothing or at least not much of anything.".

He turned back to Charga. "Unless, like I said, you or Taccio did something that really pissed them off.".

Charga shook his head. "No, Mike. It's just like I told you, they just popped up and came at us.".

"Doesn't figure." Dunne half whispered. He again stroked his moustache, it was a sign he was thinking. "Just doesn't figure." His voice trailed off, he paused momentarily, then spoke aloud. "Well, we'll get to the bottom of it somehow." he went on, using a well known poker players' terminology, "the river card hasn't been dealt yet!".

Charga nodded, then pointed to the small clothing closet next to the hospital room door. "Check in there. See if my clothes are in there.".

Street moved toward the closet, his long legs covered the distance in three generous strides. He opened the closet door. "Yep." He looked at Dunne. "Should I give 'em to him?".

Charga had already removed the oxygen cannula from his nostrils and was sitting up on the side of the bed, undoing the linen hospital robe.

"Might as well." Dunne answered. "We can't keep him here. If he wants to go, well that's his prerogative.".

Street tossed the clothes onto the bed, then stooped over, picked up Chargas' shoes and socks and dropped them at Chargas' feet.

"You'll need these too." he said, "If you're walking out of here.".

Charga anxiously checked for his wallet, after all, he had been carrying quite a roll. "Good." he thought, it was intact in the inside breast pocket of his jacket. His phone and watch were also there, in the side pocket. He took a quick peek into the leather billfold. OK. The cash was all there. He took a deep breath and immediately began dressing, shorts, undershirt, pants, shirt and holster. He rubbed his feet just a bit before he slipped on his socks, then stepped into his shoes and looked up. "That nurse said the doc should be here soon, if he doesn't show in a few minutes I'll just sign myself out.". He stood up, wobbled some, steadied himself, then slid into his blue suit jacket. "I've got a date tonight . . ." he added with a mischievous smile, "and I intend to keep it.".

"Always the ladies man." Dunne growled, "I see that hasn't changed, but you do what you have to do and we'll do what we have to do. Now let's get those names again. You said the one who lived just below Taccio was Ahkmed, right?".

"Right.".

Dunne motioned to his partner. "Brad, write this down."

He turned back to Charga. "Last name?".

"I saw the name Basara on the mailbox downstairs, figure that's it.", then added, "And he works at the track.".

Brad Street had his notepad in hand. He asked for the exact spelling of that name, letter by letter. "B, A, S, E, R, A?".

"No E" Charga answered, "All A's.".

Dunne broke in. "And what was the name you said Taccio called out in that store?".

"I think it was something like Bin Haseed.".

"You think?" Dunnes' tone was all business now. He wondered, had his former partner forgotten his police training regarding positive remembrance, or was it that crack on the head he had sustained back on that concrete floor. He decided to press the subject. "What do you mean you think? You should know! Now, think back. Remember! Get it right!".

Charga sat quietly for a brief moment. "Yeah! That was it." he said, now confidently, "Bin Haseed.".

"Got that Brad?" Dunne asked as he pointed to Brad Streets' notepad. "Haseed." he repeated.

"Very common Arabic name." Street answered as he continued making notes, "Like Smith or Jones here.".

"We'll give the L.A.P.D. this info, meantime we'll follow up at the track regarding the assault on Harborstone, but you know L.A. homicide will want to talk to you about this triple kill. Maybe you should wait for them. After all, it's totally their case now, and you should just keep out of it.".

Charga said nothing in response. He simply nodded.

Mike Dunne knew his former partner well enough to know he wouldn't just leave this case to the police, especially since he was now so deeply immersed in it himself. Dunne went on, "Or am I just wasting my breath here?". It was a rhetorical question. He already knew the answer and Charga validated his thoughts.

"Mike, you know I don't like loose ends, particularly when I'm one of those ends.", he stood up, then started unsteadily toward the door. "Gonna give me a lift?" he asked.

"Yeah, sure. Let's go." Dunne replied. He turned to detective Street. "Come on Brad," he said, "We'll drop him off, then we've got some work to do ourselves.".

"You're just gonna walk right out of here?" Street asked as he pocketed his notepad and grabbed onto Chargas' right arm. "You're still not steady on your feet.".

Charga answered. "I'll be fine.". He spied the pen in Streets'jacket outer breast pocket. "City crime victim funds should cover this, but just in case . . ." he said, as he plucked the pen away. He picked up the hospital chart from the foot of the bed, removed his hospital insurance card from his wallet, and jotted down his carriers' name along with his own membership number at the top of the page. Then signed his name with the additional words 'I'm fine, bill them, thanks' and tossed the chart back on the bed. "The doc will find this soon enough.". He replaced the pen into Streets' jacket and the three men headed toward the hallway.

The hospital hall was uncommonly quiet. No doctors moving through in the usual execution of their normal rounds, no nurses or nurses aides entering or exiting patient rooms, no patients shuffling along in half drugged out states meandering thru the hall. Big Mike Dunne was first to take notice of the unusual quiet. He extended his arm in front of his two companions as if to hold them from lurching forward off the front seat of a vehicle whose driver had suddenly hit the brake. "Hold it guys!" he ordered, "Something's wrong here.". He instinctively turned to scan the hall behind them. Two figures stood at the south end of the hall just in front of the stairway. "Check it out." he said, motioning with a head bob in their direction. "Feds!".

From his previous dealings with other law enforcement agencies he easily recognized the very obvious plain clothes uniforms of federal officers. They wore blue serge suits, white shirts, red ties, and shiny patent leather shoes. The two similarly suited men stood straight backed and grim faced. One was black with a clean shaven head, while the other, a Caucasian, sported close cropped blond hair. Both were just over six foot tall and wore what had come to be known as highway patrol style sunglasses. The blond moved his left arm, positioned his hand in front of his face, and appeared to be talking into his sleeve.

"Just keep walking." Dunne continued. He pointed to the elevators at the opposite end of the hallway. "We'll take the elevators down. Should be no prob.".

Charga turned slightly and looked back toward the two suited men.

"What're they here for?" he mumbled the question, "Something going on here?".

"Beats me." Dunne answered shrugging his shoulders, "But it's got nothing to do with us, I'm sure.".

"First lady." Street interjected, "That's it!".

Before Charga or Dunne could question that statement the elevator doors slid open, and two very tall black men, also attired in what could be called the federal officers' uniform of sorts, stepped out.

They quickly made their way to the nurses' station desk just opposite the elevators, whispered something to one of the three nurses behind the desk, then turned toward Charga, Dunne, and Street.

"Come right here you guys.". The taller of the two spoke in an authoritative manner. His voice was deep and strong, like the lead singer in an Othello opera. "Right down here, please.", he added.

As the threesome approached the nurses' station area, Charga noticed his own Oriental nurse standing to the rear of that area.

"Hello, My Ling.", he made a saluting gesture as he spoke, "And how are you doing?".

My Ling smiled, then turned her gaze to the floor, and a slight blush ran across her face as the other two nurses giggled.

"This floor is supposed to be clear.", the big man with the big voice boomed out, "What are you doing here?".

"We were just leaving." Mike Dunne answered, then showing his badge, added, "We're Arcadia P.D.".

That statement seemed to take the edge off, as both big black men exhaled a deep breath and relaxed their posture.

"And we're federal agents.", came the reply. The two men flipped open wallet sized identification and flashed them cockily in a show of superiority, as if to demonstrate their higher standing in the area of law enforcement.

"What's going on?, Dunne asked.

"First lady." Street whispered, "I told you, first lady.".

"That's correct." the big man answered, "The first lady will be touring this hospital.".

"I told you." Street interjected.

The federal agent continued, seemingly ignoring Streets' comment.

"We're securing the building.". He turned to his partner. "Agent Johnson will escort you down.".

Then he nodded toward the elevators. "Take 'em J J." he said.

Agent Johnson touched the elevator call button and the elevator doors opened almost immediately. "Let's go." he said.

Charga, Dunne and Street followed him into the elevator.

"So long My Ling." Charga said loudly as he waved a slow goodbye wave. "Maybe another time, okay?".

The elevator doors closed and agent Johnson hit the button marked 'lobby'.

"I tried to tell you," Street murmured, "You know how the first lady is in to the health care situation . . .".

"Yeah! Yeah!" Dunne cut in, then added jokingly, "Did you take a smarty pill today? How come you suddenly know so much?".

"I just know, that's all." Street replied. A sly smile changed his normally very serious facial expression to that of a mischievous teenager. "I just know." he repeated.

"So tell me, just how did you know about this deal with the first lady?" Dunne continued in his questioning mode. He spoke in a mocking brusque tone. Street recognized that intonation. It was Big Mike Dunne's penchant toward friendly banter, and so Street answered in kind. "I really didn't know." Street replied. He raised his chin in a move indicative of self congratulation. "Simply put two and two together," he paused, placed his right index finger to his forehead, then continued, "I knew she was in L.A. and I know she's big on this healthcare issue, so when I noticed the hospital hallway clear of activity, and feds on the scene, well it just figured.".

"That's good deductive police work." Charga chimed in, "Maybe you've got a better partner than you know, Mike.".

"And now you're helping Duke here walk, holding him up, so what's with that?" Dunne asked, again in a frivolous insouciant tone.

"Well" Street answered, "In some Oriental cultures when you save someone's life, then you're obligated to take care of that person from that moment on.".

"Oh, so now you're an expert on Oriental customs as well as Muslim cultures, is that it?".

Street nodded. "I told you there were lots of things you don't know about me".

"He's a good man." Charga added, "Be happy about it, Mike.".

"I know." Dunne acknowledged, "Just pulling one of his long legs.".

The elevator stopped with a jerk, and the doors slid open.

"After you." Agent Johnson held the doors open as Dunne, Street, and Charga stepped out. The hospital lobby was awash with federal agents. Two were stationed at the front entrance doors, two more just outside the elevator, four at the lobby desk, and another agent at the door leading to the stairway.

"Sure have enough security for her here." Street exclaimed, taking note of the nine federal officers positioned around them.

Agent Johnson led the threesome thru the lobby toward the front doors. "Okay gents." he said, "You're on your own from here." He then brought his left hand up in front of his face and spoke into the miniature microphone located discreetly inside his jacket sleeve. "Subjects are out. Ten four."

"Check it out." Charga whispered, "A few more outside, too."

Another group of six men, three black, three Caucasian, were assembled just outside the hospital entrance. All were attired in similar blue suits, white shirts, and red tie combinations, and were wearing the same highway patrol type dark glasses. All had very similar crew cut style hair.

"For sure these guys can't go undercover." Charga added jokingly.

Dunne and Street chuckled. "You're right on that, Duke." Dunne agreed.

They gingerly walked the fifty foot path to the unmarked Arcadia RD. vehicle. "Take the wheel, Brad." He opened the rear door. "Get in Duke." he said, "We'll stop at the L.A. lab first, get your Glock, and you can give them your statement while you're there. Then back to your place.

We'll have you home by six the latest."

"Sounds okay." Charga replied, "Thanks for the lift."

Charga almost hopped over the three steps leading to his apartment front door. The throbbing, dull pain in his head due to his earlier slight concussion had subsided somewhat, but the burning sensation from the knife cut in his left arm seemed to be worsening. He glanced at his watch. Five fifty five. Big Mike Dunne had called it just about right, and he had said it wouldn't take much for Charga to retrieve his weapon. Dunne had dealt with the L.A. CSI lab before, and was well aware of their modus operandi regarding weapon retrieval. Charga hadn't really believed him about that, but claiming his Glock was, in fact, really quick and easy, merely a formality of signing a proof of legal ownership, and right to carry form. His oral and written statement to the L.A. homicide detectives also went uncommonly smooth. They seemed almost disinterested in the whole situation. Charga had gotten the idea they weren't really going to investigate any aspect of the incident. One of the L.A. detectives had made an offhand comment, "Those crazies are always cutting each other down there", and Charga had noticed one of the detectives stuffing his written statement into the back space of a file cabinet, just as the other was telling him "Okay. That's it. We've got it. You can go, mister Charga.". It was obvious this case was not going to be one of their priorities.

He heard his phone ringing just as he stepped into his apartment.

"Maybe Sylvia." he thought, "Making sure I remember.".

Quickly closing the door behind him, he tossed his keys and cell phone on the living room coffee table, and picked up his land line receiver just as his answering machine kicked in. "You've reached Charga investigations. Please leave a message after the tone, and I'll call you back as soon as . . ." He cut in. "I'm here. Go ahead.".

The sound of a feedback squeal sent a sharp jolt thru his ear, and reactivated the dull pain across his forehead. "Hold on." he said over the rasping screech, "I'll move away from the answering machine.". He stepped into the kitchen. "Okay. Go ahead now.".

It was a female voice, but not that of Sylvia Cortez.

"Allo, Dukay. It's Adriana.".

"Adriana! What a pleasant surprise! But I was expecting you to write.".

"Oh, Dukay," Adriana purred as she spoke, "You know sometimes I just wanta talk with you.".

"Well, that's great!" Charga blurted out excitedly, "Just the sound of your voice makes me feel good!". Suddenly his headache seemed to ease and his arm just didn't hurt as much as it had a moment earlier.

"I've been thinking of you a lot lately." she continued, her soft slight accent was like music to Charga's ear.

"And me, you." he replied.

Adriana went on to describe in detail her days at the university, how she was now into post graduate study of economics and Italian national politics, and her plans to help change the world. Charga was impressed. She was not only beautiful, but smart as well. This was a lady with big ideas and strong convictions, actually not all of which he agreed, but that inner strength of hers was another facet of her character he found attractive.

"So what have you been doing?" she then asked, "How is your investigation business going?".

Charga described his P.I. business, and how he was making pretty good money at it, then he told her of his latest encounter down in Little Lebanon. She appeared very interested, and Charga laid it on thick, the action, and the potential danger, in a very macho braggadocio fashion. "Oh yeah, baby," he went on, "And I intend to find out what's really going on down at that racetrack.".

She cut him off abruptly. "Oh, Dukay, I will fly in and be with you.".

Charga smiled. It made him feel even better to know Adriana cared so much for him that she would fly twelve hours, across two continents and an ocean, just because she felt he may be in some personal danger. "It's okay." he said, "You don't have to do that, anyhow what about your school?".

"Oh, Dukay, that's no problema. We're on break for two weeks. I will be with you tomorrow.".

"Well, I'd love to see you here, but . . .". Before he could finish what he was about to say, she cut him off again. "I will call you," she said very quickly, "Got to go, bye now.". Click. Dial tone.

"That was odd." Charga mused, but before he could even begin to think about the sudden ending of that call, his cell phone began buzzing and vibrating across the slick coffee table top. He caught it just as it reached the table edge. "Hello?".

"Hello Duke.". It was the unmistakable voice of ADA Sylvia Cortez. "Hi, Sylvia.".

"Say, Dukey, I'll be leaving my office in a few minutes, so I should be at Garlatti's in about twenty minutes. Is that okay?".

"Yeah, sure Sylvia. It's fine if we get there just a bit early."

"Are you sure?" she asked, almost apologetically.

"Absolutely. No prob.".

"Been thinking about it all day." she purred, "It'll be good to be with you again after so long a time.". They hadn't had dinner together in several months.

"And I've got lots to tell you," Charga replied, "I've had a very interesting day.".

"Oh, did you find who you were looking for?".

"Oh! Did I!" Charga almost shouted the words. "But I'll tell you all about it when we meet.".

"Okay, Duke. Should I wait at the door if I get there before you?".

"No, Sylvia. Just go on in and get a table. It's not that big of a place. I'll see you," then he added, "and I'll do the same if I'm there first, okay?".

"Yes, okay Duke. See you then. Bye.".

"Later" he answered. He pocketed the phone, removed five one hundred dollar bills from his wallet, and carefully laid them atop his TV. "Won't need all this cash at Garlattis." he thought. He then hurriedly went to his bathroom sink and doused his face and hair with cold water. It was refreshing. He ran his comb thru his hair just to smooth it out a bit, dried his face, and was once again ready to be off and running. "Almost as good as new." he said to himself.

It was his own tepid attempt to convince himself that his aching head and cut arm no longer hurt, and it didn't fully work. He rubbed his forehead, then looked down at his arm. "Almost. Just almost." he mumbled, and out the door he went.

Mike dunne had said the Dynasty was parked in back, in the resident parking area. Charga scooted around the apartment building, squeezed the de-alarm button on his auto lock key, and heard the horn chirp. He turned in the direction of the sound. His black beauty was all by itself in the guest parking area. He liked the fact that Dunne had parked it away from the other vehicles, and that it was straddling the painted stall lines, and parked in such a way as to be taking two spaces, thus discouraging any other motorist from parking next to it. It was as if Mike Dunne knew how Charga felt about his vehicle.

"But more likely he was just in a hurry." he thought, "That's probably more what happened.". He checked the vehicle. No marks, no scrapes. He patted the roof. "Good girl." he said aloud as he opened the driver side door and slid in behind the wheel. "Okay, let's go!".

The engine turned over and started unhesitatingly with just the touch of the ignition key. "That's my baby!" he thought as he steered the black beauty onto the street.

Sunday late afternoon traffic was ordinarily light, but on this day it was exceptionally so. No traffic to speak of on either the freeway or the side roads all the way down to Anaheim. He was at Garlattis restaurant in fifteen minutes. He parked just thirty feet from the restaurant front, and headed on in. On his way he noticed the new Mercedes, parked right in front of the place, with California vanity plates that read 'SC-ADA'.

"She's here." he said to himself as he gently touched the hood of the Mercedes. "And it's still warm. Must have arrived a few minutes ago.".

The sweet aroma of Garlattis Sicilian cooking once again filled his nostrils and activated his gastric juices. His appetite was always easily aroused by that Sicilian scent, and especially so on this day, as it dawned on him that the only thing passing his palate on this day was that one lonely cup of black coffee in the early A.M. "No wonder my stomach is growling." he thought. He stepped inside. The Garlattis had some good business on this Sunday. Just two tables empty. He spied Sylvia Cortez seated at a table just in front of the kitchen area doors. She looked up, their eyes met, and she smiled and waved.

Angelo Garlatti bounded to the entry door and welcomed him. "Back again? Good! Just set yourself up at one of these tables." he pointed to the two patron-less tables, "I'll be right with you.".

"That's okay, Ange." Charga waved him off, "I'm here to meet that lovely lady back there.". He nodded toward Sylvia Cortez. "Oh!" Angelo Garlatti looked back, "Very nice.". He formed a circle with his thumb and forefinger, "Bella." he whispered admiringly, "Bella!".

Charga sauntered back to Sylvia Cortez. He paused momentarily as he approached the table, then bent forward to plant a kiss on her cheek. "Hi, Sylvia.".

She turned her head suddenly, and promptly kissed him on the lips. It was a hot kiss, a wet kiss. He made no effort to pull away, fully enjoying her generous show of affection. Her right hand found its way to the back of his neck, and she pulled his head more firmly toward her. The kiss went on for ten, then fifteen seconds. It seemed much longer to Duke Charga, but as far as Sylvia Cortez was concerned, it was not as long as it could have been, or should have been. Once again, as was the case in the past, she was showing no compunction about demonstrating her most obvious romantic feeling toward him.

Dinner had been momentarily suspended at the nearby tables, as heads were turned and mouths remained agape, embarrassingly exposing partially chewed spaghetti, meatballs, and veal parmigiana. She released her grip and slowly pulled back, the kiss ending with a squishy sounding pop, much like that of a moistened rubber ended dart being pulled off a glass surface. "Ahh, amore!" came the call from a diner at a nearby table, "Buono fortunato!", followed by a smattering of gentle applause. Chargas' face remained just inches from the still moistened lips of Sylvia. "Thank you for that." he whispered to her, then he turned. "And thank you all as well." he said loudly, smiling broadly, "You can all go back to your dinners now. Thanks.". He slid onto the bench seat opposite her. "You look great!" he said. She smiled. It was obvious she had already taken a few minutes to spruce herself up. Her hair was neatly brushed, hanging loosely, yet perfectly framing her classically lovely Latino face. Eyebrows, lashes, lips, all refreshed with liner, mascara, and lip gloss, and all symmetrically perfect. He had almost forgotten how stunningly handsome a woman Sylvia Cortez really was.

"Why in hells' name did I pass on her?" he wondered. In an instant she reminded him. "So do you really keep in touch with that Adriana girl?" she asked., cocking her head slightly, and emphasizing the active verb.

Detective Street checked the vehicle clock as he turned the ignition key. He looked over at his partner. "It's a little past six, Mike. So where to?".

"I'll cali the BCH stable." was the answer, "I've got the number here somewhere.". He fumbled with his daily activity report papers. "We'll check to see if that Basara character is still there, or if he's gone home. I want to talk to that guy.". He paused, "Right now he's the key. Should have something interesting to add.".

He lifted the police vehicle phone receiver. "H Q? Okay. This is Dunne. Connect me to this number.". He read off the BCH stable phone number. The connection was made. Two rings and the phone was picked up at the other end. "BCH. Zella aqua.".

Dunne cupped the phone. "Got it." he said, "It's that Zella guy.".

Street nodded. Dunne continued, "This is detective Dunne. I spoke with you before, remember?".

"Si. I remember." came the reply, "What can I do for you ahora?".

"I need to know if there are any other BCH stable hands there with you.".

"Ahora? No senor. Solimente me.".

"Everyone gone home?".

"Si. Now just me and a few other race track people here. Nobody from BCH. Mister Colton, he no like paying extra to anybody, so everybody goes home right after the last race.".

"Okay, thanks." Dunne answered quickly. He had what information he needed. "That's all for now. You can go back to whatever you were doing. Maybe we'll talk with you again later in the week, just in case we need to fill in some details, so don't go anywhere.".

"Where am I gonna go?" Juan Zella asked in a confused tone, "I'm the numero uno trainer here now. I don't go anyplace now, solo aqui.".

"Bueno!" Dunne replied, then using just about all the Spanish he had acquired thru the years, added, "Hasta luego!", and set the mobile phone back in its' cradle under the dash.

"Back to Little Lebanon!" he ordered, "Let's find Basara.". Little Lebanon was normally about a half hour drive from Century City. "Step on it, Brad." Dunne added, "Let's move it!".

They were there in fifteen minutes. "Atta boy!" Dunne congratulated his partner as they entered the Muslim section of the big city. "That's what I call driving!".

The golden California sun, which had drenched all Los Angeles with its' brightness and warmth throughout the day, was beginning its' descent down and beyond the stucco sided buildings of the inner city, casting long ominous looking shadows on the concrete canyons of Little Lebanon. It was not yet dark enough for the street lights to click on, thus making the dimly lit, shadowy streets of this neighborhood even more foreboding and intimidating than they had appeared to be in the midday sunlight.

"Looks different around here at night." Dunne remarked. He was carefully scanning the sidewalks and buildings. Street nodded in agreement. Only a few store front windows were lit with small neon lights advertising 'Pepsi' and 'Lotto Sold Here' in English lettering. Most lit store displays were in Arabic. The zither and flute music seemed louder, and more menacing. Street had markedly slowed the vehicle and was now proceeding at just under the local thirty mile per hour speed limit, and was checking the avenues and side roads as they passed, taking notice of the fact that all were almost devoid of vehicular or pedestrian traffic.

"Must be prayer time." he said, then nodded knowingly, "That must be it.".

Dunne questioned. "Prayer time?".

"Yeah." Street answered, "Muslims pray five or six times a day at regular times and regular intervals.".

"Really?".

"Yeah, Mike, they . . .".

Dunne interrupted. "Oh, right! I almost forgot! You're the Muslim expert.". He motioned to their right. "Here's Compton. Turn here.".

Street parked just to the right of the building numbered 632, halfway between that building and the fruit and vegetable store where Charga had had his earlier nearly deadly encounter. That store was closed, locked and doubly secured with bolted iron bars and metal roll down grates to protect the large glass front windows.

Yellow crime scene tape remained criss-crossed over the door.

"Quiet down here now." Street declared in a whisper, "Just that damn strange music".

Dunne nodded, then questioned, "Don't they ever stop it?".

He was not at all knowledgeable about Muslim culture, and Brad Street seemed to know quite a bit on that subject. Dunne expected an answer of some sort, but Street remained momentarily silent.

"Well, do they play it like this all night long?" Dunne asked again.

"Don't really know that." Street replied. He shook his head slowly emphasizing his negative response, "Just don't know." he said.

Dunne smirked. "Oh, so you don't really know everything Muslim, now do you?".

"Never said I did." Street shot back as he pulled open the red painted metal door numbered 632. They stepped inside the small vestibule. Dunne checked the mail boxes. "Here it is.", he said, pointing to the box marked 'BASARA 2R'. "Follow me.".

Big Mike Dunne un-holstered his snub nosed .38 special Smith and Wesson, and began to slowly ascend the stairs inside. The stairway creaked and moaned with his every step. He turned. "Quiet." He whispered.

Street shook his head. "It's not me." he whispered back, "It's you making these steps talk.".

Dunne rested his free hand on the wooden banister for extra support and balance. The railing tilted outward almost three inches.

"Stay off the railing." he ordered. He spoke softly, but authoritatively at the same time., a subtle reminder of his position as lead detective on this team. As they reached the second level hallway, the door marked 2R opened just a crack.

"Achmed?". The voice was that of a woman, a seemingly very apprehensive woman.

"Not Achmed." Dunne answered, "Police!". He already had his size thirteen shoe wedged in the door opening. The sixty watt incandescent overhead hall light gave just enough illumination so that Dunne could make out a pair of frightened eyes peering at him through the four inch opening.

"We're looking for Achmed ourselves.".

"No! He's not here.". The dark eyes widened, "Go away!".

"He's not in any trouble." Dunne went on, "We just want to ask him a few questions.".

"Go away!". Dunne could feel the extra pressure on his foot as the woman behind the door attempted to push the door shut.

"We're not immigration." he added, "Don't worry about that.".

That comment had an effect. The pressure on his foot eased.

"What do you want?".

"Just want to talk." Dunne answered.

"About what?".

"Something happened down at the track today, and maybe Achmed can help sort it out.".

In a clever move designed to dispel undue anxiety, Dunne was discreetly holding his weapon behind his back, and out of this woman's line of sight. "She seems frightened enough" he thought, "without her having to see a cop with a gun at her door.". His non threatening, matter of fact demeanor seemed to be working. Her voice was calmer now. "At the race track? Where he works?".

Her hands and body which had been pressing and leaning on the door totally relaxed, and the pressure on Dunne's foot ceased completely. "Someone was hurt. But, now, don't worry." Dunne replied. He spoke slowly and reassured, "It was someone else who was hurt.".

The woman sighed. "Oh, thank Allah!" she exclaimed.

"So when do you expect him home?".

"He is usually home by now." came the reply, "But sometimes he stops at the Husene market to pick up some fresh food for us.".

"The Husene market?".

"Yes. That is the vegetable store down the block.".

Dunne could sense the woman was very relieved that one, they were not immigration officers, and two, that her Achmed was in no trouble, and three, neither had he been hurt. She went on, now appearing eager to talk, "Sometimes he stops there and talks with the men there.".

Brad Street, who had been all the while standing on the top step of the stairway, now sidled up next to Dunne, and interjected, "Didn't you hear what happened there today?".

"No. I do not know. What?".

"You live just a few feet away, and you don't know what happened?". Street was becoming impatient. This was almost unbelievable to him.

"Slow down Brad." Dunne pressed his palm against Street's chest, "Just slow it down.".

Brad Street stepped back, and Big Mike Dunne continued with his soft spoken questioning.

"Excuse him ma'am," he almost whispered in an apologetic tone, "he's in a hurry to go home to his own wife. But really, how is it that you haven't heard of the incident at that market?".

"Achmed does not allow me to go out alone.".

"Don't you have a radio or a TV?".

"No. We are not permitted.".

"No radio or TV?" Dunne questioned while thinking and almost speaking his thoughts aloud, "In nineteen ninety three?". "No. These things are tools of the Shayateen for the evil infidels to listen and watch.".

Big Mike Dunne turned to his partner. "What's she saying?" he asked.

"She thinks we're all listening to Satan. Shayateen is Muslim for the devil. These people believe that the U.S. is the great Satan! They're just nuts!".

"She sure does look scared." Dunne said. He decided to project an atmosphere of calm. "It's okay, ma'am." he assured, "We won't harm you.". He pocketed his weapon, then raised both hands slightly, palms up, and smiled. "We really don't want to frighten you." he continued, "but we have to be sure Achmed is not here, so we have to step inside." He paused, then added, "That is if you don't mind.".

"Achmed is not here.".

"Well, we still have to check. We won't touch anything and I promise we'll be in and out in just a minute. Please unlock and open the door.".

He removed his foot from the doorway, then added, more forcefully, "You must co-operate." he said, now holding his detective badge up in plain view, "We are the police.". The door slowly closed. Dunne and Street could hear the sliding chain lock being disengaged. The door opened just wide enough for Big Mike Dunne to barely squeeze through the doorway.

"Thank you ma'am." he said and he quickly stepped into the small, meagerly furnished apartment. Detective Street followed him in, but remained at the open doorway. Dunne was slightly taken aback as he took notice of how this woman was dressed, and momentarily hesitated in his tracks as he eye balled her up and down. She was covered head to ankle in a black linen like wrap around cloth, with only her brown eyes exposed and giving clear evidence of her inner fear and distrust of these two strangers in her home. Dunne turned, looked back at his partner, then nodded toward the woman, "Check this outfit." he said almost inaudibly.

"A burka." Street whispered, "It's a Muslim burka.".

Dunne checked the bathroom, the bedroom and the bedroom closet. He knelt down and looked under the bed. "Clear." he said to his partner, "Let's go.".

Dunne turned back to the woman. "Sorry to disturb you." he said. Then he physically spun Street around and just about pushed him into the hallway. "We're outta here!". The door slammed shut behind them.

"Loads of cock roaches under the bed." Dunne said, wiping his hands with his handkerchief, then just tossing it on the steps. Street ignored the show of mock revulsion. "Should we go on up to Taccio's place?" he asked as he hesitated at the stairway, ready to go up or down on Dunnes' direction, "Well? Is it up or down?". "Not up. I don't think so.". Dunne pointed to the street level, "Let's just go down and wait for mister Basara outside.". They exited the building quickly, and walked to their vehicle. Street stopped suddenly. "Hey!" he said gazing up and down the avenue, "Notice that? No more music. They must end it at sundown.".

Dunne smiled slightly as Street unlocked the vehicle doors. "Much better." he answered, "I was getting sick of it anyway.". They both settled in their vehicle and began their stakeout watch. "How long do you figure we'll have to sit here?, Street asked as he stroked the stubble growth on his lean face, "I need a shower and a shave.".

Dunne glanced at his partner. "Aww. You don't look so bad.' he paused, then added, "And you don't smell yet, so you're okay.". They sat quietly for almost forty minutes. Street had almost dozed off when a Los Angeles police black and white drove up and parked just in front of their vehicle. Dunne elbow nudged his partner. "Wake up!".

Street straightened up and shot back, "I'm not sleeping!". He yawned widely and stretched his arms out and up over his head, "Just resting my eyes.". "Yeah, right." Dunne said, "Whatever.".

"So what is it?".

"Check it out." Dunne motioned toward the black and white whose driver had kept the motor running while his uniformed officer sidekick stepped out and headed straight toward the building numbered 632.

"Cops, so?".

"Stay here." Dunne ordered as he exited their own unmarked auto, "I'll find out what's going on.".

He trotted after the officer and was by his side in a matter of moments.

"Officer!" he called out, then showing his badge, "I'm detective Mike Dunne, Arcadia P.D.!".

The uniformed officer hesitated and peered down at Dunnes' badge. "A bit away from home aren't you?" he asked sarcastically, "What are you doing down here, detective?".

"Was here following a lead.".

"What lead? For what?".

"Wanted to talk with this guy, Achmed Basara. He lives here in 632.".

"That's funny.".

"How so?".

"I'm here to notify his next of kin.".

"Next of kin?".

"That's right, his body was found lying by the side of the freeway about a half hour ago.".

"Traffic accident?".

"Nope. Homicide. Had his throat cut.".

Charga commented on the meal. "The food here is always really good!" he said as he removed the cloth napkin from his lap. "Don't you agree?".

Sylvia Cortez nodded in agreement. "Exquisitely so." She answered, "But then, sometimes the company helps make the meal.".

Angelo Garlatti had ambled over to their table and began to hover over it. He smiled broadly, then bowing slightly, he asked, "How was everything?".

"Fine as usual." Charga answered as he dabbed the last vestige of Sicilian meat sauce from the corner of his mouth. "Thanks.".

Sylvia Cortez smiled and once again nodded in agreement. "Excellent." she added, "Simply excellent.".

Angelo Garlatti began removing the dinner plates from the table. "You like spumoni?" he asked.

"No Ange, I don't think so.".

"Okay, I bring the anisette in justa minute.".

"Fine." Charga replied, and he leaned back and took a deep breath.

It had been a fine dinner. He had ordered one of his favorites here at Garlatti's, the Sicilian veal parmigiana. Sylvia had chosen the ziti with sausage in sauce. Both had enjoyed a small salad on the side, heavily drenched in Italian olive oil and wine vinegar dressing. A large bottle of imported Chianti complimented the main entrees. Both their selections had been appetizing in their presentation, and savory and flavorous on the palate. Almost as savory and flavorful as Sylvias' so very sexually appetizing running commentary which she had so purposely pursued throughout the meal. She had waited for him to get settled in his seat, then had slowly unbuttoned her suit jacket under the pretext that it was okay to keep it tightly closed while at the DA's office or in a courtroom, but that it was quite confining and somewhat out of place to do so in any social setting. "Anyway," she had said, "at this point, I feel hot!".

Charga had taken quick notice of her very low cut orange colored Blouse. She had gently touched and rubbed the top of her partially exposed chest. "Much better." she said as she glanced down and lightly tugged on the silken blouse. Her now half exposed chest, and her body language movement appeared to be geared to intentionally displaying her full, firm breasts in a manner that conveyed an invitational message.

"I like that blouse." Charga had commented facetiously, "Can't seem to take my eyes off it.".

Sylvia had chuckled. "Thanks. The orange color just reminded me of juicy Florida fruit.".

"That so?".

"You know I come from Florida.".

"That so?".

"Yes, and the color is so refreshing and tasty looking, don't you think so?".

And so it had begun. Her conversation throughout the meal had been replete with double entendres and not so inconspicuous sexual references. It was plain to see her highly caffeinated estrogen levels were playing havoc with her female hormones, and she was making no effort to control or contain them. She had always been very self assured and confident, never harboring any self imposed compunction about revealing her position on any issue, public, political, or personal and that included her own personal romantic designs toward Duke Charga. Now, since she had been elevated to the level of a strong front running candidate for the office of city district attorney, she seemed even more forthright and forward than ever. At the beginning of this dinner she had shown much interest in Charga's recent romantic connections and liaisons, especially his contact with Adriana, the young Sicilian university student with whom, she was aware, he had been involved, and who she considered her own main competitor in any quest to win Charga's affection, but Charga had insisted on curtailing much talk regarding this one liaison. Charga had momentarily taken control of the conversation, and after initially recounting his extraordinary and rather dangerous exploits of the day, Sylvia had, in return, insisted on no further police or business talk as well.

"So, what do you want to talk about?", he had asked.

She had lightly touched her lower lip with her ring finger, simulating the movement of a flirtatious and playful teenager contemplating a serious answer to a not so serious question. Then, grinning a devilish grin had replied, "You, me, and what we maybe can do together.". She softly kissed the edge of her finger, and added, "You'd like that, wouldn't you?".

Charga had hesitated. "I guess so." were the only words that had come to mind. She had chuckled, and the game was on. She had long since kicked off her shoes, and began purposely stretching her long, shapely legs under the table in order to playfully touch Chargas' ankles and calves, and had followed this move with a question of Chargas' shoe size, adding, "You know what they say about shoe size in relation to masculine size, don't you?".

Duke Charga was well aware of the erotic inference, and found it most difficult to ignore, much less suppress, the warm tingle that had begun surging thru his loins. Her remarks and motions then became even more titillating. At one point during the meal she took her fork and carefully separated the ziti and sausage in her plate, then dramatically lifted the entire four inch sausage and brought it to her mouth, sensually nipping at the tip of the sauce covered meat while sweetly purring about how succulent was the Italian sausage taste. She then capriciously acknowledged Chargas' own heredity. "You're Italian, aren't you?". Not waiting for an answer, she continued, "Will you taste as delicious?".

It had been quite a meal, he thought, quite a meal indeed.

Sylvia Cortez interrupted his thoughts. "I know I suggested dinner and a show," she said, "but how about we skip the show?".

"That's okay with me." Charga answered. He drank down the final drops of his Anisette. "But then what?" he asked.

"I can give you a personal show." Sylvia whispered, leaning toward him. She crossed her arms in front of her body and pressed her bust atop them, causing her well rounded size thirty six C cup breasts to surge invitingly forward. "Follow me home." she murmured, then in an even quieter whisper, added, "And stay the night.".

Charga smiled. An invitation like that was really difficult to refuse. His male instinct was impelling him to jump at the chance, but should he? During this moment of indecision his cell phone began vibrating and buzzing in his pocket. Charga checked the caller ID number on its' display screen and immediately recognized it as that of the Arcadia P.D. dispatch board.

"One minute Sylvia," he said, "I think I should take this.".

"Must you?" Sylvia pleaded, "I had hoped this night would be exclusively ours.". She sighed heavily, and her deep breath caused her breasts to thrust further upwards toward his most receptive eyes.

"Wouldn't you want that too?", she asked, her whispery tone now even more husky and suggestive than ever.

Charga was no fool when it came to the ladies and their intentions. He had early on taken notice of her inviting tone of voice, and her apparent male hungry gaze. Throughout the meal she had purposely presented herself as a Puerto Rican passion flower yearning to be plucked. Her colorful, eye catching, low cut blouse had added to the incitement, and her erotically charged verbiage with obvious sexually based double entendres, along with her sensual body language and provocative movement, had been telegraphing a message of open desire. Charga could not wipe that stupid smile from his face. "But this could be important." He answered.

"Aren't I important?" she purred, and again playfully touched her lips with the tip end of an index finger.

"Just hold that thought." Charga replied as he tapped the receive call button on his phone. "Charga here."

"Duke?". It was Mike Dunne on the other end. He was calling from his vehicle phone. He had had his police unit mobile call forwarded thru main dispatch. Charga recognized the voice.

"I'm here, Mike, go ahead.".

"Okay, Duke," Dunne went on, "Something happened that I thought you'd want to know.".

"What?".

"That guy, Basara. Someone did a Taccio job on him.".

"A beat down?".

"Nope, worse than that.".

"Dead?".

"Yep. Throat cut and dumped. I'm figuring he was on his way home when he was whacked.".

"Well, now, that sure is something. Taccio had said Basara was the one who first approached him and set up the meeting with Bin Haseed about the Harborstone beat up.".

"Yeah. Maybe somebody figured he might spill whatever he knew.".

"I don't think he actually knew much, Mike. I'm thinking he was just a go between, a patsy of sorts, but anyway, what about the missus?".

"She was okay last I saw. Brad and me were just up there a few minutes ago.".

"Oh yeah?".

"Right. Brad and me were waiting for him in front of his apartment And a street cop drove up and he told us the news. He was on his way up to notify the spouse about it.".

"So, now what's next, Mike?".

"I don't know yet. Brad and me will get back to Arcadia and try to sort things out, but you should just keep out of it now for sure. This Harborstone deal may be more than a simple assault case, so don't press it on your own. As far as you're concerned this case should be closed.".

"Well, that's your opinion, Mike.".

"No! That's my advice, Duke! You'd be wise to take it.".

"Sure, sure." Charga answered sardonically, "Well, thanks for the info anyway.".

"I really think you should butt out of this.".

"I'll take your suggestion under advisement, thanks.".

"Okay, just figured you'd want to know.".

"Thanks, Mike. Talk to you later.". He tapped the end conversation button and turned to Sylvia Cortez.

"Okay." he said, "Let's go. I'll follow you.".

Chapter Three

A Federal Case!

MONDAY . . . 7 A.M.

Sylvia had awakened early, showered, dressed, and prepared a nice bacon, eggs, and coffee breakfast. She had called Charga, who by then was just awakening, told him breakfast was on the table, and that she had to leave right away since she had an early morning appointment to see the local Independent Party group before going on to court. The meeting concerned her possible candidacy for D.A. She was gone before Charga had even rolled over in bed.

Though only half awake, Charga had definitely noticed a profound change in Sylvia Cortez' after hours night time attitude, and her much more serious morning, business personna. Almost all through the night she had been like a nubile estrogen charged teenager, anxious and willing to happily experience any and every intimate sexual position and act. She was a changed woman in the morning, all business, career minded, curt, cool, and composed He almost felt like he had been had, physically used and sexually abused. "But," he rationalized, "sometimes it's actually a pleasure to be abused!".

He threw back the bed covers, stepped up and strolled into the adjoining bathroom. It was bigger and more ornate than he had expected. An extra wide countertop, two sinks, one wall almost totally mirrored, with both a standard commode and a sitz bath seat as well. The over size shower featured imported Italian marble Walls with gold plated shower head and hot and cold water controls. "This is a helluva bathroom!" he thought as he adjusted the water temperature in the shower, "ADA's must be making more than I figured.".

After a quick shower he toweled off, dressed, then found his way to the dining nook off the main kitchen where Sylvia had set his breakfast. He sat at ther little table nearest the side window overlooking the rear garden. "Must be a pretty view when there's not too much fog." he said to himself as he wolfed down the lukewarm bacon and eggs. He took a quick sip of coffee. It was cold. Then he exited out the side door and hopped out and into his vehicle. He looked up. It had been forecast to be an unusually cool and dreary day and the heavy morning fog was lending significant credence to that ill received prediction of the sudden change of weather. Charga steered his Dynasty out of the driveway of Sylvia Cortezs' five hundred thousand dollar mini mansion, and onto the dampened streets of the Los Angeles hills, then onto the freeway. Looking back over the last twelve hours brought on a subconscious smile. The evening had been an interesting and very enjoyable interlude away from the intensity of the previous day. The cut on his arm was healing nicely, his head had ceased its' throbbing, and his entire body felt rejuvenated, a very positive aftermath of the preceding nights most pleasureful activities. While those recent memories were picture perfect and clear in his mind, he became aware that the view thru his Dynastys' windshield was not. It was fogging up. He activated his vehicle windshield wipers, set the heater on medium, and the window defogger at maximum power, and kept these three units operating all the way to Century City, down Irving street, and into his apartment complex parking area. He parked neatly in his designated space, exited the vehicle and scurried quickly across the lot and up to his front door. He was moving a bit faster than normal this morning in order to minimize the bone chilling effect of the unusually cool fog which, this day, hung over all southern California like a wet towel left outdoors overnight. "Damned chilly!" he thought as he slipped his house key in the lock, "Sure will be nice to get some real rest in my own bed!".

He swung open the door and was immediately greeted by the sweet aroma of freshly brewed coffee. "What's this?" he questioned mentally. He was certain he had not set his Mister Coffee machine timer to start a new brew cycle, and anyhow, he remembered, Big Mike Dunne had completely unplugged the machine from the electrical outlet. His right hand moved instinctively toward his strapped on Glock. He stepped inside, slowly, cautiously, while at the same time quickly visually scanning his apartment living room.

No one. No movement, then . . . "Welcome home mister Charga." A smooth New England accented voice boomed out from the kitchen. "You made good time.".

Charga turned. In the kitchen was a rather tall, over six foot, physically fit gentleman sporting a gray pin striped suit, white shirt, collar unbuttoned, and with a red and blue striped tie, dotted with a group of little white stars, hanging loosely around his neck, so very nonchalantly pouring the freshly made coffee into a cup. He was about forty, clean shaven, square jawed, with short, almost crew cut style blond hair, and deep set ice blue eyes. Charga readily took notice of the large biceps, pectoral muscles, and broad shoulders, all straining to burst thru this strangers'jacket.

"And who the hell are you?" Charga blurted out, his hand remained firmly clutching his weapon.

The man smiled, then gently placed the cup on the countertop, and flashed a wallet size identification card. "Special agent Michael Mitello, N. S. A."

"National Security Agency?".

"Right!". He slipped his I.D. into his suit breast pocket, and lifted the coffee cup to his lips. He took a sip. "How come you got no cream?" he asked.

"Never mid that!" Charga replied with a tone of annoyance, "How come you're here, and how did you get in, in the first place?".

"Door was open," Mitello chuckled just a bit as he answered, "I just walked right in.".

"I don't think so, the door was locked. I know it, I locked it myself.".

"Well now," Mitello paused, took a sip of coffee, then went on. He spoke slowly, succinctly, "I say it was unlocked and as you can see there are no signs of forced entry.".

"You picked it!".

Mitello smiled, his oversized teeth almost as intimidating as his tone, "I'm NSA. Get it?".

"Yeah, I get it." Charga acquiesced, "But why are you here?". Agent Mitello did not answer. He merely unbuttoned his suit jacket, straightened his back, then sauntered into the living room, eased himself down onto the sofa and leaned back.

"Comfortable." he murmured, "Very comfortable.".

The swishing sound of the bathroom commode spilled thru the apartment as the bathroom door opened and an older, gray haired gentleman strolled out and joined Mitello and Charga in the living room. "Hello." he said with a smile as he hooked a wire framed pair of eyeglasses onto his ears and positioned it at the edge of his nose. His hair was unkempt, his face half hidden beneath a graying full beard and moustache. He was fidgety and appeared somewhat ill at ease. "I'm doctor Fredricks.". He offered his hand. Charga accepted it. It was a limp handshake. "I'm with the N. E. S. S. T.".

"And what the hell is that?" Charga shot back, "Never heard of it!"

"Well, er, er . . ." Fredricks stumbled over his words, "that's er . . .".

Agent Mitello cut in and answered for him. "That's the Nuclear Energy Subversive Support Team. They're working with us.". "Working on what? What the hell do you guys want with me, and by the way, what was that crack about me making good time?".

"Well, L. A. Hills to here in less than thirty minutes, that's what I call good time.".

"What?".

"We've been on you since you left the hospital.".

"Following me?".

"Yep. Sorry.". Mitello crossed his legs and his right pants trouser pulled up revealing a strapped on ankle holster carrying a five round .22 caliber pistol. Charga noticed and pointed to it.

"Your underwear is showing" he quipped with a smirk.

Agent Mitello ignored the comment. He looked up toward doctor Fredricks. "The coffee is made," he said, "Cups are in the cabinet above the coffee maker.", then added, "Try not to break anything.".

Charga motioned toward Fredricks. "Nervous type?".

"Yeah. He takes a light soporific to keep himself calm and . . ."

Charga interrupted. "Not interested. The question remains why are the two of you here?".

Again agent Mitello seemed to totally ignore Chargas' comments, he simply continued, "unlike you who likely lives on yarsagumba . . ."

Charga, now clearly agitated, interrupted once again, "Now what the hell are you talking about?".

"Yarsagumba. It's like yohimbe, only more potent. Comes from Nepal . . ." he paused, took one final sip of coffee and held out the now empty cup. "Here's your cup, mister Charga, thanks. I just needed a cup of Java.". He smiled, widely this time, baring his full set of symmetrical evenly edged dentition. When Mitello exposed his big teeth in this way he reminded Charga of a whinnying race horse. Now Charga smiled as well, "What a horse face!" he thought, and he restrained himself from laughing out loud.

Mitello noticed Chargas' attempt to stifle laughter, which had not been completely successful. "Something funny here, mister Charga?" he asked.

Charga didn't answer, altho still smiling he simply shook his head.

Their verbal tete a tete was interrupted by a loud shuffling sound eminating from the adjoining room. "Guess I'll just sit here, okay?", Fredricks asked as he stepped out from the kitchen and stood next to the dining area table.

Mitello looked back at him. "Sure, just sit there." he answered, then addressing Charga in a whisper added, "He's out of his element. Put him in a lab and he's a genius.". He held the empty cup up higher. "What do you want to do with this?".

Charga took the cup and set it down on the coffee table. "Leave it here!" Charga said curtly, "Now just go on. What does Nepal have to do with you being here?".

Agent Mitello adjusted his tie, tightening it just a bit. He looked up. "How do you like my tie?".

"It's great! Now get to the point!".

"Well, I was stationed in Nepal a few years back." Mitello began, "Didn't like it much tho. Only good thing there is the yarsagumba. Helps you keep it up, know what I mean?". He didn't wait for an answer, but continued rambling on, "Well, you should know, I guess. You spent the whole night with that woman, didn't you?".

"What's that got to do with anything?".

Agent Mitello raised his arms, palms up, toward Charga in a motion of mock surrender. "Hey! Take it easy! I'm not saying it was a bad thing. Actually, no! Good for you.". He paused momentarily, removed a miniature cigar from his suit breast pocket then asked, "Mind if I smoke?".

Charga nodded. "Yeah." he said, "I do mind. Put it away.".

"Okay." The big white teeth flashed again, "Wouldn't want to upset you.". It was a facetiously sarcastic remark. Charga was obviously already perturbed and annoyed by Mitellos' condescending arrogance. Charga folded his arms across his chest and cocked his head to one side. "Get on with it!" he demanded.

"Just tell him!", Fredricks called out from the adjoining room, "just tell the young fella why, why we're here and then let's, let's get going. Let's, let's get this invest, investigation on the road!".

Charga and agent Mitello turned their gaze toward the gray bearded gent who was at the dining table nervously fingering the hot coffee cup. Just for an instant Charga thought he caught the vintage aged gentleman winking at him from beneath that set of bushy gray eyebrows. He quickly realized that the winking was nothing more than a nervous tick. He watched closely as this venerable old gent, who had introduced himself as 'doctor', brought the cup to his lips with both hands trembling like those of an unfortunate advanced stage Parkinson patient. Charga stroked his own unshaven chin, as he wondered what possible assistance could this old man offer in any criminal investigation involving the NSA? Doctor Fredricks appeared rather frail, a bit disorientated and thoroughly discombobulated, plus that hesitant start and stop stuttering speech pattern was terribly disconcerting. But then again, Charga also knew from past experience that appearances and first impressions were often deceiving and unreliable. He decided to reserve judgement regarding doctor Fredricks. Agent Mitello had surreptitiously taken notice of Chargas' apparent befuddlement concerning his investigative partner. "Can you believe it?" he asked, almost jokingly, "He's a whiz at disarming bombs.". He nodded toward Fredricks and added, "When he's disengaging a detonator he doesn't shake at all.".

"So, he's with the bomb squad?".

"It's a bit more than that. N E S S T deals with more powerful explosives. He can also diffuse miniature nuclear devices.".

"By that, you mean like suitcase atomic bombs?".

"That's right, mister Charga. That's absolutely right.".

"But he seems ready for retirement.".

"He's not as old as you may think. It's his work that aged him. Turned prematurely gray.". Mitello paused, took a deep breath "He's still one of the best in the business.".

"If you say so . . .".

"I do say so!" Mitello continued, "You wouldn't know this but, his assignment as support person with the NSA is because of a presidential order issued by the last president. He's a carryover from that order. You may not know this either, but before our last president became vice president and then president, well he was head of the CIA, and before that, right after world war two, he worked with the CIC, that's the Counter Intelligence Corps, and before that he was our own American James Bond. Yeah, he sure was a commander in chief, unlike our current top guy right now.".

Charga interrupted Mitellos soliloquy, "All very interesting, but what's it got to do with your being here?".

Agent Mitello reached into his suits inside breast pocket, removed a small note pad and riffled thru the first few pages. "Says here you were involved in an incident yesterday down in Little Lebanon.".

"That's right. I got sliced in the arm and knocked out.".

Mitello cut him off. "We know all that.". He looked up sternly, the omnipresent big smile had vanished. "Turns out one of the goons who ended up on a slab . . ." he paused, then pointing directly at Chargas' face and accentuating each word with short jabbing motions, continued, more slowly, more deliberately, his voice lowering an octave or two, "actually it was the one you shot in the balls, well, turns out he was what we call a person of interest, stemming from that World trade center bombing in New York city a few weeks ago.".

"Oh, yeah, I remember that.".

"Everybody does! Well, this guy kinda dropped off our radar back there. Funny how he resurfaced here on the west coast." he paused again, then sighed a sigh of disappointment. "His turning up dead doesn't do us any good though . . ."

"Better him than me!" Charga interjected, "Much better!".

"Figures you would think that.". The wide fake smile reappeared, "But still, NSA would rather he be able to talk some.".

"Maybe you should be out looking for the number one itchy bob of that group.".

"By that I assume you mean Ach Bin Haseed, right?".

"Yeah! That's him alright! He was definitely the top dog.".

"Well, we've had our eye on him too. We've been watching him, but now . . ."

Charga interrupted. "Watching him? For what?".

Agent Mitello shook his head slowly as if to indicate some frustration, then almost in a whisper said, "You don't get it do you?".

"No! Maybe I'm not getting it.". Now it was Charga who was expressing frustration. He paused and took in a deep breath. "But, "I'll tell you both what I am getting. I'm getting tired of having uninvited guests coming at me asking questions. Yesterday it was the local police, today it's you two feds. What should I expect tomorrow? A visit from Interpol?".

He paused once again, removed his suit jacket, stepped into the dining area and draped it across the back of one of the chairs. His oversize Glock 360, holstered just below his left armpit, was fully exposed. Agent Mitello noticed. "Now it's your underwear that's showing." he said mockingly, and a contemptuous smirk curled his mouth. Charga ignored the comment, stepped back into the living room and once again stood directly in front of his munificently toothed guest. "Okay, now. What's the story?" he asked, his hands placed defiantly on his hips. "What exactly is going on?".

"That's classified," Mitello answered, "and I'm not apologizing, but we've all got a job to do, and talking to you is part of it. After all, you are involved.".

"Involved? Involved in what?".

"Again, classified." Mitello replied. He rose from the sofa and deliberately removed his own jacket in order to purposely display his personal, government issued, matte finished, sixteen round newer model Glock semi-automatic firearm. The ivory, finger grooved, hand grip was a bit off center in its' holster. Mitello hitched it up a notch, smiled and shot out a wisecrack question.

"How do you like my baby?", he asked sarcastically, as he gently patted the weapon. "More compact than your oversize shooter, and much more accurate, if I do say so myself.". He paused, then stepped past Charga, roughly brushing against him as he did. "Excuse me.", he whispered in a tone dripping with condescension, "Thanks.". The phony smile was gone, and the former talkative personna had morphed into an all business, pensive personality with attitude. He draped his jacket over his shoulder and sauntered across the room with the cocky smugness of a Spanish matador strutting into a bullring. He stopped in front of the TV, facing the window, and momentarily just stared out into the morning fog.

Then peered back over his shoulkder, again closely resembling a bullfighter eyeing a hapless and ignorant bull. "Yeah." He murmured, "I guess you really don't get it at all.".

"Now just wait a minute!" Charga cut in, "I'm not stupid.". He nodded toward doctor Fredricks, "With you and Fredricks here, I'm getting a pretty good idea of just what it is.".

"Oh, go ahead and tell him." Fredricks chimed in, "I think he's figured it out by now anyway.".

"It's classified info, doc!" Mitello shot back, raising his voice in response, "It's on a need to know basis.".

Fredricks slammed down his coffee cup, almost hard enough to crack it. "Don't stand on protocol man!" he shouted, "This man may be able to help us in some way.".

Charga took note, the stuttering had suddenly disappeared.

"He's right. Maybe I could help, so I need to know exactly what's going on.".

Fredricks stood and walked toward Charga. He placed his hands on Chargas' shoulders. "You are a patriotic American, aren't you?".

"I would say so." Charga replied.

"Okay." Fredricks turned to his partner, "Go ahead, Michael," he said very authoritatively, "tell him.".

"I don't know if I should.".

Fredricks straightened his back. "I'm the senior in charge here." He exclaimed, "And I say just do it.".

Agent Mitello nodded. Charga was surprised, to say the least, by Fredricks sudden transmutation from a person who just moments earlier had appeared to be a fumbling, bumbling, over the hill agent, into what could only be described now as a man with character and strength, exuding a sense of self assuredness. The stuttering, shaking, and apparent absence of personal resolution had evaporated, and in its' place was an air of confidence and authority. Even the nervous blinking tic was gone.

Fredricks noticed the look of bewilderment that had crept across Chargas' face. "It's a wonder what modern drugs can do, isn't it boy?", Fredricks smiled. "I took my pills with your coffee." he said as he gently stroked his gray beard. "They work really fast when taken with a warm drink. Thanks.". He turned to agent Mitello.

"Go ahead!" he ordered again, "Tell him what's going on.".

Agent Mitello responded reluctantly, "I really shouldn't be telling you this, but yes actually, he is the boss.".

"I'm interested to hear it, so just go ahead.".

"Well, we had an idea Haseed might be linked to a group of Islamic Jihadists based here in the L. A. area, and that he may have knowledge of the whereabouts of a small amount of nuclear explosives we suspect may have been smuggled across our Mexican border.", he paused and shook his head slowly in the conventional movement indicative of disapproval, "But now, because of your interference . . ." he continued slowly, "well, now he's likely gone underground deeper than a mole after a rainstorm."

"Are you talking about a bomb?".

"Right, mister Charga, a bomb.".

"Here in California?".

"No!" Mitello answered facetiously, "Over in South Africa! Of course here in California! More specifically here in L. A.!".,

Charga motioned toward Fredricks. "So that's where he fits in right?".

"Right again, mister Charga." Agent Mitello replied.

Doctor Fredricks chimed in. "And as soon as we locate it, I will defuse it!".

"Got any idea of the possible target?" Charga queried.

Agent Mitello looked to Fredricks for permission to go on.

Fredricks nodded, and Mitello then continued. "We've tripled security around the San Onofre power plant, and doubled it at the airport. Also we have extra agents at the Galleria Mall and in the downtown Los Angeles business district."

Fredricks joined in. "Don't worry. We're doing what has to be done.". His tone seemed to combine confidence with a certain sense of urgency.

"Well, that's something." Charga interjected in agreement, "but . . .".

His mind was working overtime, and his investigative instincts had already kicked in . . . bigtime! He was about to offer up his own theory as to another very possible target location. Since it had been Haseed who had actually been the one behind hiring Tony Taccio to take Harborstone out of commission, and since Harborstone was a top trainer at the Arcadia track, "Well" he thought, "Two and two makes four every time!".

Agent Mitello stepped directly in front of Charga. "We figured maybe you heard something while you and your buddy Taccio were grappling with that bunch in that fruit store. That's why we're here.".

"First of all, Taccio was not my buddy, and second, I turned in a report on the whole incident.".

"And we did read it, but it was just a little too superficial. What was the real reason you and mister Taccio were together?".

"Well," Charga answered with some annoyance obvious in his tone, "I was working on a case where Taccio was involved. It was a smack down for hire and he was the bruiser.".

"Yeah! Yeah! We know all that. What else can you tell us now?".

"Well, it seems mister Haseed wanted Taccio to bang up this thoroughbred horse trainer.".

"And why was that?".

"Not entirely sure." Charga replied, "Taccio mentioned something about his mark not hiring somebody down at the track.".

Agent Mitello removed a small pocketsize tape recorder from his jacket side pocket. "Speak into this, okay?", he asked as he clicked the handheld recorder on. "Now what was that again?".

Charga repeated his previous words.

"Not hiring who?", Mitello then asked, speaking somewhat louder, ensuring his voice be clearly picked up by the mini recorder.

"Don't know. And I don't think big Tony knew either.".

"On a first name basis?", Mitello shot back, "Thought you didn't know mister Taccio.".

"I didn't. At least not until yesterday." Charga paused, looked over to doctor Fredricks, then added, "But I did kinda like the big lug!".

"Happens like that sometimes." Fredricks whispered, "Happened to me a few years ago too. Met this turncoat Israeli Hagganah agent. Liked him quite a bit, but," He shrugged, and sighed, "I still had to take him out!".

Chargas' eyes widened. He was once again taken aback and impressed by doctor Fredricks now self assured, assertive, and cold hearted personna. "No wonder he's in charge here." he thought. He decided to direct his words to him from now on. "Ever consider the race track as a possible location for a terror attack?".

Fredricks answered in a matter of fact tone. "Could be, but I know attendance has been off lately, and the crowd is spread out quite a bit on the grounds, in the infield area, the grandstands, the box seats and all around, right?".

"But," Charga continued, "You're talking a mini nuke. Wouldn't that take it all out?".

Fredricks nodded affirmatively. "Sure would, along with surrounding buildings, but it's likely not a prime target. The limited blast wouldn't cause that much damage if the track was the blast center point. Too much open space.".

"You said limited blast, what do you call limited?".

Fredricks shrugged again. "Maybe just twenty square city blocks!".

Charga stepped back, and gulped, a hard gulp. "Just?" he asked.

That's right my boy, and that's why we need all the help we can get!".

Chapter Four

Sylvia, The Candidate

Sylvia Cortez steered her black Mercedes off Los Angeles boulevard, and into the underground parking garage of the downtown Los Angeles Tyler Moss office building. She quickly spied a vacant parking space just twenty feet from the elevator, and immediately pulled in there. She checked her watch. It was 7:45 A.M. Commuter traffic had been unusually sparse this Monday morning, and so she had arrived a half hour early. Her appointment with the Independent Conservative Party representatives had been scheduled to begin at 8:15. She checked her hair and makeup in the visor lighted mirror, concluded all was okay, then nodded to herself, picked up her briefcase from the passenger seat, took a deep breath, and smiled to herself. Miss Cortez was feeling doubly exhilarated this A.M. contemplating what could very well take place at this meeting, and thinking back to what had already taken place the previous evening. Both the anticipatory thoughts, and the passion filled remembrance were pleasant indicators of who the 'real' Sylvia Cortez really was. She had come to the conclusion that she had indeed become an irresistible force, both personally and politically. Sylvia Cortez was now confident that she could get whatever she might want. It was almost certain the Independent Conservatives would endorse her candidacy for D.A. That, along with the publics' dissatisfaction with the incumbent, and with her nomination by the second largest political party in the city, the Republicans, an almost foregone conclusion, she was, barring some unforeseen, unfortunate occurrence, a definite shoe in to win it all. The Independent Conservatives controlled the swing vote in the county, their endorsement would definitely seal the deal. She had thirty minutes time to kill, and so decided to stop at the lobby coffee nook before heading on up to conference room 701. Sylvia knew this building well. It was here where she had interned in the law offices of Tyler Moss Inc. while attending her final year of law school. That internship had been a great training ground for her. At first she had been nothing more than a go-fer for the corporate staff, traipsing up and down between the coffee shop in the lobby and the offices on the second floor. Eventually the incremental rise in importance of her duties there included letter opening, filing, and typist duties before having been brought in to study and evaluate legal motions, and defense strategies. And that was where she had excelled. By working with corporate and criminal case lawyers mainly involved in the defense of so called white collar criminals, or as they had put it, presenting valid defense arguments on behalf of individuals alleged to have perpetrated acts inconsistent with established rules, practices, or guidelines, universally accepted in normal business transactions, she had gained an abundant knowledge of legal defense tactics. Sylvia had employed that knowledge, first as a defense attorney, and now as an assistant district attorney where she had the ability to anticipate and blunt most possible legal defense maneuvers. Upon her graduation from law school she had gone on to become a surrogate court clerk, and subsequently, after passing the state bar exam in her initial attempt, was hired on as a lower court public defender. Almost immediately she had applied for a spot on the L.A. county legal team, and following that six month stint as a defendant advocate, which to her had seemed an interminable stretch of time, she was at last given the opportunity to work the other side of the courtroom as a prosecutor for the district attorney office. Her first assigned cases as an A.D.A. were minor felony proceedings. Eventually she was assigned as second chair on major case trials, and finally, as lead prosecuting attorney, her present position, where she excelled and earned a stellar reputation as a clever prosecutor with an unblemished 100% conviction rate.

The elevator doors slid open and Sylvia Cortez stepped out gingerly and headed to the coffee bar.

"Good morning, miss Cortez.". Sam, the ten year veteran building security guard remembered her. "Haven't seen you in a while.", he said, a wide smile spread across his face. His white teeth seemed brighter than she remembered. Maybe that was because she had never previously noticed that he was an African American. She had always thought of him as a genuinely nice person, and that was all, but now, since working as a prosecuting A.D.A., and since the majority of defendants she had prosecuted were black, well, now she took notice. She stammered just a bit in her answer.

"Well, er, hello Sam.". She smiled back at him. "It really has been a while hasn't it?".

Sam nodded and tipped his cap. Sylvia did not stop, or even slow down her pace, merely nodded in return and hurried on by.

Sam Smiled again.

A well dressed forty-ish man sidled up to him. Sam didn't really know this guy, although he had seen him around in the building recently, coming and going. "Nice looking lady, eh?".

Sam nodded affirmatively. "Sure is,", he said, and they both watched intently as she quickly walked to the coffee stand, her high heeled shoes aiding in the smooth sashaying of her hips and derriere. Anyone could tell that beneath that straight laced gray business suit was a body nearly perfect in proportion.

"So tell me, how do you know her, Sam?".

Sam shrugged. "Used to work here.", he replied, Worked for the big shots on two.".

"For Tyler Moss?".

"Yep. That was a few years back. Wasn't a full fledged lawyer back then. Names Sylvia Cortez.".

"I'd love to have a date with her!".

Sam shook his head. "Don't even think about it." he said, "I don't think she's interested in dating.".

"She's a lesbo?".

"Naw! Not that.". Sam had seen all types of people pass thru, in and out of his lobby, and he had learned to determine character simply thru daily observance, casual conversation, and body language. Over the years he had seldom been mistaken in his evaluation and final conclusion as to who and what these people really were. "Not that at all," he went on, "But ain't no way she'll give up her one love.".

"So then she does have someone, or doesn't she?". "Not someone.", Sam lowered his voice to almost a whisper, "I get the feeling she's in love with her career, will do anything to further it. Very ambitious.", he paused, "I think maybe she wants to be California's first female governor.".

"Really?".

"Yep. That's how I got her pegged. She's an assistant D. A. now, there was a rumor she had the hots for some rogue cop, but nothing came of that. Likely nothing will. Story now is she's up for D.A.". "Wow! You don't say, no kidding?".

"No kidding!", Sam replied, "No kidding at all.".

"A knockout and smart too, what a combo!".

"That's for sure." Sam agreed.

Sam's new acquaintance pursed his lips. "Teh Teh!" he said, "One thing is definitely for sure.".

"What's that?" Sam questioned.

"That seems such a damn waste of beauty!". He turned and strolled to the lobby elevator, pressed the call button, and almost immediately, the doors slid open. He grinned as he stepped into the elevator and pressed number seven. Sam had visually followed this guys' movements into the elevator, and was looking up, checking the lighted elevator floor number indicator. He had already begun forming an opinion on this guy. Their short conversation was innocuous enough, still Sam suspected this person's interest in Sylvia Cortez was energized by more than a simple testosterone charged arousal. The lighted numbers stopped at seven. Sam mentally checked off the corporations located on that floor. "Myers Stock Fund, Gold and Silver Inc., Conservative Party head Office . . .". He smiled to himself. "That's it! He's a politician!". Meanwhile Sylvia Cortez had picked up her coffee along with the morning newspaper, and had found an unoccupied lobby lounge chair. She settled in comfortably and checked her watch again.

Twenty minutes to kill. She opened the paper to the local news page, totally skipping past the headline story which read 'President To Visit Area'.

The Independent Conservative headquarters occupied one third of the 7th floor offices, suites 700 thru 703. In suite 700 were the executive offices; President, Vice President, Secretary, Treasurer, and their legal counsels and advisors. These were the policy makers of the Independent Conservatives who decided upon the nominees, public statements, and campaign strategies of the party. 701 was the main meeting and conference room, with restrooms in the rear. The local party chair people, community organizers, and area team captains in charge of campaign work assignments were situated in 702. 703 housed the phone bank and volunteer workers whose duties included sign and poster distribution to the parties county wide storefront annexes, and the sorting and forwarding of the party direct mail campaign notices to the various postal zip code areas in which the party had candidates on the ballots.

701 was a room almost devoid of furniture save for a large mahogany table, and twelve chairs evenly placed around it, five on each side and one each at the ends. There were several stacks of five additional chairs along the north and south walls. Some pictures of past party officers and successful party candidates added some color to the brown panel wood walls. Already around the table were three well dressed men, with party President Mark Bremer, his wire framed eyeglasses, as usual, hanging low on his bulbous nose, and his oversize frame just barely squeezing into the captain style chair, seated at the head of the ten foot conference table. To his right was Joseph Peters, the thin faced party Vice President, whose emancipated looking body gave the impression that he was a person badly in need of a hearty steak dinner. At the first chair to Bremer's left sat the Conservatives legal counselor Rudolf Cort, looking prim and proper in a gray pin striped Brooks Brothers suit. Bremer glanced down at his pocket watch. "He's late again!" he grumbled, and shifted slightly in his seat.

The double doors to 701 suddenly swung open and party secretary John Folsom enthusiastically bounded into the room, smiling widely. "Good morning gents!". He waved, then made a saluting gesture.

All three answered Folsom's greeting in unison. "Good morning, John.".

John Folsom pulled out a chair and sat next to Cort. He continued wearing a wide grin.

The big man at the head of the table cleared his throat with a stifled gargle, then began, "What's the reason for the big smile, may I ask?".

Folsom leaned forward and gestured with his hands in a double thumbs up move. "We've got the right person this time!" he said gleefully, "I told you that Cortez woman was perfect, and she is!".

Vice President Peters squirmed a bit in his seat. "And why do you think so?" he asked. There was definitely a caustic tone to his words. Peters was the only one of the party hierarchy who had been opposed to endorsing a woman for the position of county District Attorney. He had preferred endorsing the current county sheriff for that position, maintaining that a female candidate might alienate a portion of the male vote.

Folsom answered with an air of confidence. "I got a real good look at her downstairs in the lobby," he said, "and your fears of losing a part of the male vote are totally unfounded.".

"What do you mean by that?" Peters queried, his thin frame seemed to quiver as he spoke. "I know Cortez will likely be the candidate for the repubs, but what makes you so sure . . ."

Before he could finish his thought, Folsom broke in. "Have you ever seen her in person, Joe?", he asked.

"No, but I've seen some pictures.".

"Well, you'll know why I'm so sure about her when you do, don't worry. She'll definitely win and win big, or I don't know men!"

Rudolf Cort placed a folder atop the well polished mahogany table and opened it quickly to display several photos of Sylvia Cortez.

He picked out a photo which he had personally taken discreetly in the courtroom while she had been addressing a jury with closing arguments in a recent organized crime racketeering case. He slid the photo in front of the party vice president.

"You've just seen news pictures," he said, "check this out.".

Folsom glanced down at the photo.

"And she's smart as a whip too.", Cort continued, "She'll definitely get the boys into the voting booths."

The big man seated at the head of the table pushed his eyeglasses up on his nose just a bit, delicately using one index finger. They almost immediately slipped down again and he simply peered over them as he spoke. "I know she's a very handsome lady.", he paused, then asked, "but what's with her personal life? Any scandals? Skeletons in her closet? What have you uncovered in that area?". He was addressing everyone at the table, but the question was directly primarily at the party lawyer Cort, who had been assigned the task of thoroughly vetting Sylvia Cortez prior to their possible endorsement.

Cort spun the folder and slid it toward Bremer.

"Here's the complete report, Mark. Up to date as of Saturday night. My investigators didn't miss a thing. I compiled it all yesterday.".

The big man smiled as he perused the several typewritten pages and additional photographs in the folder. His bifocals were so perfectly placed at the edge of his nose he had no need to move his head to look down, but merely focused his eyes downward on the report in front of him. "Very good." he said.

"It's complete." Cort interjected, "Parents emigrated from Cuba to Puerto Rico in 57, good hard working middle class people, moved to California in 69. Miss Cortez was raised well. No trouble in school, never associated with any organized Los Angeles gangs, excellent college record, and also excellent work and personal ethics.".

"I see that." the big man answered, "What I don't see here is much of a personal life, why is that?".

Cort shook his head. "That's 'cause she really doesn't have a personal life to speak of. No male involvement.", he paused momentarily, took a deep breath, then added, "I would say she's actually, well . . ." he stammered a bit searching for the correct descriptive word, "well, actually I'd say she's celibate when it comes to a sex life!".

Heads turned as Folsom sighed a loud disconsolate sigh. "Such a waste!", he half whispered, "Such a damned waste!".

Cort continued. "It appears miss Cortez is more interested in her career than any diversionary male relationships.".

Bremer cleared his throat once again. "So what's this note in here about an affair with a disgraced police officer a year or so back?".

"Oh, that?", Cort replied, giving the impression he was not at all bothered by that tidbit of information in the report. He shook his head. "Nothing! We checked it out. She had made some comments and kinda worked out a deal on that cops' behalf, but that's the job of any ADA, to protect and defend the department. They've had no follow-up contact that we know of, so likely more just a case of unrequited infatuation. It went nowhere.".

"That's good." Bremer mumbled, more to himself than anyone else. He once again adjusted his eyeglasses, and they once again almost immediately slipped back to the edge of his nose. He again peered over them, looking directly at counselor Cort.

"She has to understand that she must stay away from any kind of relationship that could even remotely be construed as improper or immoral. We are the conservative party after all.".

"I'm well aware of that." Cort answered, "and judging by her history I'm sure she'll agree with that condition herself. She seems very ambitious and . . ." Folsom interrupted.

"No problem there!", he blurted out, "Even the lobby security man knows that. She'll give up anything to become the county D.A.".

"That's right!", Cort added, "Everyone we interviewed says the same thing. She's career crazy! Wants to prove something, I guess.".

"Okay then," Bremer spoke authoritatively, "It's agreed. We'll back her!". He glanced over to the lean faced party vice president who seemed mesmerized by the photo he held in front of him. "Alright Peters?".

The thin man nodded. He did not look up. "Uh, oh yeah, alright, I'll go along.".

"She should be here any minute." Folsom said as he looked at his watch, "She's already downstairs. Probably on her way up now, so come on let's have that photo back.".

Cort reached over toward Peters, who was reluctant to let loose of Sylvia Cortez' photograph. "Uh, you said she's on her way up, right?", Peters asked almost breathlessly. He straightened his tie, and smoothed down his suit jacket. Then let loose the photo.

"Yeah, she's on her way.", Folsom replied with a smirk, "Just contain yourself now, boy!".

Bremer, Cort, and Folsom glanced back and forth and chuckled.

Cort whispered, "And he wanted us to endorse who?".

He nodded toward Peters whose face was now flushed with color.

They laughed together.

Peters lowered his head and simply smiled abashedly.

The coastal eddy low hanging clouds and morning fog had finally been burned away by the bright southern California sun. It was gradually rising to its' highest afternoon point, and was generously splaying its' springtime warmth over all Orange county. Streams of gold sliced between the horizontal blinds of Duke Chargas' apartment front window, painting everything in the room with a bright coppery hue. The bands of sunlight were stretching across the coffee table top, and beginning to bathe Chargas' face. He became aware of the gradual warming sensation on his cheek, and sensed the brightness thru closed eyelids. Instinctively, he turned his face away, and almost immediately heard a muted crackling sound, and felt a hot, painful flash drive up along the back of his neck. "Ouch!", he opened his eyes, blinked a few times, then peered down at his wrist watch. One thirty. He had fallen asleep sitting up. Well, sure, he thought. It had been a rather long evening. One in which he had not slept that well. It was true, no matter how comfortable one may feel, it's almost always a bit more difficult to get a good nights sleep when not laying on ones own familiar mattress. Sylvia Cortez had kept him up physically, in more ways than one, until well past one A.M., and the subsequent 7:30 A.M. visit by Fredricks and Mitello with their questioning and re-questioning of his recollections of the previous day, had worn him down as well. Those two had demonstrated no real concern that he was, in fact, still recovering from a hospital stay, albeit a brief one, having suffered a concussion and laceration of the arm, and was not yet 100% either physically or mentally. Therefore he had, immediately after their departure, sat his tired self down on the sofa, planning to relax his body for just a few minutes before contemplating any plan of action on his part for the days and week ahead. They had grilled him for two hours with a continuous barrage of questions regarding his association with Tony Taccio, and the happenings at the fruit and vegetable market in little Lebanon. Charga felt many of the questions, and his own answers, had been irrelevant and superfluous, but he had answered them all anyway. Throughout the interrogation agent Mitello had maintained an air of condescension and aloofness, but Fredricks was more intent and focused on Chargas' answers and observations. Fredricks had explained that, based on the history of terror attacks, the terrorists' real aim is to either cause as much economic disruption as possible, or to instill as much fear, to as many people, as possible. Therefore, areas of significant business activity, and places accommodating large numbers of people, must be considered primary targets. Charga had suggested, that if that was truly the case, then ballparks, local amusement centers, and the areas' lone racetrack site should certainly also be considered as possible targets of such an attack. He had also raised the point that the Anaheim Angels baseball schedule had them playing the L.A. Dodgers over the coming weekend, and that match up had repeatedly been a sellout series. There could be 55 thousand plus at the ballpark for every game. Charga had also suggested that the sudden assault upon himself and Big Tony Taccio could be an indication of some sort of connection to the Arcadia racetrack. Mitello was reluctant at first to accept Chargas' theory concerning the racetrack, but when Charga mentioned the phone call from Mike Dunne regarding the homicide of the shedrow worker named Basara, and Fredricks had nodded and whispered, "the pres!", Mitello had quickly changed his tune.

"Definitely some kind of tie in there!".

"That's the reason we are here." Fredricks had said. "We're already covering all the hard targets and the most logical soft ones, including the ballpark and the tourist attractions, but it sure does look like something may be going on up at Arcadia.".

He then removed the government issued cellular phone which was hooked on his belt, extended its' antenna, touched just one speed dial button, and was immediately connected to the local NSA. After a few minutes of hushed conversation, he addressed Charga once again. "We'll have boots on the ground in Arcadia within the hour.". Charga nodded. "Good idea.". Charga was satisfied that he had contributed all he could to their ongoing investigation. "Glad to be of some help." he said, "Now let's get these guys before they . . .".

Fredricks had cut him off. "Oh, we'll get them okay.". Just as the pair seemed ready to leave, Fredricks had turned and added, "Let me tell you this, mister Charga. You've been a great help, but if what you suspect regarding the racetrack is true, then you may already be involved too deeply in something that is over your head, and I would recommend you stand down and allow us to do our work, after all, we are the experts here, understand?".

Mitello had chimed in. He was not as diplomatic in his commentary. "Listen Charga, your poking around may simply impede our progress.", he snarled, "Like I said before, you've already driven one of our main leads into deep cover. You're one of those guys who just attracts trouble, so just stand back and butt out!".

"Butt out? No way!", Charga thought, "They don't know Marion Charga!". The prior days' assault that had landed him in Compton general had churned up his innate, congenital sense of Latino/Italian revenge. He had already decided, while laying in the hospital bed the day before that, in spite of Mike Dunnes' admonition to the contrary, he was going after these people on his own, especially that Bin Haseed character.

"Someone told me the same thing yesterday." Charga said in response, "and I'll tell you the same thing I told him.".

"And what was that?".

"I'll take your suggestion under advisement.".

The two NSA agents had visibly grimaced at that wisecrack, and Fredricks had turned to add one last comment as he stepped out the front door. "You'd be wise to step back, mister Charga. These people are downright barbarians. Think about it!".

"Yeah, okay." was Chargas' response as he closed and locked the door behind them. He then settled back on the sofa in an almost exhausted state. "Good riddance!" he said aloud.

Now he was gently rubbing the sleep from his eyes. He stretched his right arm and soothingly massaged the back of his neck. It was still a bit stiff and hurting, a consequence of his awkward 4 hour sitting up while sleeping position. He yawned widely and took a deep breath. There was a distinctive odor of something burning which had spread throughout the apartment.

"Say now, what's that?", he mumbled to himself. He stood up and followed the smell into the kitchen area. "Damn it!".

His early morning visitors had almost emptied the coffee carafe, replaced it on the coffee maker, but hadn't turned the darn thing off. The bottom of the glass container was blackened with burnt on coffee.

"Almost ready to crack!", he thought as he depressed the 'off' button.

"I sure hope those guys are more cautious in their professional line of work. Guess I'm going out for coffee today.".

Charga then hitched up his pants, tightened his belt and adjusted his shoulder holster. He checked his Glock, making sure it was snug in its' place, then retrieved his suit jacket which he had earlier draped over the back of one of the dining room chairs, and headed on out.

Just as he grasped the front door knob his landline phone began to ring. He quickly stepped back into his apartment kitchen area and lifted the receiver. "Charga investigations. Charga here.".

A breathy female voice returned his greeting. "Oh, mister Charga, I'm so glad I got you.".

The voice was familiar, but from those few words, Charga just could not connect the face. "Yes, how may I help you?".

"I need you.", came the purring reply, "It's about my husband again.".

"Aha!", Charga thought, he had it now. "Mrs. Micelli?".

"Yes, it's me.". The tone was inviting, it was Micelli alright. "I'm so glad you remembered.".

"How could I not? I was just in your office two days ago.".

"Yes, that's right.". There was a momentary pause, then she almost whispered her next words, "but you left before I could properly thank you.".

Charga ignored the obvious implication. "Okay.", he answered, his own tone of voice was cordial but formal, "What can I do for you now?".

"Well, it's my husband.".

"Yes? What happened? Did he hit you? What?".

"Oh, you just must come to me.". Again the sexually charged whisper. "You must, you just must.".

"I was just on my way out to get some coffee and a bagel.", Charga said in return, "I can see you in about a half hour or so.".

"But I have coffee and sweets here in my office.". It was a not so veiled invitation. "And what I have for you is so very important for both of us.".

"You mean it can't wait thirty minutes?".

"No! Not at all." The seductress intonation was unmistakable.

"I just can't wait!". She repeated her words slowly with much emphasis on the first person pronoun. "I., just., cannot., wait!".

"Could be another easy five bills." Charga thought, "Why the hell not?". He happily acquiesced to her demand. "Okay.", he said, "I'll head right on down to you now, be there in ten, maybe fifteen minutes, okay?".

"Ohhh!", she purred, "That'll be wonderful. I'll expect you then, very soon.".

Charga attempted to end the call right there. "Right! I'll see you in a few min . . ." She cut him off abruptly.

"Great!", she blurted out excitedly, "And I'll certainly be ready for you.". Click!

"Now that was strange.", he thought, "Wonder what it is she really wants.". He replaced the receiver, then quickly stepped out and locked the door behind him. He scooted out and jogged around back to his designated parking space, unlocked his Dynastys' doors and slid in behind the wheel. Just a touch of the ignition key in place, and the starter instantly kicked in. The straight six cylinder engine turned over and was idling just as smoothly as the day Charga had driven it out of the showroom. He affectionately patted the dash panel. "That's my reliable Dyna.", he said aloud as he set the transmission in reverse and gently pressed down on the accelerator. It was not yet two P.M., and traffic was light at this time of day. It was at least two hours before the normal rush hour freeway congestion would start.

Charga decided to take the 5 freeway, and exit on Montrosia rather than travel the local streets and stoplight regulated avenues. He arrived at Mrs. Micellis' building in Duarte within fifteen minutes, parked just outside the main lobby door and was on the elevator up to her office in another two.

The lettering on the suite entry door read 'Maxem Real Estate'. Charga pulled open the door and stepped in. The outer office and reception area was unmanned. No one at the front desk or in the work area. "That's unusual for this time of day.", he thought as he walked past the empty desks and headed straight on in toward the door marked 'M. Micelli, Mgr'. It was ajar. He didn't knock. Mrs. Micelli was seated in her oversize leather chair behind her desk, she was facing the rear window, her back to the door.

"Well, I'm here.", Charga announced cheerily.

Mrs. Micelli swung around in her chair, stood up, and took several steps around her desk and toward him. "And I'm so glad you are.". She moved slowly, teasingly, and there appeared to be an aura of lasciviousness about her every word and motion. "I really needed to see you." she said, "Really!". Chargas' eyes widened. She was dressed to kill in a loose fitting red silken blouse which set a pleasant contrast in color to her flowing blonde hair. It was obvious she was braless since her every movement caused her breasts to jiggle like two size 34B mounds of freshly made Jello beneath the delicate shiny material. A straight form fitting, black polyester skirt served to accentuate the smooth cellulite free curves of her backside, hips, and thighs, while black patent leather high heeled shoes gave emphasis to her long attractively muscular legs. A light minty glow of fresh eye shadow highlighted the deep green of her eyes, and her lips appeared invitingly wet and ablaze with a fiery red sheen.

"A very sensually handsome lady.", Charga thought as his eyes drank in a full measure of her almost overwhelming and copious beauty. Her skirt was pulled up to mid thigh, possibly an effect of her prior sitting position, and he naturally and instinctively focused on the accidentally exposed area of leg. In his mind, he questioned whether this was really an accidental exposure of skin.

He raised his thumb as if hitch hiking. "How come no ones in the outer office?", he asked, motioning back over his shoulder.

"Oh, I gave everyone the rest of the day off.", she replied softly, "I wanted the two of us to have some privacy.".

Charga spied some freshly brewing coffee set up on a small table standing just to the right of the big mahogany desk.

"That for me?", he asked as he nodded toward the still dripping coffee maker.

"That's right.", she answered. She placed her hands at her waist, then smoothed down her skirt along her hips and outer thigh, and slinked a few steps closer. She purred. "It's ready for you, and like I told you on the phone, I'm ready for you too.". Her tone and her smile now purposely sensual and obviously inviting.

Charga took notice but did not let on or acknowledge he had, instead he proceeded to casually fix himself a cup of coffee, maintaining an air of dispassionate nonchalance.

"Smells good.", he said, and he began stirring in the cream and sugar. "Haven't had cream with my coffee for quite a while.".

His eyes remained fixed on his cup.

"You know," Micelli whispered as she stepped in closer to him, pressing her body against his left side, "You could have more than just cream with that coffee.".

Charga stepped away. "No offense." he nodded toward his left arm, "But I've got a bad cut on my bicep.". He glanced around the office. "So where's the donuts?", he asked.

171

"I didn't say I had donuts.", she answered with a smirk, "I said I had sweets . . .". She paused momentarily, then added in a slow, throaty tone, "You haven't yet tasted my sweets.".

Charga glanced back at her, and grinned as she brushed away a wisp of golden blonde hair which had fallen across her eyes.

"Wouldn't you like to taste my sweets?", she asked with a wink.

Charga shook his head slowly, not in a negative motion but more in bewilderment. As a man he was both pleased and perplexed. That women found him attractive was always ego boosting, but trying to figure out their thought process was a continuous challenge. This cougar had already come on to him once before, so her sexually aggressive demeanor was no real surprise, but he wondered, was that female hunger the only reason she had called him back?

"You mentioned a problem with your husband, right?", he asked, seemingly ignoring her double entendre comment and suggestive body language. "So what did he do, exactly?".

"Well, I told him I had your report.", her body stiffened some as she spoke, "and he just packed up and left yesterday.".

"Yes, and so?". Charga could see no problem so far. "Isn't that what you wanted him to do?".

"Well, yes and no.".

Charga sat down on one of the office chairs and took a sip of coffee. Now he had to digest that last statement. He looked up at the statuesque, handsome lady, and wondered just what was going on in that beautiful head. She smiled at him, and once again began advancing toward him, sensually swiveling her hips in exaggerated fashion. She was breathing heavily, and his focus was naturally drawn to her heaving breasts whose teats were visibly outlined and pressing out against the silken blouse.

"Yes and no, what do you mean by that?", he asked while forcibly averting his stare from her bodice to her face.

"Well,", she replied, lightly stamping her foot, "He never even made an attempt to make up, or say he was sorry.".

"What?". Charga almost choked on his coffee. "Women!" he thought, "Who could ever understand them?".

"Well, I wanted him to at least try!", she continued, "After all, look at me. How could someone just give me up like that?".

"But,", Charga mumbled. He was almost incredulous. "He was nothing but a player. You hired me to find that out for sure.".

"That's right.", she went on, "But I just wanted him to know I was on to him, and . . .".

"Okay!", Charga cut in, "So what do you want me to do now? Make him come back?".

"No, not that.".

"So what then?".

"Well, he hadn't touched me intimately for several weeks.".

"And?", Charga was becoming less confused now. He thought, "Maybe it's just that this lady is simply hot to trot!".

"So?", he asked, "What then?".

"But you see, we were together for almost sixteen years, and he knew I needed a certain amount of attention.", she paused again, then almost whispered, "You know, intimate attention.".

"And so, I'm here now for what?", Charga asked as he stood up and set the now empty coffee cup atop the desk. It was really a purely rhetorical question, he had a pretty good idea of what it was she wanted from him.

"Don't you find me attractive?", she asked in return. She stepped closer to him and pressed her body against his chest. "Stay with me." she continued, "I will even pay you for your time, that is, if you like.". She brushed her lips on his cheek, then moved her mouth close to his ear and whispered, "Just tell me how much, I really want you, and I want you now.".

Her sensual tone and slinking movements rolled over him like the caressing touch of a full body massage being performed by a naked Swedish female masseuse. He had rejected her once before, but on this day the tingling sensation running up thru his loins told him that this time he just could not resist. He became both relaxed and aroused at the same time. He held her by the waist and smiled, a smile of great expectations. "Why not?", he thought, "Why the hell not?". Then, in a soft voice, acceptance and lust oozing conspicuously with each word, whispered "Let's just say that cup of Java is payment enough, okay Mrs. Micelli?".

"Call me Marilyn.", she murmured in his ear. Her arms were now wrapped around his shoulders, her hands pressing the back of his neck. Her lush, moistened lips found their way to his mouth. She kissed him once, then once again, forcefully pulling his head to her, and pressing their bodies together. Charga slid his hands around to her lower back, then slowly downward until they rested on her buttocks. He gently grasped her perfectly proportioned rear cheeks, and drew her body tightly against his own. Now their lower torsos and the full length of their thighs were touching, and Charga could feel the warmth of her most intimate feminine area.

"Just do me.", she said, almost pleadingly, "Do me. I need it. I need it now!".

Chapter five

Go Figure!

B ig Mike Dunne and his partner detective Brad Street shot each other a perplexed glance, then stared back to Arcadia 1st precinct Captain John Dunbar, who was seated in his usual, almost majestic pose, behind his desk, which was, as usual, covered with randomly scattered police papers and file folders. They had been summoned in for what captain Dunbar had labeled a 'little talk'.
"Have I made myself clear?", he growled up at them. They nodded in tandem. "Good! Now get your asses out of here!".
"Right, captain.", Street answered meekly. Mike Dunne merely nodded once again.
"Go check the incoming assault reports.", Dunbar ordered, his gruff voice had risen an octave for emphasis. "And don't slam the door behind you.".
Together, Dunne and Street turned and exited Dunbars' office.
They stepped into the precinct squad room, and Big Mike Dunne made it a point to shut the office door with just a bit extra force.
They heard Dunbar call out. "I said not to do that, Dunne!".
"Yeah, yeah.", Dunne grumbled under his breath, "I heard ya!".
"Now that was unexpected, wasn't it?", Street said looking back over his shoulder.
"That's an understatement.", Dunne mumbled, barely audibly, "First time!", he added, "First time!".
"First time?", Street questioned.
"Yep! First time in seventeen years I've been ordered off a case.".

"I've heard of things like this," Street said, "But I didn't figure it would be so soon for me.". That was true. Street was relatively new in the department of detectives. He had only been with the investigative unit for less than one year, first six months in robbery detail, then six months here with Dunne on assaults.

"Any idea why cap Dunbar did it?", he asked.

"Well," the veteran detective replied, "I figure he got orders from up the ladder. He wouldn't do something like that otherwise. But you know . . .", he shot a quick look to his partner Street, and shook his head slowly, "I just hate folding my hand before I see the flop!".

"So, what do we do now, Mike? Just forget it?".

Dunne didn't respond, he merely stroked his moustache and began thinking aloud. "Not even an important case.", he said, as he pulled out his chair at his desk. He plopped himself heavily into the old wooden swivel seat, stared up at his tall partner and continued his soliloquy. "Just a simple beat down," he paused, and rubbed his chin while contemplating the assault and associated homicides.

"Then there's that deal with Charga and Taccio, and the incident at that vegetable place, and to top it all off there's Basaras' takeout! They're definitely all connected!".

"Sure they are!", Street added enthusiastically, "Each one goes with the other!".

"Seems right! But what's behind the whole thing?" Dunne queried. The question was as much for himself as for his partner.

"Definitely more than meets the eye here.".

"Well, what are we gonna do? Can't go against the boss. What?".

Detective Street felt a friendly slap on the back.

"Going against the boss are you?". It was his former partner, sergeant Paul Carson. "So Brad," he went on, "How you been? How do you like working triple A?".

Since Street had been transferred from robbery division, he and Carson had been working different shifts and had rarely run into each other. This was an unusual meeting.

Street turned. "Hi Paul".

Carson was of Norwegian descent. His parents had long before changed their name from Karlson with a K, to Carson with a C, and without the middle L, to more easily assimilate into the American culture. He was big, almost as tall as Street, but with a solidly built torso, very similar to that of Mike Dunne. That's where their similarities ended. Carsons' skin color was as white as a Scandanavian coastal iceberg, and thinning light blonde hair, streaked with some gray, combined with that pale Nordic complexion made it appear that his face was devoid of eyebrows.

Steel blue eyes, set deep in their sockets, along with thin light pink lips offered the only contrast to his otherwise colorless and always expressionless face. With no jacket or tie, and wearing a white shirt, he looked like an unfinished snowman awaiting the coal chip eyes, carrot nose and corn cob pipe. It was no wonder he had earned a CB nickname of 'whiteface'.

Dunne looked up. "Oh, hello Whitey.", he said.

Carson nodded.

"Accidents and assaults isn't so bad.", Street began, "Never know what you might run into. How about you, still in robbery division?".

"Yeah,", Carson answered, "We've got five open cases right now. Mostly crash and cash, they're the toughest to crack, you know. Perps just bust a window, grab whatever they can, and they're outta there in a flash. It's usually just the greasers and niggers that do it.".

Street was thinking. "Still a racist! How and why does P.D. keep him on?".

"So," Carson continued, "What are you and fat Mike here working on?".

"Past tense please. That should be what were we working on. Just was instructed to stand down and drop the case.".

"What? Really? And why was that?".

"Don't rightly know. Started out as a simple assault, what it turned into is a mystery to us.".

"What do you mean, a mystery?".

"Ended up with four homicides and another attempted one.".

"And how the hell did that work out?", Carson asked with a slight chuckle.

"Beyond me. Ask Mike, or better yet, go ask captain Dunbar.".

Carson looked down at Mike Dunne, who was quietly seated at his desk writing out the final report on the Harborstone assault case.

"Say, Dunne, nice to work with a real white American, now ain't it?".

Dunne didn't look up. "Watch it carson.", he said. He was already somewhat rankled by his orders to stand down and was in no mood for Carsons' bigoted remarks.

"Whatever happened to that spic partner of yours? Heard he's chasing ambulances now.".

Dunne shot him an angry stare. "Just watch it! Unless you're just looking for trouble.".

"Aw, calm down.", Carson said in return. "Here . . .". He reached over to a nearby table, picked up a half empty box of donuts, and tossed it on Dunnes' desk. "Have a donut, relax!".

Street hurriedly picked it up, closed the box top and started to set it back on the nearby snack table. "We'll pass, thanks anyway.".

Dunne pointed to his desk top. "Hold it a minute, Brad. Just leave 'em here.". He glanced up to Paul carson. "Always knew you were good for something.", he said with sarcasm dripping off every word.

Carson waved a goodbye motion. "Yeah, sure.", he said, "Just enjoy 'em.". He turned back to his former partner, "See ya, Brad.

Take care and just let me know when you want to get away from fatty here.".

"What was that?". Dunne stood up, straight backed. "What did you say?".

Carson chuckled once again, and simply swaggered away, looking back over his shoulder with a grin.

Street stared at his partner and shook his head. "Just sit down, Mike.", he said as he pulled out the chair on the opposite side of their team desk. "You guys never did get along, did you?".

Dunne returned to his seat. "AW!", he said, as he sorted thru the half dozen donuts in the box, finally settling on a sticky honey covered one, "He's just an asshole, well you should know that. You worked with him.". He held up his donut choice. "This one's good, They call this a bears claw, I love these.".

"You love 'em all!", Street cracked with a smirk.

"Guess I'll call Duke Charga and let him know what's going on here with us.", big Mike said as he chomped down on his donut.

"Do you think he's going to follow up on that Harborstone case?".

"Think? No! I know it!", big Mike laughed. "He'll never let go of this deal until he finds out what it's really all about. I know Duke

Charga, and those characters made a big mistake when they went after him.".

"How so, Mike?".

"They got him mad!", Dunne lowered his voice to almost a whisper "They got him really mad!". He picked up his desk phone. "He's likely out on his own right now, I'll call his cell number.".

"Okay.". Street stood up and nodded toward the white assignment board at the far end of the squad room. "I'll check the latest assault and accident assignments, if any.". He paused, then added, "I'll grab a cup of coffee too, you want one?".

"Sure.", big Mike answered as he began picking thru the remaining half dozen or so donuts until finally settling on a honey glazed type. He held it up high. "I'll need some Java to wash this baby down.".

"How do you want it Mike?", Street asked. He stepped to Dunnes' side of the desk, and hesitated there. "Cream and sugar?".

"No. Just cream.", Dunne replied patting his rounded stomach. "I've got to try to watch my calorie intake, ya know?".

"Yeah, I know." Street smiled. "I noticed how you're doing that.".

Dunne didn't respond to that wisecrack. He was focused on his little pocket size telephone number book. "Here's his cell number,", he mumbled, and began pushing the buttons on his desk phone.

Street returned in a few minutes with a container of coffee in each hand. He placed one in front of his partner. "There you go, Mike.", he said, "Cream, no sugar.".

Mike Dunne wasn't talking, just quietly holding the phone to his ear. He grunted and nodded.

"Didn't get him yet?", Street asked.

"Nope. It's ringing, but nothing yet, not even a voice message.".

"Maybe call him back later.". Streets' suggestion went unanswered. He returned to his seat, then added, "Nothing in on triple A's, so I guess we'll just chill for a while.". He leaned back and sipped on his coffee. "Might as well enjoy the lull.".

Duke Charga had just gotten to his cell. "Hello, Charga here.".

"Finally!", Mike Dunne called out, "How come it took you so long to answer? Something wrong?".

"No, nothing's wrong.". Chargas words came in rapid fire staccato mode. "I'm just into something, Mike. What the hell do you want?".

"You sound out of breath.".

Charga cut him off. "I'm okay, what's up?".

Mike Dunne was anxious to tell his former partner of the earlier meeting with captain Dunbar. "Something came up here this afternoon . . .".

Charga cut him off again. "Something came up for me just a few minutes ago, and actually it's still up right now, so make it quick!".

"Need any help?".

"No, not really, Mike. I'm on it! So, now what is it?".

"Well, I figured I got to tell you what's going on up here.".

"Okay!", Charga shot back, "Just don't expect me to be telling you what's going on down here. Go! Shoot!".

"We were bumped off the Harborstone case.".

"Figured!", Charga grunted back, "I know why.".

"You know?".

"Yep! I'll tell you about it tomorrow.".

"That sounds good, when?", Dunne questioned, then as an afterthought asked, "And how the hell do you know anyway?".

"Not now Mike!", Charga was panting between his words, "Later!" He paused momentarily, then continued, his words blurting out faster than before. "Should've never answered this phone!". Click!

"Now, that was strange.", Dunne said aloud, yet mostly to himself. "Charga seemed very distracted.". He took a sip of his coffee, then unbuckled his pants belt. "Ahh, that's better.".

"Pants too tight, Mike?", Street chided sarcastically, "No sugar in the coffee doesn't seem to be cutting it, eh?".

Big Mike Dunne shook his head. "That's not it.", he answered. "It's that damn dry cleaner. Uses too much cleaning chemical.". He took a deep breath, and finished his second donut.

"Makes the clothes shrink, you know?".

"Right, Mike.", Street chuckled, "Makes 'em shrink!". He tossed his own empty coffee container into the trash basket under the desk. "Well, what are we going to do now? There's nothing' on the schedule.".

"I'll tell you what we're gonna do.", Dunne replied as he pushed his body away from the desk. The wheels on his rolling chair squeaked like an alley cat in heat.

"Oh yeah? What?", Street asked.

"Starting tomorrow, we're gonna become hardcore horseracing fans, that's what!".

Duke Charga placed his hands, palms up, on either side of Marilyn Micellis' torso, which laid almost motionless atop the oversize mahogany desk. He pushed himself up and paused momentarily to visually drink in and admire her overall physical attractiveness. The shiny red blouse was unbuttoned and laying out along her sides, exposing Aphrodite like breasts which, despite her supine position, remained upright and firm, their symmetrically perfect and rigid teats like two pinkish nipples begging to be suckled. Her unclothed lower body was glowing with an even tan, and her skin felt as soft and smooth to the touch as warm silk on a sunny southern California afternoon. Despite her disheveled hair, and somewhat smudged and slightly faded makeup, her innate movie star facial beauty remained intact. "She's right!", he thought, "How could anyone give up this work of art without a fight?".

He stepped back, tripped over his Florshiem size eleven wing tips, and fell backward into one of the soft leather office chairs, right onto his BVD undershorts, and his suit trousers which he had earlier tossed, rather haphazardly, on the seat. He sat still for a few seconds, then took in a deep breath.

"That was good.", he said aloud.

"No!", came the throaty response, "It was better than good.".

The semi clothed beauty stretched her arms over her head, then sighed a long sigh of contentment.

"It was wonderful.", she whispered, "Simply wonderful.".

She lifted her head and extended her arms toward him. "Come back mister Charga. Come back to me."

Charga sat up. "Call me Duke.", he said, "I think we know each other well enough now to be on a first name basis.".

"Okay, then Duke.", she replied as she propped herself up on her elbows. Her legs were bent at the knees, and remained hanging just off the front edge of the desk. She moved them further apart.

"Come back.", she pleaded, "Come back to me, Duke . . . now.".

"Hold on now!", Charga said as he slumped back in the chair. He was not at all ready to start all over again. "I think I just want to eat now.".

Micelli smiled widely, and tossed her head back, fluffing up her hair. "Don't make promises you may be unable to keep.".

"Uh oh! I mean a real meal!", he replied, and he began pulling up his undershorts, then his pants. "In a restaurant.".

He picked up her skirt and undies, and tossed them over her thighs. "Here. Get dressed.", he ordered, "We're going out for dinner.".

"And after dinner . . . what?", she asked flirtatiously as she wriggled into her nylon panties and hip hugging skirt. "My place or yours?".

Charga laughed. "We'll discuss that later, okay?".

He retrieved his Glock and shoulder holster from the back of the chair, strapped them on, and draped his suit jacket over his shoulder, partially covering both.

She pointed to his weapon. "You walk the streets with that thing showing?", she asked, as she slipped into her high heeled shoes, "Is that legal?" . . .

"It's legal.", Charga answered, "But I'll put my jacket on before we get outside.".

Micelli took hold of his arm and pulled him close, purposely pressing her still exposed breasts against his right side. "So where are we going?", she asked while rubbing her body against his, "I mean, after dinner?".

Charga struggled to ignore the suggestive commentary and sensual bodily contact. He looked down at her open blouse. "Button up.", he said, "We're going to Garlattis for dinner. It's my favorite place to eat. Know where it is?".

"Not really, but I've heard of it before.".

"Best Italian food around.", Charga said. He slipped into his suit jacket and removed his car keys from the side pocket.

"I'm parked right out front. Let's go.".

Moments later they were down the stairs and on the front sidewalk. He unlocked the side passenger door, swung it wide and held it open for her. "Hop in, babe. It's just a short drive down to Anaheim, and I definitely need to refuel.".

They were at Garlattis within fifteen minutes. Angelo Garlatti was standing out front smoking an El Ropo little cigar. He noticed Charga and his new lady almost immediately, and gestured to them.

"Buon journo, mister Duke.", he called out.

Charga returned the greeting. "Buon journo Ange. This is miss Micelli.".

"Un otra donna Italiano?". Angelo Garlatti half bowed. "Buono!".

He took her hand in his, and brought it up to his lips.

"Ahhh, bella.", he whispered as he touched the back of her hand with his mouth. "Bella donna.".

"That's so sweet.", she gushed, "So continental!".

"Yeah, right.", Charga nodded, "He's a Sicilian lover alright!".

She smiled and purred, "You mean., like you?".

"My minds on food now.", Charga replied with a wink, "Let's just go and eat.".

It was still early so they had their choice of table selection. Charga pointed to an empty table situated at the front window.

"Let's take that one.", he said, and began leading her toward it.

All conversation in Garlattis seemed to suddenly cease, heads turned, and all eyes were focused on Micellis' sensually swiveling hips and derriere as she slinked along behind Charga, her every step keeping almost perfect time with the beat of the Dean Martin classic 'That's Amore' being played on the restaurant sound system.

"You sure do draw a helluva lot of attention.", Charga remarked, and they sat themselves down just as Deanos song hit its' final notes. She didn't respond verbally, but a smile lit her face as if Charga had gifted her with the greatest of compliments. He scanned the restaurant. The conversational buzz had begun again, and with the momentary Micelli temptress show ended, Garlattis Monday afternoon diners were back to savoring mamma Garlattis tasteful home cooking. Now she became aware that the entire restaurant was enveloped with the flavorful scent of mammas' Sicilian style cuisine.

"Smells wonderful here.", Micelli whispered, "If the food is as good as it smells, it's no wonder why you come here.".

Charga nodded. "Been coming here for years.".

"By the way," she continued, "What was all that Italian talk between you and that guy out front?".

"Oh, you mean Angelo. He's one of the owners. Said you were lovely.".

"Okay, Dukey, not that I really care that much, but what was that crack about another woman?".

"Oh, you caught that did you?".

"I'm not only married to an Italian," she smirked, "My father was Italian too.".

"No wonder she's so hot!", he thought, "It's in the blood!".

Back at Arcadia RD. big Mike Dunne was checking his watch. It was three thirty. He signed the team daily report log, and tossed it across the desk to his partner. "Here Brad.", he said, "Check it out, sign it, and file it away.".

"Got it.". Street gave the report a quick glance. "You sure made it short and sweet.". He initialed the bottom. "Probably best since nobody will be seeing this anyway.".

"You're right about that.", Dunne agreed, "This report may very likely simply disappear out of Dunbars' office. That's what usually happens when an investigation gets aborted." He paused, and took a deep breath. "And I don't like it, not a bit!".

"Nothing much we can do about it though, is there Mike?".

Dunne raised his hand in the universal motion signifying 'stop'.

"Not officially.", he said, "But then again . . ." His voice trailed off. "Who's to know . . . ?".

He tugged on his pants. "Damn dry cleaner.", he mumbled. Street stood up, report in hand. "I'll put this away, then what?".

He didn't wait for an answer, instead he walked directly to the set of file cabinets just outside captain Dunbars' office, pulled open a drawer, and dropped the file in its' appropriate space.

He tapped on the captains' office door.

"Come!", Dunbars' gravelly voice bellowed out.

Street opened the door and poked his head in. "I filed the Harborstone report in cabinet two, okay cap?".

"Fine.", Dunbar answered. He did not look up. "I'll check it later.".

"Okay. Figured you'd want to know.".

"Fine! You told me. I'll take care of it, now just close the door.".

He paused for a few seconds, then added, "And don't slam it!".

Street returned to his desk where Mike Dunne was already standing, readying to call it a day. "Let's wrap it up for today.", he said. "I've got to get down to the mall and pick up some new clothes.". He took another deep breath, and again tugged on his pants belt. "I need some pants that fit right, and are pre shrunk.".

Detective Paul Carson, who had been standing nearby, strode over to him. "Heard you say you're going to the mall.".

"Yeah, that's right, so?". Dunne replied. "What's it to you?". Carson took a step back. "Take it easy. Just interested to know which mall, the north Arcadia mall maybe?".

"That's what I was planning.", Dunne replied. He was not at all pleased by Carsons' intrusion into his private conversation with his partner. "Like I said, what's it to you?".

Carson snickered. "Hey! I don't really care, except that it might be a wasted trip on your part.".

"What do you mean by that?".

"Just got word the mall is in lockdown. The state police are evacuating all the stores. No one gets in or gets out without being checked.".

"Really? What happened?". Dunne asked, his interest was piqued.

"Don't really know.", Carson answered as he slipped into his suit jacket. "But I've also been called in to check out the scene. Maybe a robbery attempt.".

"I'd like to check it out as well.", Dunne said, and he began walking alongside Carson as he headed for the squad room door. Carson stopped and turned, his face just inches away from Dunnes. "You're not in robbery, chubby.", he chided as he poked at Dunnes' barrel chest. "So just step back and eat yourself another donut!". That crack rankled big Mike to the point where his right hand instinctively balled into a fist. He was just about ready to pop this antagonistic character, but before he could move he felt his arm being held from behind. It was Brad Street. "Relax, Mike.", Street whispered, "Forget it. Let's just do what you said, and call it a day.".

"Yeah, I guess you're right.", Dunne reluctantly agreed, "Maybe he's not worth it.".

Carson shrugged, and smirked, then turned and exited the squad room without another word.

"He's a jerk!", Dunne turned to his partner. "I'm okay." he said. Street chuckled. "You may be okay, but you're starting to act like your former partner. What am I going to do with you?".

Dunne smiled. He patted Street on the shoulder. "You're okay, Brad. You're a good partner. Thanks.".

Duke Charga lifted the cloth napkin from his lap and dabbed the corners of his mouth, wiping away the last lingering particles of Mamma Garlattis tomato sauce and mozzarella cheese. He had scarfed down her Sicilian style meatless lasagna in a matter of mere moments. Marilyn Micelli was delicately picking at her Caesars salad. She looked up.

"You really were hungry.".

"I told you I needed to refuel.". Charga balled up the napkin and placed it in the now empty lasagna bowl. He sat back in his seat.

"I just love the food here.".

"It is very good.", she agreed with a nod, "But I really wasn't that hungry . . . . for food that is.".

Charga caught the innuendo, understood it, but opted to ignore it at this time. Angelo Garlatti was ambling toward them carrying two double shot size glasses of the traditional Sicilian after dinner drink.

"Ahh.", Charga said, "Here's Angelo with the final touch.".

The portly waiter placed the two Anisette drinks on the table, and began removing the empty plates. "Everything okay?", he asked.

"Fine, as usual, Ange.", Charga answered, "But the lady isn't finished.".

Angelo Garlatti looked down at Chargas' dinner companion.

"That's okay, senora, take your time.". He lingered for just a few seconds, his eyes focused on her obviously braless bosom.

"I'll come back.", then added, still wide eyed, "Don't rush.".

"Okay, Ange.", Charga said, "And when you come back, bring me the check.".

Angelo turned and slowly made his way to the rear of the restaurant, took a final look back over his shoulder, then disappeared behind the doors marked 'kitchen employees only'.

Charga quickly downed one of the Anisettes, then picked up the second. "Do you want this?", he asked.

Marilyn Micelli shook her head. "No thanks.".

"Good! I'll take it.". Charga drank the second glass of Anisette in one gulp. "You know, Ange likes you, I can tell.".

"Well . . .", Micelli began, "I think . . .". The conversation was broken by the buzzing sound of her own personal cellular phone.

"Hold on.", she said, "It's my phone.".

She reached down and picked up the small red leather bag she had inconspicuously carried with her.

"That's an awfully small pocketbook.", Charga nodded toward it. "What is it? A makeup bag?".

"It's called a clutch.". She unzipped the bag and removed the small pink colored phone. She checked the caller ID screen.

"It's from my home phone.", she said, "I better take it.".

"Maybe one of your kids?", Charga asked. He knew from his recent surveillance and investigation of Micellis' husband that there were two teenagers in the family. She shrugged and touched the talk button on the phone. "Hello?".

Her face suddenly lit up. "It's my hubbie!", she called out gleefully, then quietly into the phone, "Yes dear?".

Chargas' eyes widened. "What the hell is this?", he wondered, "She's thrilled that her two timing husband is calling?".

"You're home?", she continued, "Okay.". There was a long pause . . . She smiled. "And I love you too.", she whispered.

"Yes! Yes, I'll be there.". Another pause, then, "And I'm sorry too dear. Yes. Okay. Bye.".

Charga signaled Angelo Garlatti, who had returned to the restaurant front. "Check!".

Angelo nodded his acknowledgement, pulled a pad from his apron pocket, made some notations and tore off a sheet.

"Here you are mister Charga.".

Marilyn Micelli waved a backhanded wave. "I'm done.", she said, "You can take this away.". Then, addressing her remarks to Charga, "Take me back to my office so I can get my car and get home, okay?".

Charga nodded. "Sure.", he replied. "Whatever you want.". He was feeling both a bit dejected and somewhat confused.

"How fickle women can be.", he thought, "One never knows what's in their mind.".

The bill was twenty six dollars. He dropped three tens on the table. "There you go, Ange.", he said, "All yours.".

"Thank you mister Charga, and buono serra to you and your lovely lady. Buono serra.".

"Right.", Charga replied, "And good night to you too, see you soon.".

The drive back to Micellis' office building was a quiet one. Charga sat stoically and silent, just occasionally glancing over to his good looking, but rather confusing companion, mulling over the phone call which had precipitated their earlier rendezvous, and subsequent sexual interaction, and wondering what this afternoon had really been all about. She now appeared anxious and fidgety, a blank stare almost distorting her comely facial attractiveness.

Charga steered his Dynasty into the office building parking lot.

"We're here.", he said, "Where's your car?".

She pointed to a newer model silver Buick. "Right there.". Then she leaned over and planted a love tap kiss on his cheek. "Thank you Dukey.", she whispered, "I'll call you if I need you again.".

"Yeah, right.", Charga mumbled. The feeling of again having been used by a woman crept over him. "Just call me anytime, and we'll see.", he added as she threw open the passenger side door.

"Isn't it wonderful?", she gushed. Her face was once again bright and beautiful. "John really loves me!".

"Right. Wonderful!".

She almost leapt out of the car. "See you!" she exclaimed happily, "I'm going home!".

"Good.", Charga answered, "Go home. Good luck!".

Charga headed back to century City. He was feeling a bit light headed, a cumulative consequence of the two glasses of Barbarone wine he had drunk with his lasagna, followed by the two double shots of Anisette, plus a lack of some sound sleep, his recent nighttime, then afternoon, activities with the ladies, and the encounter in the fruit and vegetable store the previuos day which had landed him in the hospital. While Duke Charga had always prided himself in keeping his body and mind in a well maintained condition, this combination of events was taking its toll on his overall physical and mental state. Now, a pictoral collage of the past few days happenings were swirling furiously in his brain. It had been one individual incident followed by another, and yet, he sensed they were all somehow connected, commencing with the Saturday meeting in Marilyn Micellis' office, and the subsequent excursion to the racetrack, the early Sunday morning visit by Mike Dunne and Brad Street, his own visit with the horse trainer John Harborstone in Duarte general, the track audio visual room, Tony Taccio and the encounter at the vegetable market, his own short hospital stay, Sylvia Cortez, Adrianas' phone call, NSA agents at his apartment, topped off by the call from, and rendezvous with, the alluring Mrs. Micelli. Things had been moving so fast around him, he was finding it difficult to get a handle on what it all meant, and to where these events were leading. Although his appetite for food and sex had been satiated, still he felt dissatisfied emotionally, "maybe this is what the ladies feel when they think they've been used simply as a 'love toy'", he thought as he turned into his apartment parking lot. But no. He almost immediately reversed his thinking and opinion, and decided that was not the way for him to view this situation. "Sometimes it's a pleasure to be used once in a while.", he said to himself. It was an effort to rationalize his actions and ameliorate his innermost feelings. It worked. "I'll think more about that in the morning, right now I just need some rest.".

He simply planned to finally get himself a good nights sleep. It would be the first good night of real rest in three days!

Charga parked in his designated space and gave his Dynasty a loving pat as he noticed the three day film of dust which was now dulling its' new car ebony black shine finish.

"I need to get my baby washed!", he said aloud, "Tomorrow for sure!". He was talking to his vehicle like it was alive. "Good thing there's no one near me or they might think I'm a bit goofy!", he thought. He turned and began to lumber laboriously thru the parking lot area and around to the front of the apartment complex. The lasagna was laying just a bit too heavily on his stomach. Instead of giving him the extra energy he had sought, it was actually working in an opposite manner and slowing down his metabolism. He was feeling almost totally exhausted as he slid his door key into the lock. "Need to get some rest.", he thought again, "Sure will be good to lie down in my own bed.". He stepped inside, closed the front door behind him, and immediately threw off his suit jacket and removed his shoulder holster. He tossed both on the couch. Normally, the oversize weapon had felt a part of him, today it felt burdensome. It was the first time where the big Glock felt weighty on his frame. He quickly undressed down to his shorts, gave his face and upper body a fast wash over the bathroom sink, toweled off, and dropped face down onto his bed. In a moment he was fast asleep.

Chapter Six

Incident at the Mall

The Arcadia mall was alive with chaotic activity. Bright multi-colored store display and sale signs, many in green and gold hued neon, along with the flashing red and blue police vehicle roof mounted lights, and the whining sirens of other approaching law enforcement vehicles combined, creating an eerie symphony of foreboding sounds and colors. Uniformed officers, swat team and hazmat technicians in their respective blue, all black, and all white uniforms were rapidly moving to their assigned positions around and inside the mall. TV remote broadcast trucks, with twenty foot tall antenna and lighted newscasters added to the apparent semi-confusion. The southside of the Arcadia mall had already been cordoned off with police vehicles and the familiar yellow caution/ crime scene tape. Local police, FBI and NSA officials had earlier been deployed in the mall itself, and had blocked the shopping promenade midway in the heart of the mall interior.

Detective Paul Carson parked his unmarked Arcadia PD vehicle as close to the yellow crime scene tape as possible. His newest recently assigned partner Mel Gordon, with just under three years on the force, immediately opened the car door and was about to step out.

"Another eager beaver!", Carson thought. That was usually the case, the younger less experienced probies were almost always the most eager to get into some action.

"Just hold it, Mel!", Carson said, and he grabbed hold of Mel Gordons' left arm. "What's the time?".

The young officer Gordon checked his watch, then answered, "It's six thirty, mister Carson.".

"Okay, just stay in the car.", Carson ordered as he unhooked the microphone on the vehicle remote police band radio transmitter. He depressed the speaker button. "Unit seventeen. We're ten twenty at Arcadia mall at ten thirty six, eighteen thirty.".

The scratchy reply came back. "Ten four, seventeen.".

"You stay here, Mel.", Carson said, "I'm going to check on what's happening.".

"Yes sir!".

Gordon pulled the car door shut, and meekly sat back in his seat.

Carson actually took pleasure in knowing that he could easily intimidate this new partner with a simple change in vocal tone.

"I'll let you know if I need you.", he said, a smirk curling across his lips, "Just stay put for now.".

"Yes sir!".

Carson stepped out of the vehicle and walked up to the nearest uniformed policeman standing just beyond the crime scene tape.

He flashed his Arcadia PD badge.

"Who's in charge here?" he asked.

The officer pointed to a group of men standing near a black and white police cruiser. "Check with them.".

Carson looked in the direction the officer had pointed. Five men.

Three of the five wore plain street clothes, T shirts and blue denim jeans, with badges of different designs and shapes hanging around their necks, their silver and gold finishes glittering off and on in the glow of the blinking lights atop the nearby vehicle. Another wore a dark blue suit, and the other was in what appeared to be a regular police uniform, but with many gold stripes along its' sleeve and a big gold star on the cap. "Possibly a high ranking officer of some sort.", Carson thought. He quickly approached them, his PD badge held high in front of him.

"I'm Carson.", he announced, "Robbery, Arcadia.".

The group nodded acknowledgement almost in tandem. The suited gent smiled, flashing a set of oversize teeth. "NSA.", he said. He stood erect and spoke with confidence. Carson immediately understood. He was obviously the leader of the five.

The big toothed man continued. He pointed to the uniformed member of the group. "This is captain Drake, Arcadia mall security.".

Drake was an unusually big man, broad shouldered with a barrel chest. His face was weather-beaten and leathery, and the deep wrinkles crawling out from the corners of his steely blue eyes and thin lipped mouth gave evidence of decades of outdoor exposure. Wisps of gray hair were visible, peeking out from under his ornate cap. He offered his hand to shake. Carson backed off just a bit, then sneered. "A mall cop, eh?".

The big man did not respond, but simply pulled back his hand, removed his cap, revealing a full head of graying hair cut in military style. He handed the cap to one of the plain clothes officers. "Hold this please.", he said calmly, "Thank you.".

He then took one step forward, his right hand folded into a tight fist, his chest appeared to expand like that of a blow fish thrown onto a dry docked rowboat. "Twenty years marine, special ops.", he said, poking Carsons' chest with the index finger of his left hand. "And now, what was that you were saying?".

Carson stepped back. "Uh, nothin'.", he replied, "Nothin'.".

The big toothed man smiled a wry smile. "My name's Mitello.", he said. Then, holding Drake back with one hand, began pointing toward the three others in the group, and continued with his informal introductions. All three stood about six foot tall. One was Caucasian, clean shaven and neat, wearing a knit cap, the second sported a seven o'clock beard and long hair, and appeared to be of Hispanic heritage, while the third of the group was the most formidable looking, an African American, muscular, with a clean shaven head. "This guy with the skull cap is Jackson, FBI", Mitello went on, "This is Special agent Arroyo, federal secret service, and the black dude here is Lincoln from Tobacco and firearms.".

Carson nodded. Mitello continued, "Your own captain Dunbar has already deployed two swat teams and all available regular street cops from Arcadia.".

"Uh, okay.", Carson sputtered, "Hello fellas.". He was still feeling the hurt on his chest from Drakes' forceful finger poking. "Well, looks like the gang's all here.", Carson cracked, "So what's going on anyway? You all sure didn't come out just for a robbery.".

"Bomb in the mall.", Drake said, then added proudly, "We got a threat and so I called it in.".

"A bomb?".

"That's right.", agent Mitello answered, "My partner's in there now, checking it out. If it is a bomb for real, he'll defuse it.".

"So, you actually won't be needing me around here, right?", Carson asked. He was anxious to turn the whole affair over to the federal officers. "No need to get involved here.", he thought, "If the damn thing does go off, I want to be as far away from this place as possible.". Captain Drake took back his cap, positioned it atop his head at just the right angle, stepped forward and began speaking. His tone was imperious, almost threatening. "Well, now that you're here, you might want to help with the logistics and crowd control . . .".

Carson cut in abruptly, "That's okay!", he said, "My partner and I will just scoot on out of here. We're on robbery detail. We're not part of the bomb squad.".

"That figures!", Drake said in return. There was an obvious sarcastic tone to his words.

Carson stepped back two feet, made an about face and very quickly returned to his vehicle. He slid in behind the wheel, grabbed hold of the radio mike and called in. "Unit seventeen returning to base. Ten thirty six, eighteen forty. Ten four?".

"Ten four, seventeen.", came the reply.

"Let's get outta here, Mel.". Carson started the car and set the transmission in reverse. He stepped down hard on the accelerator.

"What's going on, mister Carson?", his young, newly assigned partner asked inquisitively.

"Tell you later.", Carson replied, "Right now I'm getting us away from this mall".

Drake had watched Carsons' obvious retreat. "Yellow!", he called out, "Punk!".

Agent Mitello held Drakes' arm. "Take it easy, bud!" he said, "Just let him go.".

The squealing sound of the car rear wheels pierced the night air as Carson steered his vehicle thru a rapid U-turn and out toward the main thoroughfare. Mel Gordon's eyes widened and he glanced over to his senior partner. "What?" was the only word he could squeeze out. Carson offered his explanation.

"There's a freakin' bomb in there somewhere, and I don't fancy getting my ass blown off for nothin'!". He pressed down hard on the accelerator and switched on the vehicle siren. "This'll clear the road!" he added, "We'll be outta any blast range in a minute!".

The murmur of the spectators who had gathered around just beyond the yellow police crime scene tape began to rise as four figures clad in astronaut like outfits emerged thru the Arcadia mall main entrance doors. They were the haz-mat team who had been first dispatched to the area. In their midst was an older gentleman in a plain blue suit, sporting a beard and a head of unruly graying hair.

"What's the story, Fredricks?" Mitello called out as the haz-mat team returned to their own vehicle, and the gray bearded man approached the group. "What's going on?".

NESST agent Fredricks shook his head and joined the five. He had completed a reconnaissance of the bombs' reported location.

"Nothing." he announced, "The whole thing was a ruse.".

"No bomb?" Agent Arroyo asked.

"Nope. Just a suspicious looking box at Friedmans jewelers.".

Mitello turned and gazed over the crowd which had gathered outside the crime scene tape line.

"They're probably out there." he said.

"Who's out there?" Lincoln asked as he spun his shiny dome around toward the crowd.

"I think it was a test." Mitello explained, "They were just checking our response times.".

Fredricks nodded. "We know who they are, or at least what they are."

"And what's that?".

Fredricks took a deep breath. "Terrorists." he said, "We have active terrorists right here in southern California.".

"You mean to tell me there's a terror cell here?" the big black man asked, "How come T and F never heard about that?".

"This is the first I've heard of it, too!" Arroyo interjected as he nervously rubbed the stubble on his cheek, "Keeping that news a secret?".

"We were coordinating the operation with them." Mitello answered, motioning to agent Jackson.

Jackson nodded and acknowledged the fact. "Yeah, we knew." He said, "We've known for a few weeks.".

"And so, what's being done about it?" Arroyo asked.

"We've got the situation in hand." Mitello assured, "Jackson here can fill you in on what we've done so far.".

"I'll give you all the details later." Jackson turned and looked at mall security captain Drake. "You really don't need to know this.".

Drake nodded affirmatively. "I got it." he said, and he began walking back toward the mall entrance.

"Well, I will tell you guys this," Jackson continued, "We've intercepted a message that the group we're concerned with is expecting some big shot to arrive in L.A. sometime this week.".

"And," Mitello added with a confident note, "We hope to round them all up before they can do any damage.".

"And just how are you guys going to do that?" agent Arroyo asked.

"We have our ways." Mitello answered, again in a confident tone, "We've already recovered half their explosives, and we're pretty confident we can get the rest before they can use it, and when we do, we'll pick them all up as well.".

"Is that a promise?".

"Well," Mitello replied, "Almost!".

Back in Century City, Duke Charga rolled over on his bed. He covered his head with one of the pillows in an effort to block out the sound that had awakened him. "What is that?" he thought, as the ringing sound continued. "I didn't set the alarm.".

Then, realizing it was his land line phone, he threw the pillow to the floor and hopped out of the bed. He checked his bedside clock.

It was 7 P.M. "Aww!" he said aloud, "Who could that be?".

He stumbled, half naked, and still only half awake, thru the hallway and into the kitchen. He lifted the phone receiver.

"Uhh, hello?".

"Hallo, Dukay.". The feminine purring intonation massaged Chargas' ears with a most recognizable European accent, and he instantly pictured the face that went along with the voice. The blemish free olive complexion, the long shiny black hair, and the sexy, and lush, ruby red lips.

"Adriana!" he shouted excitedly, "Are you here?".

"Oh, no sweetie." came the soft voiced reply, "I'm at Midway in Chicago."

"Oh, but you're on your way, right?" Charga asked enthusiastically.

He was anxiously looking forward to renewing their previous amorous, though relatively short, relationship. They had never slept together, still he had already considered the possibility that this gal could very well be the one permanent gal in his life.

"When will you be arriving in California?".

"Oh, my sweet one. I won't be in Los Angeles until eleven forty five tonight, that's California time." Her tone was as soft, melodious and mesmerizing as a slow waltz played by the Lester Lanin orchestra. Until this moment he hadn't realized just how much he really missed having her near.

"That's awful late." he blurted out, "But I'll come pick you up, okay?".

"Oh, no, Dukay, that will not be necessary. I have already made plans. A good friend of mine will be waiting for me at the airport."

"In one way, that's good." Charga murmured as he began rubbing the sleep from his half open and half awake eyes.

She heard. "Why do you say that's good?".

"Ooops!" Charga thought, "Maybe I shouldn't have said that, but what the hell, I might as well tell the truth, or at least most of the truth."

"Well, er, I" he stumbled over his words. "It's just that I haven't been getting much good sleep lately," he wouldn't say just why that was, but continued, "and I just laid down to get some rest a few minutes ago."

"It's okay, my sweet. I will see you tomorrow."

"But, where will you stay tonight? In a hotel?".

"Oh, no! My friend has a spare bedroom. I will be fine."

"Where exactly?".

"My friends' place is on Compton and sixth. I will call you from there tomorrow."

"Compton and sixth? Do you know where that is?" Charga asked.

He was concerned. Compton and sixth was not in what could be considered one of the better neighborhoods within the L.A. city limits. "That's little Lebanon." he went on, "There are lots of mean people around there."

"Oh, don't be silly. I'll be fine.".

"No. I mean it!" Charga replied, "That's where I was banged up by those damn crazy Muslims.".

"Oh, now Dukay. Be nice. Don't be calling people names just because you may not understand them.".

"But, it's true!" Charga insisted, "Even the local cops said those people are nutso! And . . ." He was cut off before he could continue.

"Oh! So sorry, Dukay, my plane is ready. I will call you in the morning, okay?".

"Well, er . . . sure Adriana. Call me as soon as you get up.".

"Okay, I will do that, my sweet." A short pause, then she almost sang her last words. "Bye" she whispered, "So until tomorrow, my sweet.".

"Yes." Charga answered, "Until tomorrow.". He held the phone to his ear until he heard the hangup click on the other end, then gently replaced it in its' cradle.

"How in hell am I going to sleep tonight?" he thought. "Maybe a beer would help.".

He opened his refrigerator and removed the one last, lonely bottle of Miller High Life, twisted off the cap, and took a long swig of the golden brew right from the bottle. One more long gulp and all twelve ounces were gone. He tossed the empty bottle into his trash container, and headed back to the bedroom.

"What a day!" he said aloud to himself as he rolled back onto the bed, "What a helluva day!".

Chapter Seven

Long Day Tuesday

Tuesday. Duke Charga rolled over in bed. A shaft of sunlight had sliced thru the bedroom window blinds, and was reflecting off the dresser mirror and splashing across his face, He opened his eyes just a bit, and blinked several times. He could still feel an occasional twinge of pain in his left bicep. That cut was healing, but not as quickly as he had hoped. He was uncertain whether it was the morning brightness or the hurting of his arm that had awakened him. "What time is it?", he thought as he slowly lifted his head off the pillow. Normally he would set his alarm for 7 A.M., but he was almost totally exhausted the night before, and hadn't touched the clock before retiring, nor had he checked what time it was when he had at last laid down and fallen asleep. He rubbed his eyes, and focused in on the clock sitting atop the bedside nightstand. 7:45! "Not too late.", he thought. He rose up and made his way to the bathroom, relieved himself of excess fluids, and immediately stepped into the shower. He showered cold, carefully twisting and turning his body so as not to soak the bandage on his arm. The tingling feel of the cold water reinvigorated his body and revitalized his mind.

"That was refreshing", he thought as he quickly toweled off. Then he wrapped the towel around his waist, ambled into the kitchen, and set up the Mister Coffee machine to make three cups.

"Think I just need a little extra boost today.", he said aloud and he poured in the water, set the filter in place, and spooned out the coffee. "Three cups should do it.".

Returning to the bedroom, he picked out a new set of underwear, shorts and top, a fresh light gray sateen shirt, and a pair of clean black socks. He scanned his suit closet and chose the gray striped gabardine. "Been told I look really good in this.". That thought brought a slight smug like smile to his lips. He dressed quickly, but left the suit jacket on its' hanger. He strapped on his shoulder holster, checked his Glock, and slid it snugly in its' place.

Over the years he had become so accustomed to wearing this oversized weapon, he felt almost semi-naked without it. "Ahhh.", he sighed. Now he was comfortable and ready to start another day. He pulled on his socks and slipped into his shoes. "Let's check the news." he said to himself, "Let's see just what's happening today.".

He returned to the kitchen, pausing just a moment in his living room to locate the TV remote and click on the local channel news. "There was a day," he thought, "not that long ago, when the morning paper delivered the news to your doorstep, but now, with all the local channels offering up a morning news program, and with twenty four hour news channels on TV, daily newspapers had become almost unnecessary, and in a way that's a shame.". The morning TV news was the main reason he had opted for weekend only newspaper delivery. Charga checked the coffee. It was made. He rinsed out one of the coffee cups which had been sitting in the sink, poured himself a cupful, sweetened it with two teaspoons of sugar, and took a sip. "Hmm. Black coffee.", he thought, "I'm starting to like it like this.".

He stepped into the living room and eased himself onto the couch facing the TV, being careful to not spill a drop of the almost full cup of hot coffee. The local news story revolved around the false alarm bomb scare at the North Arcadia mall. The video report included some quick shots of the bomb squad which had been called in. Charga took notice of the group of people reported to have been in charge of the investigation there. He immediately recognized the tall, bearded older gent. "Fredricks!" he said aloud, "I'd know that old coot anywhere!".

He finished his first cup of Java, placed the empty cup atop the living room coffee table, yawned widely and stretched his arms up and out, then pulled them back to flex his pectoral and back muscles. "Ahh. That felt good" he sighed. He stared intently at the TV. "Wonder who those other guys are." he thought as he grabbed his coffee cup, stood up and began ambling back into the kitchen to refill it. The TV news voice over answered his mental question. "Officers from the NSA, FBI, tobacco and firearms division joined with local law enforcement and mall security personnel in the investigation of this incident".

"Seems like they're pulling out all the stops" he said aloud as he poured himself a second cup of black coffee. "Well, Fredricks did say they were determined to get whoever these characters are." Just as he started back into the living room his land line phone began ringing. "Adriana!" he blurted out and he stopped in his tracks and eagerly lifted the receiver. "Hello my honey" he half whispered, "I was waiting for your call."

"Well, hello sweetheart," the gruff voice of Big Mike Dunne was unmistakable. "Sooo good to hear you too" he continued facetiously, "Are you dressed?" he asked with a chuckle, "I'd love to see you."

"Okay Mike." Charga replied, "What is it you want at this time in the morning?"

"Turn on your TV" Dunne answered, now in a serious tone. "The news on channel four".

"I'm watching it now Mike. About the mall?" "Right." Dunne went on, "The bomb story." "So?"

"Something's going on in this burg Duke."

"I know" Charga said in response. He took a sip of his coffee, then continued, "I know all about it."

"Really? What do you mean by that Duke? They reported it was likely just a crank call."

"Is that right?" Charga questioned. He knew better. If Fredricks and Mitello were on the scene, along with FBI, and Tobacco and Firearms agents, well then, it was certainly not being considered or handled as a simple crank call.

"That's what they said on TV. Did you hear that?"

"No. I just turned the TV on a minute ago."

"Well, remember Carson? He was there last night," Dunne paused, then continued more slowly and distinctly, exaggerating his verbal enunciation of each word, "He said the Feds were all over the place. All kinds of feds and . . ."

Charga broke in. "Yeah. I just heard that, Mike, and?"

"Well, the news kinda just dismissed it, but I'm not buying the bluff. I've been doing what I do for quite some time, you know?"

"Yeah, Mike, I know"

"Well then Duke my boy, let me tell you" Dunne went on, "Something's up, something important." His tone now seemed fraught with a certain level of apprehension, very uncommon for Big Mike Dunne, the grizzled tough police veteran. "Two NSA men were here this morning. They pulled our Harborstone report and the related incident reports, then met with Dunbar in his office. A few minutes later Dunbar issued a notice, nobody goes on leave this week."

"Figures" Charga half mumbled, and he took another long swig of coffee. "Did he say why?"

"Something to do with the Feds, but he didn't say what."

"Mike, the two NSA guys, did they say their names?"

"No. They just stood in the background."

"One guy with big teeth, the other, older, gray haired, wearing bifocals?"

"That's them alright. But how did you know that?"

"They visited me yesterday. They're tracking a terror cell. Those goons in the vegetable store were part of it."

"Yeah! I figured it was some kind of a federal deal when Brad and I were ordered to back off the Harborstone case."

"Right Mike, There's definitely some kind of connection with Harborstones smack down, but I can't figure what it is."

"It's all those Arabs working down in the stables at the track."

"What do you mean Mike? There's nothing but Mexicans and Latinos down there."

"Ahh. See? You don't know squat! They just look like Latinos, but there's a bunch of towel heads working there now, especially at the stable where Harborstone worked."

"I didn't know that."

"At least half of that crew seems to be Arabic! That guy Zella can't even talk to one of 'em, had Basara, that dude who's now on a slab down at the morgue, had him interpreting instructions. You do know that one of the owners of that stable is a sheik, right?"

"Well, no, I didn't know that either . . ."

"Well, Duke my boy, maybe you don't know what you've gotten yourself into. I did tell you to stay out of the Harborstone case didn't I?"

Charga finished off his second cup of coffee, took a deep breath, then answered. "That you did Mike, that you did."

He knew Mike Dunne was right. Had he just kept his nose out of the whole affair, he wouldn't have tracked down Taccio and wouldn't have ended up in Compton general. Then again, he thought, maybe he wouldn't have hooked up with Slyvia Cortez either.

Charga was never one who believed in circumstance. "Things happen because they're supposed to happen" he thought, "There's a reason for everything".

"Okay Duke, I just thought you might want to know what's going on down here. Figured I'd clue you in, and" . . . Dunne paused momentarily, then continued in a more somber tone, "advise you once again to step back. Let the feds take it from here."

"That's what they told me too, when they were here."

Dunne recognized the defiant tone. "Not gonna do that are you?" he asked. He knew what Chargas answer would be, he knew Charga.

"Got to go Mike" Charga answered, "My cellular phone is 'ringing'.

"Maybe that's your honey" Dunne remarked sarcastically, then added "I'll talk to you later. Bye lover boy.". He almost slammed the phone onto the receiver, and pushed the phone across his desk.

He looked over to his partner. "That's my hard headed ex partner alright! You just can't talk to him! Just won't butt out! Plus he's got women calling him every day, every night and even early in the morning!"

Brad Street smirked, and shook his head slowly. "You're just jealous." he said "But you still love him like a brother! I know it, and . . ." he pointed at Big Mike Dunnes barrel chest "you know it too."

"Yeah" Dunne had to admit it. The bond of friendship which had built up over the years between himself and Marion Duke Charga was as strong as ever. "Yeah. I guess you're right Brad, but sometimes I worry about him. He just won't learn!"

Charga quickly set the phone receiver back in its' cradle, placed the empty cup in the sink, and hurried into the bedroom where he had left his cellular phone overnight in its' charger. He got to it on the fourth ring just before his voice mail message would have kicked in. "This has to be Adriana now" he thought, "She must have tried the other line, found it busy, then dialed my cell, but I wonder how she got this number?"

He hit the talk button.

"Hello honey" he said, "How did you get this number?"

"What? You gave it to me." The voice on the other end was feminine alright, but it was not the voice of Adriana Messina.

"Oh, that's right. Hello Sylvia."

"Well, that's a hell of a way to answer the phone." There was a tinge of estrogenic jealously in Sylvia Cortez's tone, "And just who is your honey?" she asked coldly.

"I knew it was you". Charga lied. "I've got the new caller ID feature on this phone". It was true. He did have that feature on his cellular phone service, but in his anxious impatience to answer hadn't noticed the number which had flashed on the phone display screen. "I just forgot that you had this number. You're up early, what's going on?"

"I had to call you" Sylvia replied, then continued rather haltingly, "There's, uh, something I, er, I must tell you."

"Okay." Charga said, "I imagine it must be important or you wouldn't be calling at five minutes to eight in the morning. What is it?"

"It's about you and me."

"Go on."

"Well, you know I was seriously contemplating running for district attorney, right?"

"Yeah Sylvia, I know."

"So there's good news and bad news." she paused for a few seconds, then went on "Good news is I've already gotten the Conservative endorsement and it's almost a certainty I'll get the nomination from the Republicans so I'll be a candidate on both lines and . . ."

Charga broke in. "That's great!" He was genuinely pleased to hear that news. "So congratulations are in order."

"You may not think it's so great in a moment."

Chargas' curiosity was piqued. "Go ahead. So what's the bad news?" he asked.

"Well, you know as an official candidate the liberals will undertake an extensive investigation into my background, my career . . ."

"Yeah, so?"

"Remember the deal I brokered with that felon you slapped around?"

"I remember."

"Well, I proffered that deal and the D. A. signed off on it. Not unusual. The D.A. makes deals every day with criminals and felons, and that was just another one of them. No one would bring it up since it did result in a major case conviction."

"Yeah, so? I'm listening. You said this is about you and me, so?"

"Okay. Let me explain. If we are seen together, the opposition could then link that deal with your escaping criminal charges and they could then use that against me. They would bring up the possibility that I did what I did for personal reasons. That could be viewed negatively by the public at large. It could be considered an abuse of my office. It could cost me the election and . . ." There was a momentary pause. Charga heard Sylvia take in a deep breath, then let out a long sigh. He sensed Sylvia Cortez was on the verge of an 'I really like you., but' comment. He was right. "Well Duke" she continued, "It's just that we just shouldn't see each other. Not for a while, at least not until after November sixth, understand?"

"That'll be tough" Charga replied, "Really tough after Sunday night. Didn't that mean something to you? A little something?"

"Really Duke" she answered almost totally unemotionally, "I needed someone that night, and I'm glad that someone was you, but this involves my future, you know?"

"She needed someone?" Charga thought. "Does that mean she may have slept with almost anyone that night?"

"And I'm also glad that someone was me Sylvia" he said in return, "but still, that's not a very ego building comment, don't you think?" The disappointment in his tone was obvious. She immediately recognized that she had inadvertently wounded his sense of masculinity and sex appeal, and so, deftly ignored the comment and changed the subject. "More good news is that when or if I do get to be district attorney, well then I'll elevate Mike Petrone to lead A.D.A. That should please you, right? You two have been friends for some time, yes?"

"Sure" Charga answered. He was certainly glad for his old friend but remained a bit downhearted about Sylvia Cortez' last comment.

"Yeah. That would be good for him. He deserves it I guess. He's a good man."

"You do understand the situation, don't you?"

"Sure Sylvia" he answered, "I understand, good luck."

"Thanks Dukey, well then, goodbye."

"Later" Charga said. He hit the call end button and set the cell phone back in its' charger. "Women!" he said aloud, "You just really can't trust them!" He strapped on his wrist watch. "After eight now" he thought, "Adriana should be calling soon." Then as an afterthought "Now she's really hot, and I really like her an awful lot, but I wonder what's in store for us?" He laughed to himself. "Whatever" he thought, "One never knows!"

He returned to the kitchen. There was another half cup of coffee being kept warm in the glass carafe on the coffee maker. "Guess I'll finish this" he thought. He emptied the carafe into his cup, hit the off button on the Mister Coffee machine, then went in and sat himself down on the living room sofa. The news had ended and a nonsensical game show of some kind was now on. He stared at the TV but his mind remained on Sylvia's call. "It was just a simple brush "off" he thought. It was apparent Sylvia's career was her number one priority. "Guess I can't blame her for that" he philosophized to himself, "Everyone has their own mission in life. Difficulty is in discovering what that mission may be." He leaned back and relaxed. Someone had just won a bedroom set. "Good for her!" he said aloud, "Good for her!"

Adriana Messina was seated on a cushioned bench at the boudoir dresser contemplating her reflection in the lighted dresser mirror.

"Forty eight, forty nine, fifty." She had counted each brush stroke and had completed her morning ritual of brushing her shoulder length silky black hair. Now she gently and carefully laid the hair brush on the dresser top in its proper position alongside the comb and hand mirror which made up the set.

"Okay Sabani" she called out, "I'm done. Thanks for the use of your comb and brush."

"I knew you were finished" came the response from the adjoining room. "You said you were going to brush your hair fifty times and I heard you rattling off the numbers." Sabani Kattar and Adriana Messina had been school mates when they attended Southern California University at Long Beach as foreign exchange students some years back. Although completely dissimilar in appearance, Adriana being a stately, shapely, very good looking young lady, while Sabani was a small girl, just five foot two in height, weighing no more than one hundred and five pounds soaking wet. Still, a strong bond of camaraderie had grown between the two when they found they shared not only classroom study programs, but a similar outlook on life in general. They had kept in close contact ever since, even though Adriana had decided to go on and continue her education in Europe while Sabani had opted to remain in the United States to pursue a working career in or around the Los Angeles area. Born in Libya, Sabani was brown skinned, with dark brown eyes and semi curly black hair which she always kept cut short. Being a Muslim she naturally migrated to this section of the city where, with the help of an outreach neighborhood Islamic council, she eventually secured employment at a local tax assistance office and settled into this neat two bedroom apartment at the southern edge of the area known as Little Lebanon. Since moving into this district Sabani Kattar had become immersed in the Islamic way of life and was now following a more fundamentalist Muslim female lifestyle.

She was dressing in the adjoining bedroom.

Adriana, looking closely in the dresser mirror, took notice of the beginnings of a facial pimple which had sprung up on her forehead just below her hairline. "Damn!" she muttered, then called out, "Sabani, could you come here a moment? I want to ask you something."

Almost immediately Sabani pushed aside the colorful beaded strings acting as a room divider between the two bedrooms, in place of a door, and joined Adriana in the master bedroom. Sabani was dressed in traditional Arabic attire, a dark robe that almost totally covered her body from neck to ankles, and a dark head scarf which covered not only her hair, but most of her forehead as well, and was tied tightly under her chin. Adrian saw her friends' reflection in the mirror. "You wear a Chador everyday now don't you?*She asked.

"Never mind that." Sabani answered. She had become used to similar questions concerning her choice of dress and was not at all bothered or upset when such questions came her way. "It's my heritage" she said, then asked "What is it Adri? What do you want to show me?"

Adriana slid to the side just a bit, then patted the space she had made on the bench. "Come sit beside me." she said, then pointing to that newly discovered blemish asked "Does this look very bad?"

Little Sabani sat next to her, looked at her face, and chuckled. "No Adri." she answered with a half smile, "It's not even noticeable, unless you're looking for it."

"That's good. I guess I'll just apply a little extra makeup on that spot."

"It wouldn't be noticeable at all if you would dress like a woman should."

Adriana laughed. "I could never dress like you." she said shaking her head to loosely fluff up her hair. "I could never blend in to the American lifestyle if I dressed like you."

"Like I said before," Sabani answered, "It's my heritage and I know my place"

"Well, sure. It's okay if you stick in this neighborhood, but if you want to move around in America, and not stand out like a sore thumb, it's totally NG!".

"But I'm not interested in moving around like you. I'm satisfied right here",

"Well, good for you Sabani, but I've got other plans, you know, that."

"Yes, I know." Sabani replied. She sniffed the air. The aroma of some kind of sweet meat wafted thru the room. "I'm already preparing our dinner, can you smell it?"

"Yes, smells really good too."

Sabani stood up, "Come into the kitchen" she said as she took Adrianas hand, and both started towards the hallway leading to the front of the apartment. "I'm making kofta kari. I'll put it in the fridge and we'll heat it up after my evening prayer."

"That's ground beef meatballs right?"

"You remember?"

"I remember." Adriana replied, "You made this a few times back at Long Beach. I'll be sure to be back for dinner tonight."

"You're meeting with that same young man you dated before?"

"Yes. But I plan to just have lunch with him, and find out just what he's up to. You know, he's not an official policeman anymore. Just a private detective now" she paused, then added "He should be easier to manipulate now than he was before when he was a real cop!"

"Be careful!" Sabani cautioned. They hugged for a brief moment, then Adriana Messina pulled away. "I've got to call him now." She said, "But I'll be back tonight. I don't want to miss out on that home cooking." She paused and smiled. "It smells just like one of grandmas meals."

"Be careful." Sabani repeated, "Just be very careful."

Duke Charga had settled in on the living room couch, comfortably watching the channel four morning programming schedule, and somewhat to his surprise, found himself actually enjoying the colorful inanities and exuberance of the game show contestants and the reaction of the audience members, both of whose main interest in life, or so it seemed, was to walk off with a new stove or microwave as a prize, or to see someone else do the same. They seemed totally impercipient of the goings on in the city, country or world, and it appeared if they did have a scant clue of the happenings beyond the scope of the game show, they couldn't care less about it.

"Must be nice in a way" he thought, "to be so innocent and naive." He chuckled lightly and took a final sip of his now almost room temperature coffee. Just as he set the coffee cup on the end table next to him, his land line phone began ringing once again. He popped up off the couch like a Mexican jumping bean on a hot plate. "Now that has to be Adriana" he said aloud as he trotted back into the kitchen and picked up the receiver. "Hello!"

"Oh hello Dukay". Finally it was whom he had expected. "Adriana."

"Yes, si. It is me." came the reply. The softly accented voice was almost musical in its cadence. "I'm here in Los Angeles at my friends home and I'm well rested, so how shall we meet? I'm really anxious to see you once again."

"And me you" Charga said. Notwithstanding all his many exploits and sexual encounters with other ladies, he still found himself yearning for Adriana's company. Was this because they had never slept together, he wondered. They had come very close several times but had never intimately consummated their affair. Would this desire dissipate once the testosterone powered urge was satiated? He didn't believe so, but for several reasons beyond the obvious, was anxious to find out.

"Adriana, do you have a car, or do you want me to pick you up somewhere?"

"No, I've got no auto" she replied, "but just tell me where you are and I'll find you okay."

That seemed a bit strange to him. If she had no car why wouldn't she want him to come pick her up?

"Will you be taking a taxi then?" he asked.

"Well, I could do that, or I can get a ride from my friend. Don't worry. Just tell me where you want to meet."

"Oh, okay." Charga agreed reluctantly, "How about we have lunch at that Italian place where we went before. Garlattis. Remember?"

"Oh my sweet," she purred back, "Of course I remember, and I remember where it is too. I think of it as our own special place."

"She sure does know how to make a man feel good" he thought.

"That's great." he said, and he began to feel a warming sensation building in his loins. Just the thought of being close to her was physically arousing. He peered down at his watch. Eight minutes past ten. Had he been watching those semi mindless game shows this long? "Must have" he thought. "Okay Adriana" he said, "It's a bit past ten now, how about we meet at eleven? Can you make it there by then?'

"Oh sure. That's perfect, my sweet."

"Okay, good, can't wait!" Charga went on rather excitedly, "Love to see you again, It's really been a while since I held you close, er, ah, yeah, good!"

He immediately recognized how desperate and discombobulated he sounded, but at that moment was powerless to contain or conceal his so very obvious prurient excitation. It was uncommon for him to react in this manner and she quickly picked up on that fact.

"Yes Dukay, that will be perfect." she repeated in response. She paused momentarily, then added softly, "I'm excited to see you again too. I've missed you"

Charga took a deep breath, and a few seconds to re-compose himself. "And I missed you too" he said, "More than I realized" he thought, "Much more."

"I know" she whispered, "I can tell in your voice. See you soon my sweet."

"Right." he said, his speech pattern and tone now back to normal, "We'll meet at Garlattis, okay."

"Okay, bye for now sweet."

It took just moments for Charga to slip into his suit jacket, and hop on out to the residents rear parking area.

"My baby sure needs a cleaning" he thought as he approached the sleek lined Dynasty which was now covered with a combination of street dirt, racetrack dust, and the normal everyday film of Los Angeles area smog soot. "Got to stop and run her thru a car wash".

He quickly unlocked the door and slid in behind the wheel.

Considering a fifteen minute stop off at the Century City automatic car wash, Charga determined it would take about forty five minutes total to get down to Anaheim, still plenty of time to be at Garlattis by eleven. "Have to take care of my baby" he thought, and so he headed straight down Century boulevard to the two dollar quick wash drive thru, ran his baby thru, then took the freeway and was at Garlattis by ten fifty eight.

Angelo Garlatti was just unlocking the resturant front door as Charga drove his now shiny, clean black beauty into the lot.

"Buono journo" the portly resturantuer called out as Charga exited his vehicle. "Como sta? You're here early today, no?"

"Hello Angelo" Charga replied, "Here for lunch today."

"Alone?"

"Nope. I'm meeting someone."

"Business or pleasure?"

"Strictly pleasure, Ange. With Adriana. Remember her?"

"Oh ma sho" Angelo Garlatti replied, "I no forget, una otra bella donna" he pointed to the local red and white taxi which had just pulled into the lot. "Looka, Shesa here"

The rear taxi door opened and Adriana Messina stepped out, slowly, gracefully, dressed in a light green blouse, above the knee length black sateen skirt, three inch heels, and carrying a small green leather purse, she was as lovely as a living Venus de Milo.

Her golden complexion was perfectly framed by the silky smooth jet black hair that seemed to shine in the southern California sunlight, her dark brown eyes meticulously lined with a green hued mascara, and her plush red lips more sensuous than Charga remembered.

"She's as beautiful as ever." Charga thought, "Maybe even more so." She hovered for a moment just beside the drivers door, then leaned in, causing the black skirt to pull up just a bit, exposing an extra few inches of skin, and pulling it taught against her upper thigh and buttocks. She then turned slowly, and began walking towards the restaurant front door where Charga and Angelo Garlatti were standing. The taxi pulled out and drove away. Both Duke Charga and Angelo Garlattis eyes were focused on her swinging chassis as she approached.

"Hallo" she said with a smile, "I'm here!"

Angelo Garlatti was first to return the greeting. "Buono journo".

Charga stepped forward with open arms. "Welcome back, Adriana." he said as they embraced and Adriana planted a soft kiss on his cheek. "Hallo Dukay" she whispered in his ear, "I'm so happy to be with you again."

Charga held her close. He could feel the firmness of her breasts pressing against his chest, and the contact of their lower bodies stimulated a momentary sexual arousal. "Come. Let's go. We've got a lot to catch up on."

Angelo Garlatti held the door open and they strolled into Garlattis restaurant. "You our firsta customers today." he said, "Go ahead, you picka your table."

"Right here by the window" Charga pointed to a nearby table. "It's the best seat in the house" he added with a wink. It was the table where he had sat with Adriana on their very first official date.

She smiled. "I know why" she said, "I remember."

"You want a menu?" Angelo Garlatti asked.

"What's the lunch special, Ange?" Charga answered the question with one of his own.

Angelo looked at Adriana. "Tu es una Siciliano, no?"

"Si" she smiled. "Yes. But we're in America now. We should speak Anglais, no?"

"Okay" Angelo replied, "So for you I'm a make a special pizza. I'm a make a Piazzi pizza."

"A what?" Charga queried, "Never heard of it. Something new?"

"It's a special with black olives, sauseega, and extra fromage. It's named after Giuseppe Piazzi."

"And who's that?" Adriana asked, "Who's Giuseppe Piazzi?"

Angelo Garlatti stepped back, his hands held up in the gesture of surrender. "Momma mia!" he said, "Tu es una Siciliano and you don't know Giuseppe Piazzi?"

"I don't think so." Adriana answered, slowly shaking her head in a negative motion.

"I never heard that name before either." Charga chimed in.

Now it was the portly restaurant owner and waiter who shook his head. "Momma mia!" he said again. "Giuseppe piazzi is only the most a famous astronomer in Siciliano history!"

"Really?" Charga said, "Famous for what?" he asked.

"Giuseppe Piazzi?" Angelo pointed to the ceiling. "He discover the little drawf a planet a called Ceres. That's a way back in January first a in eighteen oh one." He turned to Adriana who was sitting quietly and just staring down at the folded napkin and food utensils which were laid out on the table. "Ima surprise," he continued, "All Sicilianos know about a Piazzi. That's a learn in the fifth a grade."

"Uh, er, oh I guess I just forgot." Adriana Messina smiled apologetically, paused for a few seconds, then added, "But I think that's a good idea. I could go for a few slices of a good Sicilian pizza, and how about we have some wine to go with it?"

"Buono!" Garlatti, replied, "I bring a the best Barbarone okay?"

"Perfect." Charga answered, "And bring a whole carafe." He tapped the table top, "Right here."

"Okay, just a one minuto" Angelo Garlatti turned and quickly walked to the rear of the restaurant and thru the swinging doors leading to the kitchen area.

"He's a great character" Charga said as he nodded towards the kitchen doors, "We've become pretty good friends."

"I like him too" Adriana replied as she clasped her hands in front of her face, resting her elbows on the edge of the table, "But now you must tell me what you've been up to since you left the police. And lately, what's going on with you in your life?"

Charga began recounting his past private investigation cases.

Adriana listened intently, nodding acknowledgement in the appropriate places. "So interesting" she said, "So you've been pretty busy, no?'

"One could say that." Charga answered. He spied Angelo approaching with a tray holding a carafe of dark red wine and two oversized wine glasses. "Here's the wine" he said.

Angelo placed the two glasses on the table, filled them both, and set the now half empty carafe in the center of the table. "I bringa you the big a glasses, okay?" he asked.

"Sure, fine." Charga sipped the Barbarone, "And the wine is fine as usual."

"That's a nice" Angelo said as he looked toward Chargas' beauteous companion. Adriana hadn't touched her glass. "What's a matter?" he asked, "You no like Barbarone? Maybe you want Chianti?"

"Oh no" she answered, "It's just that, well, could you put an ice cube in it to make it cool?"

"An ice a cube?"

"Yes, thank you." she smiled, "I like it a bit cool."

"Okay, an ice a cube" Angelo garlatti turned, began walking back toward the kitchen. He slapped his forehead, and mumbled to himself. "Ma, gisto yenna bazza. Cold a vino, just a bazza."

Angelo disappeared momentarily into the kitchen but re-emerged quickly and walked to the restaurant front door where he took up the position of greeter and host in anticipation of the expected lunch special crowd. Momma Garlattis restaurant was locally famous for its' $3.99 meatball hero lunch special served from 11:30 A.M. to 1 P.M. every weekday. They normally served from 50 to 100 of these special lunches within that time frame and this day was no different. The restaurant began to fill very quickly. It was Mike Garlatti who returned to Chargas' table with a glass full of ice cubes. Mike was the Garlatti senior son who normally worked as the chef in the family restaurant and rarely ventured out into the restaurant dining area to take orders or wait tables. He loved to cook and his 350 pound rotund body was conspicuous evidence that he also loved to eat. The once white linen apron he had tied around his barrel shaped belly was stained with spots of dried tomato sauce, and his hands were whitened with traces of flour. He wore as dopey a smile as a 6 month baby whose mommy was playing peek a boo with a hanky. He set the glass of cubes on the table next to the wine carafe without ever taking his widened eyes off Adrianas' face and bodice. She sat stoically, listening intently to Chargas' verbal rendition of the happenings of the past few days and paid no attention at all to the elder Garlattis ogling stare. Charga interrupted his soliloquy, nodded toward the overweight elder Garlatti. "That's Mike" he said, "He normally stays in back."

Adriana didn't speak, she merely glanced over, smiled, and nodded slightly, then turned back to face Charga. "Thanks Mike," Charga said, "That's all we need now."

"Oh, sure, okay" the big bellied chef turned waiter spun around and lumbered back to the restaurant kitchen. He turned back for one last, long look before pushing thru the swinging doors. The goofy smile on his face had diminished not one bit. "I think he only came out to get a gander at you" Charga whispered with a smile, "Angelo must have told him about you."

"What do you mean by that?"

"Ah, come on Adriana" Charga continued, "Take a look around. You're the most beautiful woman in the place." he motioned to the other tables and booths, then added, "Probably the most beautiful woman whose ever been in this place."

Adriana didn't respond, except to smile slightly, then she turned and scanned the restaurant. Several senior aged couples were seated at the other booths, also a group of college age boys at a table, and one lone forty something man had just taken a seat at a table directly across from their booth. Dressed in a blue suit, white shirt, and wearing a bright red tie, this man stood out from the rest of the restaurant patrons who were mostly wearing sport shirts and casual clothes. She noticed he was staring at Charga and her, and when her eyes met his he immediately looked down and picked up the menu that Angelo Garlatti had placed on his table.

"They do get a lot of business in here," she said, "like always, no?"
Charga nodded. "It's the food." he answered, "They have a great rep."
He stretched his arm across the table and took Adrianas' hand in his.
"It's really good to be with you, Adriana." he said softly.
"Yes Dukay" she whispered back and she gently squeezed his hand.
"Same here."
In a few minutes Angelo Garlatti arrived with the specialty pizza.
He moved the wine carafe to the rear of the table, set the pizza
directly in the center, and placed a small plate in front of each of
them. "Mange." he said, "Enjoy."
"Thanks Ange." Charga replied and he began selecting a slice for
Adriana, "How's this for you?" he asked, "Too big?".
"Oh no." she replied, "It's fine."
He set the first slice of pizza on her plate, then pulled off a slice for
himself and took a bite. "This is really good, right?" he said, his
mouth still half full, "What do you think?"
Adriana nodded. This special Piazzi pizza was really tasty and it was
just moments later when there remained only one lonely slice on
the metal pizza tray. Between bites Charga had been describing the
incident at the vegetable store. He pointed to his left bicep. "So that's
how I got this cut and ended up in the hospital for a few hours."
"That's just awful. Are you still hurting?"
"Nah! I'm still not one hundred percent, but now that I'm feeling
better I'm definitely gonna follow up on it." He paused, wiped
his mouth with the napkin, then continued, "I'm not telling you
everything, but let's say I know for sure the whole deal is connected
to John Harborstone and I'm gonna take a good look at what's going
on up at that racetrack."
"Oh no." she said pleadingly, "Don't go there. It could be dangerous.
You should let the police look into it."
"It won't be, bad" Charga replied, "I'm actually planning to nosey
around up there this afternoon."
"Wouldn't you rather spend the day with me?" she whispered back,
"After all we haven't been together for such a long time."
"You can come with me if you like. It shouldn't take long."
"No, I don't think I'd want to do that."

215

"That's okay" Charga took her hand again, "I'll be back and spend tonight with you, but I've got to take a look around and ask some questions. I want that Bin Haseed character for myself!"

She shook her head slowly. "I really wish you wouldn't do that." she said, cocking her head to one side and fluttering her eye lashes.

The moves were meant to influence his decision. They didn't work.

"I have to, Adriana. It's just something I have to do. Sorry, but that's just me.". He signaled for the check and in just moments Angelo came and placed it on the table. "There you go mister Charga.".

Charga took out his wallet. "Oopps!" he said, "I've only got hundreds. Can you break one, Ange?"

"We could, but it would take all our small bills. It's early you know, and you're the firsta customer today."

"That's okay Dukay" Adriana broke in, "I left the house today with four twenties, so here" she opened her green leather purse and removed a small bundle of bills. "Here's a twenty" she said. "Keep the change."

"Is this okay with you, Adriana?" Charga asked.

He was uncomfortable having a woman pay for a meal. "Will you be okay?"

Adriana waved him off. "Oh sure." she replied "I've still got sixty dollars left, see?" She held three additional twenties in her hand and added, "Plenty to go shopping with. You can just drop me off at the mall, I wanted to do some shopping anyway."

"Well, okay." Charga answered, still a bit ill at ease with the situation, "But how will we get together later?"

"I could call you." Adriana smiled sweetly, "Don't worry, it's okay."

"Right." Charga said, "I'll give you my cell phone number."

He removed a P.I. card from his wallet, and wrote his personal cell number on the back.tv Here, call me at this number anytime."

"So you are going to the racetrack, aren't you?"

"Like I said Adriana, I have to."

Angelo Garlatti took the restaurant food check and the twenty dollar bill. "Prego" he said, and he turned and headed back to the kitchen.

Charga and Adriana slid out of the booth and strolled out to Chargas' Dynasty. Neither noticed the man in the blue suit whispering into his suit jacket lapel.

The Arcadia police detective squad room was buzzing with activity. A group of detectives had gathered around the duty roster whiteboard where 'All leaves cancelled' and 'Personnel meeting 10 AM Tues' had been scrawled in bold three inch letters with red marker ink. Other detectives from the assault, bunco, robbery, and homicide division were milling at or around their respective desks.

About fifty uniformed officers had gathered in the adjacent large police shape up room. Captain Dunbar opened his office door and peeked out.

"Dunne, Street, in here!" he called. He made a 'come here' motion with his index finger, "Now!".

Dunne and Street, who had been seated at their desk, snapped up and speed walked into the office.

"Yeah, Cap. What is it?" Dunne asked.

"Close the door, Mike." Dunne replied, then ordered, "Take a seat, both of you.".

He removed a head shot photo from a stack of photos on his desk.

"Two things." he said, "First, the feds have positively identified those two stiffs from that vegetable store.".

"Well, about time!" Street cut in, "And so?".

Dunbar ignored the sarcastic tone, and went on. "Both were from Yemen . . .".

"Yemen? Where the hell, or what the hell, is that?" Street questioned.

"Little country in the middle east. Near Iraq I think." Dunbar answered. "And now will you just button it and let me talk?".

Street tightened his thin lips and nodded. "Okay, okay.".

"Okay now, just listen." Dunbar went on. "The one who ole Charga took out was a known militant connected with that Abba Ali mosque down on eighth street. You know, the one with that trouble maker leader who keeps on bad mouthing the U.S.". He pointed at Big Mike Dunne and continued. "The one you popped Mike, was the nephew of a big shot sheik, the sheik who's got money in the BCH stable down at the track."

Captain Dunbar passed the photo he had been holding to Mike Dunne. "Here." he said, "Take a gander at this.".

"Is this his picture?" Dunne asked as he examined the photo, then showed it to his partner.

"Mean looking dude." Street remarked. "Needs a shave.".

"You want this back, cap?" Dunne asked.

"No and no" Dunbar replied. "No, that's not his picture, and no I don't want it back. Keep it. Actually that's an FBI photo of Ach Bin Haseed, the third man that Charga told you about. That's right, he's real, but now he's gone underground and they've lost track of him. He's been under surveillance by the feds for some time, and . . ." he paused to emphasize his words, "they want him bad!".

He placed his hand on the stack of photos sitting on his desk.

"Feds have issued a county wide alert. They want to find him ASAP!". He patted the stack of photos. "These will be distributed to all detectives and uniforms in the L.A. county systems." He paused again, then limply sat himself down in the big leather chair behind his desk. He pointed at Mike Dunne again. "Since you're the senior detective here, I'm assigning you as liaison and coordinator between the feds and our own squad.".

"What's going on, cap?" Dunne asked. "First we're told to stand down, and now the feds want us to go full bore. Why?".

"Can't rightly say. All I've been told is that the feds want this guy really bad, and they want the local PD's to help get him."

"Okay." Dunne shrugged, "Whatever!".

"Now listen Mike," Dunbar went on, "First thing now is, you have to get on down to the fed building on Wilshire. Go upstairs, fourth floor. They've got the owner of that vegetable store down there now in their interrogation room. You should talk to them and see just what they want us to do beside dragging our precinct streets for this Haseed guy. Talk to them. I'll call 'em and tell 'em you're on your way, meanwhile I'll hand these out to our detectives and uniforms. We've got to try and find this guy and then I guess we'll find out exactly what he's up to. Get it?".

"Got it cap." Dunne answered as he stepped up out of his seat and motioned to his partner. "Let's go Brad. I guess we've got some kind of important work to do.".

In a matter of moments the two detectives were in their vehicle and southbound on the 605 freeway. They exited on Whittier boulevard and drove west. Whittier becomes Wilshire just past the 10 freeway, It was just another half mile and they arrived at their destination.

The entire trip took less than thirty minutes. The federal offices here were housed in a 1960's non descript building with a very small sign in front reading 'Federal Building L.A.'. They parked in back and entered thru a small rear door marked 'Personnel Only'.

Before they had gone ten feet, a six foot, well muscled uniformed security guard, sporting a close cropped military style haircut, and cradling an automatic rifle in his arms stopped them.

"Just hold it there gentlemen.". He stood straight and rigid, blocking the hallway.

Dunne exposed his PD shield. "We're police." he said.

"That's fine." came the curt reply. "Let's see some ID.".

Street had already pulled out his wallet ID. "Here's mine." he said.

The armed officer pointed to a desk a few feet behind him. There was another uniformed military guard seated at the desk.

"Show it there." he ordered.

Street walked up and placed his ID on the security desk. "Here's my ID.".

Dunne followed suit. "And here's mine."

The seated officer checked their identification closely, then picked up a phone. "Rear desk." he said, "Got two Arcadia PD here, Dunne and Street.". He paused. "Right sir, yes sir.", he looked up.

"Firearms, gentlemen." he said, "Empty 'em and leave them here, please, and you can pick them up on your way out, thank you.". He laid open a visitor register log. "Sign in here." he said, "They're expecting you. Fourth floor briefing room.".

Almost immediately, two six foot marines arrived on the scene. One was black, the other a very light skinned blonde. Both were clad in camouflage battle uniforms, and were cradling the newest model of government issued Browning automatic rifle and grenade launcher weapons. They also had holstered .45 caliber handguns strapped on their belts. The blonde marine positioned himself to the detectives side, the other stepped around and stood behind them. "This way." the blonde said and he began leading them at a speedy pace down the hall to the center of the building where a set of four elevators were located. The second marine followed along just a step behind. They stepped into the elevator. The black marine touched the button marked NSA. No one spoke. The only sound to be heard was the unnerving squeaking of the cables as the elevator rose up the shaft way. The lighted floor indicator showed 2, 3, 4. The elevator stopped with a jerk and the doors slid open slowly with an ominous grinding sound.

Street glanced down and back. "Our taxes at work." he said with a sarcastic tone, motioning to the elevator. Both marines stood rigid. They looked directly into Streets' eyes. They didn't speak, but their icy stare was statement enough. Street blinked, and tightened his lips. Dunne just shook his head like a daddy disappointed with the actions of a son. He and Street were then led to a set of double doors with a small doorplate marked simply 'NSA-SoCal'. "Here you are." the blonde marine said as he opened both doors wide. "NSA." he added with a welcoming hand gesture. The fourth floor of this Federal building housed the mid southern California offices of the NSA on one side, and the western headquarters of the Bureau of Firearms and Tobacco on the other. The jurisdiction of this NSA office included Catalina Island to the west, and ranged from Santa Barbara to the north, the atomic power plant at San Onofre to the south, and on out to the California-Nevada state borders to the east.

The detectives stopped at the doors and surveyed the large open room. There were six rows of ten numbered desks in each row.

The walls were of solid cinder block, no windows. At the north side, farthest away from the entrance were three interrogation rooms with large see thru one sided mirrored glass windows. The entire large open area was bristling with activity. Phones were ringing, desktop computers were beeping while displaying various Los Angeles county street layouts, and the many NSA operatives and agents huddled in groups of three or four, and engaged in animated conversations were creating an undecipherable cacophony of sounds and movement. There seemed to be an overall atmosphere of confused urgency.

"What's going on here?" Dunne asked.

The black marine answered, pointing to the far end of the room. "Desk twenty two, back there. Thank you, sir.".

The two marines then took up positions at attention just inside the double doors. Dunne and Street headed toward desk number twenty two.

"That's them." Street said, noticing the two NSA agents who had spoken in the squad room the day before. "Can't miss that gray haired old coot.".

Dunne shot him a look. "Watch how you talk here, Brad.", he said, "We don't want to make enemies of these guys, know what I mean?".

Street shrugged. "Yeah. Feds. Okay, I got it.".

The NSA agent standing at desk twenty two recognized them as well. He smiled as they approached, flashing his oversize teeth.

"Right here gents." he called out, "Take a seat.".

He pulled over a chair from a nearby desk, and set it next to the one that already was at desk twenty two. "Let's get down to business. I'm gonna brief you both, and . . ." he stepped closer and hovered over them, then continued, "And I won't pull any punches, so brace yourself.".

"Sounds serious." Dunne said, "Go ahead.".

"Well, here it is." Agent Mitello began. He motioned to the glass window behind him. "See that guy in there?" he asked, "He can't see us but we can see him.".

Dunne and Street looked over, and nodded. A small bearded dark skinned man sat nervously in the interrogation room designated as 'Int-number2'.

"Yeah. What about him?".

"He's the owner of that vegetable store where your friend Charga stirred things up on Sunday.".

"Right, that's the guy we saw running out of the store, and?".

"And it appears that store was one of the meeting places for a group of people intent on doing some harm to the U S of A.".

"Really?".

"That's right! We've been onto them for a while and we've had them under surveillance for a few months now.".

"And so?".

"And so, we've just now uncovered their real plans.".

"What's that?".

"We know they smuggled in two canisters of nuclear material from over the border with Mexico, but we weren't sure what their target was.".

"Now it really sounds serious!" Street broke in, then repeated slowly, "Really serious.".

"See that lady in there with him?".

The detectives nodded. Walking back and forth in that same interrogation room was a heavy set dark haired female dressed in a conservative dark green jacket and skirt suit.

"She's Alice Moss, a federal deputy assistant attorney general out of the Los Angeles county federal office. We've also got a federal judge on alert, being covered 24-7 by our agents, just in case miss Moss needs a warrant of any kind, she can call the judge for authorization and our agent will deliver the warrant anywhere we need it.".

"Okay, but you're saying there's possibly two atomic bombs out there, is that it?".

"Well, not exactly. We've already confiscated one canister. It's been sent to Los Alamos.".

"How in hell did they carry them over the border? They must weigh a few pounds, no?", Street asked.

"That's right.".

"Okay, well then, how many pounds do you figure?".

"We're thinking about five or six, maybe more, but still enough explosive power to take out a few square blocks, and contaminate a good portion of the surrounding area with radioactive dust.".

"Holy crap!", street exclaimed, "Are you kidding?".

"I told you I wouldn't pull any punches.".

"You said you just now have their plans, so what is their intended target? Somewhere here in the LA area I presume. Right?".

Mitello shifted his footing, stepped back and leaned his backside on the edge of the desk. He shook his head slowly, "It's not what, it's who!".

"Who?", Mike Dunne questioned, "And that would be . . .?".

"Only the president.", Mitello answered, "That's who! The president!".

"Say, I did read that the pres was flying in to meet his wife. She's been in town visiting the hospitals." Street said, "We almost bumped into her when we picked up Charga.".

"Yeah, well the president is flying in tonight. He's speaking at a fund raiser in Anaheim tomorrow night, then his plans are to go to the races with the missus.".

"What, he's gonna go to the track?", Dunne asked incredulously, "Even knowing that the threat exists?".

"No one can talk him out of it." Mitello paused, then shrugged his shoulders and continued, "You may or may not know that president Nixon was the first sitting president to attend a Kentcky Derby, well, did you know that?" Not waiting for an answer he went on, "Well, this president wants to be the first sitting president to attend the biggest race in the west, that's the western derby set to run this week. They're running it on a special day to accommodate the presidents' schedule. The track owner is a personal friend."

"Why doesn't he just change his schedule?" Dunne asked, "That way their plans would be screwed."

"He's been so advised, but he says if he changes his schedule any time there's a threat of some kind, well then, that's when the bad guys win, and let's face it, you don't get to be president if you're cowardly, and this guy has more courage than even I gave him credit for. Nope, he's not running from anybody. He's coming and that's that!". Mitello looked up at his partner "Never thought you'd hear me defending this president did you Fredricks?" he asked.

The gray haired agent, who had been standing close by, shook his head slowly, negatively, "N-no, su-sure didn't!".

"Well, on a more personal note, I'm really pissed about this whole deal!" Mitello grumbled, "Screwed up all my plans for the week!".

"Your plans? What plans?" Dunne asked.

"Well, you know all our leave days were suspended because of this perceived threat."

"So? Big deal!" Street cut in, "So were ours down at Arcadia."

"But I had big plans for this week." Mitello replied, "I was hoping to go to Sicily, where my family came from, and catch the big Praioti celebrations."

"What the hell is that? Never heard of it." Street said, "Some kind of mafia ritual?".

"Shut up, Street!" Dunne ordered, "Remember what I said before!".

"Sorry." Street slumped back in his seat, "Didn't mean anything."

"What is that?" Dunne asked, "That what you said, a prioti?".

"Praioti!" Mitello repeated, "My family comes from a town called Saint Agatha De Militello, on the north coast of Sicily. It's between two rivers, the Inganno and the Rosmarino, and was founded by a group of fishermen from Catania. The Praioti ceremony is held every year on Good Friday in thanks to the Madonna for saving them from a shipwreck off the coast. Every year they turn their small boats upside down and light fishing torches on them, then there's all kinds of music and dancing on the shore. It's a big deal!"

"Well, that's the way life deals sometimes," Mike Dunne said, his tone was sympathetic, "but priorities are priorities, you know?".

"I was hoping to get in some fishing out there on those rivers too," Mitello continued, "and . . ."

Fredricks cut in. "These people aren't interested in your personal vacation plans, Michael." he said, "Just stick to the business at hand, okay?".

Agent Mitello shifted his weight onto one leg, hoisted himself up and set his rear end on the edge of the desk. He nodded acquiescence. "Sure, okay." he continued sheepishly, "You're still the boss.". He looked at his partner.

Doctor Fredricks was standing erect with his arms folded across his chest. His body was steady and rigid and he wore a stern and earnest expression on his face. In that position, at that moment, he no longer appeared an old man. Mitello grinned. "Took your pill I see." he added, then turned his gaze back to Street and Dunne.

"Well, here it is gents," he said, "Our people arrived with the CSU down at that store, and we made a thorough search of that back room. That's where we discovered the first of the two canisters hidden behind a food crate stacked along the wall."

"I didn't know that." Dunne cut in, "We didn't see any federal people there.".

"That's 'cause you and your partner here" he pointed to detective Street, "well, you left along with the ambulance. We figure that the third man, that's mister Haseed, grabbed the other canister and took off in a vehicle down that back alley.". Agent Mitello paused, and pointed back to the two way mirrored wall. "Looks like she's done." he said, "Here she comes."

The door to the interrogation room opened and assistant Attorney General Moss stepped out and began walking directly to their desk.

An armed marine, who had been standing just outside that room, now entered it, closed and locked the door behind himself, and took a position directly in front of the bearded store owner, who was clearly glistening with perspiration.

"Get any more out of him?" Fredricks asked.

Miss Moss stood straight, in an almost military 'at attention' stance. She was tall, near six foot, and very solidly built. "Obviously former military" Dunne thought. He nodded a silent greeting nod.

She looked down at him with no reaction, instead she simply answered Fredricks question. "Nope! I think he's said everything he's gonna say, everything he knows anyhow." she began, "I don't believe he knows exactly where the other canister is or where it's heading. He said again that both of them were being kept in that back room in his store, Haseed was there so it's definite that Haseed has the other one. Where he's gone he doesn't know.".

"Did he give any idea as to where or when they're planning to use it?" Mitello asked.

She shifted her eyes to Mitello, and gave him a contorted look of disdain. "I would've told you if he did." she growled, "but no. He just said what he had said before, that they plan to take out the president!".

"Okay, then," Mitello answered. He looked back at the two Arcadia detectives. "Here it is then gents.".

"Go ahead." Dunne urged, "What?".

"You know the secret service protects the president up close, right?". Dunne nodded.

"But," Mitello went on, "when there is need for assistance, as in this case where we have what we call a credible threat, well, then all available agencies, the FBI, us, and the state and local police are called in as well.".

"Understood." Dunne nodded again. "So what is it you need us to do?".

Agent Mitello turned halfway, leaned back and picked up a Los Angeles county street map which had been lying open atop the desk. He handed it to Dunne, then continued. "The Los Angeles city PD will be securing the hotel and meeting room where the president will be speaking and these three auto routes up to Arcadia, then your own captain Dunbar will deploy uniformed officers along with other plain clothes people along these routes to the racetrack, see?". He traced the indicated routes on the map with his finger.

"Got it." Dunne answered, "But why three routes?".

"The presidents' caravan may or may not be traveling along one of these. Just another way to keep 'em guessing. Notice how spread out they are? Each one begins out of a different exit and goes in a different direction at least a mile apart from each other until nearing the racetrack."

"I see." Dunne said, "but if it's an A bomb we're talking about, and they want to take him out, they wouldn't have to be too close, right?".

Fredricks answered. "That's right." he said, "but that's why we're already scouring the areas, street by street, building by building, and room by room.".

"And that's where you come in." Mitello interjected. "We need you and your detective squad to work with us in securing the racetrack". He stood up and walked around to the opposite side of the desk, pulled open a drawer and removed a large box. In it were two dozen hand held two way communication radios. "Here." he said as he laid the box on the desk. "These are for your guys. They're pre-programmed on our wave length. We already have agents at the hotel, and we'll be sending some to the track as well. We'll be securing all entrances to both places.".

"Okay. But what do you want us to do?" Dunne asked.

"You guys, along with some uniforms, are to check and clear the stable areas, and the grandstand buildings down at the track.".

"That's a helluva lot of space!" Street complained, "It'll take some time!".

"That's why we want you to start today." Agent Mitello continued, "As soon as you clear one area, assign a uniform to keep it clear. When all areas are secure we will encircle the entire track with uniforms, agents and track security guards, and control access to it. Meanwhile our agents will already be clearing the outlying buildings."

"Sounds good." Street said as he leaned toward Dunne and examined the map. "So that means every vehicle coming into the track will be checked too, right?".

"That's right." Fredricks replied, "and all air traffic from local airports will be halted, there'll be a fly-over rule in effect over the area except for flights leaving or arriving on a coastal flight plan.".

"And" Agent Mitello added, "with the APB out on that Haseed character, his movements will be limited, and if he does come out of hiding, well," he paused, then spoke with determination evident in his voice, "well, we'll get him for sure, and if he doesn't have the canister," he smirked, "then we'll get him to tell where it is.".

"What if he won't tell?" Street asked, "Some of these guys just won't sing!".

Mitello smiled. His oversize teeth seemed to sparkle in the glow of the overhead fluorescent light.

"We have ways," he said, "We have ways.".

Mike Dunne stood up, folded the map and handed it back to agent Mitello. "Here" he said, "This is yours.". Then he turned to his partner, Brad Street. "Take the radios." he said, "and let's get the ball rolling.". He shook hands with agent Mitello, then with doctor Fredricks. "We'll handle our end." he said. He turned to the female assistant attorney general. "Miss Moss, good day." he said. She stood straight backed and made no move in response to his offering his hand. "Good luck, gentlemen," she said, "You'll need it!".

Duke Charga steered his Dynasty into the main parking area of the north Duarte shopping mall and coasted to a smooth stop directly in front of the Alexandria Women's Wear store.

"Here you go." he said, as he leaned across the front seat and planted a soft kiss on Adriana's cheek. "Have fun shopping.".

Adriana gently stroked his face. "You are so sweet." she said.

Charga enjoyed the touch. "Call me whenever you like and I'll be right here in ten minutes to pick you up. You have my cell number, right?".

"Yes, I do now." she answered softly as she opened the passenger door. "But I do wish you just wouldn't go back to that place today. Wouldn't you rather be with me?". She held the door open waiting for an answer.

Charga smiled an apologetic smile. "I would really, sweetheart, but you know this is something I've just got to do for myself, and I can only do it during the daytime.".

"But, there's nothing going on at that racetrack today." she said as she stepped out and onto the pavement. She turned and leaned back into the vehicle, and Chargas' eyes involuntarily became hypnotically focused on her now visibly inviting cleavage. Her breasts were heaving licentiously with her every breath.

"No way I can change your mind?" she asked, flashing a flirtatious wink.

"Tempting." Charga thought, but he had already made up his mind. His investigative instincts were coursing thru his body. He just had to follow up his inquiry by once again talking with Juan Zella and John Harborstone. Four bodies, all somehow involved with Harborstone and the BCH stable, were already laying out at the morgue, and he had come close to joining them. He was determined to settle this case before he became number five.

"This shouldn't take long." he said in response, "The track's only a few minutes away. You just call and I'll be back.".

Adriana shook her head. "If you must." she muttered. She closed the car door, waved a slow so-long wave, and entered the mall.

Surface streets were clear of excess traffic on this non racing day, so drive time to the racetrack was less than ten minutes. Charga turned onto the stable entrance dirt road, and slowed at the guard shack. The same disinterested security officer he had encountered the day before was on duty. He was slouched back on a webbed beach chair flipping thru the pages of the latest issue of Hustler magazine. Charga greeted him with a friendly wave. "Going to BCH!" he called out.

The security guard recognized him and nodded, then replied, "Okay, buddy, but be careful back there. They're shipping today.". He quickly returned to his magazine with wide eyes and a goofy smile. Charga drove on.

"Some security!" he said to himself, "Really solid! Ha!". Charga pulled over and parked some fifty feet before the big green lettered BCH stable. Two forty foot horse transport trailers, with their rear ramps down, were parked in the roadway in front of the open barn doors of the building. He noticed Juan Zella standing next to the wooden steps at the side of the BCH stable. "Halo Juan!" he called out as he exited his Dynasty and began walking forward, "Qui pasa aqui?".

Juan Zella turned. An unmistakable look of annoyance was painted on his face. "Mira!" he said, "The bigga boss!". He pointed to a well dressed, portly gentleman standing to the side of the open stable doors. Charga took note of the silken suited, dark skinned man. There were also two very big men dressed in white Arabic robes positioned on each side of this man, just a step behind him. "Who is he?" Charga asked.

"That's the Sheik Baddaffi." Zella replied. "He flew in this morning, and he's taking our best horses, and he said, he's shipping them up north right away!".

"Why would he want to do that?"

"I don't know!" Zella said with disgust. "I get to be trainer, and now I got no chevallos to train!". He pointed to a big gray thoroughbred being loaded onto the near trailer. "There goes our best star!" he said, and Charga watched as two men led the big roan to the horse trailer ramp. One was tugging hard at its' bridle while the other slapped it on its' haunches with a riding crop, in an unsuccessful effort to get the reluctant horse to cease balking and step up and onto the open rear ramp of the trailer.

Juan Zella almost leaped out of his shoes. "Alto!" he hollered, "Stop!". He trotted to the trailer and stepped up on the open ramp.

"I'll do it!" he said as he grabbed the bridle reins. "Let go!".

Charga stepped near and watched closely. Zella sure did know how to handle these thoroughbreds. He patted the horses' nostrils, whispered something in its' ear, and began leading it slowly up the ramp and into the trailer. Now standing close to these horse trailers, Charga took notice of two other men closing the rear of the second trailer. Both wore denim pants, gray shirts with rolled up sleeves, and baseball caps with BCH prominently stitched on the front. One was standing partially turned away, the other, whose face was turned to him, he immediately recognized as being the person he had seen up in the break room on his initial visit to Brian Colton.

Then the second man turned and looked Chargas' way. He was clean shaven, and although Charga could not immediately say why, he did feel there was something familiar about him as well.

It was the eyes! The deep set cold eyes!

"Haseed!" Charga exclaimed.

The man stood straight for a second, then whispered, "You!". He turned and began to run.

Charga reached for his Glock. "Stop!" he shouted.

The portly sheik spied the weapon as Charga pulled it out. "Gun!" he screamed, pointing at Charga, "Get him!".

The two robed assistants immediately stepped in front of the sheik, shielding him like secret service men around a president.

The bigger of the two stable hands who had been handling the big roan, jumped down off the ramp and grasped Chargas' wrist, forcing his arm upwards, pointing the Glock to the heavens. The other stable hand stepped to Chargas' left and landed a solid punch to Chargas' ribs. Charga turned slightly, and rammed his left elbow to the second mans' head, then lashed out and caught the bigger man with a left to the temple causing a loosening of his grip on Chargas' wrist. Now attaining a position of leverage, Charga forcefully raised a knee to the big mans' groin, crumbling him into a painful doubled over heap, then he rammed his Glock down onto the big mans' forehead. "That should cut you down to size!" he chided as the big guy sagged limply forward. Charga then quickly whipped his weapon around and smacked the second attacker on the side of the head, sending him reeling. He hit his head on the side of the ramp as he fell backwards, tried to rise but fell back unconscious. Now turning his attention to the bigger of the two, Charga thrust his size eleven shoe twice to the big mans' chest and ribs, sending him sprawling in a face first free fall onto the straw covered dirt. With his breath having been kicked out of him, he lay prone and motionless.

"And that takes care of you!" Charga wisecracked.

Then he looked up. Ach Bin Haseed had already hopped onto a flatbed electric cart which had been parked near the stable doors, and he was scooting away down the dirt road past the nearby barns. Charga holstered his Glock, stepped up onto the horse trailer ramp and shoved Juan Zella aside. "Sorry, Juan. I need your star!" he said. He snatched the bridle reins from Zellas' hand, grasped a fistful of mane, and hoisted himself up onto the big roans' back.

"Get up! Chick! Chick!" he chirped, and the race horse responded, bounding down the ramp and galloping onto the shed row road.

Charga heard a siren wail and glanced back for a second to catch a glimpse of a black Ford with a windshield full of flashing blue and yellow lights skidding to a stop just inches in back of the horse trailer with the open rear ramp. "Feds!" he thought, "Good!". He quickly returned his focus to the electric cart, which was now raising dust more than two building lengths away. Charga tightened his leg grip on the thoroughbreds' flanks, laid himself flat on the big stallions neck and withers, and urged it into an all out run.

Two men in dark blue serge suits, white shirts, and red ties, literally jumped out of the black Ford. They each held government issued .45 caliber automatics in their hand. From behind the two robed figures sheik Baddaffi shouted out, "Get that man! He's stealing my horse!". The two men ignored his call, hopped over the trailer ramp and sprinted after Charga and the galloping roan.

The built-in speed governor in the electric cart limited its' acceleration to 20 mph, about half that of the all out running swiftness of the big thoroughbred. Charga continued to press the horse forward, and was quickly closing the gap between himself and the fleeing Haseed.

Haseed glanced back, seeing Charga gaining he steered the cart into the open doors of the nearest stable building. Charga spurred his mount on, and followed just seconds after. Upon entering the barn he immediately commanded the big roan to stop.

"Whoa! Whoa there big boy!". He pulled back on the horses' mane and dismounted even before the thoroughbred had come to a complete stop. The electric cart was parked in front of the second horse stall. Charga sensed movement to his left, he turned to see what it was just as a metal strapped bale of hay came flying at his head. He felt the rough straw scratch his face, and was knocked backward up against the left flank of the big horse, which reared back and pulled away with a loud frightened whinny. Charga fell, the bale of hay landing at his side. He looked up and saw the bottom of a square edged shovel coming at him. He tried to duck out of the way of the swinging metal, but was just a second too late. The shovel bashed his forehead with an impact sound that reverberated throughout the stable. He rolled over on the straw covered floor, and felt another blow across his back. He glanced up. Haseed was holding the shovel high over his head, readying to bring it down in a final coup de grace move, directly into Chargas' unprotected face. Two shots rang out. Haseeds' grip on the makeshift weapon loosened; it fell behind him, and a few seconds later he followed, falling limply backward over it.

Charga felt his forehead. It was covered with a film of warm moist liquid, blood. He was on his knees and attempting to rise to his feet, but that swinging shovel to his head had his brain swirling. He couldn't gain his equilibrium, and fell forward almost completely prone on the stable floor. His face was just inches above the horse path, and he breathed in the malodorous sinus clearing fumes of the equine urine moistened straw. He shook his head briskly in a vain effort to clear his brain, and looked up. Thru unfocused eyes he could make out the blurry silhouettes of two men standing at the open barn door. They began approaching in what he saw as slow motion, seemingly weightless strides, resembling that of two astronauts walking on the moon. One of the silhouettes stopped and hovered over him. "Are you okay?", he asked.

Charga heard the words, but at first couldn't decipher exactly what was being said. It was like this man was far away, and talking thru an open ended drain pipe at 78 rpm while he was hearing at 45.

"I asked are you okay?", the voice repeated.

Chargas' eyes came back into focus. It was one of the feds. He shook his head. "Just dizzy." he answered.

The second man was already leaning over Haseed. "He's done!".

He pulled out a white handkerchief and tossed it to his partner.

"Hold that on his head.", he ordered, "I'll call this in.". He began speaking into his suit sleeve. "Unit one, this is five.".

Juan Zella, who had followed the two agents in a full out run, appeared at the open stable. "Where's my horse?", he shouted.

Then, noticing Charga now on his knees and being helped up by the suited agent, "Is mister Charga okay?".

"I'm alright, Juan." Charga said as he pointed to the other end of the stable. "The horse is down there, he's okay too.".

"Bueno! Bueno!" Zella replied. He trotted to the big roan. "Easy boy!" he said as he approached his big equine star and took hold of the loosely hanging bridle reins. "Easy now.".

The federal officer who had just reported the incident turned to Charga, now on his feet and being steadied by the second agent.

"Good thing we were on you.", he said, "I've got a bus on the way, and our unit chief and local law enforcement team will be here in a matter of minutes." He turned back to Juan Zella. "Meanwhile, nothing moves out, no horses, no trailers, no people, comprende?".

Juan Zella waved him off. "Si! Si!", he said as he patted the roans' nose. At this time it was clear Zella was more concerned about the condition of his thoroughbred than whether anyone could come or go from the stables area.

The agent continued. "I'll contact track security, and have them detain anyone who attempts to leave.".

Charga chuckled. He thought of the stable security guard. "Good luck with that!", he said aloud.

Having heard shots fired, the stable workers from the nearby barns began to gather at the open doors. "Just step back!", the agent ordered. "Stay out of this barn!". He helped Charga onto the electric cart. "Sit here.", he said. "We'll take this back to the BCH stable.".

Charga sat between the two agents. He continued pressing the handkerchief to his bloody forehead with one hand, and braced himself by grasping the front panel with the other. He was still feeling somewhat lightheaded, and appreciated being held upright via the snug fit between these two agents.

"Just in case you don't know, we're NSA. I'm special agent Beck. My partner here is agent Montclair. We've been on you for a couple days.".

Charga nodded. "I know." he said.

"Good thing for you, wouldn't you say?".

"For sure." Charga replied, "Thanks.". He nodded over his shoulder. "Is that SOB back there dead?".

"Dead as a door nail." Agent Beck replied, "I never miss!".

They pulled up just a few feet from the two horse trailers which had remained parked in front of the BCH building. The two stable workers that Charga had earlier taken out, were now up on their feet, and in conversation with the sheik and his own two personal aides. The man with whom Haseed had been working was nowhere in sight.

Agent Beck shut off the electric cart, and hopped out from behind the wheel. He removed his I.D. from his inside jacket pocket, and held it up as he approached the five men. "NSA!" he said, "Need to ask you a few questions.".

In a matter of minutes the shedrow air was filled with the screeching sound of wailing police vehicle sirens along with the distinctive on-off road clearing horn blasts of an accompanying ambulance. Several law enforcement vehicles had arrived on the scene and uniformed and plain clothes officers quickly spread out over the race track stable area.

Charga was immediately escorted to the back of the ambulance.

The open wound on his forehead required four stitches. Two ciproflaxin pills were administered along with shots of vitamin B and penicillin to retard any possible infection. The paramedics recommended he be hospitalized for further examination.

"I'll be fine!" he protested, "You've done enough.".

Now seated at the edge of the ambulances' open rear door, his legs dangling, and his feet just inches above the shedrow dirt road, he was looking down and about to step out and return to his vehicle when he sensed someone approaching.

"Hello mister Charga.".

He looked up. There was no mistaking the gray bearded older gent and his big toothed companion.

"Oh! You guys again." he said as he stood up, wobbled slightly, but quickly steadied himself by holding onto the open rear door. "You following me too?".

"Yep! It's us again. We told you we were on you, didn't we?".

Charga nodded. "That you did.".

"And you should be glad about that.". Charga noticed a certain air of self congratulation in that remark. "Fredricks here figured you to be someone who instinctively shows up at the wrong place, but at the right time. You seem to have a talent in sniffing out trouble.".

"It just seems to come to me.".

"Well, my boys saved your ass today, didn't they?".

Charga nodded. "Well, yeah. Thanks for that, but your guys took out that Haseed character, and I wanted him for myself!".

"What? They did?".

"Sure did. That was Haseed back there. He shaved his beard, tossed his turban for a BCH baseball cap, and dressed in a plain work shirt and denim pants, but I recognized his eyes, and he recognized me too, and that's why he ran!".

"Son of a bitch!" Mitello blurted out. "We figured he was the one who had the second canister.".

"Second?".

"That's right. Second." Fredricks chimed in. "Turns out there were two explosive units. We already have one, and we've already analyzed the material in it. It was a small amount of cobalt 60. Not as explosive as weapons grade uranium, but still could've caused a good deal of damage. The second one is still out there, and . . .".

Charga interrupted. "But your guys made Haseed dead, so now what?".

"Just let us worry about that mister Charga." Mitello answered holding up an open palm indicating 'stop'. "We've got it under control, and you should just sit back down and let this crew take you to the hospital. You've had another nice bump in the head.".

"But what about that second guy, the one who was working with Haseed, and what about that big shot sheik? He was taking all the BCH horses . . .".

Mitello cut him off. "We got that guy as he was about to leave the stable area. Names Salaam Mahdi. He's been on the BCH payroll for a year. He's being questioned at this very moment, and I've spoken with the sheik, and he's okay.".

"Are they both crazy Muslims?" Charga asked, "How can you trust 'em?".

"Actually, the sheik is a Christian from Lebanon. Very devout, goes to church every Wednesday and Sunday. We've got a dossier on him already.".

"Really?" Charga thought aloud, "How come?".

"FBI and immigration checked him out years ago when he first got involved in racing here. He's clean.".

"Kinda suspicious shipping out all his horses tho, isn't it?".

"Not really." Mitello answered, "When he heard there were rumors of some kind of unethical activity with his horses, well, he's so damn pious and righteous, he decided to pull his thoroughbreds out, and get this, he even plans to sever all contact with BCH stables.".

"Unbelievable!", Charga exclaimed, surprise evident in his tone, "I didn't even know there were Christian Arabs!' he paused, then added, "Well, Brian Colton won't be happy about that.".

Mitello motioned to the side of the ambulance. "The paramedics are working on the sheiks' two drivers now. One has a bad cut on the back of his head.".

"Those are the two goons I took out?".

"Yeah. That's what agent Beck told us. You did a job on both of 'em. The other one, the bigger one, well, looks like you ruptured him. What is it? Do you have a thing with testicles?".

Chapter Eight

Find that Canister!

Known terrorist suspect Ach Bin Haseed, the last person known to have had possession of the 2nd canister of Cobalt-60, had been eliminated, however the canister whereabouts remained unknown. The situation appeared to be coming to a head right there at the backstretch stable area of the racetrack. Doctor Fredricks reached in his suit jacket side pocket, removed a small pill box, quickly picked out two pink colored pills, and popped them in his mouth. He momentarily furrowed his brow as he contemplated the next course of action, then nodded slightly.

"Okay, Michael," he said, "So now here's what we'll do.". He paused, and motioned to the barn buildings. "We have to scour every inch of these buildings. Every nook and cranny, every stall, every bale of hay, so call in for metal detectors and extra personnel, and when the local PD people arrive, have them join in the search back here." He paused again, then pointed to the track. "Send out a few to check the track itself, and of course, the main grandstand and all its' walkways, stairwells, offices, and well, you know . . ." His voice trailed off and agent Mitello nodded. "Yeah." Mitello answered, "I know. I'll tell agents Beck and Montclair to start right now.". He turned and hurriedly walked toward the other agents.

Fredricks shifted his attention back to Charga. "Meanwhile you just head on out of here. My people will find that canister, and when they do, I'll personally disarm it. We don't need you around mucking things up. Anyhow, you're hurt.".

"But," Charga said in return, "I think I can help, even in spite of this head wound.".

"Thanks, but no thanks. You're no lomger a legitimate officer of the local law, so we can't involve you in this anyway, and anyhow we've got plenty people here now, including FBI and Secret Service personnel so . . ."

"Secret service?", Charga cut in, "I thought they only show up when the president is involved.".

Fredricks nodded. "That's right, and he is! He's planning to be right here day after tomorrow.".

"Here? At this racetrack?".

"That's right! He flies in tomorrow, staying in the L.A. area for two days. Thursday he'll be here in the turf club VIP room.".

"I knew he was coming in for some kind of political rally, saw that on the TV news, but they didn't mention he was planning to go to the races too.".

"That's because this is supposed to be a surprise visit. We didn't notify the media about it, but somehow, it seems, there's a group of radicals who found out, and we have credible evidence that they're targeting the presidential party somewhere, sometime during this visit in L.A. Might be they're zeroed in on his planned surprise appearance here, after all, the big western derby will be televised, and that'll give them the notoriety they seek.".

"Well, can't he just change his plans?", Charga asked.

Fredricks smiled a weak smile. "Been asked that question before." he said. "Nope. The pres won't run.". He scanned the stable buildings with a cold stare, then murmured, "We'll find it. We'll damn sure find it.".

Charga was about to protest when his cell phone began to buzz. He nodded. "This could be my lady friend.", he said as he raised the phone to his ear. "This is Charga.".

He was right. Adrianas' voice was like sweet music to his still aching head. "Hallo Dukay, well I'm almost done," she began, "I bought some nice shoes, a lovely necklace, and a beautiful head scarf, and I'm heading out now.".

"That's nice." Charga answered. He wasn't really all that interested in her shopping successes, and was surprised to hear from her so soon.

He had expected her to be touring the mall for at least an hour. That's what most American women would have done.

"Maybe European gals are different" he thought, then said, "Well, that was quick. Do you want me to come pick you up now?".

"Okay. In about twenty minutes. I'll be outside, right where you dropped me off. Is that alright?".

"Fine, Adriana. I'm on my way.". He hit the end talk button and slipped the phone back in his pocket. "Guess you're right." he said to Fredricks. "I'm outta here.".

As he began walking back to his Dynasty, another black sedan drove up and stopped just a few feet away. "Hey Duke!".

Charga looked up. It was Big Mike Dunne and detective Brad Street. "You guys here too?", Charga called out, "They're really pulling out all the stops, hey?".

"Never mind that." Dunne replied, "What the hell are you doing here?".

Charga shrugged. "Just starting trouble, as usual.".

"This is a pretty big deal!" Dunne hollered, "You don't know the half of it! I don't think you should be here.".

Charga waved him off. "That's where you're wrong. I know all about it.", he paused, then looked back to Fredricks and motioned with his head, "He told me. The pres, the threat, I know it all.".

Mike Dunne shook his head slowly, "You just have a knack for getting involved, dontcha?".

"Guess so." Charga said as he opened the driver side door of his Dynasty.

"So," Dunne hollered out, "Where are you off to now?".

Charga smiled a wry smile. "Goin' to pick up a lady.". He slid in behind the wheel, closed the door, quickly inserted and turned the ignition key, and his shiny black beauty immediately responded. He hit the window open switch. "I promised." he said out the now open window. "Don't want to disappoint, you know.".

Dunne glanced to Brad Street. "Typical!", he said, a slight tone of feigned disgust evident in his remark.

Street chuckled. "You still love him like a brother." he cracked, "And don't even try to deny it!".

Charga drove off leaving a cloud of brownish dust in his wake.

He was at the Duarte mall in a matter of minutes. Adriana was just exiting the mall as he drove up.

"You got here really fast.", she said as she opened the passenger door and slid in. Then, noticing the bandage on Chargas' forehead, she pointed to it and asked simply "What happened there?".

"Oh, nothing too much.", Charga answered. He was reluctant to explain all the circumstances that had led to this most recent injury. "I fell over a bale of hay.", he said, "Hit my head on a shovel, that's all. No big deal.".

He had delivered the explanation in such a nonchalant, dismissive manner, and since she was anxious to tell of her own little shopping spree, she simply nodded an understanding and accepting nod, and began recounting her own activities in the mall.

"There aren't many large shopping mails like this in Sicily." She said, "Well, not in the town where I was, anyway.".

Charga was only half listening.

"So much jewelry, clothing, and food." she went on, "It's really decadent!".

"Speaking of food," Charga cut in, "Where do you want to go to eat?".

"Oh, no." she replied, almost apologetically, "My old friend has prepared a meal for me tonight. I'll be eating with her at her place, and some other girls are coming over too.".

Charga shot her a surprised glance. "I thought we were going to spend some time together tonight." he said.

"Oh, sweetie." she purred, "We'll have plenty of time together in the next few weeks, but I just got in last night, and I'm still on Europe time, you know. I'll be turning in early.".

"Yeah." Charga said, "I guess you're right. It does take a day or so to get back in sync after a long flight like that.".

"And tomorrow I'll be going to a hairdresser." she rambled on, "Then tomorrow night I'll be meeting with some more old college friends for a welcome back party that they've planned for me, but I'll be with you definitely on Thursday, okay?".

"Sure." Charga replied, "Anyway the medics who took care of this today," he touched the bandage on his forehead, "Well, they said I should come in to the hospital, and have it checked out and . . .", he was rationalizing in an effort to assuage his disappointment, "I want to visit that horse trainer who's in there too, so that'll take some time. Then I'll be stopping at the Arcadia PD to talk with my former partner Mike, so I'll be busy most of tomorrow, too.".

"Okay." Adriana said in return, "So, you can take me down to my friends place now, and then we'll meet day after tomorrow. I'll spend that day with you, all day, I promise."

She planted a soft kiss on Chargas' cheek. Charga smiled. That made him feel better.

"Sure." he said, "And where would you like to go on that day? Any ideas?".

Adriana smiled. "I know!" she replied, "Since you enjoy being at that place so much, and I like it too, let's go to the racetrack, okay?".

"Sure." Charga agreed, "That's a great idea.".

He turned onto the freeway, and drove the six miles down to the Compton street exit.

"Almost there." he said, "That was Compton and sixth, right?".

"Yes, sweetie. Just drop me off at the corner. Right there!".

Charga double parked in front of a clean, well kept apartment complex, one of several along the street.

"See?" Adriana said, pointing to the three story brick faced building, "It's not really a bad neighborhood, now is it?".

Charga looked around. "Well, no." he replied, "I guess not.".

She playfully planted another love tap kiss, this time on the edge of his nose. "I'll call you Thursday." she whispered.

Charga smiled again. "Okay. Till then." he said in return, "I'll wait.".

The drive back to Century City took longer than he had expected. He had run into the beginning of the afternoon, homeward bound, rush hour traffic. It was a relief to get back to his apartment, and lay down on his own bed. That hit in the head had slowed him down more than he had at first realized. Not bothering to shed his clothes, he practically oozed onto his bed, and almost immediately passed out cold, and was engulfed in a silent, dreamless blackness.

Morning arrived in a flash! Charga awoke with a start.

The unmistakable noise of the Wednesday garbage removal trucks lifting and emptying the complex's trash dumpsters clanked thru his apartment. He glanced at the clock at his bedside nightstand.

6:30 A.M.!

Still fully clothed, he rolled over on his bed, and heard a tearing sound. The left armpit of his suit jacket had caught onto his Glock. He reached over to examine the tear. It was at least six inches on the seam. "Damn!" he said aloud, "My best suit, too!".

He slowly lifted himself up, and grumbled as he tossed the gray gabardine jacket onto the unmade bed. "Freakin' crack in the head!" he mumbled as he patted his bandaged forehead.

He kicked off his shoes, removed his shoulder holster, and almost tore off the rest of his clothes.

After a quick shower, and towel off, he slipped into a set of clean underwear and ambled out to the kitchen to set up a fresh brew of coffee. Then back to the bedroom to check out his clothes closet for a clean shirt, and a different suit. He chose his blue serge, and a gray striped tie to go along with a steel gray shirt. He strapped on his holster, checked his Glock, and slid it into place. He peeked at his wrist watch. It was now just after 7 A.M.

He figured it was too early to visit with Harborstone at the hospital, but not too early to have his forehead wound checked, so he finished his second cup of coffee, and decided to head on out to Duarte general, despite the early hour. At this time he thought it best to take the surface street roads rather than risk being caught up in the not uncommon early morning rush hour tieups on the freeway. It would take a few minutes more, but he wanted to avoid the mental stress since his brain was now pounding in his head like a drunks' hangover.

He drove directly to the hospital emergency entrance, parked in the rear, and literally staggered into the emergency room. There were only three other people in the room.

A hospital orderly ran up to him just as he entered.

"You back again?".

"What do you mean by that?" Charga asked in return.

The orderly shrugged. "Nothing much," he answered, "It's just that I helped wheel you in here last Sunday afternoon.". He motioned to the bandage on Chargas' forehead. "Got it in front this time, eh?" he wisecracked, "So how did you do that?".

"Never mind. Where's the doctor?".

"He's in the first room down the hall. Just take a seat here, and fill out this form. He'll be right out.".

Charga took a seat in the first row just in front of the registration counter. In a few minutes the doctor returned. He tended to the other three in the room first. One had a cut finger, another a hurt elbow, and the third was having chest pains and so, was immediately admitted to the hospital on a gurney. He then approached Charga. "Head wound, eh?" he said as he tore off the taped on bandage. "Stitches look good. You've healed up nicely.". He pointed to the adjacent hallway. "Just go to the first room on the right. I'll be right there, and we'll get them out.".

The stitch removal procedure took a mere five minutes. The doctor covered the now exposed cut with a small band aid. "This should do it. Just keep this on for a day or so, and you'll be just fine.".

"Thanks, doc." Charga said, "But I still have a kinda bad headache.".

"Likely a slight concussion. It'll go away.". His tone was dispassionate and unconcerned. "I wouldn't worry about it. You'll be fine.". He turned abruptly and strode back into the emergency room. Charga heard him call out. "Is that it for now? Great! I'm going out front for coffee. Call me if something serious turns up, otherwise, let 'em wait 'til I get back!".

Charga laughed to himself. "Dedicated doctor! Ha!" he mumbled as he began walking down the corridor toward the sign marked 'elevator'. The arrow pointed to the left. In just a few moments he was on the fourth floor. He peered into room 406. It was unoccupied. He then looked down the hallway and noticed a female nurse hurrying thru the hall carrying an x-ray. Charga stepped in front of her.

"Nurse!" he said, "What happened to the people that were in this room?".

She glanced at the room number sign. "Room 406 . . ." she replied, "Oh yes. Old man Carney was moved downstairs, and that other feller, well he signed himself out late last night.".

"Signed himself out?".

"That's right. The doctor in charge wasn't happy about that, but he was able to walk on his own, so it was his prerogative. He seemed in a hurry too.".

"In a hurry?".

"Yes. Said he had to see a man about a horse, but I've heard that line before. I think he just wanted to get out of here.".

Charga shook his head. "No, baby." he said, "This time I'm sure this guy really was going to see a man about a horse.".

"Really?".

"Yeah, really, and I think I know just where he's gone.".

Charga took the elevator back down to the first level, and exited back thru the emergency room. There were now four injured people anxiously awaiting treatment. The emergency room on duty doctor had not yet returned.

"Guess there's nothing too serious happening yet." Charga thought as he walked thru the room and out to his Dynasty.

He decided to head back to the track, figuring Harborstone would likely be back at BCH, and he also was curious to see what additional action Mitello and Fredricks had initiated there.

Chapter Nine

Duke Backs Off

The emergency room attendant who had earlier greeted him was standing outside smoking a cigar. He waved at Charga. "Nice seeing you again!" he shouted, "When will you be back?". He blew out a perfectly shaped smoke ring and chuckled.

"Hope this is my last visit here for a while." Charga said in return. The hospital attendant called back. "Just keep doing what ever it is you're doing and you'll be back for sure! Some guys never learn!". It was an off the cuff semi-serious wisecrack, yet it struck Charga with the voltage power of a lightening strike. He stopped in his tracks, then glanced back and saw his reflection in the glass sliding door. His forehead was bruised and sporting an oversize band-aid, and the area around his left eye was discolored and a bit swollen.

He shrugged. "He may just be right." he thought as he began mentally reviewing the events of the past few days. Big Mike had advised him to step back, and not pursue the Harborstone case. Mitello and Fredricks had advised the same. In both instances he had ignored their warnings and in both cases he had eventually landed in this hospital. Even Adrianna had asked him to discontinue his personal quest for revenge against that Haseed character.

"Well, now that Haseed is on a slab, maybe it is time for me to stand down." he thought. The Harborstone mugging incident had morphed into a major federal case, and there was no real reason for him to remain involved. He made a snap decision then and there to inform mister Harborstone that yes, he had indeed discovered who had assaulted him and why, but his own personal involvement in the case had now ended. Maybe he wouldn't even bill Harborstone for his services, after all he really had kinda pushed himself into the case to begin with.

"Maybe it really is time for me to back off." he thought. He waved to the attendant. "Thanks, but don't expect me back for a while!".

It was not yet ten o-clock, and since this was a regularly scheduled racing day with no early bird wagering available, Charga knew that the racetrack main parking lot, clubhouse, and grandstand gates would be closed until two hours prior to the one P.M. 1st race post time. "No problem for me.", he thought as he drove around back and steered his Dynasty into the stable area entrance road.

The familiar track security guard was standing outside his guard booth. Charga slowed his vehicle.

"Unusual," he thought, "He's out of his little shack.".

Standing next to the guard was a well dressed 6 foot tall African American. He was wearing a blue suit, white shirt and red tie.

"A fed!", Charga said to himself, "Definitely a fed!".

The two men waved Charga to stop, then approached his vehicle, one at each side. The security guard tapped on the driver-side window. Charga lowered it.

"What's up?", he asked.

"Sorry," the guard answered, "I told him I knew you and you were okay to pass, but I've been ordered to stop every vehicle.".

He motioned to the suited black man who was now standing on the passenger side of the car peering into the rear seating area.

The man spoke to Charga in an authoritative tone. "Please step out and open the trunk." he ordered.

Charga nodded. "No problem." he said and he reached down and pulled the remote trunk release.

"Damn thing!" the guard half whispered as Charga stepped out of the vehicle. "They're acting like I don't do my job right!".

Charga didn't comment, merely smiled a knowing smile.

The suited federal agent rummaged thru the Dynasty's trunk, then slammed it shut and walked around to Charga.

"Please turn around." he said, "Spread your legs and place your hands on the roof.". He performed a quick pat-down, and immediately took note of Chargas' Glock. "What's this?" he asked.

"Where ya think ya goin' with this?".

He plucked the weapon from under Charga's arm, and handed it to the security guard. "Hold onto this." he said.

Charga did not turn and remained facing the vehicle. "My name's Charga." he said, "I've been working with Dunne and Brad Street.".

"So what, wise guy! So you're a big shot in the stock market. Who cares? This ain't wall street!".

Charga looked back over his shoulder. "Maybe you know agent Mitello?".

The mention of agent Mitello drew an immediate reaction.

"Got ID?".

"In my wallet." Charga answered, "In my breast pocket.".

"Dammit! I told you he was okay," the guard interjected, "He's been thru here before!".

The agent lifted Charga's wallet, glanced at it, then spoke into his sleeve. "This is Coleman at gate three. Got a guy here name of Charga. Is he okay?". There followed a short pause as he pressed a tiny listening device tighter in his left ear. "Okay." he said to the security guard, "Give him back his weapon. He's clear.". Then he addressed Charga. "Thank you sir, You're clear to go on. Special agent Mitello says if you want to talk with him, he's in the main building out front, up on the press level.".

"I told you!" the guard blurted out, "I told you he was okay!".

Charga drove down the dirt roadway to the big green BCH building and parked just in front of the outdoor wooden stairway. He noticed Juan Zella standing at the stable door.

"Hola! Juan!" he called out, "Is Harborstone here?".

"Hola, mister Charga. Si! All the bosses are here ahorra.". He pointed at the stairs. "Arriba!" he added, "Upstairs in the big office!".

"That figures! Thanks!" Charga said in return as he began ascending the creaking stairs.

Charga found the big three of BCH with no difficulty since he could hear their loud angry voices the moment he pulled open the door at the top of the steps. He swiftly walked along the upper level passageway, and entered Brian Colton's outer office, then stopped momentarily to peer down thru the big glass window at the now empty horse stalls below. The sheik appeared to have made good on his plan to remove all his thoroughbreds from the BCH stable. Sheik Baddaffi's two

Omni present Arabic robed body guards stood just outside Colton's inner office door. Charga did not attempt to pass them, instead he simply stepped up to the open door and stood there in a non threatening posture with his hands semi-raised like a surrendering World War One French soldier. The two body guards also did not move, but merely glared menacingly. Charga went unnoticed for at least 5 minutes as the threesome within the office continued their intense conversation. Colton was chomping nervously on his unlit cigar between each spoken word. Harborstone, still bruised in the face, with one ear bandaged, and still nursing a swollen lower lip, was leaning against a chair for bodily support, with his head hanging low. Meanwhile the sheik, standing erect, dressed in a sleek tuxedo like suit, and sporting a black and gold necktie that screamed money, was dominating the dialogue with a continuing soliloquy on the ethics of business and the virtues of honesty. He was obviously angry with his two partners. Charga gathered that Harborstone had privately admitted to unethically administering excess medications to their horses, thus precipitating an intense investigation by the CHRB which could very well result in a major fine, and a possible ban from racing, while Coltons' lavish expenditures of BCH funds had depleted the corporation bank balance. The sheik definitely wanted out of the contracted partnership. Much to Charga's surprise, after listening in on the conversation for just a few moments, it appeared that of the three, it was this Arabian Christian who had the highest standard of honesty, ethics, and morality, and it was this sheik who actually first spied Charga at the doorway.

"You!" he hollered. "You're the one who ran off with my horse! Come in here!". Harborstone and Colton, who had had their backs to the door, spun around in tandem.

"He's the private dick!" Harborstone said. "He's the one who hustled me into hiring him while I was still under a sedative . . ."

Colton cut in. "He was up to see me too! Asked a lot of questions.".

"Never mind that!", Harborstone continued as he limped toward Charga. It was plain to see he remained in some discomfort stemming from that early Sunday morning beat down. "The black orderly in the hospital told me what you did!". Harborstone paused, then stepped closer and poked Charga in the chest. "That was very unorthodox, don't you think?".

"Had to do it." Charga answered, "I was just too curious not to.".

"Well, the Arcadia police told me you found the thug who assaulted me on that same day, and within hours, is that right?".

"That's right. I did.".

"Well, then," Harborstone went on, "If that's the case, then I'll just be paying you for that one day. What's your normal fee?".

"Two hundred a day" Charga replied, "That was Sunday and this is Wednesday, but I wanted to.".

"Don't even think about adding up those days! What you did after Sunday was on your own.".

"Hold on now! I got beat up on Sunday working your case." Charga said in return, "So maybe you owe me for . . .".

"Forget it!" Harborstone shot back. "And since you only worked a few hours on finding the person who put me in the hospital, well then, here!". He removed a wad of bills from his pocket and peeled off two fifties. "Here's a half days pay! We're even. And don't even think about asking me for more 'cause I'm not paying, see?".

Brian Colton chimed in. "And I'm not answering anymore of your dumb questions either, so you can just get your butt outta here!".

"Whoa!" Charga exclaimed as he backed up a step. He began to realize how and why these two were in business together.

"Two assholes!" he thought.

The sheik gestured with his hand for the others to stop talking.

"I apologize for accusing you of stealing my horse." he said. "Please accept.".

Charga nodded. "It seems no one is who you think they are.", he thought.

"No problem, sheik." he said, and offered his hand. "Shake! No hard feelings there.". He turned to Colton. "And I don't have to ask you anything." he said. "Because I know all I need or want to know about you.". Then he addressed Harborstone.

"Well, you're right. I did find out who busted you up, and now it seems the real reason these people wanted you out of the picture was not because you're gay, and certainly not because of any woman, but only because they wanted to get another one of their own people right into the picture, and by the way do you know that the person who actually did the beat down on you is no longer with us?". He paused momentarily, then continued slowly, "Now I'm thinking that maybe this was one time I really should've listened to my old partner, could've stood back and kept my nose clean, instead I opted to butt myself in where I shouldn't have been, and then it became more personal than anything else. Turns out it's bigger than any of your petty problems, and so I actually went to see you in the hospital this morning 'cause I wanted to tell you I wasn't gonna charge you anything at all, but now . . ." Using only his index finger and thumb, he gently removed the two fifties from Harborstones' hand. "Now I'll gladly accept this. Thank you." He smirked. "So, I guess I'm done here with you guys." He spun on his heels, took two steps toward the door, then looked back and added "A pleasure to meet you sheik." he said with a wink, "And that's more than I can say about these two!".

Charga nodded and grinned at the two body guards as he passed them on the way out.

"See you gents." he said, then wisecracked, "Don't you two ever smile?".

Juan Zella was waiting at the foot of the outside stairway. He called out to Charga. "So what did they say?" he asked, "Any news about the horses? Are we still in business?".

"Didn't mention anything like that, Juan. Sorry. You'll have to check with them, but my impression was that BCH is breaking up.".

"Maricomb!" Zella exclaimed, "I guess I'll be looking for a new job! Just get moved up and now move abacco!".

Charga shrugged. "You'll be fine." he said, "People here must know that you know your business. You'll be just fine.".

Zella walked back into the barn shaking his head and mumbling to himself.

Charga quickly strode to his Dynasty, slid in behind the wheel, then decided to call Mike Dunne at Arcadia P.D. The phone rang twice, then, "Arcadia P D. Sergeant Dunne here.".

"Mike, it's Duke.".

"Hello Duke. What's up?".

"Just wanted to let you know I'm out of the Harborstone racetrack deal. I'm backing off.".

"What? Am I hearing right? You're finally using your head for something else than a golf ball on a tee! So what brought this on?".

"Was at the hospital this morning, and got a wakeup call from one of the people there and . . ."

"So!" Dunne broke in, "You listen to strangers, but not to your friends, is that it?".

"Well, I'm sorry Mike. I guess you were right, right at the start . . ."

"Damn straight I was right!" Dunne fired back, "Now here's some more advice, stay away from that racetrack, ya hear me?".

"Yeah, I hear you loud and clear.".

"So where are you now?".

"Well, actually . . ." Charga stumbled over his words, "I'm, er, in the stable area at, er, the racetrack.".

"Son of a bitch!" Dunne hollered, "What did I just tell ya?".

"Don't worry, I'm just on my way out . . ."

"Good! Get out and stay out!" Dunne said in return, "At least for a few days!".

"A few days?" Charga asked, "Why? Something up down there for sure?".

"Just do like I said, and don't ask questions. I'll tell you all about it when it's over, or you'll see it on the TV news.".

"Okay, Mike. I'm not arguing. Just wanted you to know that I'm out, totally out!".

"Well, I really never thought I'd hear you say something sensible like that. What is it? Something wrong?".

"I'm wising up! Actually, I've got a helluva headache so I think I'll just go on home, take a few aspirin and kinda just rest up.".

"Good idea!" Dunne answered, "Keep that thought and I'll talk to you soon.".

"Sure Mike." Charga said, then added, "Say hello to stretch, okay?".

"Will do, take it easy.".

Charga heard the hang up click, and snapped his own cellular phone shut. He tossed the phone on the passenger seat and removed his vehicle keys from his jacket pocket. The Dynasty's six cylinder engine started right up with just a touch of the ignition key. "That's my reliable Dyna." he said aloud.

He made a quick u-turn, and drove off.

Arriving at his apartment complex just after 11:30 A.M., he immediately stripped and stepped into the shower. Following that quick cool water rinse off, he took three aspirin, wrapped a damp face towel around his still throbbing head, and stretched out on the bed. Within minutes Marion Duke Charga was sound asleep.

It was the ringing sound of his land line phone that awakened him. He turned over, looked up and was surprised to find the bedroom in total darkness. He glanced toward the window. It was dark outside as well. He clicked on the light on the bed set night stand and checked the time. It was almost 8 P.M.

"Jesus!" he said aloud, "I just passed out!".

He removed the now dry cloth from his forehead. "At least the headache is gone.", he thought as he stood up off the bed, and quickly trotted down the hall to the kitchen. He lifted the receiver just before his answering machine would have kicked in.

"Charga investigations. Hello?".

"Hello Dukay.". It was Adriana.

"Adriana!" he answered, "Well, now what a pleasant surprise to hear you.".

"I tried calling you earlier, but only heard the answering machine message.", she went on, "So then I called your cell phone, but you didn't answer that either. Where were you? I was worried.".

"Oh, you shouldn't have worried. It's just that I was up early this morning, went to the hospital to have my head injury checked, then I drove over to the racetrack stables area and . . .".

"The racetrack?", she broke in, "The TV news reported there was a shooting there yesterday, and that there's extra police there today because of it." she paused, "But you didn't tell me about any shooting when you picked me up . . .".

"Well, I didn't want to alarm you." Charga said in return, "But actually I was there when the shooting occurred, and I even knew who it was that got shot.".

"Really? You were? You did? Was it a friend of yours? The news didn't report who it was."

"No." Charga answered, "Not at all a friend, but I told you about him. Name was Haseed.".

"Haseed? I do remember you mentioning a name like that, but the news said it was a stable worker who was attempting to steal a horse. They said he was shot by a track security officer.".

"Yeah, well it was something like that." Charga continued, "And now they're double checking everyone who comes or goes, especially in the stable area. Now you either have to be a known track employee or a cop to get in back there.".

"Really? Then how did you get in? You're no longer a policeman."

"Easy for me. The security guard back there knows me. He vouched for me today, and I'll probably now be waved thru with no problem.".

"Really? That's good.".

"Yeah. Well, Because I was up so early, I came back and just fell asleep, that's why I was out like a light here on the bed, and just didn't hear the phone ringing, and I left my cell phone in my car, but I'm okay.".

"That's good sweetie. And how's that little bump on your head, is it okay too?".

"Sure, Adriana. I'm fine, but how come you called?".

"Oh sweetie, my friends are just leaving and I'll be going to bed soon, and I was just thinking of you and . . ."

"Well now, that's encouraging." Charga thought. He didn't interrupt and she went on. "And I was thinking about what we'll be doing tomorrow. I'm thinking I'll meet you at out favorite restaurant, then we can go together to the races, okay my sweet?".

Charga hesitated a few seconds, then answered. "Well Adriana, Yes, we can meet at Garlattis, but then no, we won't be going to the races. How about we go over to Griffith Park and spend a day out there?".

"You mean we're not going to the racetrack? Because of what happened?".

"Uh, yeah. That's right. Anyplace but there for tomorrow, is that okay?". There was a slight pause. "Adriana! Are you there?".

Another short pause. "Uh, oh, si! Yes my sweet, I'm still here.".

"So, what do you say? Griffith Park? Or maybe someplace else you want to go?".

"Uh, oh, sure sweetie. Griffith Park sounds nice.".

She didn't sound too enthusiastic, but Charga figured he'd just keep the conversation upbeat.

"Good. So we'll have lunch at Garlattis, then head on out to the park, how's that sound?".

"Uh, oh sweetie. Maybe you could come pick me up. You know where I'm staying.".

"Okay. That would be fine with me." Charga replied, "What time? Around noon?".

"Oh no. Come earlier. Maybe eleven, okay?".

"Sure. Will you be ready?".

"I'll be ready. Just come in and ring my friends bell. Her name is Sabani, Sabani Kattar.".

"Kattar? Okay." Charga answered. He was eagerly looking forward to spending a calm, relaxing day with his sweet Adriana. "I'll be there with bells on!".

"Oh, Dukay. You are such a fool sometimes.".

"What? What do you mean by that?".

"Oh, nothing really. Just that you sometimes say silly things.".

Charga laughed. "Well, maybe it's you that makes me silly. Being with you just makes me kinda happy.".

She chuckled just a bit as she spoke. "Maybe . . ." she said rather slowly, "maybe tomorrow we'll see just how silly and happy you can be.".

Charga didn't fully understand that innocuous, but pleasantly spoken comment. "Uh, alright." he said in response, "I'll try not to be too silly.".

"Until tomorrow, my sweet." she whispered, "I'll be ready for you at eleven. Bye now.".

"Good night, sweetheart." Charga said. He took a deep breath.

Adriana's lilting voice had caused a testosterone surge to race thru his loins, and since he hadn't stopped to pull on a pair of undershorts, he was now standing stark naked in the kitchen. He glanced down. He definitely had been aroused.

"Already slept eight hours," he thought, "And now this! It's gonna be really tough to get back to sleep tonight!".

He decided to relax on the living room sofa and watch some TV for a while.

It was near one A.M. when, still sitting up, he again dropped off to sleep, and began dreaming amorous dreams of the lovely Adriana.

Chapter Ten

Admission of Evil

6:30 A.M.

Charga awoke with a shiver. He blinked twice, then rubbed his eyes, loosening the sleep dust from their corners. The TV was on and a handsome blonde woman was presenting the early morning news. He glanced at his arms. They were bubbly with goosebumps.

He had once again fallen asleep sitting up on the living room sofa, but this time he had accomplished the feat wearing nothing but his birthday suit.

"Brrr." he mumbled to himself, "It's chilly in here.".

He literally jumped up, and headed back to the bedroom where he found his bathrobe and quickly slipped it on. He checked the clock on his night table.

"Plenty time to clean up, dress, and go on out to Dennys for a good breakfast." he thought, "Maybe I'll stop off and wash Dyna too, before heading down to Compton to pick up Adriana.".

He washed and shaved, ran a comb thru his hair, slipped on a fresh set of underwear, then picked out an older pair of pants, and a sports shirt.

"These will be fine for a walk thru Griffith park." he thought. He pulled on a new pair of socks, and his Uggs walking boots, then strapped on his Glock and threw on a thigh length suede sports jacket. He took a long look at himself in the full length mirror on the bathroom door.

The band-aid on his forehead seemed to be blending in to his skin tone, or maybe he was just getting used to seeing it.

"Well, anyway, I'm good to go!" he said aloud.

He slipped on his wristwatch, picked up his wallet, keys, and cell phone, clicked off the TV, and was out the door by 7:15.

After a leisurely Grand Slam breakfast, he drove to his favorite Century City car wash, ran Dyna thru it, and headed down to the big city. It was still early. Adriana had said to come get her at 11, it was now just after 10. Charga spied a roadside news seller holding a stack of daily papers at the upcoming corner. He decided to pick up a paper, sit in his vehicle and waste a few minutes with the comics and the sports sections. He opened the driver-side window.

"I'll take one!" he called out, "Thanks.".

He drove onto a tree lined side street and parked in the shade. He opened the paper. The big news in sports, aside from the Angels, Dodgers interleague rivalry, was the unorthodox Thursday running of the Western Derby, and the absence of any entry from the famous BCH stable in that prestigious race. There was no real explanation as to why this was so.

"Well," Charga thought as he read thru the article, "I sure know why. They're all gone!".

There also was no mention of the fact that, as Charga knew, this race would be attended by the President.

"Right," he thought, "Fredricks did say that this was to be a surprise visit. No one informed the press about it.". At 10:35 he folded the paper, tossed it on the rear seat, and started out down to Compton. He arrived at the apartment complex where Adriana was staying at 5 to 11.

"Perfect timing." he said to himself as he steered his now clean and shiny Dynasty to the curb just twenty feet from the apartment entry door. He stepped out and leisurely strolled toward the doorway. His mind was focused on Adriana, and he failed to notice the red and white taxi which had already been parked directly in front of the apartment, or that the driver of the taxi had quickly exited his vehicle just as Charga approached the apartment front door.

Charga pulled open the outer door, entered the vestibule, and began visually scanning the names on the postal boxes.

"Kattar." he mumbled, "Let's see. Kattar.".

The taxi driver, a medium sized dark skinned man, with a stubbly beard, and dark, deep set eyes, entered just a moment later.

Charga glanced back, smiled and nodded. "Hello.".

No answer. The man simply nodded in return. Charga turned his attention back to the letter boxes, and as he did, he felt a hard blow to the back of his neck. He fell forward, steadied himself with one hand against the set of mailboxes, then quickly turned and lashed out with a left hook to the his attackers' face. The stranger ducked just in time, and Chargas' fist went whizzing over the top of his head. Charga felt another blow to his midsection, then another to his left bicep. This one landed directly on the still healing cut. Charga winced with pain, but maintained his footing and returned a hard right to the strangers' chest, pushing him back against the opposite wall. Then he lifted a knee to the mans' groin, drew his Glock and used it as a club against the strangers' head, once, twice! The man went limp and crumpled forward against the outer door. Charga looked down. "What the hell was this all about?" he thought as he bent over to check his would be assailants' condition. There was a rustling noise behind him, and he became aware of the vestibule inner door being opened. Before he could turn, he simultaneously heard the sound of metal against bone, and felt a sharp pain in the back of his head. He fell atop the stranger. Another blow to his head, and everything went black.

Charga had no idea how much time had already elapsed when he began struggling to wake from that empty dreamless state. He grunted and moaned, then touched the back of his head with his hand in an effort to soothe the burning pain which was throbbing in unison with his every heart beat. He blinked and slowly brought his eyes into focus. "What the . . ." he mumbled as his vision fixed on the steering wheel of his Dynasty. He was sitting up in the front seat of his vehicle, and immediately became aware of a figure seated next to him. Instinctively glancing to his right, he recognized it to be Adriana, sitting stoically and grim faced. Slowly turning toward her, he felt a tightness around his neck.

"Do not move, mister Charga." came a deep voice from the back seat, "Just keep your eyes forward.". The thin wire garrote was tightened. "I can take your worthless life with a simple twist, yes?".

Charga gasped for air. "Yeah." he said, "I understand."

"And," the voice came back, "I have your weapon, and I will use it against this woman as well.".

"Okay! Okay!" Charga said, "But could you at least loosen this around my neck?".

His plea went unanswered. The pressure on his neck did not ease.

"You will now start this vehicle and begin to drive.".

"Sure, sure, but where are we going?", Charga gasped thru the words as he turned the ignition key, then out of the side of his mouth to Adriana, "Who the hell hit me?".

"It was this mans' partner." she replied softly, "But don't try to talk now. I think we should just do what he says.".

"Be quiet!" the man in back shouted, "I will tell you where we are going. Now, just drive.".

Charga put the Dynasty in gear and pulled out.

"Now what?" he asked.

"Take the freeway north to Huntington, then west.".

"West on Huntington? Going to the track are we?" Charga cracked.

"Shut up and just drive!". The wire garrote was tightened again.

Charga pressed hard on the accelerator. The Dynasty speedometer showed 70, then 75.

"Just slow down!" came the command from behind him, "Slow down or I will take her out right now!".

Charga was obliged to comply. He continued on the freeway at 65 mph, exited at Huntington and drove a speed limit 30 mph along the tree lined thoroughfare. The racetrack entrance was in view.

"Turn in the stable entry.".

Charga did not answer. He steered the vehicle onto the stable area dirt roadway, and slowed significantly as he approached the security guard shack.

"There's security here." he said, "Got to stop.".

The track security officer stepped out and stood in front of the shack. The same federal officer who was with him the day before was two steps behind. He had unbuttoned his suit jacket and was standing erect, seemingly ready for anything. The guard greeted Charga with a smile. "Hello again." he said. The man in the back seat whispered. "Just be cool or she goes first.".

"Hi." Charga answered.

"I see you've got some friends with you today.". He didn't notice the fine wire set tightly around Chargas' neck. "Yeah, right.".

"Gonna give them a little tour of the stables, eh?". "Yeah.".

"That's nice. People get a kick out of seeing what goes on back here.".

"Yeah, right.".

The guard turned and addressed the federal officer. "They're okay!" he called out, then waved Charga thru, "Go ahead." he said, "I'll see you later. Have a good day.".

The federal officer, seeing Charga behind the wheel and remembering him from the previous day, buttoned his jacket, simply nodded, and stepped back into the guard shack. Charga drove on slowly. "Now what?", he asked. "Park near the pathway leading to the rear of the grandstand." the man ordered as he released the wire from around Chargas' neck. "I have your weapon under this newspaper," he continued, "Thank you for leaving it back here for me. Now, after you park, remove the keys and toss them out the window, and remember, one false move and the lady dies. Now we shall all step out together, slowly." Charga detected a certain slight foreign accent. "Another Haseed." he thought, "That's it! Another Goddamn Haseed!".

Charga faked tossing his car keys away, instead he deftly slipped them into his pants pocket.

The stranger took a position behind Charga and Adriana. "You two walk slowly in front." he said, "We shall walk along the outer path, away from any activity. Head to that rear entrance.". As the threesome began down the pathway along the outer side of the dirt track, a familiar voice boomed out. "Hey Duke! Duke! Over here!". Charga turned. It was detective Brad Street.

He was about twenty feet away, walking along the inner turf track accompanied by two uniformed Arcadia P.D. officers.

"What're you doing down here, Duke?" he called out.

"Just keep walking." came the muffled command from behind.

"Can't do that." Charga whispered, "He knows me. He'll get suspicious.". He stopped and called back. "Hey stretch! What are you up to?".

"We're checking the railings and fences out here, and you?".

"Going to the main building." Charga answered, without really answering, "Where's Mike?".

"He's at the concession stand out front, waiting for the coffee to be brewed. You know him. Loves his coffee and donuts!".

"Say hello!" Charga called back, "And tell him not to worry, that I took his advice!".

"Advice?".

"Yeah. Just tell him, he'll know what it means.".

"That's enough small talk." the man behind Charga whispered.

Charga looked back. The folded over newspaper with his Glock under it was being pressed against Adriana's ribs.

"Got to go!" Charga called out as he waved to his friend, "See you later!", then continued walking, just a bit faster now, toward the main grandstand building. "Was that okay for you?" he whispered.

"Now you are being smart. Go right around this next corner." Came the next command, "To the elevators on the left.".

Charga realized this man was obviously familiar with the layout of the building. He had either been here before, studied the building blueprints, or obtained and learned the floor plan from someone else who had previously walked these halls.

Adriana pressed the elevator call button. The elevator doors slid open. "Step in." the man ordered, "We're going up to the fifth floor, push five.".

"Going to make a press release statement?" Charga wisecracked.

"Shut up!".

"Please don't antagonize him, Dukay." Adriana pleaded, "let's just do whatever he says.".

"Smart lady." the dark skinned man smirked, "You should listen to her, mister Charga.".

"Okay! Okay!" Charga mumbled, "You've got the gun now, so I guess right now you're the boss.".

The elevator creaked as it reached level five. The doors slid open with an ear piercing squeal.

Charga felt a shove from behind. "To the left!".

He glanced back once more. His Glock was again being pressed against Adriana's ribs. "Not time to make a move." he thought.

"Okay! Okay!" he said, "You don't have to push! I'm going!".

Big Mike Dunne, with two glazed donuts in one hand, and a large container of coffee in the other, was comfortably seated on the wooden bench ten feet from the outer fence, along the final turn of the dirt track, right at the head of the stretch run. He looked out over the track and saw his partner Brad street and the two assigned uniform Arcadia PD officers as they came trekking into the turn. They had almost completed their check of the vertical and horizontal fence posts along the inner turf course.

"Hey, Brad!" Dunne called out, "Anything?".

Street waved. "No! Nothing suspicious out here! So far anyway!".

"Good! Then when you're through out there I'll meet you guys at the finish line.".

"Okay! Right!" Street called back. He continued walking by along the turf track, then turned and added, "Oh, by the way, Mike. I saw Duke Charga.".

"What? When? Here?".

"Yeah! About ten minutes ago, back there.". Street pointed to the backstretch far turn. "He said he was heading to the main grandstand building!".

"What? The main building behind me?".

"That's what he said." Street called back, "But, he did say not to worry. He took your advice.".

"He took my advice?".

"That's what he said. Told me to be sure to tell you 'cause you'd understand!".

Dunne ran that comment thru his mind. "Last bit of advice I gave him was to stay away from this place." he thought. He took one last bite on the first donut, one more big gulp of coffee, swallowed hard, then stood up, and slammed the other donut and the now half empty coffee container into a nearby trash deposit barrel.

"Something's wrong here!" he said aloud.

He unhooked the police band radio from his belt, and called in.

"This is Dunne to post one. Meet me at the rear doors, section five.".

He spun on his heels, and began trotting back to the main grandstand building.

"Duke's at it again!" he mumbled, "Poking his nose in!".

Charga and Adriana walked along the passageway toward the audio visual room at the end of the hall. Charga stopped at the door. "Gonna check the photo finishes now, are we?".

He suddenly felt the barrel of the Glock poking him in the small of his back. "Just shut up!".

"Please, Dukay, please.", Adriana pleaded again, "Don't anger him!".
Their unshaven captor momentarily turned to check the hallway
behind them. Two men were now standing in front of the press lunch
room at the far end of the hall. One was short, gray haired, dressed
in denim pants and a flowery design sports shirt, puffing on a little
cigar and raising a bluish, white cloud of smoke around his head. The
other was bigger, and well dressed in a blue serge suit. Both appeared
to be unconcerned with the threesome at the AV door.

"Who are they?" the man whispered in Chargas' ear, "Do you know
them?".

Charga glanced back over his shoulder, and as he did, the bigger of
these two looked his way and smiled, flashing a set of oversize teeth,
then nodded and turned away. Then he quickly wrapped his arm
over the smaller mans' shoulder and they both disappeared into the
press lunch room, "They're probably press people." Charga whispered
back, "That's the press room back there. They're not interested in
us.". He had easily recognized little Charlie Cole, the assistant to AV
room manager Jack Demondo, and NSA agent Michael Mitello. It
was they who had been standing in the hall just outside the press
room, and it was apparent that agent Mitello had, in fact, recognized
Charga as well. Charga glanced back at his threatening captor. No
change in facial expression.

"Good for that." he thought. He had answered calmly, and had
successfully masked any indication of recognition.

"Go on!" ordered the dark skinned man, and he again pressed the
muzzle of the Glock into Chargas' back. "Just go on in here, and don't
make any sudden moves or else . . ."

"Yeah, I know." Charga said as he opened the AV room door, "Or else
the lady gets it.".

"Wrong! Now you both get it, so just go on in, and shut up!".

At this point Charga didn't know just what to expect as he stepped
into the racetrack audio visual room.

Meanwhile, Big Mike Dunne had just reached the grandstand
building elevators. His police radio crackled. "Dunne, this is one.
Come to the press room, fifth level. Now! Ten four?". He depressed
the talk button. "Ten four, one." he answered, "On my way!".

Charga walked slowly between the racks of VHS tapes toward the
TV console panel. A gray haired older gentleman was seated at the

panel of TV monitors. He turned slightly, adjusted his wire framed eyeglasses, and calmly questioned, "M-may I help you?". Charga found it difficult to suppress a smirk. It was none other than Doctor Fredricks. Fredricks smiled. "May I help you?" he repeated.

"Oh, yes, of course you can help." the stubble bearded man replied. He gestured threateningly with the gun. "You can just sit still right where you are.".

Charga felt another jab of the Glock, this time between his shoulder blades. "And you, you get in there and sit down too, and keep your hands on the countertop where I can see them.". Then, addressing Adriana while motioning with the gun, the man continued, "And woman! You set the latch on that door. I don't want anyone barging in on us! And remember, I can see you.".

He pushed Charga forward forcefully. "I said sit!".

"Okay! Okay!" Charga grumbled, "You don't have to shove.".

"But what is it you want?", Fredricks queried, feigning total ignorance of the situation, "There's no money up here." he paused, turned his head slightly, and discreetly winked at Charga, who was now seated a few feet away, then added meekly, "The cash is all downstairs.".

"You will find out what I want very soon, just as soon as your satanic leader arrives.".

"Satanic leader?", Fredricks asked, again faking ignorance, "What do you mean by that?".

"You shall see.", came the quick retort, "You shall soon see.".

Adriana had secured the entrance door, and was now again standing at the near end of the VHS tape racks. "What do you want me to do now, sir?", she asked.

"Just remain as you are! You have done well and will be rewarded by Allah. We shall now just wait quietly for the evil one to arrive, and upon his arrival I shall simply . . ." his voice trailed off as he took several backward steps, while quickly glancing back and forth between Fredricks and Charga, and the wall corner to their right where a 3 by 6 foot electrical panel door was situated. He stepped close to this door, reached out with his left hand and pulled it open, then grinned an evil grin. Inside this space, leaning against the wiring, was a 3 foot tall, by 10 inch in diameter, shiny steel canister marked along its' side with Arabic lettering. At the top of this canister was a simple on/off switch, set in the off position. He continued speaking, almost whispering now, in an ominous and menacing tone, "I shall simply flick this switch, and we shall then all go to Dar-es-salaam, our own individual final house of peace."

Charga and Fredricks sat almost motionless. Charga glanced over to Fredricks who appeared to be almost grinning, then they both set their eyes on their antagonist, waiting for him to lower his guard for just a moment. Adriana remained standing near the racks of VHS tapes. She was staring up at the TV monitors behind them.

Several moments passed, when suddenly Adriana cried out, "Look there!", and she pointed to the TV screens.

Charga turned and looked up at the racetrack TV monitor which was focused on the main entrance. A caravan of black stretch limousines had just driven in thru the gates.

"The President!", he thought, "He's here."

The Presidential limousine caravan had quickly entered the main gate, and was cruising to the special VIP entrance of the Clubhouse section below. Four secret service agents were jogging along each side of the second limo. Special uniformed police, along with ten more of the Presidents' own protective secret service agents, lined the ten foot long walkway leading from the parking area to this entrance. This protective force was bolstered by another array of track security officers, and local Arcadia police, who formed a double outer line along both sides of the Presidential party's path.

The President and First lady emerged from the number two limo and were hustled into the building. The entire arrival sequence was accomplished in a matter of moments.

"Ah, he is here!", the stubble bearded man whispered, "In a short time he will be in his special seat just below us. Be patient my friends, it shall just be a moment or so."

He then gazed upward, wide eyed, as if in some sort of self induced narco-hypnosis.

"Aluha Akbar!" he called out, "Aluha Akbar!".

That brief moment of mental distraction was all the time Fredricks needed. He sprang off his chair, and with a surprising burst of speed and agility that belied his appearance and meek attitude of just moments before, lunged forward, bulldozing into this obviously maniacal Islamic fanatic like a professional football linebacker attempting to sack a quarterback. The impact was enough to loosen the mans' grip on the Glock, and it went careening away, scraping along the concrete floor, before skidding to a stop at the base of a rack of VHS tapes, just inches from Adrianas' feet.

"Get the gun, Adriana!", Charga hollered as he joined Fredricks in grappling their antagonist to the floor.

"I've got him!", Fredricks exclaimed. He moved behind and grasped the stubble bearded would be terrorist around the neck, and held him in a basic police drill choke hold. "I've got him good!".

Charga stood up. "Nice work." he said to the elderly appearing federal agent, "I didn't figure you to be so damn tough!".

"I've handled this type many times before.", Fredricks replied. He remained literally lying atop his disabled prey. "And when I get them down, they stay down!". He was tightening his grip around the mans' head. "When I get 'em", he puffed out, "They stay got!".

Adriana scooped up the Glock, and in one smooth motion, tapped the ammo release tab and caught the grip loaded clip in her hand. She then visually checked the top cylinder bullet chamber, and quickly snapped the ammo clip back in the handle. The weapon was ready to fire.

Charga was surprised and impressed with the way she handled his Glock. "Just like a weapons trained pro!", he thought. Then a serious question rushed thru his brain. "How does she know that?".

Adriana took two small steps forward, and raised the Glock, pointing it back and forth between Fredricks and Charga.

"Okay, now." she said, "You've got him, old man, but now I've got the gun, so I would advise you to release him immediately.", she paused, then added in a sinister tone, "Unless, that is, you'd like a bullet in your brain!".

"Adriana!", Charga exclaimed, "What's going on?".

Adriana smiled, a strangely malevolent smile that contorted her normally beauteous facial features. Her eyes had turned cold and dark, her jaw was taut, her brow furrowed.

"What is going on is what Allah has deemed to go on!", she said.

The Glock was now pointing directly at Fredricks head.

"I said release him!", she demanded, "Release him now!".

Fredricks let go his grip, stood up and stepped back, his hands held high. He stood in an 'I surrender' posture.

"Okay lady.", he said, "Just take it easy.".

264

Adriana continued to wave the Glock threateningly, alternately pointing it back and forth from Fredricks to Charga.

"Get your hands up too, sweetie.", she said to Charga, "And step back against that counter, that's a good boy!".

Charga was stunned. With as much time as he had spent with her, it was more than scary to witness a side of this woman he hadn't ever suspected even existed.

"Adriana!", he blurted out, "What's happening? I thought we had something together. I thought we had a future. I never . . ."

Adriana cut him off. "You foolish infidel! All you ever really wanted from me was sex, and I knew as long as you didn't get that, then you would follow me like a puppy dog! Now just shut up, and sit down.".

Charga shook his head. "Who the hell are you, really?", he asked.

"I am a follower of Muhammed, the true messenger of God. Allah be praised, and as far as sex goes, there's no way I would ever lay next to you, ever, you infidel pig! Now just be quiet and sit!".

"You're a what?" Charga almost shouted the question, "But you're Italian! You're Catholic!".

"Catholic?", Adriana shot back excitedly, "And then follow that pompous Pope? And his cadre of perverted priests? Ha! Never! But yes, my father was Sicilian . . .", her words trailed off, and she paused momentarily, swallowed hard, then took a deep breath, and brought her emotions back under control. She began again, slowly, but more emphatically, thru gritted teeth. "But, my mother was a Libyan Muslim, and she and my father were both murdered by the bombs your beloved president Reagan dropped on us. Blown to bits along with my two younger brothers while they were doing nothing more than enjoying a nice home cooked dinner at our house in Tripoli! So now it's time for your own Satanic leader to feel the wrath of Allah!". She turned her attention to the stubbly bearded man who was rubbing his neck. "Get up Hasna.", she said, "And go do what you are supposed to do!".

"Yes miss Adri", he answered as he rose to his feet and began walking to the open electrical panel door. "Our Imam leader was wise to place you in charge here . . ."

"Never mind that!" Adriana ordered, "Just do it, Hasna, and Allah be praised!".

Hasna reached into the open space and placed his hand at the top of the canister. "Aluha Akbar!" he called out, and he flicked the switch to 'on'. Nothing! He flipped the switch to off, then back to on, off, on, off, on. Nothing! He turned, wide eyed. "Something's wrong!" he shouted, "Something's wrong!". Adriana appeared momentarily confused. "Wha . . . what?". Fredricks once again was first to take advantage of this few seconds loss of concentration, and lunged forward. Adrianas' reaction was just a second too late. She fired, hitting Fredricks in the shoulder, just as Charga sprung up and grabbed hold of her arm. He bashed her arm against the edge of the VHS racks, and the Glock went flying between the rows, landing just in front of the entrance door. Hasna came running at him, and Charga threw Adriana to the floor, then ducked under a swinging fist, and landed a right cross to Hasnas' face. Hasna staggered backward, tripping over Fredricks, who was on his knees behind him. Adriana was now crawling toward the door, in an attempt to retrieve the Glock. She was inches away from grabbing hold of the weapon when the door suddenly burst open. Agent Mitello, along with several additional federal officers stormed into the room.

"NSA!" he hollered out, "Everyone stay where you are!".

He looked down at his partner. "Fredricks," he said, "You okay?".

"I'm fine, just a shoulder wound. It's nothing.".

"This the leader?" Mitello asked, nodding at the stubbly bearded man who was just now recovering from Chargas knockout blow.

Fredricks smiled and shook his head. "Nope." he said, then pointing to Adriana added, "She's the big one!".

"No shit?" Mitello shot back, "I would've never guessed.".

"You would've never guessed? How do you think I feel?". Charga chimed in.

"We'll talk about that later, mister Charga, right now . . ." Mitello motioned to the other agents in the room, "Cuff 'em both!".

Adriana struggled as the agents pulled her up off the floor and cuffed her wrists behind her.

"You wouldn't be so smug if that canister switch had worked!", she grumbled defiantly.

Fredricks, obviously hurting some, was pressing a handkerchief on his shoulder wound, but managed a sly smile. "Oh, it worked alright, lady." he said, "It's just that I had already removed the Cobalt 60 explosive your people put in that canister." He paused, checked his shoulder, then looking squarely into Adrianas' face, continued. "Oh, by the way, sweetheart," he said "that was yesterday. We were just waiting to see who was going to show up today to try to set it off.". Then added facetiously, "Thanks for coming.". He turned to agent Mitello "I think we got 'em all now.".

Charga stepped to the door, picked up his Glock and slipped it back in his shoulder holster.

"I suspected you guys were up to something when I saw you in the hall." he said to agent Mitello. "Then I was sure something was up when Fredricks here was in Jack Demondos' chair, but how come you waited so long to get in here?".

Fredricks answered. "We wanted to see how this scenario would play out." he said. "And if that woman wasn't such a fanatic we maybe never would have known she was also in on the plot. She just gave herself away!".

Big Mike Dunne, and Brad Street had been standing outside in the hall, along with Jack Demondo and his assistant Charlie Cole when the NSA agents had charged into the AV room. Now, led by Big Mike, they began hurrying onto the scene.

Dunne was first to speak. "Duke!" he exclaimed, "Are you okay?". Charga nodded. "I'm fine." he said, "Just a bit disappointed.". "Why's that? You got 'em all didn't you?".

"Yeah, that we did." Charga answered, "But one of 'em was Adriana.".

"Really? I don't believe it!".

"Andldjdn't either!" Charga said, "Just didn't figure!".

Jack Demondo stormed past everyone, stepped up to the TV monitor panel and pointed to a small hole. Adrianas' shot had apparently gone clean thru Fredricks' shoulder and lodged in the metal between the TV screens.

Demondo turned abruptly. "So who shot my monitor board?", he asked, "And who's gonna pay fo it?". He then adjusted his eye glasses, and noticing that his assistant, Charlie Cole, was standing just inside the AV room door with a still lit cigar tightly clenched between his teeth, called out. "And you thar, Chorlie! Git your bee-hind outta this he-ya room with thet thar stogie! You know bettah than thet! Git!".

Charga glanced back to little Charlie and chuckled. "Yeah. Cigars are not allowed in here, but bombs, well now, that's another story." He turned to agent Mitello. "Say." he continued, "How in hell did they get it in here in the first place?".

"That's easy." Mitello replied, "That BCH stable hand Mahdi, he sneaked it in here yesterday morning just before anyone arrived. Got it from Haseed who brought it in on one of the horse trailers. Mahdi carried it up here, then simply slipped a slim jim tool between the door and the lock, and pushed the door open. Easy. It's an old fashioned lock. See how easy we popped in?".

"Really? And how do you know all that?".

Agent Mitello flashed his big toothed smile. "We picked up Mahdi yesterday, before he could leave the track, and after a few hours of our questioning, well, he sang like a canary.".

"That's right, mister Charga." Fredricks chimed in. "We already had the owner of that vegetable store. That was their meeting place. Got some info from him, then Mahdi gave us the location of this canister, and we cleaned it out yesterday, soon after you had gone.".

Charga nodded. "Impressive." he said. "Very impressive.".

"We're NSA!" Mitello said proud fully. He puffed up his chest. "It's what we do!".

"But then, what was that deal the other night down at the mall?".

"A diversion." Fredricks replied, "An effort to have us spread our people thin around the county.". He shook his head. "Didn't work tho. We figured it out! They were after the Pres! No way we would let that happen!".

"So who's gonna pay to fix ma panel?", Demondo called out, "Ah wanna know.".

Fredricks turned. "See one of those agents." he said, motioning to the several other NSA agents in the room. "They'll tell you how to apply for repair re-imbursement". Then, addressing Charga, Dunne, and Street, he continued. "You guys can take off now. We got it from here.".

"Okay." Big Mike Dunne replied. He motioned with a thumb to the door. "Let's go guys.".

Charga took two steps, then stopped in front of agent Mitello. "She was staying with a friend, Sabani Kattar." he said, nodding toward Adriana who was being held in the center of the room. "Down in

Little Lebanon. I'll give you the address. She's probably in on it too, wouldn't you think?".

"We'll follow that up.", Mitello answered, "But there's no way, at this time, to prove anything like that, and it's possible this friend may have a sense of loyalty to her own friends, and maybe to her Muslim religion as well, if she's also a Mus, and that could preclude her from speaking up. Then again, even if this friend did know of some possible plot against the government, she's under no legal obligation to inform anyone of such a possibility, not under our law as it is now. She might help us, that is, if she's not another Islamic fanatic, but we'll check her out, and keep her on our watch list, just in case. Don't you worry, like I said, we're NSA!".

Charga nodded. "Yeah. That's what you said, you're NSA!".

Dunne turned to Mitello. "Well, I guess now you can take your trip anyway, eh?".

"You know," Agent Mitello answered, "I hadn't thought about it, but yes, I'll be leaving tomorrow for sure.".

Charga glanced back to Mike Dunne. He had no idea what trip they were referring to. "Okay, Mike. Let's get!", he said, "and what's that trip comment all about?".

"Oh," Dunne replied, "Nothing really, it's just that agent Mitello is going to Italy.".

"Well, good for him. Now let's get outta here.".

Chapter Eleven

Dukes' Retrospective

Charga, Dunne and Street took the elevator down to the first level.

It squeaked ominously on the way down.

Charga pointed to the elevator floor. "I was told they're gonna fix this thing." he said.

"It better be soon."* Street half whispered, "Doesn't sound like it's going to last too much longer.".

"I'm not gonna last too much longer!" Dunne interjected, "Not if these little cases continue to blow up like this one!".

"Yeah." Charga agreed, "It really did blow up, didn't it?".

"Actually," Street added jokingly, "Actually, it really became a federal case!".

They shared a short stifled laugh as they stepped out.

"We're gonna grab a cup of coffee." Dunne said.

"And of course," Street added, "Don't forget, a donut!".

Dunne ignored the jibe. "Care to join us, Duke?".

"No thanks." Charga answered glumly. "I'll be heading on down to Anaheim. I'll have lunch down at Garlattis. That might cheer me up some.".

Big Mike Dunne slapped his former partner on the back.

"C'mon Duke, don't be so down on yourself. Everybody gets hit with a real bad beat on the river once in a while.". It was a reference to losing a poker hand on the very last card.

"Oh yeah?" Charga answered, "Well, I feel like a damn fool! There was something wrong about Adriana, and I just didn't see it, but . . ."
He hesitated for a few seconds, then continued haltingly, "but, she was just so damn beautiful!".
"And that's all you saw, eh?" Big Mike asked, shaking his head slowly in mock disapproval.
"Yeah. Guess so. Goes to show. No one is who you might think they are. Guess I never really knew just who she really was.".
"Ever get her in bed?".
"Nope. That didn't happen.".
Street chuckled, then chimed in. "So that's why! You were in a daze! She had you totally strung out!".
"You're probably right.".
"Well, we're going this way, and you?" Mike Dunne asked, "Where to?".
Charga pointed toward the backstretch. "Back there." he said.
"Okay then, Duke, see ya!".
"Right. So long Mike.".
"So long bud." Street added as he offered his hand to shake. "And good luck.".
"Thanks stretch." Charga said in return. Then he smiled a weak smile. "I mean thanks, Brad.". Their handshake was sincere. "And take care of this big guy, okay?".
"Will do." Street answered.
Charga headed toward the stable area where he had parked his Dynasty. The trek back to his black beauty seemed much shorter in both distance and time than the forced march at gunpoint which he had endured earlier along this same dirt path. A few short minutes later and he was in his vehicle. A touch of the ignition key, and his Dynasty once again proved its' reliability.
"Okay Dyna." he said aloud, more to himself than to his car, "Let's get outta here.".
Charga steered his vehicle in a wide u-turn, then began driving slowly on the dirt roadway toward the stable area exit gate. Someone called out.
"Hola! Alto! Mira aqui! Look here!, mister Charga!". Charga glanced to his left. It was Juan Zella, standing in front of a big red painted stable which had two 6 foot tall white Ls attached to its' front exterior

just above the open stable doors. He was hosing off a chestnut thoroughbred. Charga brought his Dynasty to a sudden stop, raising a small cloud of dried straw dust beneath it, then he lowered a window.

"Hey Juan!", he called back, "What're you doing over here?". Zella crimped the hose, walked to the spigot and shut the water. He looked up. "I'm working here!", he said, a wide smile crept across his face.

"You're working here? What about BCH?".

"Ahh, BCH? When the word was leaked that BCH was done, and that sheik Baddaffi was taking all his horses out, well, then I got three offers for work, and I picked this stable, the Lyons Lair. They have some really good horses here, and mister Lyon is a good man to work for.".

"I knew you'd land on your feet.", Charga said, "But what really happened over at BCH? Do you know?".

"Oh, si!" Zella answered, "I know.".

He approached Charga in the vehicle, leaned in a bit, then in a lowered voice continued. "Baddaffi quit because first, mister Colton was spending too much of the profits, secondo, because he found out that mister H was doping his chevallos, and the racing board was ready to fine BCH, and maybe stop them from racing in the state, but primera because he said there's too much crime here. One of our BCH hands was killed on his way home, another one was just arrested . . ." he paused and rubbed his chin. "Maybe he had no papers." he continued, "I don't know why the policia took Mahdi, but then you had that big fight, and the policia shot that other guy! Sheik Baddaffi said there was too much evil around here . . . And still nobody down here really knows why that guy was shot anyhow.".

Charga broke in. "I know why." he said. He didn't elaborate. Zella nodded. "Oh, si! You were there!".

"Yeah, Juan." Charga replied, "So I know about that first hand, but I can't say.".

"Well, it's okay by me. I don't really care." Zella went on. "Because now I'm the assistant trainer here, and the numero uno trainer is ready to move on, so . . ." he smiled again, "Maybe this time!", he added, "Maybe!".

"Good for you, Juan." Charga said. They shook hands. "And good luck my friend.".

"Muchos gratias, amigo!".

Charga drove off. He was genuinely pleased about Juan Zellas' situation, but that chance meeting triggered Chargas' recollection of Pepino Zella and the incidence of his so called accident in the barn area. Funny how Adriana had suddenly entered his life when he was looking into that incident. Had she appeared merely to distract him from following up on that investigation? He had always had his doubts about that death being determined accidental. Now that he thought of it, wasn't little Pepino replaced by that Salaam Mahdi character? Maybe it was Mahdi who had taken Pepino out, in a plan to replace him way back then. This group could've been planning to blow this track all along, and having the pres here would be frosting on the cake! Adriana had diverted his attention back then, and he had finally quit the investigation and acquiesced to the initial conclusion of accidental death, but that was mainly because he was so mesmerized by her beauty, and by what he now knew was a spurious affection toward him that she had so successfully faked, he was unable, back then, to keep his mind on his job.

"Well, they got that Mahdi guy now anyhow.", he thought, "He'll probably be behind bars for the rest of his life! But dammit! I shoulda figured! There was something wrong! And the clues were there all this week! I just didn't notice!"

He slapped the steering wheel, then tapped his own forehead.

"I shoulda figured!" he said aloud. He thought back to her phone call, and how she had so suddenly said she would be flying in. That was right after he had mentioned the fight at the vegetable store.

"She seemed defensive of Muslims, and was staying with a friend in Little Lebanon." he thought, "And the same cab that took her to Garlattis was parked in front of her friends' apartment. That driver was definitely the one who attacked me in the hall, and forced me to the track.".

He waved at the security guard as he exited the stable area.

"So long, bud!", the guard called out, "See ya soon! Take care!".

Charga tapped the horn twice in response, steered onto the main thoroughfare and drove toward the freeway heading south. He was at Garlattis restaurant within minutes. Turning into the parking lot he thought back to Adrianas' arrival there just two days prior. She had said she left the apartment that day with 80 dollars, but she still had that 80 bucks in the restaurant when she offered to pay the bill. That meant the cab ride was free!

"Dammit!" he almost hollered the words. "I shoulda caught that!".

Entering the restaurant, he was happily greeted by a smiling Angelo Garlatti. "Hey, mister Charga! Hello.". He looked around for a moment. "What? No lady today?", he asked, half jokingly.

"No, Ange. Today I'm alone.".

Angelo Garlatti gestured toward a booth. "Here okay?".

"Sure. Fine.".

"Say, whatsa matter. You no look too good.".

Charga shrugged. "I just found out my Adriana wasn't who I thought she was.".

"Well, thatsa no news for me!".

"What do you mean by that, Ange?".

"Firsta," Garlatti answered, holding up one finger, "She was no true Siciliano!".

"Why do you say that?".

"No real-a Sicilano would put ice in their red wine. Thasa one.".

Angelo Garlatti now held up a second finger. "Numero two, no real Sicilano would not know about the famousa Piazzi! So what is she, a Greeka?".

"Nope! Turns out she's part Libyan.", Charga paused, "And," he added, "She's a Muslim!".

"Muslima? Thasa no good. They bazza! Crazy!".

"I found that out." Charga mumbled, then aloud, "Well, we broke it off today. She was just using me.".

"Thasa okay. You still gotta the other two, no?".

"No, Ange." Charga replied. "Those two were also just using me. One went back to her husband, the other dropped me for her career! So, as of now, I've got no lady at all.".

"No worry. You'll getta one again soon. Now, you need a menu?".

"No menu. Just bring me a meatball sandwich and some red wine."

"Right away." Angelo turned and walked back to the restaurant kitchen. The TV set near the ceiling in the rear corner of the restaurant was set on a news channel and was showing views of the racetrack. It caught Chargas' eye. Their camera was scanning the stands, and the voice over commentator was explaining why there was such a large crowd in attendance. "Today is western derby day, and in attendance today is the president, first lady, and their entourage. All seated in the VIP section of the clubhouse.".

Angelo Garlatti returned within minutes with Chargas' sandwich and a glass of red wine. "There you go." he said as he carefully set the wine and sandwich on the table. He followed Chargas' stare and turned to look up at the TV. The camera was now focused in on the president. "Oh, you see? The president is here. He likes the races too.".

Charga nodded. "But he's taking a big chance, going out in public like that.", he said, "There are plenty crazy people out there who might want to take him out!".

"Nahh!", Angelo shook his head. "Nobody can get too close to him After all hesa the president! Hesa got lotsa protection!".

"Yeah." Charga said, "Maybe you're right!". He continued watching the TV while quickly finishing off the famous Garlatti meatball sandwich. After sipping the last drop of red wine, he laid a ten dollar bill on the table, and motioned to Angelo, who was now standing near the kitchen area door. "Keep it, Ange.".

Angelo Garlatti nodded, and returned a thumbs up sign. Charga ambled out to his vehicle. He slid in behind the wheel and slipped the key in the ignition. A slight turn and the Dynasty six cylinder motor responded instantaneously. He sat for a moment before engaging the transmission.

"I can handle the criminals." he thought, "But Micelli, Cortez, Adriana . . ." he shook his head." These women! I don't know.". He set the transmission in drive and pressed down on the accelerator pedal. The vehicle moved forward smoothly, its' finely tuned engine purring like a big, powerful feline machine. He stroked the dashboard, gently, lovingly. "That's my Dyna.", he whispered, as he drove off, "I guess you're the one and only lady I can really rely on." He smiled to himself as he turned onto the freeway and headed home.